Fitzwilliam Darcy, GENTLEMAN

A Novel in Three Parts

Book 2

Fitzwilliam Darcy, Gentleman

A Novel in Three Parts

~Book 2~

Duty and Desire

By

Pamela Aidan

Wytherngate Press
2004

2004 Wytherngate Press

Cover etching:
"Hunting" (Stag 1)
by Samuel Howitt
Orme's Collection of British Field Sports Illustrated in Twenty Beautifully Coloured Engravings (1807-1808)

Cover design by
Margaret Coleman

ISBN 0-9728529-1-3
LCCN 2004108428

Wytherngate Press website: Wytherngate.com
Email: WytherngatePress@crownhillwriters.com

The principal text of this book was set in a digitized version of 10 point Baskerville. Titles appear in Baker Script & Bank Gothic.

Printed in the United States of America on acid-free paper

Aidan, Pamela.
Duty and Desire/ Pamela Aidan.
240 p.; 21 cm.
Series: Fitzwilliam Darcy, Gentleman; 2.
ISBN 0-9728529-1-3
1. Regency–England–Fiction. 2. Regency fiction. I. Austen, Jane, 1775-1815. Pride and Prejudice. II. Series: Fitzwilliam Darcy, Gentleman; Book 2.

813.54 2004108428

To my sons Nathan,
Marcus, and Zachary—
my gift to the future.

I have learned so much since the publication of *An Assembly Such As This*, the first book in this series, the principle thing being that editing is a very difficult office that should not be undertaken by the author. Hence, my very grateful thanks to Kim Cheeley for undertaking this exacting job. Another thing I learned was how hard it is for a novice to learn the computer programs required for book production, especially when faced with a deadline. This mystery I gladly hand over to my husband, Michael, without whose encouragement and belief in me *Duty and Desire* would never have reached completion.

Lastly, to you, my readers: thank you for the letters, the reviews, the delight you express in my work that has led to success beyond all my dreams.

Bless you all!

Pamela Aidan

Books by Pamela Aidan

~~~

An Assembly Such As This
Duty and Desire
These Three Remain
~~~

TABLE OF *Chapters*

~ 1 ~
Natural Frailty

"...through him who liveth and reigneth with thee and the Holy Ghost, now and ever. Amen."

Darcy recited the collect for the first Sunday in Advent, his prayer book closed upon his thumb as he stood alone in his family's pew at St—'s. The morning had dawned reluctantly, seeming determined to shroud its rising with a fog drawn up from the snow-covered earth. It seeped, cold and pitiless, into the bones of man and beast, and seemed to cling to the very stones of the sanctuary. Darcy shivered. He had almost foregone the services, his temper unimproved by the passage of the night, but habit had pulled him out of bed, and knowing his staff had arisen early in the expectation of his attendance, he had dressed, broken his fast and departed.

His dark green frockcoat buttoned high against the chill, Darcy surveyed the richly appointed hall, its architecture and furnishings encouraging his eye to travel upward to the soaring ribs of the ceiling and the grandeur of the coloured light that fell from the great windows. His gaze falling, he noted with little surprise that although this day marked the first Sunday of that season of joy, the church was not overfull. It rarely was. Few of the families whose names graced sumptuous gifts of panel, stained glass, or plate deigned to grace the repository of their munificence with their actual presence. That, however, had not been the Darcy family's practice; and although he stood alone, in his mind's eye he could well imagine his forebears, standing in sober reflection in the pew beside him.

The first Scripture reading of the morning was announced and Darcy opened his book to the selection for the day to join in the reading.

"Owe no man anything, but to love one another: for he that loveth another hath fulfilled the law..."

The click of boot heels and rattle of a sword in its sheath echoed in the vastness behind him, distracting Darcy from the text. In the next moment, he was forcefully nudged down the pew by a scarlet-clad shoulder.

"Good Lord, it is wretched weather! Thought you might stay home this morning. Need to speak to you," Colonel Richard Fitzwilliam whispered loudly into his cousin's ear.

"Quiet!" Darcy whispered back tersely, half amused, half annoyed at Fitzwilliam's characteristic irreverence. He skewered a corner of his book into his cousin's arm until he surrendered and reached for it. "Here...read!"

"...if there be any other commandment, it is briefly comprehended in this saying, namely, Thou shalt love thy neighbour as thyself..."

"Ouch! Fitz. Is that bloody 'loving thy neighbour'?" Fitzwilliam looked at him reproachfully as he rubbed his arm.

"Richard, your language!" Darcy murmured back. "Just read...here." He pointed to the place, and Fitzwilliam bent his head to the text, a large grin on his face.

"...let us therefore caste off the works of darkness, and let us put on the armour of light. Let us walk honestly, as in the day; not in rioting and drunkenness..."

"That leaves out the Army," Fitzwilliam quipped to him out of the side of his mouth. "Navy, too."

"...not in chambering and wantonness..."

"Down goes the peerage."

"Richard!" Darcy breathed menacingly.

"...not in strife and envying. But put ye on the Lord Jesus Christ, and make not provision for the flesh, to fulfill the lusts thereof."

"Finished off the entire *ton* with that one." He glanced over his shoulder, "but, none of *them* are about, so here endeth the lesson."

Darcy rolled his eyes and then stepped heavily on his cousin's booted foot, for which encouragement to piety he was rewarded with an elbow in his side. They sat down, Darcy putting space between himself and Fitzwilliam. Another grin flickered across the Colonel's face as the two turned their attention to the Reverend Doctor's sermon upon the Gospel of St. Matthew, Chapter 21.

By the time the good Doctor came to the multitudes of Jerusalem spreading their garments and branches in the way, Fitzwilliam had leaned back and, with crossed arms, fallen into a pose that could well be mistaken for a nap. Darcy shifted his position, placing his boots closer to the foot warmers, and assayed to attend to the sermon that had departed from the text and now drifted into the realm of philosophical discourse. It was rather the same sort of plea to the rational mind and self-interested morality that he had heard expounded innumerable times before. The "infirmity of the nature of man" was lamented and the "occasional failings and sudden surprises" of the petty transgressions he was heir to lightly touched upon and softly laid at the feet of the "natural frailty" that resided in the human breast.

Natural frailty! Darcy stirred at the familiar expression and looked down at the tips of his boots, his lips compressed in an unforgiving line as he tested the appellative against his own experience at the hands of a certain other. The exercise produced unwelcome implications. Was he tamely to accept "frailty" as the explanation–nay–the excuse for such invidious behaviour as Wickham had visited upon Georgiana and himself? Was he expected to pity Wickham for his weakness, succour him? Resentment, as bitter as it was cold, reawakened in his chest, and the Reverend Doctor was attended to with a more critical ear.

"In such times," intoned the minister, "we must lay hold of the unqualified mercy of the Supreme Being who will, in nowise, hold us to such a strict account as will end in our disappointment, but who offers us now in Christ the cordial of a moderated, rational requisition of Divine justice. If sincerity has been your watchword and the performance of your duty has been your creed, then, with justified complacency, you may rest upon the evidence of your lives."

Evidence! What complacency could Wickham's "evidence" afford him? Surely, he is beyond any claim to mercy! Darcy's umbrage protested, a niggling unease attacking the edges of his certainty. He leaned back and crossed his arms over his chest, mirroring in knife-edged attention what his cousin did in slumber.

"And, if exempt at least from any gross vice," the Doctor continued, "or if sometimes accidentally betrayed into it, on its never having been indulged habitually, he may congratulate himself on his inoffensiveness to his Creator and society in general. Or if not even so," the Doctor delicately cleared his throat, "yet on the balance being in his favour, or, on the whole, not much against him, when his good and bad actions are fairly weighed, and due allowance is made for human frailty, he may with assurance consider his portion of humanity's contract with the Almighty fulfilled and the rewards of blessedness secured."

Darcy stared at the pulpit, his mind and body forcibly communicating afresh to him the odium of Wickham's deeds and his reanimated rage forged new links in the chain of his soul-deep resentment. Would Wickham escape even the bar of eternal justice? "On the balance...not much against...fairly weighed...due allowance!" Wickham, himself, could hardly have pled his case with more eloquence and sympathetic appeal! Darcy's jaw tightened—a dangerous, darkling eye the only relief from a chilling, stony countenance.

The Reverend Doctor continued. "To that end, 'Know thyself' as the philosopher says and, in prudence of mind, conduct yourselves according to the advice of St. James as to useful good works and, certainly, in the performance of one's duty. But always, my dear congregation, *moderately*, as befits a rational being. Thus endeth the lesson. Amen." The Doctor closed his Bible upon his notes, but Darcy could not so easily shut up his roiling anger and indignation. His whole being demanded action, but he could neither move to relieve it nor guess what course would satisfy its demands.

The choir stood to sing the recessional, the rustle of their unison movements and the triumphal cords of the organ rousing Fitzwilliam from his inattention. He sat up straight and blinked, owl-like, at his cousin. "Did I miss anything?" Fitzwilliam yawned as they came to their feet.

"It was much the same as always," Darcy replied, averting his face from his cousin. Richard would need but a glance to know something was amiss. Taking advantage of Fitzwilliam's ritualistic endeavours to shake loose from the effects of slumber, Darcy slowly retrieved his hat and book. A diversion was required. With a studied carelessness he turned to his cousin. "Save for when His Grace, the Duke of Cumberland ran down the aisle, confessing to the murder of his valet."

"Cumberland!" Fitzwilliam's eyes sprang open, and he swivelled halfway 'round before catching himself and turning on Darcy. "Cumberland, indeed! Badly done, Fitz, taking advantage of a poor soldier worn out in the service of..."

"In the service of the ladies of London, shielding them from the terrors of a moment of boredom!" Darcy snorted. "Yes, you have my unalloyed sympathy, Richard."

Fitzwilliam laughed and stepped out into the aisle. "Shall you mind me stretching out my boots under your dinner table today, Fitz? His lordship and the rest of the family left for Matlock last week, and I am sore in need of a quiet meal away from the soldiery. I think I'm getting too old for kicking up continually," he sighed. "Settled and quiet would, I believe, answer all my ideas of happiness. In truth, it is beginning to appear highly attractive."

"'Settled and quiet' was exactly what you were during the greater part of services this morning, but," he smiled tightly as his cousin protested his perception of the matter, "I'll not berate you upon that score."

"As you said, it was 'much the same as always.'"

"Yes, quite so," Darcy drawled. "Rather, tell me the name of the 'highly attractive' lady with whom you aspire to be settled and quiet."

"Now, Fitz, did I mention a lady?" The heightened colour around Fitzwilliam's stock belied the carelessness of his question.

"Richard, there has *always* been a lady." They had, by now, reached the church door and, with more reserve than usual, Darcy nodded to the Reverend Doctor. As they stepped out from the doorway, Harry, who had been watching for them, motioned for the carriage, which smartly rolled forward to the curb.

"This is the most deuced-awful weather." Fitzwilliam shivered as he waited for Harry to open the door. "I hope we are not in for an entire winter of it. Glad the pater and mater left for home when they did." He climbed in behind Darcy and hurriedly spread a carriage robe over his legs. "Bye-the-bye, Fitz," he squinted across at his cousin as the carriage pulled away, "is that the knot that cut Brummell off at the knees? Show your poor cousin how it is done, there's a good fellow. *The Roquefort* is it?"

"*The Roquet*, Richard," Darcy ground back at him. "Not you, as well!"

~~~~~~~~&~~~~~~~~

"Fitz? Fitz, I do not believe you have heard a thing I have said!" Colonel Fitzwilliam put down his glass of after dinner port and joined his cousin's vigil at his library window. "And it was rather witty, if I must say so myself."

"You are wrong, Richard, on both counts," Darcy replied dryly, his face still set toward the panes.

"On *both* counts?" Fitzwilliam leaned in against the window's frame for a better look at his cousin's face.

Darcy turned to him, his lips pursed in a condescending smile. "I heard *every* word you said, and it was *not* witty. Amusing? Perhaps, but not anything that would pass for wit." He lifted his own glass and finished off the contents as he awaited Fitzwilliam's counter to his thrust.

"Well, I shall be glad, then, to be considered 'amusing' according to your exacting taste, Cousin." Fitzwilliam paused and cocked a knowing brow at him. "But, you must admit that you were not devoting your whole attention to me and have not acted yourself today. Anything you can tell me?"

Darcy glanced uneasily at his cousin, silently cursing his acute powers of observation. He had never been able to hide anything from Richard for long; he knew him far too well. Perhaps the time had come to speak his concerns. Taking a deep breath, Darcy turned back to the warm haven of his library. "I have had several letters from Georgiana in the last month."

"Georgiana!" Fitzwilliam's teasing smile faded into concern. "There has been no change, then?"

"On the contrary!" Darcy plunged on to the heart of the matter. "There has been a very marked change, and although I welcome it most gratefully, I do not entirely comprehend it."

Fitzwilliam straightened. "A *marked* change, you say? In what way?"

"She has left off her melancholy and begs forgiveness for troubling us all with it. I am instructed—yes, *instructed*," Darcy repeated at the disbelieving look Fitzwilliam returned him, "to regard the whole matter no longer as *she* does not, save as a lesson learned."
~~~~~~~~

Fitzwilliam uttered an exclamation. "And that is not all! She writes that she has started visiting our tenants as mother did."

"Is it possible?" Fitzwilliam shook his head. "The last time we were together, she could not as much as look at me nor speak above a whisper."

"There is yet more! Her last letter was most warmly phrased, and if you may be persuaded to believe it, Richard, she offered *me* advice on a matter about which I had written her." Darcy walked over to his desk while Fitzwilliam pondered his words in stunned silence. He opened a drawer, withdrew a sheet and held it out to his cousin. "Then, when I had returned to London, Hinchcliffe showed me this."

"*One hundred pounds per annum to the Society for Returning Young Women...*" Fitzwilliam read. "Fitz, are you playing me a joke, because it's a damned poor one."

"I am not joking, I assure you." Darcy retrieved the letter and faced his cousin squarely. "What do you make of it, Richard?"

Fitzwilliam cast about him for his port and, finding it, threw back what remained. "I don't know. It appears incredible!" He looked at Darcy intently. "You said her letter was 'warmly phrased.' She sounded *happy*, then?"

"Happy?" Darcy rolled the word about in his mind then shook his head. "I would not describe it so. Contented? Matured?" He looked to his cousin in an uncomfortable loss for words. "In any event, I will join her at Pemberley in a few days' time, and I intend to keep her by me." He paused. "I bring her back to Town with me in January."

"If she has improved as you believe..." Fitzwilliam allowed his sentence to dangle as he stared into his empty glass, his brow knit.

"Do you go to Matlock for Christmas or must you remain in Town? You could then see for yourself and advise me, for I would value your opinion, Richard." Darcy's steady look into his cousin's eyes underscored his words.

Fitzwilliam nodded, acknowledging both the import and singularity of Darcy's request. "I am granted a week's leave and had not yet decided where to spend it. His lordship will be much pleased to see me at Matlock and her ladyship will, of course, be cast into transports that all her family are home. Shall you host the family for a week as in Christmas past?"

Darcy nodded and after replacing the letter in his desk, he poured his cousin and himself more of the port. He tipped the glass to his lips after saluting him, letting the pleasant burn slide smoothly down his throat as he closed his eyes. There was more he wished Richard's views upon, but how to begin?

"I have seen Wickham." Darcy's quiet announcement broke the silence like the crack of a rifle shot.

"Wickham! He would not dare!" Fitzwilliam fairly exploded.

"No, we met quite by accident while I was accompanying Bingley in Hertfordshire. Apparently, he has come upon enough money to purchase a lieutenancy and has joined a militia stationed in Meryton."

"A militia! Wickham? He must be at the end of his resources, or hiding from pressing obligations, to do so. Wickham, a soldier! I wish, by God, I had him under *my* command!"

Fitzwilliam paced the length of the room then turned and demanded, "Did you speak with his commanding officer? Tell him what a villain he's acquired?"

"How could I tell him?" Darcy remonstrated in response to Fitzwilliam's glower. I would be called upon to furnish proof that neither I—*nor you*—can ever give." Darcy held Fitzwilliam's blazing eyes with his own until the latter's shoulders slumped in acknowledgement. Darcy indicated the armchairs by the hearth, and both sat down heavily, their faces turned away each from the other in private, frustrated thought. For several long minutes the only sound in the room was a wind come blasting against the windowpanes.

"Richard, how do you account for Wickham?"

Fitzwilliam raised a blank face. "Account for him?"

"Explain him." Darcy bit his lower lip, then let out the breath he was holding and expanded on a question that had plagued him for over a decade. "He received more than he could have dreamt of from my father and was put in the way of advancing well beyond his origins. Yet he squandered it all, even as it was given, and repaid all my father's solicitude with the attempted seduction of his daughter." He paused, took another swallow of the port then continued in a lowered voice, "Would you call it a 'natural frailty'?"

"Natural frailty! He's a blackguard, and there is the beginning and end of it!" Fitzwilliam roared. He stopped, then, and mastered himself before continuing in a more subdued tone. "And so he was from the start, as you have cause to remember. I may be only a year older than you, but I saw him playing his hand against you even when we were children."

"My father never saw it." Darcy swirled the liquid in his glass.

"Humph," Fitzwilliam snorted. "As to that, I am not entirely convinced. Your father was an unusually perceptive man. I cannot help but think he had Wickham's measure, although why he did not act, I cannot say. But in one thing he *was* deceived. I do not believe he could ever have conceived of Wickham's harming Georgiana. Nor could any of us! We knew him to be a sneak thief, liar, and profligate, but," Fitzwilliam pounded the arm of his chair, "even we, who suffered his tricks, could not guess the depths of his viciousness!"

"Perhaps he only fell into it accidentally. The pressures of his debts...time against him..." Darcy recalled the morning's sermon.

"Accidentally fell into it! Fitz...it was a cold-blooded, carefully planned campaign! Probably was about it for months!"

"But Richard," Darcy faced his cousin directly, his countenance awash with confliction, "human frailty cannot be so summarily dismissed. I make no claims to be immune from its effects, and you, surely, do not, as you appeal to it regularly! We all hope that, given its consideration, the balance will weigh out in our favour for our attention to duty and to charity."

Fitzwilliam cocked his head to one side and looked deeply into his cousin's eyes. "That is true, Fitz," he replied slowly, "and I am no theologian...or philosopher, for that matter. That is rather your line than mine. But, if you are asking me whether we are to excuse Wickham's behaviour to Georgiana because he could not help himself, or if, in the end, his scale will be tipped to the good, I beg leave to tell you, Cousin, you may go to the Devil! For, barring sudden and immediate sainthood, the creature's a rogue of the deepest dye and will remain so. Even the Army can't change that!"

A knock at the library door prevented Darcy from addressing his cousin's position. He called permission and Witcher entered carrying a silver tray on which lay a folded note.

"Sir, this just came, and the boy was told to wait for a reply."

"Thank you, Witcher," Darcy replied, plucking up the note. "If you would wait a moment, I shall pen a reply directly." The seal broken, he unfolded the sheet and immediately recognized Bingley's scrawling hand.

Darcy,

It is the strangest thing, but Caroline has removed to Town and shut up Netherfield saying she cannot be happy in Hertfordshire! And intends to stay in London for Christmas—

> Louisa and Hurst as well. Needless to say, I have removed myself from Grenier's and am now comfortably at home. (As comfortably as may be, in all events) Therefore, please present yourself in Aldford Street for dinner on Monday evening, as I will be quite absent from the hotel. That is, unless you would rather dine at the hotel. Please advise me!
>
> Your servant,
> Bingley

Darcy looked up at Fitzwilliam. "It is from Bingley. He desires my advice on whether we should dine at his home or elsewhere." He rose from the chair and went to his desk.

"Thunder an' turf, can't the puppy decide even where he will eat without your help?"

"It would appear not," Darcy chuckled mirthlessly, "but I cannot fault him at present as I have been the instrument of his misdoubt." He reached for his pen, inspected the point and dipped it into the inkwell.

"You have been encouraging him to depend upon you far too much, Fitz," Fitzwilliam warned him.

"That is the irony of it." Darcy wrote his reply that Aldford Street was acceptable. Miss Bingley would, he knew, be quite incensed with him if he avoided her at this juncture. "Until a few weeks ago, I was pushing him out from under my wings. But something arose in Hertfordshire that proved beyond his powers and I am forced to play Mother Hen once more. Here, Witcher." Darcy sanded and folded the note, then placed it on the tray. "Now, let us leave the subject!"

"I am yours to command, Cousin!" Fitzwilliam sketched him a bow. "What do you say to a few racks of billiards before I must report back to the Guards? And perhaps," he added slyly, "we might agree to a little wager on the results?"

"Shot your bolt already this month, Cousin?"

"Blame it on the ladies, Fitz. What's a poor man to do? Natural frailty, don't you know!"

"A few racks of billiards" later, Darcy found his purse a bit lighter and his cousin's smile correspondingly broader. Although, for Richard's benefit, he made a show of chagrin at his losses, he was in nowise displeased to part with the guineas that would see Fitzwilliam comfortably through to the end of the quarter. Darcy knew his cousin to be generous to a fault with the men—boys, really—under his command, particularly those who were younger sons, as he was. Richard looked after them rather like a Mother Hen himself, making sure they wrote home, rescuing them from scrapes and roughly cozening them into creditable specimens of His Majesty's Guard. But such shifts required expenditures that his quarterly allowance could not always cover without curtailing Fitzwilliam's own varied activities. Applying to his lordship for additional funds was not a course his cousin desired to pursue on a regular basis. Therefore, Darcy unfailingly made his box available to his cousin for interests that they shared, such as the theatre and opera and, for those they did not, the occasional wager on the roll of a ball or turn of a card provided what was lacking. This arrangement was never acknowledged by either, of course, but was understood, the funds needed being generously lost on the one hand and graciously received on the other.

"Well, old man, I shall display some unwonted mercy and take myself off to the Guard before I win Pemberley from you." Fitzwilliam stretched out his shoulder muscles before reaching for his regimentals. He slid the guineas into an inner pocket and shrugged into the scarlet.

Darcy feigned a grimace. "So you keep saying, but the day has not yet come, nor will it, Cousin." He picked up his own coat and led the way out to the stairs, Fitzwilliam behind him. "You will come, then, Christmas week?" he asked.

"Depend upon it," Fitzwilliam replied as they descended the stairs. "You have me confounded with this news of Georgiana, and even did I not share guardianship of her, I should be concerned on the basis of our close relationship alone. Besides, it has been too long since we have shared Christmas! Her ladyship will be in high gig to have me home *and* spend Christmas at Pemberley again." They reached the hall, and Fitzwilliam turned a serious mien upon him. "She has been concerned about you, Fitz, about both of you, really. This invitation will, I am sure, ease her mind."

"My aunt's solicitude is appreciated," Darcy assured Fitzwilliam, "and I confess I have been negligent in my correspondence with her of late. That will be remedied. I shall write her tonight!"

"Then, I'll leave you to it. Do me a kindness and tell her you saw me today and that we dined together, et cetera, et cetera." A sudden thought seized him. "And don't fail to mention I was in church, there's a good fellow! She will be glad to hear from you, of course, but doubly glad to know her scapegrace of a son spent a sober Sunday. I would write her myself, but she will *believe* you."

Witcher opened the door at his master's nod, and the cousins gripped each other's hand in a firm, familiar manner. "I shall so write, Richard," Darcy promised solemnly, but then laughed. "Although retrieving your character to my aunt seems rather a lost cause at this late date." At Fitzwilliam's answering crow, he added mischievously, "Perhaps if you made attendance a habit..."

"Ho, no! Thank you, Cousin. Just write your little bit, and all will be well. Good-bye, then, until Christmas! Witcher!" Fitzwilliam nodded at the old butler and, pulling his cloak tight, ran down the steps of Erewile House and into the hack summoned for him while Darcy turned back to the stairs and the not unpleasant task of writing his Aunt Fitzwilliam.

The sun had long surrendered in its battle against the clouds and fog. Vacating the field to his sister moon, he had already retired to observe what she could make of it when Darcy committed the final syllables of his letter to paper. As he sanded and blotted the missive, he noticed the darkness with regret. Now, not only the weather but also the light was against any notion of a brisk turn about the square to work out the cramped sinews of his limbs and the perturbation of his mind. He laid the letter on the silver servier for Hinchcliffe to post in the morning and arose from his desk with a groan.

"Wickham!" Darcy went to the window and, leaning one arm against the frame, peered out into the night. The square before him was unnaturally silent, the sound of any horse or carriage passing by being muffled by the pervasive fog. The morning's sermon had caught him off his guard and unsettled what had previously been a fixed disposition of mind. The sensation was most disagreeable, and his attempt to reason it out with Richard had proved utterly useless. The question still remained: How *did* one account for Wickham and men like him? Further, was he prepared to believe that Wickham was in little worse a position in the eyes of Eternity than himself?

Richard had misunderstood him completely, thinking he wished to find excuse for Wickham's actions. He could not have been farther from the truth! Darcy's hot resentment of the man rose effortlessly, testifying that it was as implacable as ever it was, perhaps more so as he seemed to be intimately involved in Elizabeth Bennet's poor opinion of him. No, Richard had not recognized the debater's form he had adopted to explore the issue in a safe, objective manner, but had responded with the heat of a passion revolted with such niceties. Now were added to that resentment feelings of injustice at the hands of a Supreme Judge who would allow such a villain to pass Heaven's bar merely by the addition of a few paltry good deeds performed, no doubt, to his own temporal advantage. The entire idea was intolerable! But, there was no one with whom he could puzzle it out, leastwise not immediately at hand, and it was getting late.

Darcy straightened, walked back to his desk and blew out the lamp upon it. Standing motionless in the dark library, he wearily reviewed the morrow's duties. In the morning he must clear his desk of any remaining items of business. Then, at half-past two, present himself in Cavendish Square and commission Lawrence to paint Georgiana's portrait on their return to Town. Lastly, he was expected at Aldford Street for dinner with Bingley and his sister.

He closed his eyes and another groan escaped him. Bingley! If all went well, *that* coil, at least, would be cleared. He prayed that Caroline Bingley had followed his directions precisely and restricted herself to disinterested affirmations of the doubts he had planted in her brother's mind. If she had tried to bully him into giving up Miss Bennet, Darcy knew that all his subtleties of suggestion would have been for naught and he would be confronting a Bingley with heels dug in and head lowered in mulish obstinacy.

The thought chilled him. He had not considered failure. If, against his family and friend, Bingley insisted upon Miss Bennet.... Even in the darkness, Darcy's gaze easily found the shelf on which the book containing the embroidery threads reposed. He did not need to see them; he knew the count of the colours: three green, two yellow and one each of blue, rose and lavender. Would he cut the connexion or stand by Bingley? Stand by him, surely! But at what cost? Perhaps, very little. It well may be that Bingley, the married man, would no longer be interested in the attractions of Town and, as relations between the wed and their bachelor fellows did tend to thin... Darcy shook his head. No, Bingley would remain Bingley. Although his company at some events may fail, Darcy could not doubt his continued warm regard. And that would mean....

"Elizabeth." He had not meant to think it, let alone to say the name aloud, but it echoed in the darkness of the library and fell softly against his ear. Darcy gripped the edge of his desk with painful force and commanded himself not to be a fool. "She dislikes you, idiot! That should provide proof enough against being in her company." Before he could berate himself further, the door to the library suddenly swung open and the blaze of a lamp held aloft caused Darcy to blink and cover his eyes.

"Mr. Darcy!" The lamp was lowered and set on a hall table. "Your pardon, sir. I heard a sound, and as the library was dark, we could not think what it could be." When his eyes had finally adjusted Darcy was able to discern his butler in the doorway with one of the sturdier footmen behind him armed with a kitchen faggot. "With that business in Wapping, sir. All those poor souls murdered in their beds."

Darcy looked askance at his staff. "It is quite all right, Witcher. Understandable, I suppose, but we *are* a goodly distance from Wapping!"

"Yes, sir." Witcher bowed his head, "I guess it is the fog, sir. Has everyone a bit nervous not knowing what is behind or a'fore you. Just the kind of weather for mischief." He motioned the footman away to his post and then bowed to Darcy. "Your pardon, again, sir. Shall I leave you this lamp?"

"No, you may take it with you. Good night, Witcher."

"And to you, Mr. Darcy." Darcy waited until the elderly servant descended the stairs to the servants' floor before starting up them to his bedchamber. Sleep would be his only recourse of escape from the piercing uncertainties of this day. "'To sleep' but, dear God, not 'to dream,' I beg you."

~2~
The Hand of Providence

Darcy settled back into the dark green squabs of his traveling coach as the tollgate at Hampstead vanished behind them in the half-light of early morning. Unbuttoning his greatcoat only enough to reach inside his waistcoat, he pulled out his pocket watch and held it up to the feeble light. It was a quarter past seven, which meant that they had taken less than an hour to navigate the streets of the city and pass through the toll. Now, the road before the horses lay wide and free. The smart snap of his driver's whip cracked against the approaching dawn, assuring Darcy that James Coachman was not unaware of these excellent conditions or of his master's impatience to be home. The coach surged forward.

Home! Darcy closed his eyes and relaxed into the dip and sway of the coach. He had barely allowed himself to think of Pemberley or even the journey there until the truth of their departure made itself apparent to all his senses. Now, he *could* think of it, for the obstacles had all been swept away yesterday as if by miracle.

Hinchcliffe had laid the last bit of business before him by eleven, giving him ample opportunity for a light luncheon and an invigorating turn about the square before his appointment with Lawrence. That interview had gone surprisingly well, and Darcy left Cavendish Square for his club with the famed artist firmly commissioned to see Georgiana for preliminary sketches within a week of their arrival in Town. A multitude of carriages in the street and servants about the doors forewarned him that Boodles would be crowded and, for distaste of more undesired attention, he almost turned away. But as he made his way around the salons and card tables, all the talk had been all of a young peer newly-returned from the Continent whose maiden speech before Parliament had sent the Tory majority into a choking fury.

"The fellow's a lunatic," voiced more than one of Darcy's fellow members. "Or worse," was the usual rejoinder concerning the impassioned but ill-judged speech in defence of the loom-smashing followers of "General Ludd" against the current Bill which called for their summary execution.

"He must relish living dangerously," Lord Devereaux ventured as he threw down his hand in response to Darcy's king of diamonds, "for he also is in a fair way of becoming Lady Caroline's new pet... and Lamb's latest humiliation. Did you observe them at Melbourne's on Friday?" Darcy's ears had pricked up at the reference.

"Good Lord, yes! What a display!" replied Sir Hugh Goforth, "Thought Lamb would call the fellow out for encouraging his wife in such an outrageous start. If she were *my* wife, the lady would now be stitching handkerchiefs behind locked doors on my remotest estate, and my Lord Byron would be awaking about this time in the hold of an India-bound ship."

A chorus of nods had agreed with this avowal and, not long after, the game broke up. Darcy called for his coat and took his leave shortly thereafter without even one inquiry about the accursed knot. As Boodles' door closed behind him, he thanked heaven that the actions of the dangerously foolish Lord Byron had so quickly displaced his notoriety in the public mind.

The last appointment of the day had been the one he had most dreaded. His preoccupation with the coming evening could not have been more obvious. Fletcher, while carefully preparing him for dinner at Aldford Street, had been forced to issue discreet instructions in order to get the task done. All his concentration on the evening ahead of him, he had not noticed his funereal appearance until he had entered Bingley's drawing room at the appointed hour and was greeted by a pair of startled looks.

"What is this, Darcy! No bad news, I hope!" Bingley had risen and quickly come to his side while Miss Bingley had laid a hand to her heart and brought a handkerchief to her lips.

"Bad news?" Darcy stared at the two in confusion. "I should think not! Why should you think that?"

"Your dress, Darcy." The worry on his friend's face changed into amusement. "For a moment I thought the King had died! What is your man thinking of, turning you out like a great black crow?" He laughed as he circled round him to observe the entire effect.

He had looked down, then, at the unembellished, unrelieved black of his costume and pursed his lips in ire with Fletcher, but there was naught he could do. *What cannot be mended must be borne,* he reminded himself, but his valet's message was very clear.

"Mr. Darcy looks like nothing remotely resembling a crow, Charles." Miss Bingley had recovered herself and advanced toward them. "It is the fashion now for gentlemen to dress with such understated elegance, *a la* Brummell. Mr. Darcy is merely in advance of the style, which you would do well to emulate, Brother." Darcy bowed over her hand and was surprised to feel it grip his own in signal, but of what, he knew not.

"Well, if not a crow, then a raven...a very *Brummellian* raven, if you must have it so, Caroline!" Bingley laughed, but the smile behind his eyes was faint. "But, come, Darcy. Dinner is ready and it is just the three of us tonight." He sighed then, and lapsed into silence as they crossed the room and hall.

"You must wonder to see me in Town, Mr. Darcy." Miss Bingley eyed her brother nervously and her voice quavered. "Charles was most surprised, thinking he had left me well situated in Hertfordshire, which, of course, he had. But, alas, I am not as enamoured of the country as my brother...at least, not of Hertfordshire. I ask you sir, what would I *do* with only Louisa and Hurst for company! And at this season!" She laughed, but its pitch rang false. Darcy noticed Bingley flinch at the sound.

"The neighbourhood was at your feet, Caroline," Bingley said quietly. "You would not have lacked for company, I am certain."

"Perhaps you are right, but I should have greatly missed our friends in Town. And the shopping, you know! What is Meryton to London for shopping?" Miss Bingley had looked to Darcy for confirmation.

"I would gladly have squired you on a shopping expedition," Bingley replied before Darcy could come to his sister's assistance. "There was no need to close Netherfield." She began to protest, but he cut her off. "But this is ground already covered, and I am sure we do not wish to bore Darcy with family squabbles." Miss Bingley coloured at his words, casting a brief, pleading look in Darcy's direction.

Darcy hesitated. The atmosphere was fraught with tension, and for perhaps the first time, he was finding it difficult to read his friend. *Had Miss Bingley followed his instructions or had the two gone toe-to-toe over Miss Bennet?* Bingley offered him no clues; his eyes focused down upon his plate as servants flittered about, performing the well-choreographed motions of serving a gentleman's dinner. Miss Bingley delicately cleared her throat.

"How went your interview with Lawrence today?" Bingley's eyes came up, his countenance suggesting that he was willing to be amused.

"Quite well, actually," he replied, thankful to be relieved of the responsibility of lighting upon a topic of conversation. "I expected to be treated to all manner of high, artistic sensibilities and nerves, but Lawrence was quite civil and his studio was in every way respectable."

"No paint thrown against the walls or scandalously-clad models lying about, then?"

Darcy laughed. "No, nothing of the kind. I am sorry to disappoint you, but it was all rather businesslike. I was shown to his study, offered tea and asked what sort of portrait I had in mind. We then repaired to his studio where he showed me samples of his finished work and some in progress. We agreed upon a date for Georgiana's first sitting, I was thanked for my patronage and shown out the door. Done and done in a matter of three quarters of an hour!"

"Shocking! All my notions of artists are tumbled over," Bingley quipped in a manner more like himself. "I suppose I must content myself with Lord Brougham's description of *L'Catalani's* hysterics on Friday last to sustain my impression of the artistic temperament."

The rest of their dinner was taken in the same light manner. Miss Bingley relaxed and talked somewhat as they ate but refrained from her customary domination of the conversation. Instead, she occupied herself with indulgent attention to her brother's stories, punctuating them with meaningful glances in Darcy's direction, the content of which he could only guess. By the time Bingley had excused Darcy and himself to his study after dinner, she was biting her lower lip, but whether in vexation or agitation of nerves, Darcy could not tell.

Charles again fell silent as they strolled to his study, and not finding a creditable way of relieving it, Darcy had followed suit. The study door had not even clicked behind them before Charles was extending a heavy, cut-glass tumbler of light amber liquor toward him. His own, he held up in salute and downed it entire as Darcy looked on in consternation.

"Charles..." he began, but was stopped by the closed eyes and uncharacteristically grim line of his friend's mouth. Bingley opened his eyes then and tilted his head at him.

"Do you remember our conversation at the coaching inn last week? You warned me there of my propensity to exaggerate." Bingley's gaze bore into his own, and it required a good deal of command on his part not to look away.

"Yes, I remember," he replied quietly.

"Also, you cautioned me of becoming so enthralled with the phantoms of my imagination that I would render myself disgusting to my family, friends, and society in general." Bingley withdrew his gaze and turned to pour another round from the decanter.

"You were more than tolerant of my advice, Charles," he offered, still unsure of his friend's state of mind. Bingley held out the decanter to him, but he refused it.

"I have thought a great deal about what you said, Darcy. I have argued with myself and, in my mind, with *you* as well." He bent and snatched away the scattering of papers from the chairs by the hearth and then indicated they should sit down. "I have spent the last two days since her surprising arrival testing what I believed true against Caroline's observations."

He remembered squirming in his chair at this point in Bingley's narrative, but he hoped it had not been so. Bingley had paused and looked into the flames of the hearth for so long a time that he had been hard put to maintain a disinterested attitude. Then, with a small sigh, his friend had continued.

"I have also thought long on Lord Brougham's admonition, and in the light of the love my friends and family bear me, I have come to a conclusion." He lifted his eyes again and with a self-deprecating smile confessed, "You were right, Darcy. I have greatly misled myself in believing Miss Bennet offered anything more than her friendship. It was all my own doing. No blame should ever be attached to her, ever." He took another swallow from his glass. "She will always be my ideal of womanhood…her beauty, her gentleness. I shall carry her always with me but to further *my* desires would only cause her distress; and that I could not bear," he ended in a whisper.

As the coach sped north through the gathering dawn, Darcy recalled how he had looked down into his glass, unable to think of what he should reply. He had achieved his object with, as it seemed, fewer tedious confrontations than he had feared and had retained Bingley's friendship in the bargain. Yet, he could not entirely rejoice in his success. Relief, he concluded, was his chief emotion. There was little danger of encountering the Bennet sisters ever again. Charles would survive his heartbreak and not blame him for it. But it pained him to see Charles dispirited so, whose habitually sunny disposition had supported his own more reserved one on so many occasions.

"It is for the best," he had finally uttered, and he found himself repeating the solecism now.

"Mr. Darcy?" In the opposite corner Fletcher struggled to attention from a doze that had begun mere blocks from Grosvenor Square. "Pardon me, sir. Did you say something?"

"'It is for the best,' Fletcher. It usually is; is it not?"

His valet gave him a brief, curious look before sliding back into his restful position against the cushions. "If it has been placed in the hands of Providence, sir, it is invariably so."

~~~~~~~&~~~~~~~

"Heigh-yup, there!" Darcy leant forward, almost pressing his face against the coach's window as James Coachman encouraged the team's leader to take the curve that would bring them into Lambton at a safer pace. He knew their temperament as the horses were Darcy's own, kept against his return at the last posting inn before Lambton; and their eagerness to return to their familiar stable boxes was keeping James well occupied with the ribbons. Snow lying a foot deep glinted and winked at Darcy under a brilliant but chill winter sun as the coach jounced and laboured through the ruts carved into the road. It was late afternoon as they approached the village, yet despite the dusting of new-fallen snow that morning, Lambton still bustled in its own country way, shaking out its apron and getting on with its small concerns as confidently as any great London establishment.

The horses were reined in to a walk as they entered St. John Street and passed the village's now-frozen pond. Several big lads armed with brooms were ranged against each other on its icy surface waiting for one of their mates to launch the stone down a path cleared of the morning's offering. Before they were lost from view, Darcy saw the stone curled and the other lads furiously brushing the ice to assist its slide.

"Strapping curl, that," Fletcher commented as he sat back again after joining his master at the window. Darcy grunted a cordial agreement, his attention already engaged in taking note of any changes in the village since his departure in early fall. A new thatch here and a bit of whitewashing there were the only differences, but
~~~~~~~

the snow hugging the corners and o'er hanging the eaves of the snug houses and familiar establishments of Lambton framed a view for him second only to Pemberley itself in dearness.

A shout from the street caused Darcy and Fletcher to look ahead. With effort Darcy repressed the smile of anticipation on his face as the innkeepers of both the Green Man and Black's Head inns emerged from their doors on opposite sides of the street at the same moment. For several years now it had been a point of honour between the two to be the first one to greet any Darcy equipage that passed through the village. Last fall Matling, of the Black's Head, had hustled out his wife to add her curtsy to his tug of the forelock when he had left for London, causing old Garston of the Green Man to look daggers at his rival as the coach had passed. Today, Darcy could see, Matling had his wife by his side once more as his coach drew near, and he nodded an acknowledgment of the pair's greeting as he passed by. But as Matling looked to the steps of the Green Man to crow his victory, Darcy observed the pleasure his regard had brought fade away to be replaced with a terrible scowl.

"Mr. Darcy, look sir!" Fletcher's voice almost choked with the laughter as he motioned out the opposite window. There on the steps of the Green Man, arranged from the oldest to the youngest, were all of old Garston's grandchildren, curtsying or tugging, with Garston himself beaming and tugging behind them.

The children gave a cheer as Darcy, shaking his head at the innkeepers' keen rivalry, waved to them. When the carriage turned the corner he settled back into the seat with a grin the match of that upon his valet's face. The horses were permitted to pick up their pace a bit as they reached the end of the line of shops on St. John and turned onto King Street. In moments they passed the village well, its pure waters famous for staving off the Black Death of one hundred and fifty years before. Next came the tree-bordered lane which led up a gentle hill to St. Lawrence's Church, whose embattled tower and spires had stood against the world for five centuries, answering to heaven for three of them for the well-being of the Darcy soul. Then, it was over an ancient stone bridge spanning the Ere, which met and then meandered along Pemberley's border, and on to the gates of the park five miles beyond at as spanking a pace as the road would allow.

"It will be good to be home, sir," Fletcher offered, as Darcy once again turned to the window, eager for the long-desired sight of his ancestral lands and home.

"Mmm," was all he replied as the coach pulled into the lane and up to the imposing gates that were, even now, being flung open in welcome. Pemberley's gatekeeper waved the team and coach through and, pausing to tug at his forelock, lifted a wide smile in greeting to the travellers before scurrying to close the wrought-iron barrier behind them.

"Is that a sprig of holly in Samuel's cap, Fletcher?" Darcy nodded appreciatively at his gatekeeper's warm welcome.

"I believe it is, sir. Yes, indisputably holly. Entirely appropriate, because of the season, sir."

"Ah, yes...the season." Darcy fell silent once more, his attention wholly focused on their passage down the long drive. The private lane wove its unhurried way through the wood that girdled the outer reaches of the park. Designed a century ago under the aegis of Darcy's great-grandfather, it required approaching visitors to slow their horses to a collected trot and then rewarded their patience with more than a few charming views of the secluded glades and tumbling streams that formed the natural beauty of Pemberley's lands.

The great trees o'er hanging the lane were heavy-laden with snow, and in the late afternoon sun, they cast long, lavender shadows across the lane and into the wood beyond, enveloping the coach in a frosty stillness that defied the reality of its steady progress. Darcy opened the window and took a deep breath of the sharp air, savouring the familiar, tangy taste of it like a fine wine. They were almost there. The team quickened its gait, their excitement transmitting itself to the occupants of the coach moments before they broke free of the wood at the crest of the hill. Suddenly, all of Pemberley lay before them, glittering like a fallen star upon a crystalline sea.

The mellow walls of the west facade glowed rosily in the light of the setting sun, the corners cooling to violet as they glanced away from the fading glow. Despite that orb's impending retreat, the windows of Pemberley seemed to gather the remaining fire. Themselves ablaze with reflected glory, they mirrored the red-gold rays out upon the surrounding snow, the effect immeasurably heightened by its twin reflected in the frozen pond below. Seeing it, Darcy felt his heart turn over and the weight of the past weeks lighten.

They began their descent from the crest immediately. The horses, a-tremble with desire for home, broke into a canter from which no one in the coach wished to dissuade them. The pounding of their hooves beat at counterpoint to the creak of leather and wood and the rattle of glass as they reached the bottom of the hill. Rounding the last curve of the lane, they flung stones and mud about in a grand show of homecoming. Reaching the straight-laid approach to Pemberley Hall, Darcy could hear James calling to the leader as he worked the ribbons upon the team's tender mouths. The horses slowed to a trot, then a fast, stiff-legged walk and, finally, to a collected stroll that brought the coach to a gentle stop before the arched entrance of Pemberley's enclosed courtyard.

Well before they had come to a stop, the courtyard had erupted into activity. Grooms from the stable caught at the ribbons of the leader, welcoming the horses home with rough affection. A small army of footmen appeared to wrest the trunks from the coach's boot while Reynolds, himself, opened the coach door.

"Welcome home, Mr. Darcy! Welcome home, sir!" The butler's voice shook slightly as Darcy climbed down from the coach.

"Reynolds! It is good to be home...more than good." He smiled back at another of his people who had known him since boyhood and then looked up at the greenery that bedecked the archway into the courtyard. "You have received my instructions, I see."

"Yes sir! We have made a beginning, but Miss Darcy wanted to consult with you more particularly before we proceeded any further with decorations." Reynolds leant forward conspiratorially and whispered, "She's been happy as a grig, sir, going through all the gewgaws in the attics and inspecting the Christmas linen and plate. Thanks be!" He straightened then and turned to direct the disposal of the trunks while Darcy strode through the archway.

As Darcy lengthened his stride toward the double-flighted stair leading into the hall, he looked up to catch a flash of colour at the second floor window that commanded the most favourable view of the approaching. He stopped and with narrowed eye searched the window for another glimpse. None was vouchsafed to him; so, with a smile to himself, he proceeded up one of the stairs, his hands already working at his greatcoat buttons so as to divest himself of encumbrances as soon as he was inside the doors. The task was completed as the doors swung open and the coat neatly shrugged off into the care of a footman, but to no purpose. Georgiana was not in the hall. He looked about questioningly, but recalled himself as Mrs. Reynolds and the upper staff bowed their greetings to the master.

"Mr. Darcy, welcome home, sir!" Mrs. Reynolds repeated both the words and heartfelt sincerity of her husband's greeting.

"Mrs. Reynolds! Thank you. It is very good to be home, ma'am." Darcy grinned down into the face of a woman who had been intimate with the life of his family since he was four years old. "Is Miss Darcy not here to greet me?"

"Miss Darcy will receive you in the music room, sir, as is proper, she being no longer a moppet-miss, a-running down the stairs the moment you come home," Mrs. Reynolds scolded him affectionately. "Now it is you who must run! Up to the music room with you, sir, to a sight that will gladden your heart." Her words caught in her throat for a moment as her old eyes misted, "…as it has gladdened this old soul's." She quickly whisked a handkerchief from her apron pocket and wiped them as she motioned with the other hand to the stairs. "Go on with you!"

"Yes, ma'am," Darcy responded obediently, then qualified it with a sly smile, "if you will have dinner early this evening. The talents of the new cook at the Leicester Arms were somewhat questionable; thus, I have not partaken of more than bread, cheese and local brew since before noon."

"No more than we suspected, sir," Mrs. Reynolds sniffed. "Miss Darcy has planned a fine welcome dinner that will be ready at six o'clock, if it pleases you, sir."

"Miss Darcy has?" Darcy looked up the stairs in wonder. "You will excuse me, ma'am." He nodded to her curtsy and made for the stairs to the rooms on the second floor. A spark of hope made common cause with his ever-vigilant caution in all things touching his sister as Darcy hurried up the stairs to the music room. A few quick strides from the top he slowed his pace in happy expectation of being welcomed with enticing strains from the pianoforte or a soft, melodious voice, but neither fell upon his ears. Only the tick of the great hall clock celebrated his approach.

What was Georgiana about? His brow furrowed in puzzlement. She had not come down to welcome him home, nor, would it appear, was she occupied in greeting his arrival with song. Perhaps Mrs. Reynolds was mistaken and she did not await him in the music room. He stopped at the conjunction of the hall he now traversed with another which led to the private family rooms and bit his lower lip as he peered down each in turn, the accumulating silence preying upon his hopes. Could it be that he had deluded himself? Had the changes in her letters been merely his wishful thinking?

In an unease, which increased with every step, Darcy continued down the darkening hall until he reached the edge of the softly glowing island of light that fell from out the music room door. He stopped just outside its reaches and vainly tried to throw his senses before him, as if he might, in some way, gain some premonition of what awaited him within; but no impression was gifted to him. Denied even a modicum of foreknowledge, he took a deep breath in preparation for whatever might come and quietly crossed the threshold.

She was sitting on one of the pair of divans that faced each other across a low table, her back to the window, her figure erect but pliant. She was attired becomingly but quite simply in a fine blue wool frock edged with knitted lace, which, while modest, left no doubt that she had bid girlhood *adieu.* Her eyes were downcast, apparently fixed upon her delicately formed hands that lay in her lap, allowing him only a view of the dark, glossy curls that framed her brow. *There has been no change.* Darcy's shoulders sagged, his disappointment a keen-edged threat to the hope he had nurtured for the last several weeks. The temptation to despair nearly overtook him, but he thrust it away. Georgiana needed him, needed his strength; and in this, he vowed he would not fail her.

"Georgiana?" he ventured softly.

At her name, Georgiana's head came up and, to Darcy's amazement, merry stars danced for joy in the eyes that met his own. She rose gracefully from the divan, a shy smile wreathing her face and, without a word, stretched out her arms to him. Without knowing how he came there, he found himself across the room, standing over her. "Georgiana!" he choked out and in the next moment his arms were entirely full and wonderfully engaged in holding the dearest of sisters against his heart.

"Dear Brother," Georgiana breathed gently against his waistcoat. Darcy blinked rapidly several times before allowing her to pull away sufficiently to look up into his face. "I cannot tell you how happy I am that you are home!"

The purity of expression upon her face, so completely in opposition to her woeful melancholy of the summer past, bereft him of speech. He could only look with thankful wonder into the placid depths uplifted to him. Georgiana blushed at his scrutiny and rested her burning cheek once more upon his chest before he could assure her of his own joy in being home.

"I had meant to receive you properly," she murmured against the haven within which he still held her. "I had meant to be quite formal, you know, and say, 'So, you are home, Brother' and 'How was your journey?'" She pulled back from his embrace. "But it all flew out of my head when you came and stood over me. Oh, dear, *dear*

Brother!" The smile she bestowed then upon him gave Darcy's heart to turn again within his chest and once more, he could not speak.

"Will you have some tea now before you dress for dinner? It is all here on the table."

"Y-yes," he managed to respond, "tea would be perfect." He released her with reluctance and allowed her to lead him down onto the divan beside her. The dimple they both had inherited from their father peeped out from her softly rounded cheek as she set about pouring. It deepened yet more as she turned to present him his cup.

"There, you have not been gone so long that I have forgotten how you like it, but do tell me if I *have* remembered amiss." He took the cup and sipped at it cautiously, determined to pronounce it 'perfect' regardless of the taste. There was no need of prevarication. It was just as he liked, and for some inexplicable reason, that fact seemed to loose a wave communicating sweet relief from the heavy, haunting guilt he had carried since spring. The sigh that escaped his lips was unquenchable. Georgiana laughed softly but, at the curious light that arose in his eyes, lowered her own to her cup in some confusion.

"You have remembered exactly, Dearest," Darcy hastened to assure her, hoping to see the dimple again, but Georgiana remained preoccupied with her cup. Although a hundred questions concerning her transformation fought each other to be voiced, he hesitated to broach the subject, fearful that their mention would shatter the wonderful peace that sheltered them at that moment. It would be better not to stray outside the bounds of polite social intercourse, he decided, until he was more sure of her condition. "Should you like to hear of my journey home?" he inquired gently, "or would you rather hear of London?"

At his question, her delicate chin rose slightly, but she still did not look at him, preferring instead to examine the intricacies of the tatting of her napkin. "Truly, Brother, I should like most of all to hear of Hertfordshire." Her gaze flickered quickly to his face and then away. Darcy could not guess what she saw there, for his surprise at her request was complete and he had had no opportunity to school his features.

"Hertfordshire!" he repeated, somewhat hoarsely. Something inside of him clenched and a sudden remembrance of lavender and sun-kissed curls sent shards of longing to pierce and shred what remained of his equanimity.

"Yes," she replied, her dimple returning as she tilted her head and looked directly at him. "Your letter from London told nothing of the ball. Was it well attended?" The re-animation of her manner put Darcy in a quandary. How devoutly he wished to forget Hertfordshire or, at least, to relegate it to those times when he was safely alone and able to come to grips with the memories it conjured up. So quickly its mention had discomposed him, sending him into places he dare not go without great care. Yet this dangerous subject was the one thing that his sister most desired of him!

"Yes," he answered her, looking away, "it was extremely well attended. It was not long before I began to believe that the entire county was in attendance." He hoped his dampening tone would discourage any further probing of that evening.

"And Mr. Bingley? He must have been pleased that so many honoured his invitation." Georgiana smiled in anticipation of her brother's affirmation of Bingley's pleasure.

"Bingley was quite pleased." Darcy paused, ostensibly to indulge in more of his tea, but in truth, to order his thoughts. "I should say that Miss Bingley was pleased as well. At least at the start of the evening," he amended. A questioning look appeared on Georgiana's face but she did not pursue his qualification. Her interest, as he would discover, lay elsewhere.

"Did he dance with the young lady you wrote of? Miss Bennet?"

"Yes," Darcy replied curtly.

"Did he show her any particular attention?" Darcy looked closely now at his sister, but could detect no ulterior interest in Bingley's affairs in her bright eyes. *No, she does not ask this for herself,* he decided. *She does not think of him as anything other than my friend.*

"He very nearly made a fool of himself over her, I regret to say," he replied in a voice rather more harsh than he had intended, "but he has come to his senses and put Miss Bennet behind him. I do not believe he will return to Hertfordshire," he ended firmly, but softened at his sister's paled countenance. "It was nothing *very* shocking, Georgiana, just poor judgment on his part, I assure you. He is well out of it and a wiser man for it."

"As you say...but, poor Mr. Bingley!" Georgiana's face clouded and she looked down into her cup. After a few moments of silence between them, wherein Darcy deemed the subject closed, he put down his own cup and, relieving Georgiana of hers, possessed himself of her hands. They lay soft and compliant in his strong, corded ones and she did not resist as he brought first one and then the other to his lips in tender salute.

"Do not concern yourself, Dearest. He is a man grown and can take his knocks. You know his happy nature. He will recover."

Georgiana returned him a serious regard. "But what of Miss *Elizabeth* Bennet? Did she correct her opinion of you? How shall I meet her if Mr. Bingley does not return to Hertfordshire nor wish to renew the acquaintance?"

Darcy almost dropped her hands in astonishment. "Is *this* the meaning of your distress? You wish to meet Miss Elizabeth Bennet! Pray...why, Georgiana?"

Georgiana gently pulled her hands from his grasp and, with her brother's eyes intent upon her, rose from the divan and walked to the old pianoforte at the window. She ran her fingers along its smooth, polished side before turning back to him and his question.

"I told you in my letter that I cannot bear to think that someone you admire does not return your admiration and, indeed, thinks ill of you. I would know whether she admitted her error." She looked to him for confirmation, but seeing his face hurried to add, "Oh, not in words, perhaps, but in her regard? Did you part on amiable terms?"

"As a gentleman, I cannot say whether the terms were regarded amiably on Miss Elizabeth's part. That would be for her to affirm or deny," Darcy replied carefully, his curiosity at his sister's interest in Elizabeth overcoming his determination to put away all thoughts of her.

"Were they amiable on your part, then?" The innocent, hopeful look she cast him gave him to wish he had tried more faithfully to follow her sisterly advice.

"I followed your advice to the best of my poor ability." he smiled ruefully as he joined her at the instrument. "I was as amiable as I am able to be on a ballroom floor."

"You *danced* with her, then?"

Darcy could have groaned. The more he attempted to conceal, the more she seemed to learn. At this rate, she would soon be in possession of the entire story. He looked in wonder at her as she stood there before him, her eyes so alive with interest. Her transformation was astonishing—nay—miraculous, and Darcy meant to know exactly how it had taken place. He would start tomorrow, but he had not yet the nerve to tax Georgiana with it. He made a mental note to interview at first light the woman under whose care Georgiana had overcome so grievous a wound.

He shook his head at her, refusing to answer her question, and then smiled down into her upturned face. "My dear girl, if you would have a moment-by-moment account, you must provide me greater sustenance than a dish of tea. Now, what have you ordered for this dinner Mrs. Reynolds spoke of? For, I warn you, I am *that* hungry!"

The dimple that cleft his cheek was swiftly matched by its feminine counterpart as Georgiana returned his loving gaze. Softly, she slipped into his arms once more. "Oh, Fitzwilliam, I am ever so glad you are home!"

His arms tightly woven about her, Darcy looked thankfully to heaven and then, burying his face into her gathered curls, could only find the strength to whisper in reply, "No more than I, Dearest. No more than I."

~3~
The Uses of Adversity

Sitting back in the chair at his study desk, the corner of his lower lip caught between his teeth, Darcy perused the letters he held in his hand once more. Satisfied that he had committed all the particulars of the first to memory, he laid it aside and proceeded to the second as the baroque clock on the mantle struck an half-hour past eight. As regular as that timepiece, the door to the study opened, admitting Mr. Reynolds and a footman bearing a tray laden with Darcy's morning coffee and toast.

"Reynolds." Darcy looked up from his reading and motioned the footman to lay the tray upon his desk. "A moment of your time."

"Yes sir, Mr. Darcy. How can I serve you?" The older man signalled the footman to depart and to close the door behind him.

Darcy laid the remaining letters upon his desk and looked up intently at the most senior member of his Pemberley staff. Reynolds' knowledge of the inner workings of life at Pemberley was comparable to none and, during and after the elder Mr. Darcy's illness, his unfailing guidance in all things pertaining to the great house had been as necessary to Darcy as Hinchcliffe's had been in the financial arena. In short, he was a man who held the Darcy name and family almost as dearly as Darcy did himself and Darcy trusted him implicitly.

"I find that I must place you in a deuced awkward position, Reynolds, but the matter is of such import that I must ask you to bear with it and assist me."

"Of course, sir!" Reynolds affirmed his willingness, although his face registered some surprise at his master's preamble.

Darcy looked away from the kindly face, his embarrassment about the request he was to make acute. "Well, there is no delicate way to put this, so I shall be straightforward with you." He turned then, back to him, "What can you tell me of Mrs. Annesley?"

"Mrs. Annesley, sir?" Reynolds' eyebrows shot up. He slowly rocked forward on his toes and back again before answering, "Well, sir....she be a fine woman, sir, quiet-like and dignified."

"And...?" Darcy prodded, as uncomfortable with insisting upon more answers as Reynolds was in giving them.

"And what, sir?"

"The woman has been in residence for four months," Darcy observed grittily, annoyed with the man's obtuseness. "There must be more you can tell me of her!"

Reynolds frowned from under bushy, white brows as he brought his finger to his stock and pulled at it. He took a few more moments to clear his throat. Then, bringing himself up painfully straight, he addressed Darcy in a tone fraught with disapproval. "I don't hold with gossip, Mr. Darcy, as you should know. Don't listen to it and don't pass it." He squinted down into his young master's countenance and, seeing the dissatisfaction etched upon it, added carefully, "All I will say is, she don't give herself airs and she's kind to all the staff, from top to bottom, sir." He fidgeted a little under the focus of Darcy's silent, searching gaze before bursting out, "Miss Darcy is wonderful fond of her." He looked for a reprieve from any further expectations and, finding none, seemed to wrestle with himself for a few moments before confessing finally, "And I bless her, Mr. Darcy, bless her morning and night for what she's done for Miss; and there, sir, is the end of it."

"That will be all then, Reynolds." Darcy dismissed him, his lips quirking at what was for his butler, a spirited defence of the lady. Mrs. Annesley had Reynolds' approval, and there was much in that. Perhaps he could put more credence in the degree of glow that issued from those references that lay before him on his desk concerning the lady. He reached over and poured some of the fresh cream into his cup and then filled it to the brim with the fragrant brew before picking up the letters again, searching out the third. Bringing his coffee to his lips, he blew on it gently as he committed the facts of the third letter to memory. The contents of the letters were not unknown to him. He had read them just as diligently upon their arrival five months before when he had been frantic for a new, trustworthy companion for Georgiana; but this time he looked for something more revealing of the lady than impeccable qualifications and unexceptional testimonials from past employers. That "something" still eluded him.

He tossed the letters down again and rose with his cup to contemplate the soothing view from his study window. Before his passing, the study had been his father's private preserve, its carved, wood-panelled walls a place of mystery during Darcy's childhood and later, a place of judgment during his adolescence. It was an intimate room and had served as the estate's book room until three-quarters of a century before, when a new, grandly appointed library had been included in his great-grandfather's plans for Pemberley's improvements. Now, although the study continued to house treasured tokens of Darcy patriarchs, it served principally as an archive of Darcy's personal book collection as well as the papers and folios that recorded the business interests and estate affairs of the family since such records had been kept.

Added to the masculine amenities of sturdy chairs and tables, displays of exquisitely crafted edged weaponry and hunting prints was a superb view out of the study's several windows. His shoulder propped against a frame, Darcy stared out into the sunken garden laid out many years ago by his grandmother. It lay bedecked in a shimmering gown of snow, its pristine whiteness in artful contrast to a variety of evergreens within the garden's design and the red brick walk that meandered delightfully about it.

As pleasing as was the view, it soon disappeared from before Darcy's eyes, transcended by visions of Georgiana at supper the night before. The dinner she had ordered was more than satisfying, consisting of many of his favourite dishes and a fine wine that had complimented all. The table had supported a tasteful arrangement of flowers and greenery prepared, he discovered upon his mention of it, by her own hand. She had blushed faintly in pleasure at his approval and thanked him with a graciousness of temper that he had never surprised from her in the past.

Their conversation had been of local matters: children born to his tenants, deaths in the village, the harvest festival in Lambton and the annual service of thanksgiving at St. Lawrence's three weeks previously. All the while he had observed her, gingerly testing the extent of the changes in this new creature that was his sister. There were moments still of shyness and hesitancy. His teasing remarks were occasionally answered with a glance of uncertainty; yet she had replied to his questions concerning their tenants, and neighbours in sure tones, a gentle, newfound compassion suffusing her countenance as she spoke. By the end of their meal, he could only sit and marvel at her.

She had risen when the last cover was removed to leave him to a glass of port, but he had refused, declaring that surely she *must* have a piece to play for him after all these months and *several* letters professing her diligence. She had laughed, her happiness in his company transparent in her face, and allowed him to lead her back to the music room where she had played for him a full half-hour. Then, bringing forth his much-neglected violin, he had joined her at the pianoforte and they played duets until their fingers ached.

Darcy looked down at his left hand, flexing it against the remaining soreness, but a sound at the study door brought his head up. His lips pressed into a firm, straight line. The lady was early, but all to the better. Perhaps he could now get some answers.

"Enter," he called, but the only response was a shuffling back and forth of the doorknob and a strange tapping noise. "Enter!" he called again, and the doorknob turned just enough to allow the door to fall away slightly from the frame. Confounded, Darcy straightened and took a step, "What the…?"

The door suddenly burst aside on its hinges and a large blur of brown, black and white launched itself across the floor. Darcy bolted to his desk and dropped his cup before the whirlwind could come upon him. "Trafalgar—SIT!" he bellowed and braced himself for certain impact, but the moment the words left his lips the hound's hindquarters hit the polished wood floor. The animal skidded the last several feet, his front feet wildly pawing for purchase before coming to rest against the toe of his boot. A large pink tongue flickered over the black tip before the animal raised deliriously happy eyes to his master's face.

"Mr. Darcy! Oh, sir…I am so sorry, sir!" Darcy looked away from the ridiculous grin upon the face of his errant beast to behold one of the junior grooms standing in the doorway seesawing from one foot to another while wringing his cap between his fists. "I was bringin' 'im in, as you ordered, Mr. Darcy. He gave me the slip, sir. He's *that* canny."

Darcy looked down at Trafalgar, who, meanwhile, had turned his head back over his shoulder to observe the groom's recital. If he had not known better, Darcy would have sworn the hound was laughing. He shook his head. "You may leave him with me, Joseph, but should he escape you again, march him back to the steward's entrance rather than letting him into my study. He must be made to learn *some* manners." Darcy leaned down and grasped the hound's muzzle, lifting it to his gaze. "That is, if you wish to continue a *gentleman's* companion." Trafalgar snuffled a bit at his tone, but then barked his agreement, sealing it with a surreptitious lick of Darcy's hand.

"But, Mr. Darcy, I never let 'im in!"

"You did not open the door, Joseph?"

"No, sir; never sir! He was in your study 'afore I reached the hall corner." In unison, both men looked sharply at the hound, who was totally occupied at the moment with exhibiting behaviour appropriate to a beast belonging to the most discriminating of gentlemen.

"You mean to tell me that he opened the door himself?" Darcy demanded incredulously. The young groom twisted his cap again and shrugged his shoulders.

"Excuse me, but it is quite possible the hound *did* open the door on its own," a smoothly modulated, feminine voice interrupted gently. "I have seen it done as a trick, although the animal must first be trained to it." At the voice, the groom moved away from the door and tugged his forelock at the lady as she came around him. She smiled and nodded to him before turning to Darcy and making her curtsy. "Mr. Darcy."

"Mrs. Annesley!" Darcy glanced at the clock, which faithfully displayed the fact that the time was indeed nine and his appointment with Georgiana's companion was upon him. This was definitely *not* how he had envisioned their interview to begin. The consternation he was feeling at being caught off-guard was deftly hidden. "Please come in, ma'am." Darcy stepped back and indicated a chair.

The lady inclined her head and entered the study, walking gracefully past the groom. Trafalgar looked at her with interest and rose to carry on an investigation, but the impulse was quelled by a stern look from his master. He lay down instead at Darcy's feet, his muzzle on his paws and his eyes flicking from one to the other in anticipation.

Mrs. Annesley appeared to Darcy much as he remembered her from five months before, save, perhaps, for the amused twinkle in her eye as she surveyed Trafalgar, who had taken upon himself guard duty of his master's boots. Last summer, Darcy had not looked for a merry heart in a companion for his sister, but a steady character whose motherly understanding and firm principles might rescue Georgiana from the melancholy depths of heartache and self-recrimination into which she had fallen after Ramsgate. Apparently, the lady had possessed such a heart in addition to his requirements and had succeeded beyond all his hopes. Whatever her method, he thought as he followed her back into the study, he was prepared to be extremely generous.

"Mrs. Annesley," he began as he took his seat and then looked at her across his desk, "am I to understand you believe this misbegotten beggar has learned to open doors?"

"It is quite possible, Mr. Darcy," she replied with a gentle smile. "My sons taught their dog all manner of tricks; opening doors was one of them. Although," she looked down into the hound's attentive face, "I think we may allow in this case that the last person to leave your study may not have brought the door completely shut. But, with one such success, I have no doubt that an intelligent animal like Master Trafalgar will continue to try his luck."

"I fear you are right." Darcy cocked a brow down at the "beggar" who took the moment to yawn and innocently blink back his regard. "You mentioned sons," he continued, "Are they at school?"

"My younger son, Titus, is at University, sir. He was admitted to Trinity last year under the sponsorship of a friend of his late father. Roman, my older son, is graduated and serving a curacy in Weston-super-Mare. If it pleases you, sir, I hope to spend Christmas there with them both." She returned his gaze pleasantly, the openness of her request inclining Darcy to grant it immediately and further, to offer her transportation to the very doorstep. "You are very kind, Mr. Darcy," she responded, the light in her hazel eyes glowing warmly before she bowed her head.

"It is the very least of services I would offer you, Mrs. Annesley." Darcy rose from his chair and stepped to the window, his jaw working as he searched for an avenue that would take the interview where he wished it to go. "I am very much in your debt, ma'am. My sister…" His throat seemed to close up at the remembrance of his joyful homecoming. He began again, "My sister is so wonderfully changed, I can scarce believe it! You know what she was when you came to Pemberley, so broken…" He turned away to the window behind him, determined to maintain his dignity. "But even before that horrible business, she had been shy and retiring. Only in her music did she express herself freely. Now…!" He turned back to her sympathetic eye. "How did you do it, ma'am?" His eyes bore down upon her as his voice gained stridency. "My cousin and I did everything in our power, all we could conceive of, to recall her to herself;

but it was for naught. You have succeeded where we had failed, and I would know how!"

The lady gave him no immediate reply, but the compassionate cast of her countenance gave him to know that his imperious words had not offended her. "Dear sir," she began quietly, "I am sure you did all that you could to aid Miss Darcy. But sir, her sorrows were deep—deeper than you know—deeper than it was in your power to reach. You must not berate yourself or your efforts."

Darcy sucked in his breath in surprise. *How dare she patronize him? Not in his power!* He drew himself up, looming over the small, seated woman. "Then, ma'am, I must inquire, by what 'power' did *you* descend to my sister's great depths and pull her out?" he returned stiffly, his lips curled in a sneer. "Will charms and potions be discovered among Miss Darcy's bonnets and reticules?"

Mrs. Annesley's eyes widened briefly at his tone, but her composure did not desert her, for she returned his bold look, albeit not his incivility. "No sir, such things you will not find," she replied firmly. "The human heart is not so easily mastered. Trumpery will not turn it aside of its course."

Darcy's face darkened, his brows slanting down in distaste. "You speak of her feelings for…" He hesitated and then spat out the words, "her seducer?"

The lady did not recoil at his frankness but answered in kind, "No, Mr. Darcy, I do not. Miss Darcy's melancholy was never from lovesickness for that man. When you discovered them at Ramsgate and confronted Mr. Wickham, Miss Darcy's eyes were opened to his character. She has not spent these months in regretting him."

While she spoke, Darcy resumed his seat at the desk, his lips pursed in dissatisfaction. "You have revealed what Miss Darcy's thoughts were *not* and, for what it is worth, I am relieved on that score. But you have yet to reveal what they *have been*, or what you have done to effect their remedy. Come, Mrs. Annesley," he insisted, his shoulders stiff with hauteur, "I require answers."

The lady's brow wrinkled slightly as she looked him back, her lips pressed together, in apparent consideration of whether to meet his demand. Taken aback at her hesitancy, a niggling doubt arose in Darcy's breast that the woman before him would comply with his wishes. Accompanying that thought was the conviction that the merry heart he had detected earlier might just beat before a backbone made of steel.

"Mr. Darcy, do you give any credence to Providence?" That she had answered him with a question startled him no less than its subject did.

"Providence, Mrs. Annesley?" Darcy stared at her in incredulity, his late dissatisfaction with the ways of the Supreme Judge hardening the set of his features. *What had Providence to do with this?*

"Do you hold that God directs the affairs of men?"

"I am fully aware of the meaning, Mrs. Annesley. I was well catechised as a child," he rebuked her icily, "but I fail to see…"

"Then sir, how does it go? Do you remember?"

Darcy's eyes narrowed dangerously at her challenge. Through clenched jaws he recited quickly, "'God, the great Creator of all things doth uphold, direct, dispose, and govern all creatures, actions, and things, from the greatest even to the least, by His most wise and holy providence.' I had forgotten, ma'am, that you are the widow of a clergyman. Doubtless, you are used to seeing all about you as directly from the hand of the Almighty, unlike the majority of us who must strive in the world of men."

His sarcasm went wide of its mark, for she only smiled gently at his answer. "Very good, Mr. Darcy. You were quite perfect in your recitation." She rose from her chair, her movement exciting Trafalgar's interest once again. The hound pulled himself up, shook himself thoroughly from ear to tail and looked to Darcy expectantly.

"Mrs. Annesley." Darcy scowled darkly as he also stood. "You have in nowise given me a satisfactory account. I am indebted to you, certainly, but I am not accustomed to obtuseness from my employees. I insist upon a straightforward answer, ma'am."

"When my husband died of a pneumonia contracted from his parish work, Mr. Darcy, leaving me with two sons to raise and no means to keep a roof over our heads, I was cast into a deep sorrow much like Miss Darcy's." She bowed her head for a moment, whether to collect herself or to escape his disapproving scowl, Darcy did not know. Raising her head, she continued with feeling, "I was recalled to the ways of Providence by a friend who reminded me of two convergent truths. The first was from Scripture. It begins, 'And we know that all things work together for good to them that love God…'" She looked intently up into his eyes, her memories kindling her face aglow. "The second, comes from the Bard:

Sweet are the uses of adversity,
Which, like the toad, ugly and venomous,

Wears yet a precious jewel in his head.

You ask me what I did for your sister, Mr. Darcy, and I must tell you *I* did nothing, nothing more than my friend did for me. It was not in your power or mine to comfort Miss Darcy and bring her from sorrow to joy. For that, you must look elsewhere, sir; and the place to begin is with Miss Darcy herself."

Most definitely made of steel! Darcy looked down into the small woman's steadfast countenance. She was correct, after all. The answers he wanted could only come from Georgiana whether this woman had performed magic or had merely quoted Scripture to her. Whatever the case, he would have to dare the permanence of his sister's recovery. The thought chilled him.

"You are a plain speaker, I see, when you finally come to the point, Mrs. Annesley," he drawled as he came around his desk. "I will take your advice concerning Miss Darcy, although I will admit to being disinclined to tease her about it at present until I am convinced of her complete recovery." He stopped before her and inclined his head. "I do truly thank you, ma'am, for whatever your influence has been over my sister. You came highly recommended by your previous employers and my own staff sings your praises." Darcy had begun stiffly, but as the truth of his words made itself felt in his own breast, his voice softened. "Please accept my sincere gratitude."

Mrs. Annesley smiled graciously at his speech and dropped him a curtsy before fixing him once more with twinkling eyes. "Your gratitude is received with welcome, Mr. Darcy. Miss Darcy is the loveliest young lady I have had the pleasure to know and she will, I have no doubt, grow into a noble womanhood. Do forebear quizzing her, as you have said, but give her your time and love. She will blossom, and you will discover all."

"May it be as you say, ma'am." Darcy inclined his head, signalling that the interview was at an end.

The lady responded in kind and turned to leave, but stopped short at the door and faced him once more. "Pardon me, Mr. Darcy."

"Yes, Mrs. Annesley?"

"Did you wish Master Trafalgar to have the freedom of the house now that you are returned?"

"That is my habit, Mrs. Annesley; although, he usually stays by me." Darcy looked around the study, but the hound was nowhere to be seen. "Did you open the door just now?"

"No, Mr. Darcy, it was open already. I think Master Trafalgar became impatient with us."

A high-pitched wail echoed through the hall beyond the study door followed by the drumming sound of paws hitting the wooden floor of the stairs and then pounding down the hall.

"Step back, Mrs. Annesley!" Darcy warned just in time as Trafalgar rounded the corner and shot through the doorway. At the sight of his master, the hound checked gracefully and approached him at a slow trot, skirting 'round him and coming to heel just behind his boots. "What have you done now, Monster?" he sighed. Trafalgar delicately licked his chops as Darcy's cook came to a breathless halt at his study door.

~~~~~~~&~~~~~~~

All thought of putting Mrs. Annesley's advice to the test was laid aside as the remainder of Darcy's first week home was filled with the necessity of attending to estate business. Having been absent during this year's harvest, Darcy had much to do to acquaint himself with the conditions of Pemberley's numerous farms and concerns. His steward was most anxious for his attention to be lavished upon the quarterly books, as well as for the opportunity to make his report on the success of that season's venture in the application of Mr. Young's *New Agriculture*. Darcy had never been one of that company of landowners satisfied with mere bookkeeping; thus, more than one afternoon was spent on arduous tours of inspection and discussion with workers and tenants alike on the results of their season's labours. Then, of course, there was Mrs. Reynolds, to consult concerning the Pemberley household, Reynolds, to discuss the servants and the expenses of the hall, and a myriad of staff to interview on the preparations for a return to the traditional celebration of Christmas at Pemberley and arrangements for the family visit of his Uncle and Aunt Fitzwilliam.

By Saturday night, Darcy was exhausted and his mind benumbed with facts, figures and the innumerable details requisite to making those decisions which would lead Pemberley and its people to a prosperous future. After his last appointment with his stable manager, Fletcher had anticipated him and, thankfully, provided a
~~~~~~~

relaxing bath followed by correct but comfortable dress for his dinner with his sister. They had dined quietly, but the assurance and modest grace with which his sister conducted their meal generated more questions in his breast, questions which clamoured against all the others residing there for resolution. She could not have missed his distraction, so great was it that he contributed little more than a few syllables to their conversation. Georgiana, a loving smile gracing her face, assumed that responsibility and entertained him with accounts of events at Pemberley during his absence until, noting his fatigue, she had sweetly offered to play for him when their meal was through.

Sitting back now on the divan in the music room with his eyes closed, Darcy briefly considered his sister's easy confidence at table and her womanly solicitude for his comfort. Her kind attention to his mood and need for diversion seemed further evidence of the efficacy of that agency about which Mrs. Annesley had made only inscrutable hints. He made a fleeting attempt to reason it through before he surrendered to the music, giving himself to it and allowing it to spread its soothing balm over his weariness. It was not long before he knew himself to be drifting into that seductive otherworld that called to the unwary caught between wakefulness and sleep. Too tired to pull back from its borders, the music enveloped Darcy's attenuated senses and began playing tricks upon them. The figure at the pianoforte shifted curiously and dimmed, gently transforming herself from one dear to him into another, whose dearness in more cogent hours he would not allow. But now, at this moment, that dearness seemed perfectly reasonable; and he welcomed her appearance with a languorous smile and a deep, inner sigh.

Contentment at Elizabeth's presence in his home, with her ease at the pianoforte playing for him, and with the notion of their companionable seclusion warmed his frame like the effects of a fine brandy. He was sure that if he moved his foot just so he would fetch up against her embroidery basket, and if he had the strength to slide his hand along the divan, he would find her lavender-scented shawl carelessly draped over its back. His eyes still closed, he turned his head and breathed in slowly. *Yes,* he smiled again; he could detect that reminder of her drifting to him from within its silken folds.

The music continued from her hand, softly flowing, seeking out all his hollow places to fill them with longing for what only she could bring to him. "Elizabeth," he breathed, his voice low-pitched as he acknowledged her power. The music hesitated, then continued on its intimate exploration of his emotions. He knew himself to be enthralled, just as he had been at Sir William's and later, during the evening of the ball at Netherfield. He knew it, and rather than pushing it away, he welcomed it with a joy that he now saw mirrored in her eyes. They were strolling through the conservatory, his parents' Eden, lush with blossoms, and she was whispering of something that necessitated leaning down close.

"Fitzwilliam." His name on her lips, so close that her breath fanned his check, was a most agreeable sensation. The answering surge of blood through his veins emboldened him to reach for her hand.

"Elizabeth," he murmured, returning her whisper with feeling.

"Fitzwilliam?" The question in her voice was not what he was expecting, nor was its timbre. "Brother?"

Darcy's eyes flew open as, with a jolt, he came back to himself and to the reality of Georgiana perched on the divan beside him, valiantly attempting to suppress the cascade of giggles that threatened to spill over fingers pressed tightly to her lips. He blinked at her, for a few moments unable to comprehend that what he had felt, so real that his heart still beat powerfully in response, had all been a dream. He looked desperately beside him on the divan, but no shawl reposed there, nor was an embroidery basket to be seen at his feet.

"Brother, what are you searching for? May I be of help?" Georgiana had sobered somewhat, but laughter still danced in her eyes and her lower lip was firmly caught in droll amusement at his disordered state.

Darcy eyed her with sudden horror. *What had he said as he sat here dreaming? How had he allowed it to happen?* A lingering warmth suffused his body, reminding him of the strength of the inducement he had withstood until fatigue had breached his defences. If he was to recoup his losses, he must needs rally immediately; but the freezing retort died, stillborn before it reached his lips, as he stared in new awareness at his sister. When had Georgiana ever dared to laugh so? When was the last time he had been brother to her, rather than guardian-father?

His bemused regard of her was too much a test of her equanimity. Georgiana's laughter spilled forth in beautiful swells that brought tears to her eyes and, when he allowed himself a rueful quirk in response, she sank helplessly against the back of the divan. "Oh, Fitzwilliam!" she finally managed, "I pray you will forgive me, but I have never seen you so!"

"Yes, well…I believe that I must have fallen asleep," he offered uncomfortably as he straightened his posture from the traitorous one that had encouraged his indiscretion.

"*Well* asleep…and dreaming, I should imagine," she replied, looking at him keenly through tear-brightened eyes. She continued softly, "Will you tell me about Miss Elizabeth Bennet now, Brother?"

Darcy peered down into her open, earnest face for several moments before looking away. *Tell her,* a voice within him urged. In truth, what is there to tell? We quarrelled, we called a truce, and we danced and quarrelled again. *Finis!* He returned to his sister's hopeful countenance and abandoned immediately any idea of offering her such a prosaic account. It would not do, nor was it entirely the truth.

"What is she like, Brother? Should I like her?" Georgiana's smile became wistful as she gently pressed him.

Darcy felt his reticence slip, and his heart expand as he beheld her so. "So many questions, my dear," he murmured as he took her hand. "Do you truly wish answers to them all?"

Her hand turned in his and squeezed it briefly. "I have tried to be content with your wish for privacy, Fitzwilliam, and not tease you. But so often you are distracted. A certain look crosses your face, and I sense you are thinking of her." She blushed as he started at her assertion. "At least, I believe that is so."

"Distracted? How so? I am sure you must be mistaken," he denied swiftly, but it did not dissuade her.

"Were you not, just now, dreaming of Miss Elizabeth?"

Darcy knew he was fairly caught. She was asking for his trust, requesting that he make trial of her. This change in her both excited his admiration and alarmed him. Her new wholeness was all and more than he could have wished for; but he could not understand it or bring himself to question her concerning it. Nor could he, for fear of the fragility of her newfound confidence, withstand her plea for anything that was clearly in his power to give. It was surely "check and mate." How could he be anything less than truthful with this precious one entrusted to him by heaven and their father? Darcy took a steadying breath.

"I will tell you what you wish to know as far as I am able." He held up a warning hand at her bright smile. "But I warn you now that you will find it all rather disappointing. I am not a 'romantic.' Although I do not pretend to know her mind, on *that* subject the lady in question would surely agree." Darcy paused to assess the effect of his caution, but the dimple on Georgiana's cheek only deepened further. "Where should you like me to begin?" He sighed in resignation.

"Tell me what she is like! Miss Elizabeth Bennet must be a singular lady to have earned your regard." Georgiana settled back on the divan, awaiting his answer as she had awaited the stories he had read to her as a child.

"Miss Elizabeth Bennet is…" Darcy's brow wrinkled in thought. He had never tried to quantify her. She did not precisely belong within any group of women of his acquaintance. She was…Elizabeth! "Miss Elizabeth Bennet is a female who defies the usual categories of society." He frowned into space. "That is to say, she is unusual. But," he hastened to add, "you must not imagine she is an Antidote or one of those dreadful Unconventional Females." He smiled to himself. "One of her neighbours, a squire, spoke of her as a woman of 'uncommon good sense wrapped up in as neat a package as could be desired.' The description does not do her justice, but it is not far off the mark."

"She is pretty then? Beautiful?" Georgiana prodded him.

She a beauty? I would as soon call her mother a wit! He flinched at the memory of his injudicious words and wondered that he had ever thought so.

"I did not think so at first, but that was because she is not formed in the classical manner and I did not have the wit to appreciate her." Darcy found himself becoming more expansive as he concentrated on answering his sister truthfully. "As I grew to know her, however, I found her very pleasing. Very pleasing, indeed! It was her eyes, I think, that first arrested my attention. They are very expressive, and when she lifts her brow, they speak volumes to those who can…" A giggle interrupted his soliloquy.

"Forgive me, Brother," Georgiana apologized sincerely. "Do go on."

"She is beautiful, yes. I think so, at any rate." He finished abruptly. "What more do you wish to know?"

"Is she kind as well as beautiful?" Georgiana's voice trembled a little.

Alert to her apprehension, Darcy was thankful for his answer. "Miss Elizabeth Bennet is a strong-minded young woman," he admitted, "but also a most kind one. Her attention to her sister who fell ill at Netherfield was unflagging. Nothing was done for Miss Bennet that Miss Elizabeth did not do herself." Recollecting other scenes, he continued, "I have seen her set crusty, old majors at ease and buck up the confidence of shy misses and country-bred youths almost in the same breath." He laughed at the memory of that evening and then almost immediately sobered. "But, I must say that she does not suffer fools or toady to those who may or may not be her betters. She is polite, of course, but she can hold her own. To that, my own experience can testify!"

"Yes," his sister responded eagerly. "And were you able to regain her good favour?"

Darcy's brow wrinkled once more as he pressed his lips together, considering her question. What should he say? What was the truth? "I truly do not know, my dear," he confessed. "She accepted my hand at the ball, or rather she acquiesced for politeness' sake, and we seemed to get on; but then, for various reasons, the accord we had reached began to unravel. Afterward, events so transpired that she would not have welcomed my company on any terms."

The pleasurable sensations Georgiana's questions had conjured in his breast faded as his narrative reached the point of their true state of affairs. Their place remained empty as they took flight and left him with only his duty and the ache of a frustrated desire. He should not indulge these memories, he told himself severely. Was not he, himself, the assassin of any inclinations in that direction? There was no purpose to this; it was against all reason that he should tease himself thus.

"I have not seen or spoken to her since that night," he continued brusquely, "and, as Bingley has recovered from his infatuation with her sister, it does not seem reasonable to expect that she will ever come in my way again. And that, my dear sister, is all there is to that!"

"You will not seek her out?" Georgiana looked at him with a mixture of surprise and regret. "You will not preserve the acquaintance?"

"No," he replied, choosing the plain, unvarnished truth over a softer answer.

"I shall never meet her, then?" she asked sadly.

The droop of her shoulders at his reply gave Darcy pause. "I shall not say 'never,' dearest," he retreated, "but it is not likely. Her fortune is very small. She would not move in the same circles of society in which we do."

"I should still like to meet her, Brother" she whispered.

"I think I should like that as well, Georgiana," he returned. "Although why, and to what purpose, I do not know, save that I believe you could not find a truer friend." The idea surprised in him a comforting hope. "Perhaps that is enough." He leaned over and kissed her forehead. "Now, if you will excuse me, I must take myself off to bed. Sherril has nearly killed me with clambering over grain sacks and up and down loft ladders, and I do not wish to fall asleep in public again!"

He left her looking after him with a pensive air upon her sweet face. When he reached the door, he looked back to give her a last, bracing smile; but she was no longer aware of him. Her slim, regal bearing was bent in contemplation of the hands in her lap in such an attitude that a shiver of apprehension shook Darcy at the sight. What had been the effect of his words? Had he overburdened her or disappointed her in some fashion? Perhaps she was merely fatigued. In truth, he had been so caught up with the business of Pemberley that he had not seen to her ease or enjoyment. Rather, she had spent herself in entertaining him! He continued to his chambers and pulled at the bell, deep in self-excoriation. The morrow would be spent at Georgiana's command, Darcy vowed as he awaited Fletcher. The business of Pemberley could damn well wait!

Zealous to put into action his resolution to be at his sister's service, Darcy awoke earlier than was his habit the following morning. Lying there among his night-tossed pillows and quilts, he wondered that sleep had ever claimed him. The half-dreams he had experienced during Georgiana's music had re-animated and, worse, exposed that portion of his heart that he had thought successfully packed away. In truth, he had reconciled himself to the fact of his admiration for Elizabeth Bennet. Its veracity was attested to by the silken keepsake resting within the pages of his book. But the "sight" of her at home in his home and the degree of satisfaction that notion had brought to him in his unguarded state were appallingly dangerous to his future peace.

"Very dangerous," he spoke aloud, lecturing his errant whimsy, for Georgiana had been more correct than he had acknowledged. The source of at least some of his distraction *had* been fancies of Elizabeth, as he had begun looking at all that was familiar to him—all that was Pemberley—with what he imagined to be her critical eye. He repeated his pronouncement of the evening before, "It will not do, sir!"

The sounds of drawers opening and shutting from behind his dressing room door broke upon his consciousness. *What? Why was Fletcher about so early?* The question of arising thus decided for him, Darcy flung back the quilts; and, rising smoothly from his bed, he quietly moved across the room. Pulling open the door to his dressing room, he found his valet already within arranging his clothes, a ewer of steaming sandalwood-scented water standing at the ready.

"Fletcher!" he growled, pulling his dressing gown about him. "You are early this morning!" He stopped to stifle a yawn, "You have ever been mindful of your duties, but this is more than scrupulous attention!"

"Ahem." Fletcher cleared his throat and flushed an alarming shade of red, "Yes, sir. It is my…ah…pleasure, Mr. Darcy."

"Your pleasure! Are you ill, man? Tell me if you are ill at once! I will not have you attending me if you should be in bed. One of the others can assist me."

As red as Fletcher's face had been, it now turned quite pale. "Oh no, sir! I am very well!"

Darcy examined him sceptically, "You do not look it! Come, man, physic yourself and be done with it!"

If possible, Darcy's advice caused Fletcher to blanch even further. "I assure you, sir, I am not ill, and the last woman I want to see is Molly!"

This information caused Darcy's brow to shoot skyward. "I thought you and the herb woman had an understanding of sorts, Fletcher."

Fletcher sniffed, "Molly is of the same opinion, sir, but I never gave her my promise." He turned to his barbering instruments, plunging them into the hot, scented water. "Nor have I done wrong by her!" he added emphatically. "We were never alone, sir!"

"But things have changed, have they?" Darcy crossed his arms over his chest, dismayed that this sort of unpleasantness was occurring among his staff. Lovers' quarrels between servants caused tensions to percolate throughout a household.

"Yes, sir, they have."

"And this excessive attention to your duties?"

"It's the 'green-eyed monster,' sir," Fletcher sighed. "Everywhere I go, it's either Molly's anger, or her friends giving me a piece of their mind, or it's another woman suggesting we keep company now I'm 'free.' You have no idea, Mr. Darcy!"

"I believe I may have an inkling," Darcy snorted as he sat down in the shaving chair. "What do you propose to do?"

"If I may, Mr. Darcy, I would like to take my holiday early this year. I'd like to travel a bit before seeing my parents." Fletcher peered at him furtively as he placed the warmed towels around Darcy's neck, "I could then be here during the festivities Miss Darcy is planning."

"Lord Brougham's largesse burning a hole in your pocket, Fletcher?"

Fletcher coloured up again. "No sir, not at all, sir." He grasped the boar's hair soaping brush and swirled it vigorously in the cup. "I'm looking rather to invest it, sir."

Darcy pursed his lips, but was denied further questioning by the lathered brush being liberally applied to his face. As Fletcher stropped the shaving blade, Darcy considered whether he should probe further into the man's strange fluctuations in complexion and his cryptic answer.

"If you would lift your chin, sir." Fletcher turned back to him, the bright blade clasped firmly, ready to begin. Darcy settled back into the chair, lifted his chin and decided, under the circumstances, to leave the matter unexamined.

~4~
The Quality of Mercy

Darcy gave the ribbons another sharp snap, causing the pair pulling the sleigh to surge forward. As a result, a fresh powdering of snow filtered down upon them as they sped through the sparkling countryside. He looked sideways at his sister, but her eyes were still straight ahead, and her delicate chin continued to resemble that of a marble statue. He turned back to the horses, the stony attitude of his own chin a match for hers.

They had quarrelled! He could scarcely believe it! Try as he might, Darcy could not recall anytime in the past in which they had come to such a pass. Georgiana had always looked to him for wisdom and been guided by his wishes, but today…! The fact of their quarrelling was only a little less shocking than what they had quarrelled about, and their presence in the sleigh at this very moment was proof of whose will had prevailed. Darcy glanced at her again. She did not appear to be enjoying her victory. If truth be told, the moisture at the corner of her eye was probably due more to her disappointment with him than the sting of cold air as she had claimed.

It was that woman's fault, Mrs. Annesley! Darcy's lips twitched in anger as he laid the blame squarely upon that absent lady's shoulders. Who else could have influenced Georgiana to engage in such odd behaviour or encouraged her into such excessive sentimentality? Surely, not the vicar at St. Lawrence's, he reasoned. The Reverend Goodman he had known well for ten years at least, and never a word of such a business as this had been heard from that man's pulpit. Darcy forcefully released a chestful of pent-up air. To be out in the cold, sharp air on "errands of mercy" when a perfectly good fire blazed cheerfully in the hearth at home was not a possibility he had considered in his bid to make amends. Fletcher's troubles that morning should have warned him of what was to come.

Georgiana had joined him at breakfast with a smile and, scorning the chair at the other end of the table, had sat at his right to partake of her chocolate and toast. She had asked whether he had slept well. "Quite well, thank you," he had assured her with a dampening look, but she had only smiled back before sipping her chocolate.

Deciding that there was no better time than the present, he set down his cup. "Georgiana, I have been negligent of you since I arrived home." He shook his head at her gentle protest, "No, it is true, my dear. Not being here during the harvest set me back prodigiously in the execution of my affairs, but that is at an end. I am determined to make amends for my preoccupation and so place myself at your command. What should you like to do?" He laughed at the look of surprise on her face, but sobered when her features took on a dubious air. "I assure you, dearest, I stand by my word. Whatever you like. You may call the tune." He sat back into the chair then, an encouraging smile upon his face, awaiting her answer.

"I do not disbelieve you, Brother," Georgiana hastened to inform him. "It is that…well, today is Sunday."

"Yes," he replied, picking up his cup again, "but the snow has made a journey to Lambton difficult. I believe we will have to forego services this morning."

"I am sure you are right, Fitzwilliam," She looked down at her plate for a few moments before addressing him again. "There is something I should like to do…something I *have* been doing and wondered how I ever should be able in this snow. But you are here and could drive the sleigh."

"Drive the sleigh!" He looked at her in amused disbelief. "You want to go out driving in the snow?"

"Not driving, precisely." She looked up at him briefly, but then turned her gaze away. "Remember, I wrote to you that I had begun visiting our tenants and the families of our labourers as Mother did?"

"Yes, I recall you did," he protested, "but Georgiana, our mother never actually 'visited' them. It was more a formal affair, held quarterly on the grounds of the largest tenants." He looked disapprovingly at her. "You do not mean to say you pay calls?"

She quailed a little at his tone, but returned, "Every Sunday afternoon. I have divided up the estate, you see, and visit them in turn on their respective Sunday. Well, not all, but the poorer ones and especially those with little children…"

"Georgiana!" Darcy choked out, aghast at what he was hearing. "Good God, what can you be thinking?" He pushed back his chair and practically leapt from it while his sister's countenance grew pale at his outburst. Running a hand through his hair, he looked down at her incredulously. "It is beyond all expectation that you should expose yourself so or behave so familiarly—a Darcy of Pemberley! You will cease these 'visits' at once!"

"But, Fitzwilliam…"

"And what of disease?" he interrupted, beginning to pace before her. "Although I pride myself on the good condition of Pemberley's people, contagion is not unknown in the lower classes…even here." The possibilities caused Darcy to shudder, but a new thought quickly gripped him. "You cannot have been alone in this. Who has aided you in this madness? I want…"

"Brother!" Georgiana's voice was quiet but insistent. "Please, hear me." The earnestness of her plea arrested Darcy's pacing. "Please," she repeated, indicating his chair. "It is distressing to me to have displeased you and more so when you tower over me." Her words, echoing Bingley's complaint of his 'towering frown,' served to check his temper, but not assuage it. He curtly bowed his compliance and resumed his seat.

"Fitzwilliam, I can no longer live a life of shapeless idleness," she began softly. "My music, my books, all that occupied my time were good things and served their purpose, but they are too weak to live upon."

Darcy shifted back in his chair defensively. "You have had the finest education it was possible to secure for a female of your station. How can you say it is too weak? What can you know, young as you are, to determine such a thing?" he demanded.

"I know myself, Brother, and what I almost did, despite my education and the advantages of my station." Darcy flinched as her words went home, and he quickly looked away. "After Ramsgate," she continued, "all my illusions were exposed. I saw my life for what it was, a listless, languid void filled with pretty toys. Nothing in it had prepared me against Wickham's deceptions."

"If you had had proper supervision—if I had not neglected…"

"Fitzwilliam," she insisted, "my own wretched heart aided him, filling in words of love where he had left only dangling phrases. Do you see?" She leaned forward, her eyes intent upon him. "I had to know, had to determine the worst of my case and pray that what I discovered would, in the hands of Providence, be turned to my good." She rose from her chair only to kneel by him.

"Georgiana!" Alarmed at her posture, he grasped her hands and would have lifted her, but the look of her face deterred him.

"Dear Brother, whether you had been there or no, whether it was Wickham or another, the true danger to me was not from without. It was from within. If for no other reason than this discovery, for the remedy it brought, I thank God for what happened." She stopped and looked up into his face, searching for his understanding, but he could not give it. He did, though, sense a connection upon which to vent his frustration.

"Is this the reason, then, for these 'visits' and that absurd letter to Hinchcliffe? You imagine you must atone for some sort of inner flaw with a surfeit of good deeds?"

"You told him not to disperse the funds?" she asked, withdrawing her hands from his.

"My dear girl, 'The Society for Returning Young Women to Their Friends in the Country'?" He could not prevent the disgust from creeping into his voice and so rose and poured himself more coffee from the buffet. "Wherever did you hear about such females?" he continued over his shoulder. "It is highly improper for a girl of your age to even know of such things let alone subscribe, *and* at a hundred pounds per annum! The twenty was more than generous, and that, I think, should be the total of your charity in that direction." He looked over at her then as he lifted a spoon to stir in the cream, but immediately he put it down again. That look had returned to her face which neither he nor his cousin had been able to remedy.

"Dearest, what is it?" Silently cursing his incautious bluntness, he returned to her side, reaching out to take her into his arms; but she withdrew from his clasp and regarded him fixedly.

"A girl my age, Brother? The Society rescues girls my age and younger, Fitzwilliam."

"Yes, that is true, Georgiana," he replied carefully, his brow wrinkled in concern for her, "but it need not trouble you. There are other worthy causes that you…"

"I wish to subscribe to this one particularly," her chin had come up although her voice trembled, "because I…because I might have become one of those girls."

"Never!" Darcy's outrage at the idea knew no bounds. "Whatever can you mean by suggesting such an idea!"

Georgiana shook her head. "I believed Wickham, Fitzwilliam! I believed just as those poor girls believe those who entice them into degradation. What if you had not come to Ramsgate? Would I have eloped with him?" Darcy stared at her wordlessly. "I have looked into my heart, Brother, and I confess that despite your loving care for me, despite what it meant to be a Darcy of Pemberley, I would have gone with him. I was *that* besotted, that deceived." She stopped momentarily to catch her breath.

"I would have searched for you, Georgiana," Darcy leant toward her, his voice choked with emotion, "*and* found you. Wickham wanted you both to be found so…"

"Yes, so he could hold my honour for ransom."

"What do you mean?" Darcy asked sharply.

"When Wickham gave me up so easily, I made inquiries." As she gathered herself to tell him, Darcy's heart almost stilled within his chest. "The rector who was to marry us was a stage-player. I would have come to him believing myself to be his wife, and then you would have been forced to buy him as my husband."

A blind rage shook Darcy to his very core. Turning from her, he strode to the window, but the picturesque view did nothing to soothe his roiling emotions.

"Do you see, Fitzwilliam? My situation may have differed in some respects to those I wish to help, but I had you and they have no one! Let me do what I can!" She came to stand by him at the window. Laying a hand upon his coat sleeve she continued softly, "And you are wrong about my reasons, dear Brother. I can atone for nothing, and it is for joy of that fact that I do these things and so please Providence."

The gentleness of her words gripped him, but he could not accept the truth of them. "When do you wish to go on your 'visits'?" he asked, his voice almost cracking under the strain of keeping his anger from frightening his sister.

"This afternoon, if it pleases you, Fitzwilliam." Her smile, so like their mother's, faded at his next words.

"It does not please me," he replied ungraciously, "but I and only I shall conduct you on all such excursions in the future, should any more occur. And you will abide by my decisions concerning your safety?"

"Yes, Brother," she answered in a small voice.

"Very well, then. One o'clock." He gave her a curt bow and left the room with no thought as to where he was going. The aggressive sound of his stride warned all before him that the master was not best pleased, so the halls were vacant as he moved through them. After a few minutes, the sound of claws tapping against the polished oak floors made an impression upon him, and he looked down to see Trafalgar trotting alongside.

"Well, Monster, to what do I owe the pleasure? Have you enraged Cook again or made a fool of Joseph? Or is there some other deviltry for which you need my protection against its consequences?" Trafalgar whined briefly, then pushed his muzzle against Darcy's hand until he'd gotten it underneath. "Oh, you want to be stroked, is it? Well, come on then." They seemed to have made their way to his study, so man and beast proceeded inside. Darcy collapsed on the sofa, and after only a moment's hesitation, Trafalgar scrambled up beside him and laid his great head on his lap. Darcy stared across the room, feeling everything but seeing nothing. What should he do? *About which catastrophe?* his inner voice asked sarcastically.

"O, Lord, what a muddle!" he sighed deeply. Trafalgar wormed his muzzle under his hand again, this time giving it a lick as he did so. "No, I have not forgotten you, you great ox!" Darcy began to stroke his soft head and shoulders. Trafalgar sighed in deep contentment and pushed himself even closer against his master. "Would that all *my* troubles could be so easily solved." He looked down into eyes glazed over in ecstasy. "What would you say to a ride in the sleigh to pay calls on the local mongrels?" The hound raised his head and gave Darcy a quizzical stare before yawning wide and dropping his head again. "My thoughts exactly, but if I must go, so must you."

~ ~ ~ ~ ~ ~ ~&~ ~ ~ ~ ~ ~ ~

Apart from the new regime of Georgiana's "Sunday mercies" to which he had most unwillingly committed, Darcy found the weeks before Christmas to be redolent with that season's traditional good cheer and happy customs. Every servant, from the highest craftsman to the lowliest stable lad, seemed to go about his duties with a lightness to his step and a smile upon his face that testified to their rich anticipation of the Great Day. The news of Pemberley's return to its customs of the past after observing five years of mourning for the late master had spread well beyond the borders of that estate to envelope those of its neighbours, Lambton village, and even on to

Derby. Therefore, it was not uncommon for Darcy to look up from his book or papers to see Reynolds's cheerful person announcing yet another neighbour waiting to be received in the drawing room or warning that another party had arrived to delight in the decorations of Pemberley's public rooms.

Although they were still in silent disagreement upon the subject of her "visits" and charities, Darcy could not but be captured by his sister's happy contentment as she made preparation for the holidays. Their days were now spent in fond accord as they prepared for their relatives' visit. In the evenings, the warmly lit music room swelled with duets, Darcy joining his voice to Georgiana's in song, or his violin to her pianoforte, in music filled with the joy of the season.

Darcy could have called himself well content if it were not for a peculiar disquiet that shadowed his days and haunted his nights. He found it difficult to walk through the rooms of his home, dressed as they were for the holidays and heavy with the scent of greenery and cinnamon, and not be reminded of Christmases past when his parents were still living. Their shades would tease him at the most unexpected times, causing him to look sharply and, when they had faded, to shake his head in self-reproof. Georgiana did not seem so affected, her younger and fewer memories being, he supposed, not so strong or numerous as his own. But the poignant memories of the past were not the sum of his discontent. A persistent thread of restlessness, a feeling of incompleteness invaded most every hour, the effects of which increased as the number of days before Christmas shortened.

In due course, all was made ready for the festivities and the evening before the expected arrival of their aunt and uncle was upon them. Georgiana quietly practiced her part of a duet they would perform, but Darcy roamed the music room, unable to settle himself into the embrace of any of his usual activities while waiting for Georgiana to finish. Finally, the music stopped.

"Brother, is something troubling you?" Georgiana's voice arrested his rambling.

"No, merely restless I suppose," he sighed, "or anxious that all is well with our uncle's journey." He turned back to her and reached for his violin. "Are you ready for me to join you?"

"Restless, Fitzwilliam?" She frowned gently. "If that is so, then you have been 'restless' for more than two weeks." Darcy tucked the instrument under his chin and drew the bow across the strings, checking the tuning.

"Two weeks! You are mistaken, I am sure." He dismissed her concern. "Regardless, it will pass." He took his position behind her at the pianoforte. "Shall we start at the beginning?"

"Shall we, indeed?" Georgiana replied, placing her hands in her lap and turning to him. "I wish you *would* start from the beginning, and tell me the truth. What is it, Fitzwilliam, that distracts you so?"

"I beg you to believe me when I say you are mistaken, Georgiana." He would not meet her gaze but stared steadfastly at the sheet of music behind her. How could he tell her what he did not know?

"I *believe* that you are lonely and are missing someone," Georgiana persisted in a soft voice.

"Lonely?!" Darcy sputtered, putting away the violin from his chin.

"And I *believe* that the 'someone' is Miss Elizabeth Bennett," she finished with certainty.

Silence lengthened between them as Darcy stared at her, his mind wholly engaged in testing her theory against his emotions. Patting his arm, Georgiana rose from the bench and went over to a table, retrieving a book from which dangled a rainbow of embroidery threads. Opening it carefully, she plucked the knot from between the pages and turned back to him, displaying it in the palm of her small hand.

"This is a rather unusual bookmark for a gentleman, Fitzwilliam." A knowing smile played about her face as she spoke. "Unless it is also a keepsake, a treasured token from a special lady." She advanced upon him and took his hand. Upturning it gently, she laid the knot in his palm. "You gaze off into the air or study a room or look out upon the gardens, covered as they are with snow, and it is as if I am not there. Or rather, as if someone else were. The most interesting expressions cross your face then: sometimes wistful, sometimes stern, and sometimes your eyes speak of such loneliness that I cannot bear to behold it."

He looked down into his palm at the bright threads coiled there, then, hardening his heart, he closed his fingers upon them. "Perhaps you are correct, Georgiana, but you should join with me and pray it is no so, for the lady and her family are so decidedly beneath our own that an alliance is unthinkable. It would be an abasement of the Darcy name, whose honour I am foresworn to uphold in all respects to make her my wife and the mother of the heir of Pemberley." His voice choked at the image his own words conjured.

"Oh, Fitwilliam, it cannot be thus!" Georgiana cried, clutching his arm. "Miss Bennet cannot be so low-born that both your happinesses must be denied."

"Not both," Darcy laughed mirthlessly. "The lady does not look on me with much favour and, if she discovers what…" He stopped short. "She has little reason to change her opinion," he finished. "Do not paint me into a tragic figure, my dear. I would wear the part quite ill." He bent and kissed her sweet brow.

"But the token, surely that means something," she exclaimed.

"Stolen, sweetling!" He tucked the knot into his waistcoat pocket. "She forgot it at Netherfield, and I appropriated it," he confessed. "You see, it is more pathetic than tragic. Or, mayhap, a comedy; I know not which. I must consult Fletcher," he mused. "He would know."

Georgiana looked up into his face, her eyes still troubled. "Do you love her?"

"I hardly know," he said quietly and paused. "I have little experience with that particular breed of emotion." He drew her down to the divan. "I know what love is in many of its aspects: love of family, love of home, love of honour. But this tie between a man and a woman…" he paused. "I have seen it in its most sublime form in our parents and, occasionally, in other marriages; but it seems the exception. Men and women routinely profess themselves violently in love, only to disavow the same a month later. Was it love? I suspect not! Infatuation, an incitement to passion by a pretty face or a fashionable address, more like."

"Then," Georgiana drew the word out, "do you put down Miss Elizabeth merely as a pretty face who has incited…"

"Here, here, my girl." Darcy shifted uncomfortably, flushing at the import of what his very young sister was about to suggest. "I do no such thing, and anything more on the subject would be most indelicate!" He glanced at her and, noting her dissatisfaction with his forestalling of an answer to her question, continued, "At least, I do not think of her in that way 'merely,' as you put it." He returned her triumphant smile. "I admire her wit, her grace, and her compassion as well. I like the manner in which she looks me in the eye and tells me exactly what she is thinking or wishes me to believe that she is thinking. It is difficult to distinguish the two at times."

"And you miss her; that much I already knew. Yet, you are not ready to call it love?" Georgiana prodded him.

"I dare not and will not," he replied firmly. "To what purpose?" he answered her small cry of dissent. "I have explained to you all the reasons why, for both Elizabeth and me, such a declaration would be profitless!"

"But would you," Georgiana persisted, "before God, be well content to cleave only to her?"

Darcy's eyes widened at her forthright question, but soon the sight of her earnest face was replaced by images of his own weaving, images that he'd tried to put aside but could not. *Well content?* His hand went to his waistcoat pocket and drew out the knotted silken threads. Fingering them, he counted them off: three green, two yellow, and one each of blue, rose, and lavender bound in a most cunningly shaped knot.

If her beautiful eyes were to look at him, in truth, in the way he'd imagined... He almost allowed himself to drift with the thought but was brought back to reality when the image before him changed to a very different one.

"Bingley!" he groaned, startling his sister.

"Mr. Bingley?" repeated Georgiana, recalling him to his surroundings. "Does Mr. Bingley love Elizabeth too?"

"No, he does not," Darcy returned adamantly. "But he does play a material part in this puzzle which I am not free to divulge." Anticipating her, he continued, "And no, Elizabeth does not fancy herself in love with him. With *that* you must be satisfied, and *I*, my dear, must find what contentment I may in another quarter regardless of my inclinations." He tucked the strands back into his pocket and rose from the divan. "Now, shall we practice this duet?" He held out his hand to her, which she gratefully took. Guiding her to the pianoforte, he pushed the bench in closer for her and retrieved his violin.

"Fitzwilliam, would you object if I made this a matter of prayer?" Georgiana's compassionate care for him touched him deeply, and although he could not understand this new turn in her life, he was not immune to the love with which it was expressed.

"No, Dearest, no objection at all." He bent and kissed her check. "Mortal men are notoriously ill-equipped for managing affairs centred in the heart." He straightened then and tucked the violin once more beneath his chin before adding, "But I would be remiss if I did not remind you that we do not live in the age of miracles, and it would take no less to sort out this tangle."

~~~~~~~&~~~~~~~
~~~~~~~

"Richard, by heaven, it is good to see you!" Darcy grasped his cousin's hand and pulled him forward into Pemberley's hall and out of the snow-laden air. "The journey, was it terrible? How is my aunt?"

"Well enough, Fitzwilliam, to answer for herself," came the reply from behind the colonel's voluminous greatcoat. "Yes, it was terrible; journeys this time of year usually are." Lady Matlock's austere countenance finally appeared from behind her son's shoulder. "But that does not mean we are sorry to have come. Christmas at Pemberley is worth whatever trouble the weather can conjure." Darcy stepped to her, bowed over her hand and then bestowed a salute upon his aunt's upturned cheek. "There, my dear," she returned warmly. "It is wonderful to see you again. Your uncle and I have not seen you this age." Lady Matlock pulled at the ribbons of her bonnet and gracefully deposited it in the waiting arms of one of the army of servants hurrying to unload the carriages and wagons that had transported the Earl's family and servants.

"I was in the country, ma'am," Darcy replied, "visiting the newly acquired estate of a friend."

"And the hunting was good," his aunt supplied for him as she pulled off her gloves. "Yes, yes, I have often heard that story.

"Just so," Darcy smiled back and turned to greet his uncle. "Welcome, my lord."

"Darcy!" The Earl of Matlock and the master of Pemberley exchanged proper bows before his uncle clasped his hand and gave it a firm shake. "Your aunt is correct." He turned slightly in his wife's direction, "As you usually are, my dear." She curtsied in reply to this astonishing admission as his lordship turned a keen eye back upon his sister's son. "We have not had the pleasure of seeing you the greater part of this fall. Now, if it is true that good hunting has kept you from us, then I shall insist upon the right as head of the family to know the whereabouts of this paradise."

"In due time, Pater," interrupted his younger son. "Brrrr! It is as cold as a witch's…ah, nose, out there! Fitz! Anything inside to warm a fellow's blood? My brother could use something bracing about now, eh, Alex?"

Lord Alexander Fitzwilliam, Viscount D'Arcy, cast him a withering look, before making his bow to his cousin. "Pay no attention to him, Darcy. We sent the puppy into the army, and he still has not learnt to behave as a gentleman."

"And here I was only looking out for your best interests, Brother!"

"Richard, do not make me the excuse for your bad manners!" D'Arcy glowered back.

"As you can see, Fitzwilliam, your cousins still cannot be in the same carriage for above an half-hour without quarrelling as they did when they were children." Lady Matlock turned a severe countenance upon sons who quite towered over her. "But where is Georgiana?"

Darcy offered his arm to his aunt. "She awaits us in the Yellow Salon, ma'am, among the multitude of dishes she deemed appropriate for your welcome..." He looked back over his shoulder to his cousins and uncle adding, "…including some 'bracing' teas and coffees which, should it be desired, I shall be pleased to supplement with even stronger fare."

Upon hearing the last, the colonel's countenance underwent a glorious transformation. "Lead on then, Fitz! Must not keep my cousin waiting!" Darcy laughed and escorted his aunt and relatives up the stairs to the Yellow Salon. They entered a room painted in the palest of lemon and edged with a creamy white plaster wainscoting artfully shaped in the form of twining ivy vines and roses. The hearth's mantle was also faced in the same manner, the sides rising above the mantle to enclose a magnificent mirror, which caught and reflected the light airiness of the room and the delicate chandeliers of gold and crystal. Designed by the late Lady Ann, the Salon had the happy capacity to project warmth in cold seasons and refreshing coolness in summer and thus was one of the favourite places of gathering in the house. Dressed as it was for Christmas, the effect on the visitors was immediate, and as Georgiana came forward to greet her family, she appeared an angel amidst the festive reminders of the season.

"My dear, dear, child!" exclaimed Lady Matlock, before Georgiana had even risen from her curtsy. "What magic is this! You have grown into a young woman while your brother has buried you in the country!" She dropped Darcy's arm and went to her niece. Gathering her hands in her own, she turned to her nephew. "Fitzwilliam, why has your sister not been in London?"

"Ma'am!" Darcy protested, "She is but sixteen years old."

"Sixteen! Only sixteen! Well, there it is; but it must not continue so. It is not good for a young lady to know nothing of London and

Society before her first Season. Whatever can you have been thinking, Fitzwilliam?"

"Aunt, please…you must not be cross with my brother," Georgiana hastily intervened. "It was my own desire to stay quietly at Pemberley." She smiled into her aunt's disapproving eyes. "But he has kindly insisted I accompany him back to London after Christmas."

"As well he should, my dear." Lady Matlock bestowed a rueful smile upon her nephew. "I should not wonder you have had little time or opportunity to chaperone a young girl at your age, Darcy, *and* keep after your cousin."

"Mater!" objected Fitzwilliam.

Lady Matlock ignored her younger son. "You shall bring her to me when his lordship and I return to town. She must be introduced to D'Arcy's fiancée as soon as possible."

The response of brother and sister to her announcement was all the lady could have wished. "Fiancée?" Darcy and Georgiana exclaimed in unison as they rounded on their cousin, who received their congratulations with a stiff smile.

"Oh, Alex, how wonderful for you!" Georgiana continued.

"Yes, well…of course, you are right," D'Arcy replied, then sent his sibling a warning look before adding, "Lady Felicia is all I could wish for in my viscountess."

"The daughter of Lord Lowden, Marquis of Chelmsford," Lord Matlock interposed, "is unexceptional, a credit to her family and, soon, to ours as well. It is an excellent match."

Darcy eyed his cousin intently as Alex accepted his hand at the news. Lady Felicia Lowden was, in his experience, all and more than his uncle had praised. She had been, in fact, the toast of the previous Season, celebrated for her beauty, conversation, ancestry, and fortune. He had been one of the favoured, escorting her to the opera and several balls, but he had soon apprehended that the lady required more admiration than one man could be expected to bestow. Not a man who aspired to make up one of a court, he had ceded his place to those who were so content, although not without some little regret. Lady Felicia was a prize by all of Society's strict standards, yet his cousin seemed ill at ease with his success. Mystified by what he saw, Darcy cocked a brow at Fitzwilliam, but he was answered with no more than a quick grimace.

Another time, then, he promised himself, and joined his sister in performing the duties of a proper host. The burden of these duties,

Darcy found, was light indeed, as before his eyes Georgiana undertook her role as hostess with a shy, but determined smile. In truth, his only contributions consisted of offering the crystal decanter of brandy to his male relatives and enjoying their conversation. Occasionally he would sense her eye upon him, a question expressed in their depths for which he would go to her side. But for the most part, a smile from him was all that she required to buoy her new confidence. Fitzwilliam, Darcy noted, glanced her way repeatedly until his curiosity finally overcame him. With admirable discretion, he worked his way over to the divan where she conversed with his mother and cautiously sat down in a neighbouring chair. When at last he rejoined the other members of his sex, it was with the air of a man who had come upon an unexpected enigma.

Darcy's desire for a private interview with his cousin was fulfilled sooner than he had expected when, during his usually solitary breakfast, Fitzwilliam's face appeared over his newspaper. "Richard! Rather early for you, is it not?" Darcy lowered his paper and indicated the steaming dishes on the sideboard, adding, "Pray, avail yourself," before returning to his newspaper as Fitzwilliam shambled to the board. His cousin proceeded to pour himself a cup from Darcy's strong personal blend and, snatching a sweet roll from a delicate basket of bone china, joined him, falling into the chair at his right with a yawn and a sigh.

"Rest is vouchsafe only to the just, I believe," Darcy commented dryly after Fitzwilliam's third yawn. He folded his paper and laid it aside as the colonel shot him a killing look over his coffee cup.

"Which, I take you to mean, I am not," he returned wryly. "In that you may be correct, at least when it comes to my brother. I ever did enjoy bedevilling him." He leaned back into his chair in philosophic reflection. "It is his perpetual state of aggrieved affrontery, I believe, which excites that less worthy aspect of my character into loosing against him any dart I find at hand."

"You blame your behaviour upon his?" Darcy shook his head reprovingly as he lifted his own cup to his lips. "Richard!"

"Not at all, Fitz! I merely subscribe to the well-known universal that to every action there is an equal and opposite reaction. And, as I am certainly Alex's equal, save his being the eldest…" He sat up then, squaring his shoulders in demonstration. "I hold myself *justified* if not just. It is all a simple matter of physics, Cousin!" The colonel chewed on his sweet roll in complete satisfaction with his theory, seemingly oblivious to his cousin's difficulty with his last sip of coffee.

Setting down his cup and reaching for his napkin, Darcy choked out, "Richard, that is sophist nonsense and…"

"Tell me of Georgiana," Fitzwilliam interrupted in a voice that was low but lacked nothing of command in its tenor.

Darcy pressed the napkin to his lips, his eyebrows curled in perplexity. "I am not sure where to begin, Richard, because I am still puzzled myself."

"She appeared perfectly at ease yesterday, conversing with my family as easily as may be. I could hardly believe it was the same girl who, mere months ago, could not bear to look any higher than my waistcoat buttons." Fitzwilliam sipped at his coffee meditatively. "What was she like when you first arrived?"

Darcy leaned forward. "At first there was some awkwardness between us which I mistook as a continuation of her past melancholy, but it is as you say. She is not the same girl, Richard! Certainly not the same since Ramsgate and, I dare say, not the same girl she was before."

"Did you speak to her about her charitable venture?"

"To be sure." Darcy rolled his eyes. "She is adamant about it, *and,* you will be astonished to learn, she has added weekly Sunday visits to the poorer of my tenants."

"Good God!"

"Precisely," Darcy agreed. "Can you make any sense of it, Richard?"

His cousin shook his head slowly, "Seems a rather odd start. I have heard of something like, but *that* cannot be." In silence, the two sipped at their coffee until finally Richard broke it. "Fitz, Georgiana is dear to me—you know that is true—and her happiness is an object with me scarcely less than it is with you." He waited for Darcy's nod of assent before continuing. "I cannot say why or how but I *can* tell you that from deep in my bones I am sure that Georgiana is truly happy, that the shadow cast by Wickham over her life is gone. My advice to you, old man, is not to question it! "

"Rather the opposite advice given me by her companion!" Darcy mused aloud.

"Companion?"

"Mrs. Annesley," Darcy returned, "a clergyman's widow who came to me last summer with impeccable references." Fitzwilliam shrugged his ignorance. "She visits her sons in Weston-super-Mare for the holidays. It was she advised me to ask Georgiana, but I have not yet dared to do so directly."

"Well, there you are, Fitz—that explains it! A clergyman's widow!"

"Perhaps," Darcy replied, "but she claims not!" He set down his cup, his cousin doing likewise, and both rose to their feet. "So here we are at *point non-plus* with neither of us possessed of enough courage to do more about it."

"Let it rest, Fitz." Fitzwilliam clapped him on the shoulder. "Mother was entranced with her last night; his lordship said it was like seeing his sister returned to him. It is Christmas—let it rest!"

"You will continue to observe her…watch over her?" Darcy demanded.

"Here's my hand on it, Cousin." Fitzwilliam took Darcy's hand in a sure grip. "Now, I have a puzzle for you. My door, which I distinctly remember shutting last night, was found open by my man this morning and, Lord help me, but one of my boots has gone missing!"

~~~~~~~&~~~~~~~

"O Lord, raise up, we pray Thee, Thy power, and come among us, and with great might succour us..."

The words of the collect for the fourth Sunday in Advent echoed from the old stone walls of St. Lawrence's as all who were able of the farms and estates of the region crowded within its holy precinct. The ancient church glowed as the candlelight reflected off silver and gold plate and illuminated the shining woodwork of the rail and chancel, festooned now with holly. The beauty of the sanctuary did not deter most eyes from observing the Darcy pew which was quite full this day, as his lordship, the Earl of Matlock, and his family were come with the master of Pemberley and his sister. The presence of his lordship's family was the crowning proof to those without the intimacy of Pemberley that the traditional celebrations of Christmas were truly once more inaugurated at that great estate. The whispers and smiling nods of the knowledgeable assured even the humblest present that a gracious welcome, a full stomach, and a few hours of merriment on the eve of the Great Day awaited them.

Darcy stood tall and grave beside his sister as they recited from their prayer books, his gaze alternating between the page and beauty of the stained-glass windows that flanked the chancel. How many
~~~~~~~

hundreds of times had he been caught up by their drama and richness of colour, he could only guess, for they had delighted him from childhood. How often had he sat beside his father, trying manfully not to swing his heels but to "conduct himself as a Darcy," and the glorious windows had saved him.

> *"...that whereas, through our sins and wickedness, we are sore let and hindered in running the race that is set before us..."*

Beside him, Georgiana's voice sounded clearly, and it was this, as well as the peculiar earnestness of her reading, that sharply drew Darcy's attention back from the windows. He looked down at her, a tight frown drawing down his lips, but her bonnet prevented him from observing her face or delivering his reprimand.

> *"...thy bountiful grace and mercy may speedily help and deliver us; through Jesus Christ our Lord, to whom, with Thee and the Holy Ghost..."*

Georgiana lifted shining eyes as she recited the collect. Able now to see her face, he followed their gaze to the same windows that were his own delight. He looked back down at her, and the sweetness of her face made him think better of his annoyance with her excess of zeal. It was good he did so, for in the next second, she turned those eyes upon him, a tremulous smile upon her face.

> *"...be honour and glory, world without end. Amen."*

"Amen," they spoke together. Darcy's smile in answer to his sister's was of equal parts affection and question. With an almost imperceptible shake of her head, Georgiana composed her features and turned her attention back to her book and the reading from an Epistle for the day, but not before Darcy perceived a certain wistfulness in them. Puzzled anew, he returned to the morning's text.

> *"Rejoice in the Lord always: and again I say, Rejoice."*

The well-known command from Scripture struck him with sovereign force, and Darcy knew with sudden conviction that beside him stood a very tangible occasion for rejoicing. For, despite his momentary neglect which had given opportunity for evil and, later, his absolute failure to rescue Georgiana from her deep melancholy, she stood beside him now, fair and whole through no agency of his own.

> *"...but in every thing by prayer and supplication with*
> *thanksgiving let your requests be made known unto God.*
> *And the peace of God, which passeth all understanding,*
> *shall keep your hearts and minds through Christ Jesus."*

He had gotten no further than "the peace of God" before the words of the text rocked him again, this time so forcibly that he lapsed into silence. Renewing his hold upon the prayer book, he brought it closer and retraced the last line. *...the peace of God, which passeth all understanding...* Darcy looked down at Georgiana, but the blasted bonnet concealed her still. Was *this* what she had been trying to tell him? He returned to the text of the Epistle to the Philippians, ignoring the fact that the good reverend now led the day's reading from St. John. *...keep your hearts and minds...* Yes, it followed—heart and mind. Had she not spoken of these things when he had tried to overrule her generosity toward her newfound charities? The events and remembered conversations of the past weeks began to fall into a disquieting pattern.

Awash in confliction over the path his thoughts had taken, Darcy was startled to feel a tug on his coat sleeve. "Brother, we may sit now!" Georgiana whispered to him, her brow creased in question at his inattention as the entire congregation waited for one of its most distinguished member to take his seat. With studied carelessness, Darcy sank down into the pew and nodded to the rector that he should continue. The reverend gentleman began his homily, but Darcy could not attend to a word of it for his private wrestling with the revelations of the last few moments. *No...it could not be! A Darcy—dare he say it—an Evangelical? What absurdity!* He shifted his position, struggling against the impulse to test immediately his preposterous notion. Then, as if in response to his unspoken question, Georgiana glanced up at him, answering his restlessness with an understanding smile. He seized upon the opportunity to search her face, but almost sighed with relief. No sign of "enthusiasm" could he detect upon its placid contours. *What did you expect to see?* came the disconcerting thought which he resolutely put away.

The remainder of the service proceeded along familiar, comfortable lines and soon it was time for the congregation to stand for the final hymn. The words being second nature to him, Darcy laid aside the hymnbook and sang with the rest of the congregants, but a flash of sunlight drew his attention once more to the glory and drama in the stained-glass panels. Their beauty assured him, comforted him that all was indeed well with the world. A small hand crept into the crook of his arm, its warmth and loving pressure more than welcome to him. He dropped his gaze from the windows to Georgiana's dear face, but the reassuring smile faded from his lips as the realization bore down upon him that the rapt expression on it was not for him; for her attention, too, was directed upon the chancel windows. *No, not upon them… beyond them!* He corrected himself, examining the young woman beside him, whom he was no longer sure he knew. *Peace that passeth all understanding…*

"A-hem." The sound of Richard pointedly clearing his throat brought Darcy back within the confines of time. "I believe her name is Georgiana Darcy. May I introduce you?"

"What?" Laughing, Georgiana looked up into her cousin's face and then her brother's.

"Your brother seems much struck with something," drawled Fitzwilliam. "If it were I, I would say it is with that very fetching bonnet. But knowing Darcy, he was likely pondering some great question and you, my dear, were merely in the way of his gaze." Darcy rewarded his cousin with a brief, freezing glance from beneath lowered brows before stepping into the aisle.

"O-ho! A weighty question it must be, indeed!" Fitzwilliam persisted. "Now what could it be?"

"Richard, desist!" Darcy commanded him in an undertone.

"Not a question, I think! No, that thunderous frown bespeaks something more warm than philosophy."

"Philosophy!" D'Arcy exclaimed, joining them in the aisle. "Did I just hear Richard say the words 'think' and 'philosophy' almost in the same breath? Darcy, you must call for the bishop, for surely a miracle has occurred within these walls. Praise heaven, my brother has *thought*!"

"A talent of mine, Alex," Fitzwilliam retorted. "Surprised you didn't know, but I am confident Lady Felicia will keep you better informed." D'Arcy immediately stiffened at the sally, his eyes darting between Darcy and his brother, his jaw locked in an alarming manner.

"Go to the devil!" D'Arcy hissed at him and, turning sharply from his relatives, he strode down the aisle and out of the church, ignoring the many gestures of respect which those gathered there offered him.

Incensed, Darcy turned then upon his remaining cousin and addressed him in a frigid tone, "I will thank you to keep your quarrelling private, Richard, and not display it for all the world to see or my sister to overhear."

Bridling at Darcy's tone, Fitzwilliam threw back his shoulders, preparing to meet the surprise attack to his flank of heretofore friendly forces, when Georgiana's large, troubled eyes met his own. "Your pardon, Georgiana," Fitzwilliam flushed guiltily. "I forgot myself—under great provocation I might add." He glanced at Darcy. Turning to Georgiana, he added, "But I should not have succumbed so easily to Alex's goading. I beg your forgiveness, Cousin."

"You are forgiven freely, Cousin," Georgiana returned softly, "but I fear Cousin Alex is very distressed, and perhaps it is he whose forgiveness you would do better to seek."

A gentle smile replaced the scowl on Fitzwilliam's face, and taking her hand lightly, he bestowed a kiss on her gloved fingertips, confessing, "You are perfectly right, my dear girl, and I will do as you bid. Darcy, you will excuse me, I trust." He bowed to his cousin and turned his step down the swath his brother had cut to the door.

Brother and sister looked after him a moment and then turned to each other, Darcy offering his arm. Georgiana took it gratefully and together they strolled to the ancient church doors. "I am astonished at the behaviour of our cousins, and cannot think how they could so grievously forget themselves in your presence, Georgiana. But I must say, you handled it wonderfully!" Darcy almost laughed. "I have rarely seen Richard brought to contrition in such a short span of time. *That* was the true miracle!"

"Miracle?" Georgiana dimpled at his praise. "I thank you for the compliment, but whether within these holy walls or without, I cannot take the credit with any degree of complacency."

"It does you honour that you say so," Darcy replied quietly. They had left the church and had now reached their carriage. Darcy handed her in and then climbed in after her. After seeing to his sister's comfort and giving James Coachman the signal to be off, he settled back into the squabs. The carriage pulled forward slowly, as James manoeuvred the team down Church Hill and through the narrow streets of Lambton. In moments they were crossing the ancient stone bridge over the Ere and tooling along for the gates of Pemberley.

Although Georgiana's face was turned to the carriage window, Darcy could see the set of her delicate jaw beneath the brim of her bonnet. He watched silently as she worked her way through whatever was disturbing her. Now and then he caught small sighs he was not meant to hear but which sorely tested his resolve to hold his peace until she should speak. Finally, she turned back to him, her manner hesitant.

"Fitzwilliam, do you recall the words of the collect this morning?"

"Which ones, sweetling?" He regarded her earnestly.

"The prayer for the grace and mercy of our Lord in the course He has given us to run." Her voice quavered a little and Darcy could see she was greatly affected.

"Yes, I remember," he answered simply.

"When you said I had caused Cousin Richard's contrition, it was not of my doing. It was that—mercy, I mean. The mercy of forgiveness, freely received as it is freely given, was, I am certain, the motivation for his contrition." She trembled so by the finish of her speech that Darcy removed his carriage robe and added it to hers.

He took her hands then, chafing them between his own. "But, Georgiana, mercy has its own power. It is above the 'sceptred sway,' if we are to believe the Bard, and of more effect than a 'throned monarch.' It is…"

"…'twice blest,'" Georgiana quoted back to him. "'It blesseth him that gives and him that takes.' Fitzwilliam, I only gave to Richard what I have received, and even in that, I am as blessed as he."

Darcy breathed out a heavy sigh and tucked her hands under the carriage robe much as he had done since she was quite a little girl. "I have a question, now, for you. The passage this morning that went, 'And the peace of God, which passeth all understanding…' Is that what you have been trying to tell me? That your recovery from…from everything is because…" He could go no further, for he did not have the words.

"Because of the mercy of God?" she supplied for him in tender tones. "Yes, my *dear* Brother, exactly that." The carriage slowed for the turn into the lane that led to the gates, but the lessening of the noise of travel did not encourage the two within to further discourse. Instead, each regarded the other in a thoughtful silence which neither had the ability to break.

~~~~~~~&~~~~~~~

By the time they had gathered in the hall and Darcy had begged his aunt and uncle to be seated at table for the glorious repast his cook was so proud to offer Pemberley's guests, it was clear that a repair in the breach between the earl's male issue had been effected. The conversation between them and the looks they exchanged bespoke a tolerance, each of the other, that caught the attention of all of those seated around the table and caused the eyebrow of their good father to hitch ever higher as the meal progressed.

"Darcy, please have the footman bring me a glass of soda and water, for I fear this surfeit of civility will put me quite out of digestion," his lordship requested finally, after yet another polite exchange between the brothers.

"Pater!" exclaimed Fitzwilliam, "I should think your digestion would be improved, now that Alex and I have cried 'truce.'"

"Truce, is it?" His lordship looked 'round the table to determine if anyone present believed his younger son's explanation of this new accord. "D'Arcy, what do you say?"

"It is as Richard says, your lordship," D'Arcy answered readily, taking a sip of wine. "At least for the present." He set down his glass with a fine precision, a smirk playing upon his lips.

"Then, may the present stretch into eternity," sighed Lady Matlock, "for I have prayed for just such a thing. I sign my name as witness to your truce, Alex." She regarded him piercingly and then, in a moment, transferred her gaze. "Richard, do you both uphold your terms *at least* until Epiphany, and I shall have my Christmas present!"

Both of her sons had the grace to flush, but it was Fitzwilliam who rose and took his mother's hand into his own saying, "It shall be as you wish, Mater. The gentlemen of our family God will rest merry in honour of the season and of you."

From under lowered lids, Darcy's glance flitted to his sister for her reaction to the unprecedented scene playing out before them. Unshed tears brightening her eyes, she watched Richard bow over his mother's hand and bestow a loving kiss upon it. When Alex joined the duo from the other side and leant down to kiss the lady's cheek, Georgiana's eyes closed. Darcy watched as she mouthed silently what he took to be a small prayer of thanks, and the tear that had hovered on the brink of her lashes broke free to trace its solitary
~~~~~~~

way down her cheek. He looked away before she might catch him at his observation.

The meal progressed in such merriment after, that the gentlemen eschewed their brandy and tobacco in favour of the ladies and the entertainment that had been promised. Georgiana rose and went to her aunt who, still much affected by the *rapprochement* of her sons, took her arm in such a gay manner that the younger lady let fall some of her hard-gained years and executed a skipping step as she led her aunt down the hall.

Darcy watched in some amusement and no little relief his sister's reversion to girl-hood as she and their aunt proceeded to the music room. But rather than follow them or D'Arcy out of the room, he elected to await the pleasure of his uncle. Turning then to inquire of his lordship's readiness he found the peer and his younger son in earnest dialogue, their hands joined in a firm clasp. Quietly leaving the room, Darcy awaited them in the hall, a knot of longing tying up his vitals and leaving him gulping for air. *It was still no good.* The ache of his father's loss, five years gone, still would catch him and deliver him such a blow that tears would follow if he did not take himself immediately and forcefully in hand.

Straightening his shoulders, Darcy started for the music room. Returning to Pemberley's rich Christmas traditions had been both balm and woe to his equanimity. The few times he was not reminded in some way of his past sorrows and his present responsibilities were those times when the joy of the season caught him up or when he allowed himself to drift into the more immediate past of his disturbing verbal engagements with Miss Elizabeth Bennet. He had relived the moments of their dance at the Netherfield ball a dozen times, pressing himself to recall her every word and nuance of manner. Of course, the pressure of her hand clasped within his and the sweetness of her lithesome form passing back and forth around him in the patterns of the dance were not forgotten either. Nor was the inexplicable sensation of intimacy caused by a shared prayer book and voices joined in psalms.

These pleasurable and disturbing memories he had found insufficient. It was true, as his sister had surmised, that he had taken to imagining Elizabeth at his side here at Pemberley. Would she enjoy his uncle and aunt? The gardens and park of Pemberley were universally admired, but would Elizabeth find them pleasing? He had even found himself in minute examination of a piece of silverware, wondering if Elizabeth would find its heavy ornamentation to her taste. And what would she think about this incomprehensible development in his sister? He was sore in need of another's comfort, he admitted finally, as his fancy brought Elizabeth again beside him, her hand resting upon his arm. He looked down and saw her, her brow cocked at him, a teasing smile upon her lips. Yes, she could cozen him out of this heaviness of spirit. Where would he ever find her like again?

The sounds of feminine laughter and a masculine chuckle broke through his thoughts, and bidding fancy away for the moment, Darcy rounded the corner of the door and joined his relatives. D'Arcy was whispering something in Georgiana's ear that sent her into renewed giggles, while Lady Matlock looked on in approbation.

"No! You cannot be telling the absolute truth, Alex!"

"Ask my father, if you doubt me, Cousin," D'Arcy replied with a knowing smile, "for your brother will never admit to it."

"Admit to what, Alex?" Darcy poured himself a glass of wine.

"To running off one Christmas Eve to join the Derbyshire Mummers just before their performance in Lambton." Darcy winced. "You were ten, I believe, and we were all at St. Lawrence's for the service when you turned up missing."

"Brother, it cannot be true!" Georgiana looked at him in wonder.

Darcy nodded slowly as the wine gently awoke his palate. "It is true, Dearest, but I *was* only ten; and you may believe that our father impressed upon me the indecorum of such an adventure."

"But our uncle…?"

"Oh, your father was forced to call upon mine to help extricate your brother from an altercation with some of the younger mummers in which he was rather outnumbered," D'Arcy supplied happily.

"Alex!" Darcy frowned at his cousin, "this is hardly fit conversation…"

"But it *is* very interesting!" came Fitzwilliam's voice from the doorway. "I remember the occasion quite well *and* cheering you on from the carriage window. Oh, it was a lovely brawl, sir, a lovely brawl!" He raised his glass to Darcy, D'Arcy and his lordship following suit. "Never let it be said you were not pluck to the bone, Fitz! One against three, wasn't it?"

Darcy inclined his head. "It was four—and I only admit it for the sake of accuracy." He turned to Georgiana. "It was an exceedingly foolish thing to do, and I was only proud of it for a very few minutes before Father caused me to see reason."

"Caused his backside to see reason!" crowed Fitzwilliam. "I distinctly remember you standing for Christmas dinner that year and being devoutly thankful I wasn't you."

"Shall we have some music?" Darcy took the opportunity of the lull in the conversation occasioned by all the young men present remembering similar exchanges with their own fathers to change the subject. For the next half-hour Darcy and his sister delighted their relatives with the duets they had prepared. Lady Matlock then arranged herself behind the grand harp and played upon the harp strings as well as the heartstrings of her dear relations as she rendered compositions that reminded them of Christmases past and loved ones no longer with them.

When she was done, Fitzwilliam led her from the instrument to her seat and then turned to the rest of his family. "I do not claim any musical talent, nor to have practiced in preparation but here it is…and join in if you remember the words" He sat down at the pianoforte and struck a chord.

All hail to the days that merit more praise
Than all the rest of the year,
And welcome the nights that double delights
As well for the poor as the peer!
Good fortune attend each merry man's friend
That doth but the best that he may,
Forgetting old wrongs with carols and songs
To drive the cold winter away.

Smiles all around attended Fitzwilliam's contribution to the evening, and his brother, father and cousin were drawn into it, joining him at the instrument.

'Tis ill for a mind to anger inclined
To think of small injuries now,
If wrath be to seek, do not lend her your cheek
Nor let her inhabit thy brow.
Cross out of thy books malevolent looks,
Both beauty and youth's decay,
And wholly consort with mirth and sport
To drive the cold winter away.

This time of the year is spent in good cheer
And neighbours together do meet,
To sit by the fire, with friendly desire,
Each other in love to greet.
Old grudges forgot are put in the pot,
All sorrows aside they lay,
The old and the young doth carol this song,
To drive the cold winter away.

When Christmas's tide comes in a like a bride,
With holly and ivy clad,
Twelve days in the year much mirth and good cheer
In every household is had.
The country guise is then to devise
Some gambols of Christmas play,
Whereat the young men do the best that they can
To drive the cold winter away.

The impromptu quartet bowed profusely to its audience with much laughter and congratulation among its members. But as Darcy looked up from another bow, he seemed to see that nuptial figure about whom he had just sung hovering at the music room door, resplendent in her bride clothes. And the lovely face beneath the twining holly and ivy was that of Elizabeth.

~5~
An Honourable Man

Upon its wheels striking the London road, the travelling coach abandoned its unpredictable jolting for a gentler dip and sway, thereby allowing its two occupants to relieve the tedium of their journey with the books they had tucked into their travelling valises. After an half-hour had passed in their separate contemplations, Darcy chanced a glance at his sister. Georgiana's lower lip was caught between her teeth and the disposition of her brow seconded her air of deep concentration on the words before her. Darcy tempered his reflexive sigh and turned back to his own reading, but it could not absorb him as it had before. Absently, he plucked up the gossamer threads of the bookmark that had rested upon his knee and wound it 'round his fingers as he reviewed the holiday now spent.

True to his wishes, Pemberley's tradition of Christmas had been upheld in a grandness of manner that more than satisfied its neighbours. Christmas Eve Day the public rooms were opened to all who wished to view the stateliness of Pemberley in its holiday glory. Visitors were conducted about in groups by the more brawny of the household servants, who pointed out each room's aspect and furnishings with proprietary pride. At tour's end, the parties were refreshed with hot cider and baked delights from the kitchen. Outside, there were games and roasting chestnuts, sleigh rides, and skating upon the lake; all accompanied by roving bands of musicians or singers. Later, every imaginable cart or wagon had been pressed into service to convey all of Pemberley's people to evening service at St. Lawrence's and then back again to the servant and tenants' ball held in the great harvest hall of the estate. Here the generosity of Pemberley continued in the provision of a great feast, complete with drink and music for half the night. Every child had departed for home with a tangy, sweet apple, a pocketful of walnuts, and a pair of thick, woollen stockings, while their fathers brought a shiny half-crown to their lips in thanks to their Maker for destining them for Pemberley.

The merry-making within the great house had been little more subdued than that without as, with the help of his aunt, Darcy hosted a small ball and late supper for the local gentry. He stood up with Lady Matlock for the first dance and Georgiana for the second; but, pleading his duties as host, he had forsaken the centre of the ballroom floor for its fringes and the task of reacquainting himself with his neighbours and their concerns. Wellesley being in Winter Quarters, the main concern of most of the gentlemen present were the Luddite raids upon the knitting industry of the region and the lack of progress in their apprehension by whoever was sent against them. Severe criticism, much the same as that Darcy had heard at his London club, was levelled also at a certain young peer from Scotland for his support of the radicals and for his shocking effect upon the ladies.

The peace between his Fitzwilliam cousins had lasted throughout their visit, being disturbed only occasionally by blunted barbs of wit at each other's expense. Although, Darcy thought ruefully, their restraint with each other seemed to encourage them into a joint effort against him. His Lordship and Lady Matlock had been welcome, charming guests. Further, his aunt's eagerness to assist in chaperoning Georgiana about Town had been a most welcome development, and Darcy had discovered a renewed respect for them which centred in their own persons rather than their connexion to him.

All had gone well—very well—considering the trepidation with which he had arrived in his own hall several weeks before. He glanced again at Georgiana as he now unwound the threads, his eyes narrowing with displeasure. Perhaps the temptations of Town would unwed her from that blasted little book! Never had he thought to find himself wishing his sister would confine herself to novels rather than engaged in his requirement that members of the fairer sex improve their minds with extensive reading.

She had received all his gifts with sweet exclamations of appreciation and her pleasure in receiving them had been well matched by his in the giving of them. The books and music she had joyed in most especially, for she *was* a Darcy, for all that was changed about her. Maria Edgeworth's next was greeted with gratitude by his sister and a knowing laugh from his aunt. D'Arcy had chortled at *The*

Scottish Chiefs, disbelieving that his young cousin would attempt so a large book and had offered to give her a synopsis of it. This Fitwilliam had advised her not to take, as he "...doubted his brother's attention could ever have been held for so long by any one thing." The new novel by the unknown author had barely been freed from its wrappings before their aunt had pounced upon it declaring that she had heard of it and begged Georgiana to lend it to her. "It is about a widow and her three daughters, my dear, cast out upon the world by a heartless step-son and his odious wife. I am almost certain it is patterned after a true story. Do you not remember the scandal, my lord?"

"No, I do not, my love," his lordship had replied as he examined the title on the book's spine, "but I do hope that 'Sense' is vindicated and 'Sensibility' reproved, Darcy."

"So Hatchard informed me," he had replied, "but I will rely on my aunt's judgment." A lively debate had then ensued among the Fitwilliams over the merits of sense against sensibility in making one's way in the world. While they had been thus engaged Georgiana had unwrapped the last of his gifts. He had been puzzled at its appearance, not being able to recall any other purchases. As the paper fell away, it came to him—it was the book he had used to excuse himself from "Poodle" Byng's fascination with Fletcher's knot. "Georgiana," he had begun, "pardon me, but that was not meant for..."

"Fitzwilliam! Oh, how can I thank you!" she had exclaimed softly and come to him to kiss his cheek, the book held tightly to her breast. "It is precisely what I wished for."

"It is?" he answered. "That is rather wonderful, as I bought it by mistake without even knowing what it was." She had looked at him then rather strangely and turned the title to his view. "*A Practical View of the Prevailing Religious System...*" he had begun to read and then looked up at her sceptically, "The title does not recommend itself to me, Georgiana. I am not sure it is entirely appropriate fare for one of your age."

"Please, Fitzwilliam," she had answered him back, "I shall abide by your wishes, but I beg you allow me this book. Its author is one of the most respected members of Parliament. It cannot, therefore, be *entirely* inappropriate, can it?" Darcy knew she had him, if not by her logic, then by her gentle bending to his will in the matter. He had acquiesced and since then, the book had been her constant companion.

Arranging the knotted threads once more upon his knee, he smoothed them out and then took up his book again. The excitement and entertainments of London were highly distracting, and they would begin clamouring for her attention almost immediately. Of that, he would make certain.

~~~~~~~&~~~~~~~

"Mr. Darcy, I beg your pardon, sir."

"Yes, what is it, Witcher?" Laying aside his walking stick and hat, Darcy began stripping off his gloves before attacking the buttons of his greatcoat. Although well into the afternoon, the winds of January had kept the day cold, so cold that Darcy was seriously considering cancelling Georgiana's scheduled sitting with Lawrence for that day. Only a few preliminary sketches had been attempted thus far and, although circumspect for one of artistic temperament, Lawrence would not, Darcy knew, be pleased with a postponement.

"A note has arrived, Sir, and the boy was told to wait for an answer no matter the time." Witcher signalled the footman to take the master's coat and gather his other belongings. "I have placed it under the blotter on your desk in the library."

Alert to his butler's meaning, Darcy nodded, "Thank you, Witcher. Please have some strong tea sent along and inform Miss Darcy that I am returned and will come to her in an half-hour."

"Very good, sir. Shall I send in a footman for your letter?"

"No," Darcy paused. There was no telling who the source of this missive might be. The fewer hands in it, the better, most like. "No," he continued, "come for it yourself, please. I shall be finished with it before going up to Miss Darcy."

"Yes, Mr. Darcy." Witcher bowed as Darcy turned his steps toward the warmth and comfort of the library of Erewile House. They had been already a week in Town and, as he had expected, upon the knocker being placed once more in its honoured place upon the doornail, they had been inundated with invitations. Although she was not yet "out," there were sufficient numbers of permissible activities designed for young ladies in just such a condition to keep Georgiana busy from breakfast until dawn. Darcy encouraged her attendance at those that survived his careful, judicious review and added to them the sittings with Lawrence, a trip back to Madame LaCoure's for the *folderols* to complement the lengths he had purchased, and evenings at the theatre.
~~~~~~~

Closing the door behind him, Darcy advanced to the great, carved desk and, pushing aside the blotter, retrieved the note that was so important to its sender that the messenger still sat by his kitchen fire, awaiting an answer. Darcy took it to the hearth where he turned it over in his hands as the fire warmed him from the cold journey back from his club. The paper was plain, and the seal reveal nothing of its author. Shrugging to himself, he sat in one of the upholstered leather chairs near the fire, broke the seal and read:

Sir,

A most Distressing Development has occurred which, I fear, will bring all our Plans to Naught! I apply to you, Sir, in this most Desperate of times, who so ably thwarted Danger in the past, to assist once more in your Friend's behalf. In short, Miss Bennet is in Town! She has sent a Note to Aldford Street! What are we to do, Sir? B. does not yet know. My Sister and I await your direction. All shall be done as you say.

C.

A surge of anger flowed unimpeded throughout Darcy's chest. The importunity of it! With uncharacteristic impetuosity he leapt to his feet, crumpled the note and hurled it into the flames. *Was there to be no end to this coil?* Resentment of Miss Bingley's repeated appeals for his assistance in this tangle followed close upon the heels of his anger and spread quickly to include Bingley's inability to exercise a proper circumspection that had brought them to this imbroglio. This, with the unwelcome leap of his own heart upon seeing the name of Bennet in the note and wondering if the lady was accompanied to Town by her sister, combined to set Darcy on a perilous edge.

Striding over to his desk, he pulled roughly at the top sheet of stationery, leaving it to settle of its own accord atop the desk as he fumbled for a quill. Finding what he required, he leaned across and flung open the inkwell. But quill in hand, poised over the well, he stopped. *What in blazes was he to advise her?* Darcy looked stupidly at the quill and paper and then sank into the chair at his desk. The acquaintance between the Bingleys and Miss Bennet *had* to be cut and in so decisive a manner as to leave no doubt on either side. It was the only means of settling the affair for once and all. Worrying his lower lip, he cast about in his mind for the best approach. In the midst of plucking up and then discarding ideas, he was interrupted by a knock at the door.

"Yes, enter," he commanded tersely.

"What! Caught you at the books again? This simply will not do, Fitz, and I am just the fellow to put an end to it!"

"Dy!" Darcy's head came up as Lord Dyfed Brougham sauntered in, a quizzing glass dangling from his hand. "What have you done with Witcher, you scoundrel?" he grumbled at him good-naturedly.

"Done with Witcher? Not a thing, old man, unless you count slipping him a golden boy to let me announce myself and, hopefully, catch you at something. *Did* I catch you at something, bye-the-bye?" Dy flashed him a curious grin.

"No, nothing!" Darcy picked up the sheet to replace it in its box, but spying the dubious look upon his friend's face, he paused and in sudden inspiration contradicted himself. "Actually, you rather did catch me. I have been asked for some advice on a matter that is just in your line."

"Really! My line, you say? And what, pray, is that?" Brougham seated himself in an adjoining chair.

"A matter of some delicacy. You remember Bingley, of course?"

Brougham nodded, "You were trying to convince him to graze elsewhere in regard to a certain young woman, if memory serves. Any luck?"

"Luck or reason, I know not which, but he *did* come 'round before I'd left for Pemberley." Darcy pulled the quill through his fingers, a frown upon his face. "But, I would not be overstating the case to say that I believe him still susceptible to the lady. Should they meet again any time soon…" He left the thought hanging as he envisioned such a meeting.

"Little chance of that! The lady resides in Hertfordshire, does she not? "

"Unfortunately, she has lately arrived in Town and desires to wait upon Bingley's sisters. They are now in an anxiety as to how they should proceed." Darcy's dark eyes settled with piercing intensity upon his friend, "What would you suggest, Dy?"

~~~~~~~&~~~~~~~
~~~~~~~

Darcy applied the final strokes of his quill upon the note to Miss Bingley and then searched his desk for a wafer to seal the single, folded sheet of the carefully worded instructions over which he and Brougham had laboured. While he did so, the aforementioned lord rambled about the library, poking a finger here at a book, there at a journal, and, occasionally, bringing his quizzing glass to his eye in bored inquiry of what he found.

"Very dull stuff you have here, Fitz."

Darcy looked up from his task in surprise. "You must not have discovered my copy of *Ciudad Rodrigo*, then. You may borrow it, if you wish. It is there on the shelf to your right. Hatchard sent it to me immediately it was available."

"Where? Ah, yes." Brougham brought up the glass again as he examined the spine. "Read it already, have you?"

"Yes, when I was in Hertfordshire."

"Humph," his friend responded, continuing to search the shelves. "Would have thought you too busy warning young Bingley off the lovely Bennet sisters to have chance to read. Here, what's this?" Darcy rose from the desk in alarm at the sight of Brougham holding a quite different volume than the one under discussion and swinging a shiny hank of knotted threads.

"Nothing!" Darcy reached for the threads, which Brougham, brow cocked in delighted amusement, danced out of his reach.

"That cannot be; it is assuredly *something*, my dear fellow, or else…"

"A bookmark then. *It is a bookmark!*," Darcy insisted, grabbing his forearm. With a laugh, Brougham handed it to him, offering him also the book in which it had nestled. Refusing it, Darcy quickly wrapped the threads around a finger, tucked them inside his waistcoat pocket and turned back to his desk. "Do you wish to borrow *Rodrigo*, then?" he asked hoping to divert his friend's attention.

"No, read it already." Brougham waggled the volume still in his hand before replacing it upon the shelf. "*Fuentes de Oronco* as well, for what little it is worth," he yawned, "although *I* did not have the enticement of such a bookmark to bring me back to its pages."

"You do not think them accurate accounts?" Darcy regarded him curiously.

"Fitz!" Brougham looked at him in true disappointment, "You cannot be gulled so easily!"

"Why? What do you know?" Darcy's interest sharpened.

"Oh, nothing!" Brougham returned quickly, his countenance suddenly closed and disappointment was replaced by a mocking derision. "Nothing that a careful reading of the absolutely *dreadful* prose wouldn't disclose. The fellow is all "guts and glory!" Never saw more than the fringes of the action, I'll wager, if that! He probably caught some of the story from the poor blighters that survived the front lines and then made up the rest."

A knock at the door interrupted them before Darcy could pursue Brougham's interesting remarks. It opened, revealing Witcher at the entrance. "Mr. Darcy, sir. Your letter?"

"Yes, Witcher, here it is." Darcy took it from his desk and pressed it into the old retainer's palm. "Now send the boy back with it, and let us hope that is the end of it. Is the tea ready?"

"Yes sir, just ready. Will you take it here?"

Darcy looked over at Brougham, "Would you care to call on Georgiana, Dy? She is upstairs."

"It would be my great pleasure," his lordship replied formally, but his voice dropped as he added, "It has been a very long time."

"Good! Witcher, have the tea sent up to the drawing room. We shall be up directly." As Witcher departed on his errand, the two mounted the stairs; but Darcy slowed when the man was out of sight. "You will find her quite changed, Dy," he began.

"I should imagine," Brougham interrupted. "It has been almost seven years!"

"Seven!" Darcy exclaimed. "Has it truly?"

"Since University! The last time I saw her was in this house at the 'do' your father gave for your graduation. He and Georgiana came down for a few minutes. I believe Mr. Darcy's health kept him from staying longer."

"Yes." Darcy nodded, his brow creasing in remembrance of those days. "It was the last time he was to appear in public. I'd had no notion of his illness until then. He would let no one speak of it, even to me." Their long, matching strides had brought them finally to the drawing room doors. "Georgiana," Darcy called out before the servant who admitted them could announce them, "an old friend has come to see you. Can you guess who it is?"

It appeared that they had caught Georgiana deeply engrossed in a lesson, for her expression upon rising from the books she and Mrs. Annesley had spread before them was of one realigning her thoughts to a quite different subject than that with which they had been occupied. She rose, smiling readily at her brother's intrusion, and made her curtsy to his companion but Darcy could sense no light of recognition in her eyes.

"Come, Miss Darcy, do not say you cannot remember me!" Brougham made an elegant bow and, rising, cast her his famous, winning smile.

"My…my Lord Brougham?" Georgiana curtsied again in confusion. "Please forgive me, I did not recognize you."

"Instantly! Who could deny anything the gracious Miss Darcy requests? But, I fear we have interrupted a lesson. Does your brother keep you at your books as he does himself?" Brougham swept his quizzing glass at the open volumes on the low table. "You must be longing for a diversion!"

"Oh, no, my lord! Mrs. Annesley and I quite…quite enjoy our t-time…" Georgiana stammered.

"Please, do not be 'my lording' me, Miss Darcy," Brougham sighed. "It fags me to death! 'Brougham' will do, as your brother will tell you." He brought the glass up to an eye and surveyed her from the tips of her slippers to the curls about her face. "But, bless me, you *have* grown, my girl."

Georgiana flushed, bewildered by the creature before her whose exquisite appearance and peculiar manners bore no semblance to the earnest youth she remembered from childhood. Stepping back a pace, she indicated her companion, "May I introduce to you my companion, Mrs. Annesley? Mrs. Annesley, Lord Brougham, Earl of Westmarch."

Brougham bowed. "Charmed, madam. Pardon me for interrupting your lesson, or was it a tête-à-tête?"

"My lord," Mrs. Annesley curtsied. "It was neither, sir. A joint study, more like, but easily deferred to another time. "

"A study!" Brougham's eyes brightened with interest. "I expected Miss Darcy to be an able scholar. Her brother and I ran neck-and-neck at University, after all. But you astound me, madam!" He moved over to the table. "What do you study, Miss Darcy?"

Looking on in consternation that, should he discover the subject of her "study," his sister might be exposed to his friend's cutting wit, Darcy stepped forward. "And when did *you* become interested in female education, Dy?" he queried as Mrs. Annesley, on his nod, quickly swept the books into a pile.

"What would a man not give to fathom the female mind, Fitz?" Brougham protested, drawing himself up into a declamatory pose as the ladies gathered up the volumes. "It is one of the original mysteries of creation, designed, no doubt, to remind us men that in our armour of logic and martial passion we are still incomplete without the female of our race. Is that not so, Miss Darcy?" Her attention engaged in assisting Mrs. Annesley move the objects of their study, Georgiana started at his sudden appeal to her. In her surprise, the books in her arms began to slide, the smallest of which escaped her desperate clutch and landed squarely upon Brougham's foot.

"My lord!" Georgiana gasped in unison with Brougham's involuntary cry of pain, and she bent to retrieve the offending tome.

"It is nothing," breathed Brougham, biting his lip. He stayed her from the book with a motion of his hand. "Please, allow me. I claim as recompense for my wound the discovery of your study, even though your brother *would* draw me off."

As Brougham bent to recover the book, Witcher arrived with the tea, and in the ensuing activity of laying out the tray and pouring the tea, it seemed to Darcy that the book had been forgotten. The conversation turned instead to the latest news and *on-dits* exchanged in select drawing rooms and clubs of Town, a subject with which Brougham was intimately acquainted and which he most obligingly shared with his hosts. Darcy knew Dy's grasp of his subject was unassailable, but when he apprised them of the news that Mrs. Siddons was to announce her retirement from the stage, he took issue.

"She has been threatening to do so for years, Dy," Darcy scoffed. "Why do you believe it to be true this time?"

"Because, Fitz, I had it from her own lips and have seen the playbill announcing her last performance," Brougham replied smugly. He turned to Georgiana. "I have also heard that you, Miss Darcy, sing and play delightfully. Would you be so kind as to honour us with a little music?"

Darcy rose as a shadow of nervous reluctance passed over his sister's face and went to her, taking her hand in his. "The piece you have been practicing so diligently, Dearest…that will be perfect. And you need not sing, if you would rather not."

"I will forego song, Miss Darcy, if only you will consent to play," Brougham urged in softened tones, his eyes smiling at her in encouragement.

Bowing her head in acceptance, Georgiana gripped Darcy's hand and allowed him to assist her to the pianoforte. As she arranged her music, he resumed his seat, offering Brougham a grateful smile before settling back into his chair. Georgiana had never performed for anyone outside of the family before. *And it was time she did,* he thought, as she laid her fingers upon the keys. She would be coming out in a year and must conquer her shyness or be outshone by young ladies with less of a gift to recommend them. *Who else but Dy would have had the temerity and address to prevail upon her to play?* He had proved himself friend twice in the space of an hour. Darcy shifted his glance to Brougham. The look of satisfaction on Dy's face was all he could have wished for Georgiana. Although Brougham's reputation as a fribble was well established, his approval in matters of music was something to be regarded, and his word on Georgiana's ability would travel swiftly through the halls of society.

Darcy looked back to his sister. The tension he had sensed in her seemed to have dissipated as her fingers caressed the keys, and it occurred to him that her selection had not sounded so well when she had practiced at Pemberley. Perhaps a better instrument should be ordered. A movement at the corner of his eye drew his gaze again to his friend. Brougham's eyes were almost closed, mere slits in his face, as he slowly brought something up from his side. A cold shiver of apprehension shook Darcy as Dy surreptitiously turned over the volume in his hand to discover the title. He knew what he would read. It was that book he had so rashly picked up at Hatchard's and which was his sister's late, constant companion. If Brougham recognized it, he would invariably write her down as a wretched "enthusiast" and, unless he could prevail upon him, so she would be labelled by all of Society before she even made her curtsy.

Darcy eyed his friend warily, his breath held in suspension, waiting only for the snigger of contempt or snort of shocked disapproval. As he watched, Dy brought the book closer to his waistcoat and, after casually looking about him, peered down at its spine. In an instant, Brougham's face paled. He frowned and looked at it again, as if disbelieving what he had read. Then, shaking his head slightly, he slid the book back into its hiding place and looked up at Georgiana, his gaze riveted upon her in a curious fashion whose meaning Darcy was at a loss to interpret.

Georgiana brought her performance to an end, the notes distilling sweetly through the drawing room as she rose from the instrument and curtsied to the applause of her small audience. Before Darcy could rise, Brougham was at her side, offering her his escort back to her chair. He saw that she took Dy's arm hesitantly, not lifting her eyes to him but rather training them upon himself in mute appeal.

"Fitz, you have been hiding a treasure!" Brougham advanced them across the room and gently assisted her into her chair. "Miss Darcy." He bowed over her hand before relinquishing it. "Allow me to say you are a very remarkable young woman." Straightening then, he turned to Darcy. "Old man, I must beg your forgiveness. I toddle off to Holland House this evening and my man has warned me that I must place myself in his hands earlier than is my habit. Therefore, I take my leave. Miss Darcy, Mrs. Annesley." He bowed to them as Darcy rose and led him to the door.

Their progress down the hall was, to Darcy's mind, disturbingly silent. His friend seemed much preoccupied with his thoughts and, apprehensive of their subject, he could not determine whether his best course lay in silence or in demanding elucidation. When they had finally reached the stairs, his agitation on his sister's future forced him to come to the point.

"Dy..."

"Fitz." His lordship spoke in the same breath. "When does Georgiana make her curtsy at court?"

Surprised at his question, Darcy stopped on the stairs and looked back at his friend cautiously. "Why, early next year, I believe."

"And who will sponsor her?"

"My aunt, Lady Matlock, will introduce her. She comes to London next week to take Georgiana in hand."

"Lady Matlock." Darcy could almost see the wheels turning in Brougham's mind. "Yes, excellent. Of the first circle in style and grace, but wholly unconnected with the fast set. Very good," he murmured.

"I am gratified to have gained your approval in the disposition of my sister!" Darcy snapped at him, irritated beyond caution.

"Oh, my pleasure, Fitz, my pleasure." Brougham preceded him down the remaining stairs. "These things need careful attention…" Reaching the bottom, he turned and looked meaningfully into Darcy's eyes. "And I would be most happy to lend you any assistance you may require."

The burden of dread he had carried for the last half-hour suddenly lifted, leaving Darcy almost weak with relief. He reached out his hand and clasped Dy's ready one in a firm grip, so firm, in fact, that it raised his friend's eyebrow.

"Glad to help, old man," Dy assured him, flexing his fingers. "Now, shall I see you at Drury Lane Thursday night?"

"Yes, Georgiana and I will be attending."

"Then I shall call at your box at intermission. If you have no fixed engagement, may I invite you both to supper after?"

"That would be splendid!" Darcy's tentative relief expanded. "But you must know, Mrs. Annesley will make a third of our party, if that is agreeable."

"Of course, Miss Darcy's companion! Yes, the excellent Mrs. Annesley is very welcome. She will do nicely to entertain my elderly cousin, who will also make up our party. A fine old lady, but a trifle deaf." Witcher and a footman appeared with his lordship's things and assisted him in the donning as he and Darcy spoke of the upcoming Chess Tourney. "Will you be competing, Fitz?" Brougham asked as he set his beaver at a jaunty angle upon his auburn locks.

"No, I have been asked to judge again this year."

"Pity, that! I would have liked to have seen you take them on!" He advanced to the door. "Oh, bye-the-bye, Fitz," his brow contracted and his voice lowered so that Darcy had to lean toward him to hear. "You never told Georgiana what I said about hiding that doll?"

"No," Darcy replied, amused by his friend's look of deep concern, "I did not. Why?"

"Good! Good, indeed. Let it remain so! Tah, Fitz!" Darcy stepped through the door, despite the cold blast, and watched Dy run down the stairs.

"Shall I close the door, sir?" The footman asked.

"Yes…yes," Darcy turned back in bemusement to the warmth of Erewile House.

~~~~~~~~&~~~~~~~~

"My dear Georgiana," Caroline Bingley pled throatily, "I beg you will be guided by me." She fingered the page they were discussing of *La Belle Assemble*. "I assure you, you will think quite differently when you are 'out' and observe that all the young ladies will be wearing their gowns so. It *is* the fashion! Anything else would be cause for comment of a most disagreeable sort."

Darcy looked up from the hand of cards which Hurst had just dealt him and directed a narrowed gaze upon Miss Bingley. *Caroline Bingley to guide his sister in her coming out frocks? Not bloody likely!* He played his card and leaned back in the chair. Georgiana smiled faintly to their hostess, but a tightness that only a brother could detect laid to quick rest the words of caution that had begun to
~~~~~~~~

form in his brain. Darcy's gaze returned to the clutch of cards in his hand as he waited for the others at the table to finish arranging theirs and meet the challenge of his first play. He had long ago eschewed the practice of arranging a hand by suit; it communicated far too much to an observant opponent and was indicative, in his opinion, of a laziness of mind.

"There!" Bingley threw down his answer to Darcy's card in exasperation. "And may you have the pleasure of it!" A warning "tch-tch" from Hurst did nothing to quell Bingley's dismay with his hand; rather, it encouraged him to look daggers at his brother-in-law's head, causing Darcy to wonder what had his friend's wind up. Hurst removed a card from his hand and, employing it as a shovel, pushed the pile toward Darcy.

"Interesting opening, Darcy," he grunted as Darcy's long fingers covered the cards he'd won and flicked out his next play.

"Darcy makes it a study to be 'interesting' at the card table," groused Bingley as he brooded over his hand. "Sets everyone else at a disadvantage, I *must* say." Sighing, he picked out a card and carelessly tossed it atop Darcy's.

Darcy arched a brow at his friend. "Poor spirits, Charles?" A triumphant "Ah-hah!" from Hurst as he slapped down his card prevented him from hearing Bingley's reply, but the set of his friend's shoulders dissuaded him from pursuing his question. They finished the hand in silence, the conversation from the ladies nearby serving admirably as an excuse for its lack at the table.

"When do you leave?" Bingley's sudden question halted all discourse in the room and brought Miss Bingley slowly to her feet.

"Monday, next," Darcy replied as he gathered the cards.

"Mr. Darcy," began Miss Bingley, "this is rather sudden, is it not? I had not heard you were to leave our company." Her eyes flashed toward her brother.

"I believe we may get on without Darcy for a week, Caroline, especially if he intends to be always winning at cards." He turned back to his friend. "But it is rather sudden, this idea to go haring off. At least, you never mentioned it to me before today."

Miss Bingley seconded her brother's words, adding "How will Miss Darcy go on if you leave her?"

"My aunt, Lady Matlock, has arrived in Town and will be taking Georgiana under her chaperonage for the week or more I am gone." He laid the pile of cards precisely on the table and, taking up the small glass of port at his right, he took a sip, allowing its sweet savour to thoroughly reveal all its pleasurable nuances before continuing. "My cousins will look in on her and my friend, Lord Brougham, has promised the same. I would never leave Georgiana without first seeing to her care." Miss Bingley paled at his rebuke and hastily returned to her journal of fashion.

"Well, then." Bingley coughed and took up the cards. "Shall we continue?" Darcy nodded and reached for the cards Bingley dealt him. His decision to accept Lord Sayre's invitation to a house party at Norwycke Castle *did* appear rather sudden and out of character, but despite its eccentricity, he knew his attendance there to be essential.

~~~~~~~&~~~~~~~

Darcy's direction to Hinchcliffe to send his acceptance had succeeded in both raising that retainer's brows and compressing his lips into a disapproving line. "Why, what have you heard?" Darcy had demanded of his secretary.

"Finances in complete disarray, sir. Shouldn't think but his lordship will have to seriously retrench in the spring. Owes money to tradesmen, bankers, and moneylenders alike. Debts of honour…"

"In other words, a typical peer of the realm." Darcy had interrupted him. "I do not attend at his invitation in order to become his banker, Hinchcliffe. Or partner him in any scheme," he quickly added before his secretary could raise the objection. "You have taught me well in that regard. I am merely in an humour to be entertained."

"Very good, sir," Hinchcliffe had replied although, through long association, Darcy took him to mean no such thing.

In complete contrast to the stiff disapproval of his secretary had been the reception of his decision by his valet. Fletcher's eyes had widened considerably at the news and his tense anticipation of the prospect had made him a trial to the entire staff of Erewile House. There, among the other masters of his art, Fletcher would be in his element, and, Darcy reluctantly conceded to him, he would be obliged to allow his man a certain freeness of hand. "Within bounds, Fletcher," he had cautioned. "I'll not turn fashion's fool to satisfy your reputation. And no surprises!"

"Certainly, sir!" Fletcher had bowed eagerly. "Nothing remarkable in itself, nothing showy or vulgar, merely a higher degree of elegance," the valet sketched out. Then after a pause, "Mr. Darcy,
~~~~~~~

sir?" Darcy nodded his permission to speak. "*The Roquet*, sir. Would you condescend to..."

"Your accurst knot?" Darcy grunted and looked away from him, all the discomfort of Fletcher's recent triumph recommending itself to his memory. Weighing it carefully against the damage a refusal would deal to his valet's pride and standing among his peers, he turned back and gave him a quick nod. "But let that be the tether-end of your invention!"

"Yes, sir. Thank you, sir!" Fletcher gabbled, barely restraining his excitement, and departed the interview with Darcy all but rubbing his hands together.

The revelation of Darcy's departure to his sister had been quite another matter. Georgiana had swiftly covered the surprise and disappointment that his awkward announcement at supper had called forth. He knew he was distressing her, and he prayed she would ask him no questions on his sudden desertion; for he could give her no coherent answer nor expect her understanding of the half-formed reasons with which he had assayed to satisfy his own conscience. For, in truth, the decision to attend Lord Sayre's house party had more to do with impulse than reason.

Darcy had known Sayre since their days at Eton and, although the older boy had never been a comrade, he had been a decent sort when it came to the younger boys at school. Later, at Cambridge, they had quartered in the same hall and the invitation to the house party had been pressed upon him in terms of a reunion of hallfellows. But it had not been Sayre's appeal to "auld lang syne" that had moved Darcy to an uncharacteristic acceptance. Oddly enough, it had been Caroline Bingley's desperate little note. In the dark hours of the night, days after he and Brougham had composed Miss Bingley's answer, the words of her missive had returned to make purchase of his mind and trouble his soul.

Miss Bennet is in Town. Although he now believed the wording of the note made it unlikely that Elizabeth Bennet had accompanied her sister, at the time, his beleaguered heart had leapt and a frisson of curious, breathless pleasure had coursed through him. The power of that momentary supposition had disconcerted him, stunned him. But then, in the quiet reflection that night afforded, he knew that the wonderfully flurried sense of intoxication he had felt contemplating her presence in London had arisen from a seeming fulfilment of the fantasy he had entertained—nay, nurtured—since their days together at Netherfield.

He reached inside his waistcoat pocket and drew out his token of her, fingering his emotions, his desires, as carefully as he did the threads she had forsaken among the line's of *Paradise Lost*. Everything about her person excited his admiration and heightened his senses: her smile, the rich colour and curl of her hair, the contrast of her dark brows to the creamy perfection of her complexion… her eyes. Easily, he conjured her as she had been the evening of the ball: her figure, heart-stopping in its womanly curves; the small, glove-clad fingers which had rested with increasing willingness in his hand. Of this he was certain: to be in her presence was to know delight in a more pure expression, to be alive in a more vivid sense than ever he had before. The depth to which his fancy had taken him was attested to by the fact that, despite his disavowals, he had not been able to leave her in Hertfordshire, but had carried her home to Pemberley to wander its halls and grace its rooms, an almost tangible presence at his side.

He caressed the threads delicately between his thumb and forefinger as he then turned to her other attractions. For the intelligence he had seen mirrored in those enigmatic eyes he had found testimony in a wit that had engaged his own sharply, substantially, in a manner that pierced him to the bone and left him tingling from the encounter. Her bold ability to rise to his every challenge and meet him with acuity that was feminine in its contours, yet unsullied with coquetry, answered all his ideas of what true companionship might be between a man and a woman. Further, she was all soft compassion to those she loved. Time and again he had been witness to it. Even, though he hated to admit it, in the interest she showed in that blackguard, Wickham, it was quite evident that in Elizabeth Bennet there dwelt no pretence, no artifice or deceit. She was herself, as she met the world, as she met him. As she came to him…

He closed his hand tightly around the silken strands at the realization of what he was doing to himself. Elizabeth Bennet was *not* coming to him. *What was he thinking?* He rose from his seat by the hearth in his bedchamber and paced the length of the room. Nothing had changed in her situation. Her place in society, her connections, the deplorable state of her immediate family all remained insuperable barriers to the contemplation of a union. He imagined the reactions of his relations and friends.

The Bennets of Hertfordshire? Who are they that the name of Darcy should be so degraded, its interests so diverted to loss? Think not only of the interest not acquired through a proper marriage.

Would you lose all that your family has achieved in the course of generations for the sake of the illusion of love? Further, shall such a mistress of Pemberley be received? Will you not, in time, regret the confined society such a wife would impose? And what of any issue of this misalliance? Who will they wed—the daughters and sons of your tenants?

He stopped his pacing before the fire and stared unwaveringly into its flames. It must end. The fantasy that he had allowed to beguile him must be put away and his duty attended to. Surely there was a woman of his own station as beautiful and blessed with wit as Elizabeth Bennet, whose charms would banish her from his mind and displace her in his heart? It was time he found her! The Darcy name required an heir, Pemberley required a mistress, Georgiana required a guiding sister, and he required… His eyes closed then, his brow contorted from a pain located where he supposed his heart rested. He was required to do his duty.

Darcy opened his fist and looked down at the token, glinting softly there in his palm. He looked back to the fire. He should surrender it to the flames and consign it to oblivion. He stretched out his hand to the fire, the strands dangling between his fingers. Duty and desire warred within his breast. It must be duty. H*e knew it must*! But before they could slide between his fingers, his hand tightened convulsively around the threads, and he turned away from the hearth. Wrapping them around his finger, he then opened his jewellery case, laid them there in a tight coil and latched the lid. Then, striding purposefully to the small table by the fire, he poured himself a finger of brandy, tossed it back, and let his mind roam until it settled on Lord Sayre's invitation to a house party. His attention to his duty would begin there. It was as good a place as any! He poured himself another and, lifting his glass to the unknown woman whom Duty would take to wife, took a sip and hurled glass and all into the flames.

~~~~~~~&~~~~~~~

"Mr. Darcy!" The hand was finished and Bingley, Hurst and the others had repaired to the refreshments recently laid down by the staff, giving Miss Bingley an opportunity to whisper to him under her breath. "I am to pay a call upon Miss Bennet on Saturday! What is your advice, sir?"
~~~~~~~

Darcy lifted the port to his lips and slowly drained the glass. Then rising, he looked down upon his supplicant, his face expressionless. "Do as you think best about Miss Bennet. I do not wish to hear the name again."

~~~~~~~&~~~~~~~

By the time James Coachman brought the ill-matched team they had been forced to engage at the last inn to a respectfully attentive halt under the portico at Norwycke Castle, Darcy was desperately weary and inclined to regret his impetuous decision to attend Sayre's house party. The journey had been fraught with incident, not the least being the acquiring of an ominous crack in the coach's rear axle. Snow-drifted roads had added inconvenience as well as time to the journey, for the lamps were already lit at the portico and in the castle's old Great Hall, where Sayre had been called from supper to greet him.

"Darcy, my dear fellow!" Sayre had expostulated upon his entrance. "What a dashed unpleasant journey you must have endured! And this, your first visit to Norwycke Castle! You must allow me to make amends!"

He had bowed to his host. "Sayre, it is I who must apologize for interrupting your supper and taking you away…"

"Tush-tush, Darcy, say no more. Old hallfellows need not stand on such ceremony! I am certain you are ravenous and the table is laid. Let my man show you to your rooms and, please, join us as you are able," Sayre had assured him with a smile as he motioned to a servant.

With Fletcher in his wake, Darcy followed the footman to an opulently appointed suite of rooms overlooking a small, walled garden now buried beneath a pall of snow. Beyond the garden the shadows of night reigned, but he expected that the moat he had crossed flowed from there to the east. They had barely time to take in the amenities of his rooms when the sound of trunks hitting the dressing room floor called Fletcher away to his duties. Soon hot water and warm towels appeared, a testimony to Fletcher's quiet efficiency, and hope arose in Darcy's breast that he was now in a fair way to shedding the discomforts and turmoil of the last several days and putting them into their proper perspective.

Proper perspective! Darcy mused as he sat back to allow Fletcher to begin divesting him of his travel-day's stubble. His fingers uncon-
~~~~~~~

sciously sought his waistcoat pocket but encountered nothing there. *What?* He started to sit up and then caught himself, but not before Fletcher's blade nicked his jaw.

"Oh, sir!" Fletcher cried in dismay as he hastily put a cloth to the cut.

"The devil!" Darcy exclaimed, spattering shaving lather in all directions as he shooed his valet away and grabbed the cloth. He looked down at the bright red splotch. Pressing it once more to his jaw, he sighed and fell back into the chair. "A fitting end for this day!" For a moment he just looked at the ceiling over his head, then turned to his man. "Can anything be done for this, Fletcher?"

Armed with a sticking plaster, Fletcher dabbed at the cut and applied the plaster, his face a study of concern. "It is not deep, sir, and should heal quickly, but I cannot say yet whether the plaster may be removed before you go down to supper."

Darcy grimaced, "I *must* go down, arriving so late as we did. It would be an affront to Sayre and his other guests to refuse to join them." He resumed his former position in the chair. "Finish the job, Fletcher. If the plaster must remain a testimony to my folly, then so be it." His valet shot him a curious glance as he retrieved the soap cup and the badger-hair lathering brush, but offered him no comment. Folly, he had called it, and folly it was. Of course, the threads were no longer in his pocket! They reposed in his jewel case where he had put them away from him. How could he have allowed them to become almost a talisman, a blasted lucky rabbit's foot! *Good God, save me from becoming any more a fool!*

Perspective. Darcy disciplined his thoughts, this time casting them back to his departure from Town the previous day and his strained farewell to his sister. Georgiana had been discomfited with his sudden announcement that he would leave her for a week or more for the company of people they barely knew. From the day of his telling her to that of his leaving, she had struggled nobly with her disappointment, bestowing determined smiles upon him which made him feel all the more guilty for his desertion. Perhaps that was why he had begun a recital of the plans their aunt had for her amusement, ending with Brougham's promise to look in on her. It was then that Georgiana had lost her composure.

"My Lord Brougham?" she had repeated, "Why would his lordship promise such a thing?" She looked up at him with an expression he could not read. "Brother, you did not *ask* him to watch over me! Say you did not!"

"No, Dearest, he offered to do so when I told him of my plans to attend Sayre's house party. He was a hallfellow as well, you know, and had received an invitation as I had."

She had turned away from him then, saying in a low, tight voice, "I am astonished that his lordship does not attend. Such gatherings are, I understand, quite necessary to his natural amiability."

"Georgiana!" Surprised at her tone, he had rebuked her. "Lord Brougham has long been my good friend, and although I cannot approve of the manner in which he has conducted his life, no man would suggest him guilty of more than the waste of a considerable intellect. That you should take him into dislike when he has condescended to protect your interests is unworthy of you."

"Protect my interests?" she had replied, her fair cheeks aflame at his correction. "I cannot pretend to understand your meaning."

"As a gently bred female, there is no reason you should," he had snapped back at her from an irritation arising more from his own guilty conscience than fault in his sister. The stricken look she had returned him then at his hasty words cut him to the quick and he cursed himself. "Georgiana, forgive me, I did not mean…"

"He knows?" she whispered as he gathered her hands in his.

"No, not that!"

"What then?" She dared to look at him, but he had not known what to reply and only looked down grimly at their entwined fingers. "Fitzwilliam, you must tell me what you mean. How is Lord Brougham protecting my interests?"

"For reasons I can only assume arise from our long friendship," he confessed haltingly, "he has refrained from exposing your 'enthusiasm' to Polite Society."

"My 'enthusiasm,'" she had repeated faintly, withdrawing her hands from his grasp. "I see." She had risen from the divan and walked to the pianoforte. "How is it that his lordship knows of my 'enthusiasm'? Have you discussed it with him?"

"No, the subject has never arisen between us." He, too, had come to his feet, but kept the distance between them Georgiana seemed to desire.

"Then how…"

"Your book! Do you not remember the first day he came? I had thought he had forgotten it, but while you played for us he very discreetly brought it out. His reaction was *quite* revealing."

She had turned away from him then, running her fingers lightly over the gleaming wood of the pianoforte in a fearful silence. "You are ashamed of me, then, Brother?" she finally spoke. "What my wilful folly and Wickham's deceit could not do, my religious affections have accomplished! And my Lord Brougham conspires with you to hide my oddity from the world."

"No, Georgiana…Dearest, not ashamed." He had groped for the words. "Uncomfortable, concerned with what this obsession may lead to…oh, I do not know," he had finished in frustration, knowing his words were not repairing the hurt he had inflicted. He tried again, injecting all the sincerity he possessed into his voice. "You must believe me when I tell you that I *know* the world in which we move, and it has no tolerance for those who step outside the accepted bounds. One day, soon, you must take your place in that world, as is your duty. I would not be fulfilling my promise to our father or demonstrating my love for you if I did not do all to insure that your duty and happiness should coincide." The depth of her tremulous sigh at his words shook her whole frame, and his heart had ached at the sight, but he had stood firm, utterly convinced of the rectitude of his words.

"I think I understand you, Fitzwilliam, and you must know, I appreciate your concern for me," she had whispered when she finally turned back to him, her eyes bright with tears. He had gone to her, then, and gathered her to him, kissing her brow. "But, Lord Brougham, Brother!" she persisted into the folds of his neckcloth, "He is so frivolous and his conversation is all elaborate nothings."

"So it is, and yet at times, so it may only seem," he had cautioned her. "There is more to Dy than the polite world knows, and hidden in his 'nothings,' I have learned, are often valuable 'somethings.'" He chucked her under her chin. "Do not undervalue him, Sweetling. If nothing else his approval will open doors through which you may one day wish to pass." She had not been able to hide her doubt of his last assertion from creasing her brow but had said no more.

As Fletcher's smooth, practiced movements with brush and blade removed the day's shadow from his face, Darcy considered again his sister's tears. Her accusation that he was ashamed of her had haunted his travel north no less than the reasons for which he was making the journey. For, despite his words to Miss Bingley and his brandy-sworn vow to himself, Elizabeth Bennet's face and voice still pervaded his thoughts. He had rid his person of her token as a step toward bringing himself to order, but he still reached for it in unguarded moments, as he had just now. Since the night of his decision to seek a wife, he had comforted himself with the thought, perfectly reasonable in its logic, that his inability to put Miss Elizabeth Bennet away was only because The Woman had not yet been encountered. Once she was met, the other would fade, perhaps be eclipsed altogether. But it had been, as the Bard had put in wily old King John's mouth, "cold comfort." This weakness of will, this lack of control over his own faculties, seemed a torment sent straight from Hades to a man who had always prided himself on his self-regulation.

Now Georgiana's troubled regard joined with Elizabeth's pensive one to further erode his confidence. *Surely he was correct in his assessment!* Fletcher had finished and handed him a fresh, warm cloth. Darcy pressed it to his face, slowly removing the remaining traces of lather as he tested the thought. He rose from the chair, discarding his waistcoat and shirt as he went to the ewer of steaming water to complete his ablutions before dressing. Did Georgiana see into his heart more readily than himself? Was his embarrassment with her devotion due more to its social consequences or to his own disquieting suspicions that such devotion was naïvely misplaced.

Darcy cupped his hands and, bending over the ewer, splashed his face and chest with the hot water. The shock of the water's heat was refreshing, stimulating, as was the vigorous application of the towel Fletcher had laid close at hand. He had been too much in thought and it clearly was dangerous! Action, activity was what his mind and body required, not these spiralling reflections, these wheels within wheels. He had come here to find a suitable wife, or at least begin a serious search, and to enjoy himself. *On with it, then!*

Fletcher held out a fine, crisp lawn shirt that he slipped up Darcy's arms and over his shoulders. "Mr. Darcy, sir," he murmured, showing him the evening clothes he had selected for his approval.

"Yes," he assented. "Fletcher, what about this plaster?" The valet looked at it carefully and, reaching for it, gave it a delicate twitch. His master grimaced.

"There is still some seepage, sir. I would not like to see your neckcloth spotted with blood while you are entertaining young ladies. Thank goodness, the cut was at the back of your jaw. The collar and knot will hide the plaster quite nicely, I'm thinking."

"The knot?" Darcy queried his valet. "What do you have in mind for me tonight, Fletcher?"

"Oh, tonight it will be rather a simple one, sir. I…that is, you would not wish to begin grandly and then have nothing to show later in your visit."

"Undoubtedly!" Darcy's lips twitched as Fletcher, outlining his campaign, helped him into his evening dress.

"I regret my inability to be more specific, sir, but we have only just arrived," he apologized. "When I have discovered your host's plans for your stay and the identity of his other guests, I shall know exactly how to proceed."

His valet's meticulous approach to his duties and pride in his employment deserved, Darcy decided, like candour on the part of his master. "There is one other factor of which you should be aware, Fletcher."

"Sir?" Fletcher's expression clearly betrayed his belief that nothing important could have escaped his notice.

"I have lately decided that it is time I took a wife."

"A wife, sir? Truly, Mr. Darcy, a wife?" A peculiar grin came over Fletcher's face. "They are here, then, sir?"

"Who is here? I have not the pleasure of knowing Lord Sayre's guest list. Whom do you mean?" Darcy demanded of his man's strange response.

The valet looked back at him in confusion. "Then, why are we here, sir?"

"Why? To look for a suitable candidate—that should be obvious! Where else should we be?"

Darcy observed his man in wonder as Fletcher's mouth opened to give him reply then shut before more than an indistinguishable syllable had escaped. His face turned pink as he choked out, "Nowhere, sir! That is...here, I suppose, sir! Pardon me, Mr. Darcy!" and turned to rummage through a drawer he had just arranged.

Darcy continued with his dressing, one eye upon the antic movements of his valet, until all that was left was the knot of his neckcloth. "Fletcher!" he was forced to call to him, "I am ready for you."

"Yes, sir." The valet approached him with a regiment of cloths over one of his arms, a signal indication of his perturbation.

"I thought it was to be simple tonight?" Darcy indicated Fletcher's burden.

"Pardon me, Mr. Darcy, but I am feeling unwell suddenly. These are only a precaution." He eased the first around his master's neck and under the moderate collar and began the fold.

"Unwell, Fletcher! Ill in my hour of need!" he quipped, doubtful that any real sickness was the cause of his valet's puzzling behaviour.

"How shall I find a wife if I am not pleasingly attired? I depend upon you, man!"

Rather than a smile at his teasing, Fletcher's response was a slight furrowing of his brow and then a cocking of one eye at his master. "Do you dance tonight, sir?"

"I have no notion. I imagine I will discover that at supper. Why?" Darcy asked in full expectation that Fletcher would match him for wit.

"If there is to be dancing, sir, I would avoid the Scotch jig or else you may find the cinque pace, thereafter, a lifetime occupation." Fletcher gave a last tug to the ends of the knot. "There sir, I think you are ready now."

"In truth, Fletcher?" Darcy regarded him. "And from which of the plays is that one? I cannot place it." Fletcher opened the door to the hall and bowed him out, but Darcy grasped the door, holding it ajar before his valet could complete his retreat behind it. "The play?" he insisted.

Fletcher's jaw worked, and the furrow of his brow deepened; but as Darcy had no intention of moving until he had an answer, he waited. Finally, the valet's eyes came up and met his. Straightening his shoulders, he pronounced, "*Much Ado About Nothing*, Mr. Darcy, and that's my opinion of it…sir!"

~6~
Dangerous Play

When Darcy entered through the doors swung open by satin-clad doormen, servants were in the process of clearing the second remove from the long table around which Sayre's guests were arranged. That great piece of furniture appeared to him as long and wide as the drawbridge that had allowed his coach and team entrance to the castle. Its surface gleamed from generations of beeswax rubbed upon its boards, the shine ably reflecting the light from the heavy, branching candelabras positioned at intervals down its length.

The company gathered there glittered as ably as the candle flames. Darcy quickly noted seven ladies and, including himself, an equal number of gentlemen before presenting his compliments to Sayre. The gentlemen of the party rose to welcome him as Sayre greeted his appearance among them with an exhibition of the genuine good humour he had been known for when they had all been together at Cambridge.

"Your place is laid down the line, my dear fellow, just beyond old Bev, there." He nodded toward his younger brother, the Honourable Beverley Trenholme. "We have finished with the light fare and are about to tuck into what one truly comes to table for." Sayre winked at Darcy, only to be brought to heel by Lady Sayre.

"La, my lord, I thought it was the company of the *ladies* for which a man comes to the table." Lady Sayre pulled her full lips into a pretty pout as she looked to the other females among them. "My dears, we have been trumped by a sirloin of beef." Protests from the gentlemen vied with laughter from the ladies as Darcy made his way to his seat. When he had gained it, it was with no little surprise that he discovered his cousin D'Arcy's fiancée, Lady Felicia, and her parents, the Marquis and Lady Chelmsford, among the guests.

"Darcy," his lordship nodded to him as he sat down, "didn't know you were a schoolmate of Sayre."

"Two years behind, your lordship," he responded as he shook out his napkin and laid it in his lap. Chelmsford answered with an incommunicative "Humph," which his daughter smoothly covered with a dazzling smile directed at him.

"Papa is second cousin to Lord Sayre, Mr. Darcy." Lady Felicia's china-blue eyes rested delicately upon him. "His lordship has often invited Papa to visit, but only this latest invitation came at a convenient time. But, I suppose, sir, you have been a frequent guest at this delightful relic?"

"No, my lady, this is my first visit." At her look of surprise he added, "As in the case of your family, this was the first convenient time." Her "Ah…" in reply was accompanied by a look suggestive of a shared understanding of his obligations and the sweetest of sympathetic smiles, putting Darcy suddenly in mind of the several times they had danced together. A very agreeable sensation of warmth took hold of him.

"Are you acquainted with all the other gentlemen?" she asked.

Darcy looked down the table. "Yes, all the others are Cambridge men. I have known Sayre since Eton and his brother as well, who was a year behind me. Lord Manning," he indicated the gentleman two away from them, "was in the same class as Sayre; Mr. Arthur Poole, a year behind them; and Viscount Monmouth was in the same class as myself, a year behind that. But of the ladies I am acquainted only with you and Lady Chelmsford." He smiled, inviting her to enlighten him.

"Well, I am not at all certain that I should introduce them," she flirted back in the accepted mode, "for then you shall be free to ask them to dance sooner rather than late." Evidently, Lady Felicia remembered their dancing as well as he did.

"As you say," he responded. She rewarded his discretion with a low-pitched laugh and turned to indicate the lady directly across the wide expanse of table from him.

"That is my mother's widowed sister, Lady Beatrice Farnsworth. Her daughter, my cousin, Miss Judith Farnsworth, is seated next to Mr. Poole." She indicated the young woman with light brown curls arranged *a la grec.* "Now, Lady Sayre, you must know, is sister to Lord Manning. But you may not be aware that they share a younger sister, the Honourable Miss Arabella Avery, who is seated next to

Lord Monmouth." Darcy nodded as he located the lady, who, upon noticing his gaze, blushed and turned her eyes to her plate.

"Upon my other side there only remains Lady Sylvanie Trenholme, Sayre's sister." Darcy's eyes followed her gracefully raised hand to behold the face of one he could only describe as a faerie princess, her black hair and grey eyes a perfect contrast to the guinea-gold goddess beside him.

"I did not know Sayre had a sister," he confessed in surprise as Lady Felicia turned back to him, effectively blocking his view.

"Nor did most," she replied. "She is the daughter of Sayre's father's second wife and has only just come back from school and an extended visit to her mother's relatives in Ireland to live at Norwycke Castle. Although she is past the usual age, Sayre intends to present her at court this Season. I am quite in sympathy with her." She lowered her eyes from his as she reached for her glass of wine.

"Why so, my lady?" Darcy looked at her curiously. The Lady Felicia of his recent acquaintance had not been one to be concerned overmuch with the problems of other young ladies. Perhaps her engagement to his cousin had relaxed her feelings of rivalry.

"It is said that Sayre wishes her off his hands as soon as possible. There was no love lost between the two brothers and their late stepmama." She gave a delicate sigh.

"Darcy!" Monmouth boomed from across the table, "Is what Sayre said true?"

"What would that be, Tris?" Darcy turned from Lady Felicia and grinned back at his old roommate.

Tristram Penniston, Viscount Monmouth, leaned his elbows on the expanse before him. "That old George has bought into a regiment somewhere! I don't credit it, not a bit of it."

Darcy's grin faded. "I fear you must. It is true." A triumphal crow from Sayre caused him to add, "I hope you have not bet on him!"

"He did!" broke in Manning. "I tried to dissuade him—reminded him of the last time he'd placed the ready with Wickham, but would he listen?"

"Which regiment did he join, Darcy?" asked Poole. He waved his fork toward their host, "Sayre bet it would be a flashy one quartered in London for George and nothing else!"

Darcy shook his head and frowned, "No, it is the —th, under Colonel Forster, quartered in Hertfordshire."

"Never took Wickham for a soldier," Monmouth sighed. "No stomach for that kind of life that I could detect. Thought he was for the Law. Twenty, was it not, Sayre?"

Darcy grimaced. "He intended to, but he did not find it to his liking."

"Who would not chuse red and gold over black and a silly, old wig?" Trenholme offered. "Wickham knows, as does any man, that the ladies go faint with admiration over a uniform. Is that not true Miss Avery?" he quizzed.

Miss Avery coloured alarmingly as the attention of the table was centred upon her. She looked helplessly at her brother, whose only encouragement was an irritated frown. "A u-uniform is n-nice," she stuttered miserably.

"Nice? Bella!" Manning's withering tone caused Darcy to wince while the others became fascinated with their silver service or wineglasses. "Good Lord, speak up, and stop st…!"

"But she *has* spoken, my lord, and much to the point!" Lady Felicia smiled gently into the swimming eyes of the very young lady. "A uniform *is* nice." She then faced the others, arching one brow. "It makes a plain man, smart; a dull man, intelligent; and a timid man, brave with merely putting it on—at least, in his own estimation!" A chorus of masculine denials mixed with chuckles that raised the spirits of the hapless Miss Avery.

"And what will a uniform do for a more talented man, Lady Felicia?" asked Lady Sayre. "I vow, it is more than 'nice' work then."

"Oh, my dear Lady Sayre." Lady Felicia looked to her hostess. "It is well-known that a uniform makes a smart man, dashing; an intelligent man, a genius; and a brave man, a hero in no more time than it takes his batman to brush it and ease him into it." A new howl went up from the gentlemen and the ladies were forced to resort to their fans. Darcy smiled approvingly. Her rescue of Miss Avery by the turning of Manning's embarrassing treatment of his sister into a clever conceit was well and compassionately done. The conversation passed on to other subjects, but Felicia smiled at him briefly before attending to the gentleman on her other side as the servants entered with the next course.

Rediscovering his appetite, Darcy addressed the truly excellent sirloin of beef set before him. It had been hours since the wretched meal at the last posting inn, and he was as ravenous as Sayre had guessed him. For several minutes all Sayre's guests, as well as the host himself, directed their attention to the sumptuous meal. Gradually conversation resumed, and Darcy observed his old college hallmates as they laughed and ate and downed glass upon glass of Sayre's good red wine. Of the six of them, only Sayre had married. Darcy had forgotten that his wife was Manning's sister and had never known that Manning had had another one, younger still. Marriage to a friend's sister had some advantages to it, to be sure. As long as the sister was tolerable, he corrected himself, as a vision of Miss Bingley as his bride presented itself. There were several sisters present, it would seem: the exceedingly shy Miss Avery and the faerie changeling, Lady Sylvanie, and one cousin, the fashionable Miss Farnsworth.

A low, intimate laugh from the lady beside him drew him once more to the fact of her presence in the group. Lady Felicia. She was certainly beautiful and, he knew, possessed of all the expected accomplishments. Tonight she had even shown him that she was possessed of a compassionate nature as well. Had he relinquished his place in her court prematurely? Perhaps he had been wrong in believing she *required* the admiration of multiple suitors? A flicker at the edge of his vision caught his attention and he looked down to find that the fringe of her gossamer shawl had fallen across his coat sleeve and was now snagged by his cuff button. She seemed not to have noticed. He reached over and gently disentangled the delicate threads, but not before she discovered him. Her eyes searched out his and the meaning in their silent expression was not lost on him.

Darcy drew back his hand from the fringe of Lady Felicia's shawl, letting it drop like a veil between them as she murmured her thanks. A number of conversations whirled about him, but his mind seemed locked upon what had just occurred, unable to move beyond the import of their exchange. He took up his wineglass and partook of a generous amount as he pretended to listen to others at the table. He was no spring lamb; he had a fair comprehension of what Lady Felicia wished him to understand. She, his own cousin's fiancée, had invited him to embark upon a flirtation.

Such relations between men and women were commonplace enough in society, valued by the participants as well as their families for the political or social advantages they bestowed. That being said, in practice a flirtation provided a safe harbour for those desiring to avoid the intrigue of the marriage mart or relief from the tedious results for those who had succumbed to it. The rules for such things were excruciatingly precise, the limits openly acknowledged; but,

Janus-like, the offering of enticements to push against those boundaries was also part of the game.

His first experience of this game had occurred at the start of his second year at University. Soon after reaching the tender age of nineteen, his father had called him down to Erewile House from Cambridge upon rumours that a Certain Lady had taken an interest in him. Although their short acquaintance had not progressed to the point of an acknowledged flirtation (frankly, he had not understood then what the lady was about) the unwisdom of being in her company was represented to him in the strongest terms. Chastened and relieved that he had not joined the ranks of callow *cicisbei* who were the lady's preferred quarry, he had returned to Cambridge a bit wiser of the world and correspondingly cautious of the female portion of it.

That predacious lady's invitation had not been the last that had come his way, to be sure. His wealth, rank, and person had attracted attention from the beginning, and in the beginning, it had been a heady experience to be the object of so much feminine admiration. But the standards he had adopted at his father's knee, the memory of the loving, respectful example of his parents, and his own native intelligence had succeeded, for the most part, in checking the passions of youth. Oh, he had experienced desire and infatuation several times over. But when the first rush of feeling had past, its object had unvaryingly been found less than worthy in the structure of her mind, the stricture of her conduct, or in his sounding of her depths in the unpredictable sea of female charity. Then, there had been the fortunes his wealth had been meant to restore, the reputations his rank was to make or heal, and the influence his name was expected to bring to bear. All these expectations and more lay thinly cloaked behind the flutter of a fan, the display of an ankle, or the dip of a neckline. It had become disgusting, and later insulting, when it was borne upon him that who he was, his self, was the least of these ladies' concerns.

It was at this dismal point in his life that Brougham had crossed his path. Already an earl upon his entrance to University, Dy had experienced the same dissatisfaction with the eligible females of their circle and had retired to the same inn as Darcy to express it by getting stone-drunk. The only student in the place at the time, Darcy had looked up from his mug of ale to see a glass and bottle being set down on his table by a fellow who then fell into the seat opposite him and introduced himself wryly as the "Rich Young Earl." Although they did not *precisely* get drunk, they managed to relieve each other's low spirits, finding a kinship of mind each in the other, and departed the tavern in support of each other in more than the making of their unsteady way back to their halls. From that point on, it had been agreed between them, the female of the race was of secondary importance and the academic race was begun.

Later, after the death of his father, the responsibilities of Pemberley and the care of Georgiana had weighed heavily upon him and the foray he had made back into the Polite World after University was cut short. It had only been in the last two years that he had made a concerted effort to return, but he had found the landscape little changed. The faces were different, but all else was ever as it had been. Perhaps it was even worse since the Continental war had claimed so many of society's young men, leading to an increasingly desperate competition among the ladies. Again, he had experienced only disappointment. Until…

Darcy flicked a glance at the woman by his side. Lady Felicia was the epitome of what Society deemed perfection in its females of rank. She had contracted a brilliant engagement with his cousin and was destined to become one of their world's influential ladies. All was before her, if not in her possession already. Yet, this was as nothing! Honour—hers, his, or his cousin's—was not even a consideration! She desired a flirtation. With him specifically, or would any man at the table serve? Darcy surveyed his fellow guests. If he did not take the bait, *would* she encourage another? He recalled Alex's unease after the announcement of his engagement and his inexplicable anger with his brother upon Richard's teasing. Had he, Darcy wondered, stumbled upon the answer to his cousin's strange behaviour? And further, should he stand silent while the lady made a fool of his cousin?

His quandary rendered the remainder of the meal tasteless, but as his body required sustenance, Darcy worked his way through course after course that flowed from his hosts' kitchen. After dinner the gentlemen were invited to repair to Sayre's gunroom for their brandy and tobacco while her ladyship suggested that the ladies retire to the more feminine environs of a salon in another wing and on the next floor. With a fluttering of fans and gathering of shawls, the ladies rose and curtsied to the gentlemen. They in turn bowed, and Sayre promised that they would not keep the ladies waiting. "For," he said as the door clicked shut behind them, "I hope to get them all safely to bed as soon as may be, so we can truly begin to enjoy ourselves." His lordship's remark was immediately understood by all, Darcy not excepted. Sayre had been an inveterate gambler at University, his penchant for cards in particular, nearly an addiction. The intervening years had not, it appeared, satiated his hunger for games of chance. It was going to be a late night.

The gunroom was, in fact, the old armoury of the castle, converted to display its owner's collection of weaponry, from pike to edge to gunpowder, in an atmosphere conveyed by appointments in keeping with a strictly masculine idea of comfort. The servants awaiting them brought forward the brandy and scotch and a selection of cigars and cheroots. Waving away the tobacco, Darcy considered the brandy but then passed it by for a smaller glass of port. If they were to gamble, he desired the command of all his faculties. Tonight's play might begin in cordiality, but it would soon take a very serious turn. Strong drink and tobacco could be dangerously distracting in the play that would occur later tonight.

"Darcy, have you seen the sabres?" Monmouth called him over to an entire wall of the sword maker's art. It was a stunning collection. The graceful blades and elegant hilts glinted in the candle light, practically begging to be lifted free of their display to have their balance weighed and their danger tested. Darcy ran a finger over a particularly lovely one from Spain, its creator's name a virtual byword for excellence among swordsmen. "A beauty, isn't it?" Monmouth commented then laughed. "I was present when Sayre won it from young Vasingstoke. His grandfather, the old baron, tried to redeem it, but Sayre wouldn't part with it. Cost Vasingstoke a month kicking his heels in the country, as I recall." Darcy let escape a low whistle. The baron's collection was legendary, but even so, this must have been a prized piece.

"Like the look of that sabre, do you?" Sayre strolled over to them with unconcealed pride in his possession of such an article. At Darcy's nod he motioned toward it, "Take it up! Tell me what you think." Almost disbelieving him, Darcy reached up and gingerly freed the sabre from its display. The weapon's hilt seemed to slip into his hand, his fingers closing around it in a perfect fit, the swirling silver bands of the wrist guard accentuating its deadly beauty. He hefted it reverently, flexing the muscles and tendons of his hand and forearm, and slowly thrust it out before him, watching the candle light play along its length as he tested its exquisite balance.

"Go on, Darcy," urged Trenholme as the others gathered around. "Show what can be done with the little beauty! My brother never was a swordsman. I'd like to see it as it was meant to be seen—in action!"

Smiling with anticipation, Darcy executed a few simple moves. The blade floated then slashed through the air, the traditional moves calling forth the weapon's own distinctive song. Perfect, he thought, or as near to perfection as a thing from the hand of man could be.

"Too tame by half!" Manning sneered.

"Show us more than nursery exercises, Darcy!" called Poole.

Checking his movement, Darcy gently placed the sabre on a table and began unbuttoning his coat. With a knowing smile upon his face, Monmouth came behind him and helped pull it from his shoulders. Shaking one arm free, Darcy stripped his other and threw the coat over a chair as he turned back to the blade. It fit into his hand as smoothly as before and, no, he had not dreamed the perfection of its balance. Stepping away from the group and stretching the muscles of his back and upper arms, he swung the sabre in increasing arcs.

"He should have an opponent," Chelmsford observed, but no one made a motion to offer his services. Instead, silence fell as the gentlemen eagerly awaited his first move. Quieting himself, Darcy drew in several calming breaths as he reviewed the steps of the exercise he had recently developed for himself. It had been well over a week…

He began slowly with classic moves that warmed his muscles and steadily increased the beat of his heart. Then the pace and complexity of the figures increased as well, until the blade was a blur as he advanced and retreated against an invisible foe. The sabre responded to his slightest wish, becoming an extension of his body. He pressed himself further.

Shouts of "Well done!" and "Good show!" slowly invaded his concentration. It was time to end. Advancing to his host, he slowed and with a flourish, threw the sabre up into the air. Catching it, he laid it across his crooked arm, offering it hilt first to a wide-eyed Sayre. His lordship took the weapon with a bow as the rest clapped Darcy upon his back, exclamations of their appreciation echoing from the stone arches of the ancient armoury.

"Damn me, Darcy!" Sayre eyed him speculatively. "Thought seven years would have slowed your sword arm. Of course, with such a blade…" He let the thought dangle as Darcy shrugged back into his coat and began on the buttons.

"Out with it, Sayre, 'with such a blade…'?" Monmouth prodded.

"Just a thought." His lordship would not be rushed. "Perhaps, Darcy, you would like an opportunity to acquire the sabre?"

His suspicion aroused at such a question, he replied casually, "Are you offering it for sale, Sayre?"

"Oh, no! Not for sale, Darcy!" Sayre regarded him slyly. "If you would have the sabre, you must win it from me!"

~~~~~~~&~~~~~~~

The gentlemen entered Lady Sayre's salon to the sound of a musical duet. The last to enter, Darcy paused in the doorway, for the scene presented for them had been artfully contrived. Lady Felicia sat at the pianoforte with Miss Avery at her side to turn her pages, while Miss Farnsworth stood behind them, drawing a bow across a violin. The music was sweetly plaintive, a popular lament, and with the performers so charmingly grouped, ideally suited to delight the senses.

It was a pleasing sight, Darcy admitted, as he found a seat. Veteran as he was of many a drawing room campaign, he was not inured to beauty and grace; and the females present possessed those qualities in full measure. All of them were good-looking women. Lady Chelmsford, the oldest, was still handsome; and her sister, Lady Beatrice, could almost be taken for Miss Farnsworth's older sister rather than her mother. Lady Sayre had been declared a "stunner" her first Season by members of the fast set who still had entry into Almack's and had been credited with bringing red hair into fashion. Although six years had passed since her triumph and marriage, her sloe eyes, womanly figure, and pouting, full lips were still more than capable of sending warm shivers down a man's spine.

Darcy turned his contemplation upon the younger ladies. Miss Avery, Lady Sayre's much younger sister, was a copy of her but in a different key. She also possessed the Avery hair, but imitated her brother in looking upon the world through grass-green eyes. The most obvious difference lay in her manner. Whereas her siblings regarded the world with confidence and complacency, Miss Avery did so with a timidity that revealed a severe doubt as to her welcome. This hesitancy was further exacerbated by her brother's impatience with her and an unfortunate tendency to stutter. She was very young and impressionable, Darcy noted. Already, her gratitude for Lady Felicia's intervention during supper had blossomed into
~~~~~~~

worship as she gazed upon the lady playing so charmingly beside her.

Miss Farnsworth, on the other hand, was a self-assured, regal beauty cast in the classical mould. Tall like her mother, she held herself with an easy confidence that bore testimony to her reputation as an accomplished horsewoman and huntress. A veritable Diana, she seemed as if she had just stepped from the forests and fields shouldering Olympus. In that, she was a perfect complement to her cousin. Lady Felicia's celebrated beauty was all of English cream mixed with Norse ancestry. Sunlight or candle, it did not matter, her hair was gloriously golden and her eyes the clearest blue. As he turned his attention to her performance at the pianoforte Darcy recalled his enchantment upon their introduction almost one year ago and his subsequent recession of himself from her court several months later. She was beautiful, of that there was no question. Her taste, her air of *recherché* was exquisite. She was the perfect consort for a man of distinction in the world. But he had relinquished his place in the lists; she was now his cousin's, and although he could still respond to her beauty, Darcy suddenly found that he was not sorry that he had stepped aside. He wanted for a wife and a mistress for Pemberley, not a consort, and especially not one whom he could not trust from out his sight.

Lady Sylvanie was the only one of the young women who was not charmingly grouped for the gentlemen's appreciation. Quickly surveying the room, Darcy found her half-hidden behind Trenholme's turned back in a corner of the salon. A heated discussion was obviously in progress as Darcy immediately recognized the signs of a man whose back had been set up. Beverley Trenholme had never been one to handle his emotions stoically. He now wove back and forth as he habitually did when in agitation, but Darcy could not fault him; for it gave him a view of the lady. His first impression of a faerie princess was recalled as he observed her cool disdain for her half-brother's words. Her black hair was plaited into a crown about her head, although cloudy wisps had come loose and played delicately about an ethereal face. Her smoke-grey eyes looked through Trenholme as if he were not even now leaning toward her, intent on making his point. Her gaze seemed focused elsewhere, beyond her brother or within herself, Darcy could not decide. No child's flower-faerie she, he concluded, but one of that more traditional, fearful caste whom men do well to treat with caution.

Knowing he should not attend to a family squabble, Darcy made to look away; but at that moment, Lady Sylvanie's eyes met his. A slow smile touched her lips. Seeing the change in her expression, Trenholme turned immediately, his features smoothing from their snarl into an embarrassed smile when he beheld the raised brow of her object. Looking over his shoulder, he said something that only caused her to laugh at him before he abruptly left her alone where she stood. Shuttering her eyes once more, the lady drifted to a chair next to Lady Chelmsford and, without another glance in Darcy's direction, appeared to give all her attention to the duet.

Finally, the last notes drifted across the salon and were answered with enthusiastic applause from the gentlemen and ladies alike. Darcy added his, but the irrepressible memory of another lady's performance at the pianoforte tempered his response. As the pair acknowledged their audience's appreciation he could not help but contrast their grand curtsies with Elizabeth Bennet's unaffected one that had thanked her listeners with such sweet sincerity. Elizabeth's performance had been no better in execution, he admitted, but her music's expression had called forth from deep within him a response that Lady Felicia's performance had been unable to touch. He closed his eyes while the remembered pleasure coursed through him.

A sudden cascade of feminine laughter brought Darcy's eyes snapping back open and a flush of heat crept up his neck. Had his lapse been noted? No, it was something Poole had said that had caused the amusement. He closed his eyes again, this time bringing his fingers to work at his temple. *Is there nothing that does not bring her to mind, or have you merely lost all your sense? You are here, sir, for an antidote to her charms, not a restorative!* He looked up again with purpose at the bevy of eligible femininity before him. Was "The Woman" who would cure him among them? He sighed lightly, feeling once more the effects of the day's travel. Perhaps he just needed rest and time to become acquainted. Then, perhaps, "She" would gently assume the guise of one of the ladies present. He could hope.

"A delightful offering," Lord Sayre complimented his guests, "as delightful as any I, or these walls, have been privileged to hear, I am sure. Do you not agree, Bev? " He turned to his brother, who by now betrayed no sign of his unsatisfactory interview with Lady Sylvanie.

"A privilege, indeed!" Trenholme agreed and offered his arm to Miss Farnsworth as his brother did to Lady Felicia, escorting her to a divan.

"Shall we have our tea, then?" Sayre looked to his wife. "My lady?"

"Yes, Sayre, I take your meaning," her ladyship gave a delicate snort, "and will not suggest more music for this night." She arched her brow as she nodded to the servants. "Drink your tea, ladies. The gentlemen have their own plans for tonight." Murmurs of disappointment issued from the female quarter, answered with nobly phrased apologies from the gentlemen. Darcy accepted his tea and sweets in silence, hoping that Lady Sayre's little rebellion against her husband's plans for a night of gambling would gain sway. The thought of a night so spent in high stakes and devil-may-care play was numbing to his travel-weary senses.

"My lady." Sayre's voice rose above the others. "Might I suggest that the ladies use this evening's separation to plan tomorrow's activities? I promise we shall be at your service whatever you decide. Shall we not, gentlemen?" His offer was enthusiastically seconded by the men and eagerly accepted by the ladies.

"Let it not be a *very* late night then, Sayre," his wife smirked in satisfaction, "or else your promise will be worth precious little on the morrow, my dear."

Sayre allowed the gentlemen long enough to do justice to his board before excusing them all from "the ladies' gentle company for the sharper air of his library." Mentally arming himself for the battles ahead, Darcy rose with the others and made his bow. The ladies wished them well with sweetly despairing smiles upon their faces.

"*Bon chance*, Papa." Lady Felicia swiftly crossed the salon to Chelmsford, who was standing next to Darcy, and bestowed a soft kiss upon her father's cheek. It was a pretty picture, and only Darcy's closeness to the exchange allowed him to observe Chelmsford's startled response before he checked himself and patted his daughter's shoulder. Lady Felicia drew back slightly from his gesture as the gathered gentlemen murmured their approval of her display of sentiment. Darcy watched in silence, his mind divided in perplexity at what he had seen.

"A most unfair advantage, Chelmsford," Monmouth grumbled playfully behind him. "I have no fair lady to wish me well in such a manner." Chelmsford laughed with the others, but his brow wrinkled slightly as his daughter rose from her curtsy.

Lady Felicia smiled archly at Monmouth. "My lord, it is true you have no 'fair' lady, but if you will soon come to the point, you might then claim the favour of one of another shade."

"Walked into that one with both eyes open," snorted Manning above his fellows' chorus of jibes at the viscount's misstep. "Take care, Monmouth!"

"Yes, do take care, my lord, as shall I." Lady Felicia turned to Darcy, detaining him while the rest of the gentlemen took their leave.

"My lady?" he inquired politely, although the hairs on the back of his neck stood up in warning at the look she gave him. Cerulean pools appealed to him from under lowered lashes as her hand came to rest upon his arm.

"As we are nearly related, Mr. Darcy, allow me to wish you well, also." His incredulity at her forwardness must have shown, or perhaps she felt his arm tremble under her hand; for she arched a brow and smiled. "But, perhaps you have no need of wishes," she murmured, drawing close to his side, "and know your way."

In a second she was gone, back to the other women, but the warmth of her hand and of the look she had cast him remained. Wheeling about abruptly, he left the room, but the churning of his thoughts as he followed after the others hampered his long stride. There was no hope of mistake or avoidance; Lady Felicia had made it very clear that a flirtation was not the sum of what she desired of him. *My God, poor Alex!* The thought brought him to a halt. No wonder he had come near to baring his fists when Richard had teased him. He knew! Had he known of his fiancée's "propensity" before he had made his offer? Surely not! His lips pressed themselves into a hard line as he looked back down the hall. Could his aunt and uncle have been so deceived as well? Darcy's eyes narrowed. To all her other talents, then, must be added that of consummate actress.

"Darcy!" Monmouth suddenly rounded the corner before him. "Coming, my good lad? I have claimed a seat for you." His old roommate stopped directly in his path and peered into his face. "Is there a problem? Good Lord, what a scowl!"

Darcy looked back at his roommate in chagrin. "N-no, Tris. Just a very long, blasted day."

"Oh, good that! Well, what I meant was, good that nothing is wrong." Monmouth clapped his shoulder. "Come on, then. It will be just like old times—you and I against all comers, eh? Although, I seem to recall, you partnered that other fellow often after our first year. Who was that? Won all the prizes when we graduated."

"Brougham," Darcy replied, the memories relaxing his features.

"Ah, yes…Brougham! Earl of Westmarch isn't he? Whatever happened to him?"

"Oh, he is still about. Flies with the Melbourne set usually, but I see him now and then." They had reached the library door, which was opened by yet another richly dressed servant.

"The Melbourne set!" Monmouth whistled. "Then it is not a wonder that I haven't seen him. M'father would disinherit me if I were to ever to…"

"Monmouth, Darcy!" Sayre's voice boomed out at them. "Hurry along, lads!"

Darcy looked about him as he came into the room, more curious to behold Sayre's library than his card tables. In shocked surprise he looked from one side of the room to the other. "I thought this was your library, Sayre."

"It is, old man." Sayre looked up briefly from the cards he was shuffling.

"Then, where are your books?" Darcy motioned to the empty bookcases running up and down the room.

"Sold 'em!" his lordship replied. "Got a pretty little sum for them, too. Who would have thought anyone would want them enough to pay for them?" he laughed. "Better the ready in my pocket than those old, fusty things doing me no good on the shelf."

"Sold them! Sayre, were there not some very old manuscripts among the collection?" Darcy looked at his lordship in amazement.

"Possibly…probably. Had a fellow in to give me a figure who was fool enough to let me see his excitement over what he had found. Got another thousand out of him." Sayre began to deal the cards. "Shall we begin, gentlemen?"

~~~~~~~&~~~~~~~

The last card of the evening was turned at three in the morning, and Darcy was thankful that he had been able to hold his own despite his fatigue and come out twenty guineas to the good. Not up to his usual play, he confessed in a yawn, dropping the golden coins on the dresser as Fletcher divested him of his evening clothes.

"Humph!" Fletcher snorted. "Better play than his lordship hoped for, I've no doubt! Begging your pardon, sir," he added quickly,
~~~~~~~

before moving to the washing stand to pour out the steaming water from the ewer.

"No, continue, Fletcher," Darcy encouraged, trying to stifle another yawn, "You have had an entire evening, and I expected you would have formed some opinions."

The valet carefully replaced the ewer before he turned and cocked his head at his master. "It would have been well with his lordship if he'd heeded old Polonius, sir. Not only has Lord Sayre's habits dulled 'the edge of husbandry,' but they threaten to lose him his patrimony altogether."

Darcy nodded thoughtfully. "Hinchcliffe told me as much before we left London, and I have seen evidence of it with my own eyes. He has sold off his library, Fletcher!"

"His library, sir?" Fletcher's face showed only mild surprise. "It stands to reason. Have you seen the gallery yet, Mr. Darcy? The gilt frames have all been removed—sold, I understand—and replaced with wood and paint."

"'All that glisters is not gold,'" Darcy thought aloud as he paced the room. Upon reaching the window, he leaned against its frame and stared out into the moonlit night. "I did see his weapons collection, and it is truly impressive. I would venture to say it is untouched."

"Yes, very true, sir, but according to my information, it is the only part of the Sayre estate either here or in London that has not suffered depredation."

"Hmm." Darcy considered Fletcher's information. "Yet tonight he held out one of his most valued swords as a prize at cards. His losses never reached that point, but…here, what is this?" He straightened and peered out into the darkness.

"Mr. Darcy?" Fletcher joined his master at the window to see a hooded and cloaked figure moving swiftly along the wall of the barren garden before disappearing from sight below them.

"A servant?" Darcy speculated.

"No, sir, not from the swing of the cloak. It speaks of a superior wool and likely lined as well." Fletcher's brow furrowed. "I regret to admit it, but I could not discern from the cut or from this angle tell you with any certainty whether the garment belonged to a man or a woman."

Despite his curiosity, Darcy could no longer deny the necessity of sleep, his next yawn so wide even Fletcher heard the crack of his jaw. He was so very tired. It was a miracle that he'd not lost his shirt at that night's play. The rest of Fletcher's gleanings would have to wait for the morrow. He drew off his shirt as he walked to the washing stand, toeing off his pumps as he went. Quickly seeing to his ablutions, he accepted his nightshirt from Fletcher and sent him off to his own rest with instructions not to disturb him until noon. The door behind his man had barely clicked shut before Darcy blew out the candles and slid his weary frame between the bedclothes of the stately piece of furniture that was the guest bed. Adjusting the pillows and quilts to his liking, he lay back with a sigh.

Lady Felicia! He almost sat up again with the sudden return of his problem to mind. Had she awaited him long or had she accepted early that he would never come? Why did she act so warmly? He had detected no great sorrow when he had left her worship those months ago. There had been a short flurry of gossip, as there always was, but they had gone on civilly after, and he had detected no particular sign of regret at his leaving. And what of discovery? Did she have no fear of exposure? Did she so discount his honour or believe Alex so besotted that he would deny the report of his own cousin? Darcy's eyes drifted shut, his fatigue an irresistible weight. And what was Sayre about? A luxurious house party and satin-clad servants when he was on the verge of bankruptcy? It made no sense! And he was so…very…tired. With a low groan, Darcy rolled over onto his stomach and, pulling a pillow into his embrace, surrendered to the insistent claims of his weary mind and body.

~~~~~~~&~~~~~~~

Fletcher's knock at precisely noon furnished Darcy with reason enough to finally abandon his efforts to draw more rest from his tumbled bed. He never could sleep into the morning, his early-formed habit of rising with the sun warring against the injudicious use of the previous evening. Looking into the sitting room of his suite, he beheld his valet, trailed by a footman with a tray of steaming dishes whose aromas performed a miracle on his perception of the day. A dressing gown was retrieved post haste, but not before Fletcher had the dishes uncovered and a cup of coffee poured and waiting for him.

"Good afternoon, sir," Fletcher greeted him quietly. "No other of his lordship's guests is stirring, and none of the maids or the gentlemen's men is to attend before two. You may enjoy your meal at leisure, sir."
~~~~~~~

Darcy looked up in surprise from his plates of steak, a rasher of bacon, toast and cups of boiled eggs. "Two! I suppose I should not be surprised that Sayre keeps Town hours in the country." He speared a bit of the steak. "Well, Fletcher, what else should I know?"

"The ladies have decided on a sleigh ride this afternoon. They wish to view some standing stones famous in the area. Then, poetry and cards are planned for this evening."

"Poetry and cards," Darcy sighed. "It could be worse."

"Sir, it is incumbent upon me to add that dancing and charades were other items on their list."

"Charades!" Darcy put down the cup he had just lifted to his lips. "Oh please, not charades!"

"I am sorry, sir, but there will be charades. Not tonight, Mr. Darcy, but every other evening this week without fail. The ladies were most insistent on that point."

"And would you know who the Charade Master or Mistress is to be?"

Fletcher drew himself up, "Of course, sir. It is to be her ladyship, Lady Sayre. Lord Sayre has his own plans for later each evening."

"Gaming." Darcy stated flatly as he broke off a piece of toast and popped it into his mouth. Fletcher nodded in assent but held his peace. "Thank you, Fletcher. I shall be only a few more minutes here."

"Very good, sir." Fletcher bowed and made for the dressing room, while Darcy chewed meditatively on his meal. Charades! Well, there was no help for it; he could hardly ask to be excused. He looked at the clock on the mantle. Plenty of time to dress and write to Georgiana of his safe arrival. Safe *arrival*, to be sure, but a rather peculiar series of experiences since! Picking up a silver spoon, he rapped the tops of the eggs and carefully removed the cracked pieces, revealing a perfectly prepared interior. Good Lord—Charades!

~~~~~~~&~~~~~~~

Fletcher's careful ministrations completed, Darcy occupied the remaining time until his fellow-guests should arise with the task of composing a letter to his sister. Such close correspondence as he had heretofore maintained with Georgiana had always made such missives a pleasure, but her new easiness did not aid him in the setting down of his narrative on the ivory sheet before him now. A portion
~~~~~~~

of his difficulty with its composition lay in the nature of their parting. The changes his sister had lately exhibited and the loss of understanding between them caused him to question the suitability of his habitual manner of addressing her. The remainder lay in the somewhat curious conduct of the gathered company as well as in his purpose for being one of their number. How, after all, did one tell one's sister that he was—what was the abominable phrase?—"hanging out for a wife?"

In the end, he wrote of his misadventures upon the road and favoured her with a short description of his hosts and their other guests, ending with an adjuration to enjoy whatever entertainments their aunt might suggest and to regard Lord Brougham's advice with the greatest solemnity, no matter in what manner it was given. Sanding down the letter and folding it, he looked about him for his seal, but search as he might, it was not among the items in the writing desk. Odd that Fletcher had neglected to notice its absence.

Pushing back the chair, he rose and crossed into the dressing room. It would likely still be in his jewel case, since he had had no use for it upon his journey. Flicking up the clasp, Darcy opened the case, his eyes scanning the interior. *Ah, yes, there it was, right next to...* The silken threads lay serenely where he had laid them. Bypassing his seal, his fingers hovered over the strands. The temptation to retrieve them and return them to his waistcoat pocket was nigh unto irresistible. He knew that if he touched them.... No! Quickly, he snatched up the seal and snapped the case shut. At all cost, he must stay to his resolve. He returned to his letter and, lighting the wax wick, let fall two drops before stamping it with the seal. Then, affixing the franking wafer, he left it and his seal on the desk for Fletcher to see to. It was now two o'clock, and drawing down his cuffs and waistcoat, he turned toward the door just as a tattoo was rapped upon it from the hall.

"Manning!" Expecting almost anyone else but the baron, Darcy greeted him with surprise. During their days as hallmates, he and Manning had not got on well and, as a consequence, had not kept in touch since the older fellow's graduation.

"A rack or two of billiards suit you before this afternoon's expedition?" Manning's cool green eyes surveyed him. "I take it you've breakfasted."

Darcy nodded and motioned Manning to lead on. "Your long friendship with Sayre and close relation through her ladyship must make you familiar with Norwycke and its environs."

"I know my way quite well, yes," Manning replied. "The billiard room, the salons, the dining room, certainly." His companion sent him an appraising glance then added, "Several of the maids' chambers are within my scope also should you desire direction."

"You are too kind," Darcy murmured back, tamping down firmly on his welling distaste.

"Not at all, Darcy," Manning rebuffed him as they entered the wood-panelled sanctum that sheltered a grandly carved green baize billiard table.

Darcy followed his lordship to a glass-fronted case that displayed a selection of cues, noticing as he passed several patches of discolouration in the panelling. It was only after he had chosen his stick that the shapes of those discolorations suggested an answer to their puzzling presence. Pictures no longer graced the walls, leaving behind their proportions in the darker shade of the panelling they had shielded from the sun. The nails were missing as well, indicating to Darcy that the pieces were not returning. More evidence, he noted while chalking his cue, that Hinchcliffe's information and Fletcher's observations had been accurate as usual.

"Do you play billiards with the same intensity as you fence, Darcy? I cannot recall." Manning's regard pinned itself upon him in an attempt to discompose him. It had been thus between them at University. For reasons known only to him, Manning had amused himself by assuming the role of Darcy's personal inquisitor. Little that he had done had passed Manning's notice without disparagement.

"Quarter is neither asked nor given," he replied evenly, refusing to be goaded.

Manning laughed. "As I anticipated. Single-minded as ever, eh, Darcy?" Darcy met his gaze coolly, the lift of one brow his only response. The baron laughed again. "But, you have learned to school your temper, I see. How long will it last, I wonder?" He lifted the rack and motioned expansively. "I offer you the break, sir. Make of it what you can."

The solid crack of the break was particularly gratifying to Darcy, as was the explosive curse of his opponent once the balls finally came to rest.

~7~
The Frailty of Woman

Although he would much rather have met and prevailed over his challenger, Darcy derived some small satisfaction from the fact that he had played Manning to a draw before they were called away to join the other guests. It was really quite ridiculous, he chided himself as he brushed down his buckskin riding breeches, but the under-classman who yet lurked in his soul and had suffered innumerable stings at Manning's hands could not help but rejoice a little.

The afternoon's expedition to a local sample of the mysterious stone circles that dotted the countryside had been enlivened by Lord Sayre's offer of mounts to those who wished to ride rather than sleigh. Therefore, with the partial success against his old antagonist behind him and the prospect of an afternoon out in the elements before, Darcy strolled across the castle's courtyard with a lighter heart than he had experienced in some time. His crop tucked under one arm and his beaver at a jaunty angle, he was pulling on his riding gloves when he joined those already gathered for the outing and arrived just in time to catch an exclamation by Miss Farnsworth's on the perfection of the weather.

"You think it 'fine,' Judith?" Lady Chelmsford addressed her niece in disbelief. "Fine for what, pray, besides freezing one to the bone?"

"It is not so very cold, Aunt," Miss Farnsworth answered in an amused voice, "and you are to ride in a sleigh with hot bricks, after all. I do not think Lord Sayre would allow that you freeze, ma'am."

Darcy raised a hand to his eyes as he looked up into a bright, crystal blue sky. He had to agree with Miss Farnesworth; it was a beautiful day. The air was chill, but the sun's rays were warm on his upturned face. Although, truth be told, the sleigh was not inviting. He would much rather ride than…

"I, for one, would rather ride on such a day." Miss Farnsworth echoed Darcy's thoughts. "And am grateful to Lord Sayre for the opportunity to do so." She turned from her aunt to smile at the gentlemen in the group and must have detected some sign of approval on his face for she paused. "I see you agree with me, Mr. Darcy. You must lend me support, sir."

"But you are such an Amazon, my dear," Lady Felicia interposed with a smile of condescension at her cousin. "Always chasing about the countryside. You must make allowances for the less *hardy* of our sex who have no wish to compete with the gentlemen in what is their natural sphere." She turned to Darcy. "Mr. Darcy was merely amused." A look of surprise and pain passed fleetingly across Miss Farnsworth's face, but not before it had summoned up a wave of indignation in Darcy's breast. So this was how it was to be! With a precise coldness he stepped 'round Lady Felicia and offered his hand to her cousin.

"May I assist you to horse, Miss Farnsworth?" he inquired.

"You are very kind, Mr. Darcy." Miss Farnsworth accepted and, with his assistance, sprang lightly into the sidesaddle, expertly gathering up the reins.

"My pleasure, ma'am." He allowed himself a slight smile. Miss Farnsworth was a pleasing picture in her smart riding habit, and her confident, easy air upon a strange horse could not but elicit admiration. "I second your sentiments and chuse to ride as well. Gentleman or lady, one can enjoy the prospects of the country far better from the back of a horse."

"I have always thought it so." She smiled back at him, inclining her head in thanks.

Darcy returned her courtesy and turned back to the other gentlemen. Monmouth and Trenholme had also elected to ride and, as their mounts were being led into the courtyard for them, Darcy swung up upon the rangy bay that was handed to him. The animal seemed biddable enough, but he as he settled into the saddle and checked the stirrups, he could not help but wish for Nelson underneath him. Satisfied that all was in order, he looked on as the other guests arranged themselves in two sleighs and noticed the absence of one of their number. Nudging the bay forward, he inquired, "Is Lady Sylvanie not joining us, Trenholme?"

"Oh, no," he replied, his voice heavy with sarcasm, "her ladyship does not deign to accompany us 'to gawk at stones.' Didn't favour the idea from the start, from what Letty—Lady Sayre—says. So, since she could not carry her point, she does not come. Insufferable little…"

"Bev!" Lord Sayre's voice snapped through the crisp air as he approached them. "Please excuse the interruption, Darcy," he said, smiling deprecatingly, "but my brother is misinformed, as is often the case with siblings." He reached up and laid a hand on Trenholme's wrist, gripping it tightly before turning back again to look up at Darcy. "Lady Sylvanie is indisposed. Just moments ago her maid informed me that she is suffering from a sick headache brought on, most likely, by the spiced apple torte at supper. It is always so when she eats anything containing cinnamon, but she was so far tempted last night that she partook of a bite. Alas," he sighed sympathetically, "that was all that was needed to bring it on." Sayre released his hold upon his brother. "But do not fear, Darcy, she will be recovered by the time we return, I am certain."

Darcy nodded and signalled his mount to back up and then turned him to join Monmouth and Miss Farnsworth in awaiting the beginning of the expedition. Finally, the occupants of the sleighs were ready and the drivers set their pairs in motion. As the horses put shoulders to harness, the jerk of the sleighs caused squeals of laughter to arise from the ladies. Exclaiming prettily, Lady Felicia fell against Manning as the sleigh jerked again, freeing the runners from ice that had already formed under them. Darcy could not, for his cousin's sake, like the knowing expression on Manning's face as he helped her to rights. But the lady had initiated the exchange, and he reminded himself that he did not stand in the place of her father or fiancée. If Chelmsford would not reign in his daughter…

The sleighs lumbered slowly out of the courtyard, but after scraping and rumbling over the drawbridge, their speed and grace were revealed the moment they met their element. The sleigh runners sighed as the teams drew them, scissoring through the glistening snow beside the packed track on which the riders now urged their mounts. It was, truly, a glorious winter day! The surge of pleasure, almost joy, which Darcy felt in it surprised him. As if reading his mind, his horse shook its head vigorously and snorted its approval of the path stretching before them, seeming to beg his indulgence in a proper gallop. Laughing at its honest enthusiasm, he allowed the horse to break into a faster gait, but it was not long before Monmouth and Miss Farnsworth were beside him.

"Ho there, Darcy!" Monmouth hailed him. "Your beast has got the rest all clamouring for a run." He flicked his glance meaningfully toward Miss Farnesworth.

"Do not hold back for my sake, gentlemen," Miss Farnsworth answered his implication a bit stiffly. "I daresay I could keep up with you."

"Miss Farnsworth!" Monmouth protested, "I have no doubt of your horsemanship with your own cattle and in good weather, but under the conditions, ma'am…"

"A trifle, I assure you, my lord." Miss Farnsworth laughed and urged her horse past them, but it was evident that she was somewhat piqued at his concern. Monmouth shrugged his shoulders at Darcy and Trenholme and then laid crop to flank. His action startled his mount, which responded with a sideways jump. Man and horse recovered, but the rider's action had not pleased his beast. In a moment, Monmouth's horse had worked the bit between his teeth and was off.

"Tris!" Darcy bellowed as Monmouth's horse made a dash for the lead. Miss Farnsworth's mount, disliking the commotion of voices and hoof beats approaching from behind, laid back its ears and swung its hindquarters out into the middle of the path, contesting the way. Foreseeing serious consequences if left to her own devices, Darcy set his heels into his own animal, hoping he could reach Miss Farnsworth before the inevitable.

"Watch out! Out of the way!" yelled Monmouth, as he sawed at the reins to no avail. Miss Farnsworth looked over her stylishly clad shoulder to see Lord Monmouth bearing down upon her at a reckless speed. Her face turned white, and she immediately began pulling on her reins, urging her mount over with a generous application of her crop. This did not sit well with the animal, who not only ignored all her commands but began to engage in a series of tight hops that positioned its hindquarters for a concerted defence of its lead position.

Monmouth's horse swung to the right, determined to pass the other, who was equally determined it should not. As he drew near, Miss Farnsworth's horse neighed out a warning and bunched its muscles. In a flash, the animal flung a well-aimed kick, causing Monmouth's beast to stumble and scream out in anger.

Darcy reached Miss Farnsworth just as her mount was preparing to answer the challenge. He made a dive for her reins, but to his chagrin, Miss Farnsworth jerked its head away, her face red with anger. “Stay away!” she commanded him as she worked furiously at the reins. “Do you think I am such a ninny! Stand back, I say!”

Astounded, Darcy paused but then made another attempt at the reins. If he could draw the animal into a tight circle… His fingers grasped only air, and then with a great leap, Miss Farnsworth’s horse was off after the other. Darcy wheeled his mount around and followed after, praying that with or without Miss Farnsworth’s help he could stop the runaway before a very nasty accident occurred.

The uproar had not been lost on those in the sleighs, but as they had not seen all, it was mistaken for a race. The passengers called out encouragement to the various riders and to their own drivers to keep up with them. Looking ahead to Monmouth, Darcy could see that he had finally succeeded in forcing his horse off the track and into the snow. Greatly impeded by the drifts, it was slowing, and he had no doubt that Monmouth would soon be back in control. He turned his attention back to Miss Farnsworth, who was still careening along the track. Confound the woman! Why had she not done the same?

Although she may not have appreciated it had she known, Miss Farnsworth had not been given the fastest horse in Lord Sayre’s stable, and for this, Darcy was soon thankful. Although the slickness of the track caused his bay occasionally to lose its footing, it recovered quickly each time, its long legs eating up the distance between them and the runaway. Cautious this time of the temper of both the horse and its rider, he eased up alongside them.

“What are you doing!” Miss Farnsworth glared at him but received no answer as Darcy edged closer and closer, forcing the other horse from the track and into the snow covered field. “I do not need your help,” she shrieked. “You’ll cause it to break its legs!” Darcy leaned over, grabbed a rein, and immediately turned his mount away, forcing the other to turn. After twenty yards thus, he was able to bring them both to a halt.

“Your pardon, Miss Farnsworth.” He restrained a desire match her glare for glare. “But I beg to disagree. It was too dangerous to allow the animal its head. Better a lamed horse than a broken neck, ma’am!” Before she could issue him the heated reply that was forming on her lips, Trenholme and Monmouth brought their mounts up on either side of them.

“Miss Farnsworth,” Monmouth began immediately, “I am aghast at the danger in which I placed you! Please, allow me to beg your forgiveness and assure you that it was not my intention to test your horsemanship for which, Miss, I must say, I salute you." The steel in Miss Farnsworth's countenance softened quickly under Monmouth's soothing speech, and by its end, she was once more the agreeable young woman who had charmed them in the courtyard.

"My lord, you are quickly forgiven, for I was in little real danger." Miss Farnsworth studiously avoided Darcy's face, chusing rather to exert her charm upon Monmouth.

"You are too modest in your praise, Monmouth," Trenholme interrupted. "Miss Farnsworth, you were magnificent!" Darcy looked between the two men in disbelief. Both incidents had betrayed an abysmal lack of caution or understanding of horseflesh on the part of both his old roommate and the lady. Trenholme's part had been wholly that of a coward, offering no help during the danger at all! Without a word, Darcy urged his mount back onto the track with the conviction that, with such encouragement as the two were giving Miss Farnsworth, the accident that had been avoided would merely be postponed.

The sleighs caught up to them in a matter of minutes, and the situation was explained and exclaimed upon for a full quarter of an hour before they re-commenced the outing to the stones. The riders took up places beside the sleighs so that conversations begun could continue. It was a question from Miss Avery that drew Darcy beside the sleigh conveying her, her brother, Lord Sayre and Lady Felicia.

"I don't know, Bella. Ask Sayre," Manning grumbled at his sister. "And mind you speak up, girl."

Miss Avery swallowed nervously as she turned her eyes upon Sayre, causing Darcy to feel a new burst of pity for her, but her curiosity must have outweighed her fear in this instance; for she blurted out her question. "My l-l-lord," she began, her voice quavering, "Lady Sylvanie s-s-said that t-the stones have a n-n-name and that w-when stones have n-names, they have a story. Is that t-t-true?"

Sayre smiled at his sister-in-law. "Miss Avery, there are always tales, nonsense really, about old things: old castles, old tombs, old trees, old stones. The King's Men are no exception. I am sure there are any number of stories about them."

"King's Men?" Miss Avery's brow creased in confusion. "Lady Sylvanie did not c-call them th-that!"

"Ah...well," Sayre responded, but then lapsed into silence.

"Miss Avery is correct, my lord," Lady Felicia said. "Lady Sylvanie called them the Knights, I believe."

"The *Whispering* Kn-knights!" Miss Avery declared triumphantly. "Yes, th-that was it! C-can you tell us the s-story, my lord?" Darcy was not the only listener to be taken by surprise with the vehemence of Sayre's answer.

"It is all rot, I tell you! Nothing to it!" His lordship's eyes stormed black in his pale face. Miss Avery cringed visibly.

"What is 'rot,' my dear brother?" Trenholme advanced his mount to take up the place on the side opposite Darcy's.

"The Knights!" Sayre huffed. "Rubbish, all rubbish!"

"I would like to hear the tale," Lady Felicia said, smiling up at Trenholme, "rubbish or no." Trenholme cocked a brow at his brother, but Sayre only snorted and looked away.

"It is a dark tale, my lady, and perhaps not fit for delicate ears," Trenholme began solemnly. Darcy rolled his eyes as the man baited his audience. As Darcy expected, Trenholme's listeners demanded he begin immediately. "The stones have been called the King's Men for only the last hundred years. From time in memoriam, they were known as the Whispering Knights."

"Why was the name changed?" asked Manning. "King's Men…Whispering Knights! What nonsense!"

"As I told you," interrupted Sayre.

"It is said," Trenholme continued, re-gathering his audience, "that our great-great-great grandfather took the opportunity to change its name when some writer fellow came through Oxfordshire gathering local tales. Our grandsire told him they were called the King's Men, made up some Banbury tale about them, and sent the fellow on his way. So, to the world outside Chipping Norton, they are the King's Men, but those who have lived here all their lives know better."

"Why d-did he d-do that?" Miss Avery's fascination was complete.

"Because of the legend, Miss Avery, the legend of the Whispering Knights. He wanted to put a stop to it, but I ask you, can a mere change of name confound a legend?" Trenholme looked to his rapt audience for an answer, but no one ventured to gainsay him except Sayre, who snorted again and shifted his bulk in his seat. Darcy bit his lip to prevent himself from laughing at the easy success of Trenholme's strategy. He was quite good, really.

"The legend, Mr. Trenholme, tell us the legend." Lady Felicia reached across and took Miss Avery's hand.

"Yes, the legend…a thousand years ago the land here was the domain of a powerful lord. Norwycke Castle faces toward his fortified hill, actually." Trenholme's voice dropped. "As with many such men at that time, he had enemies both from without and within, and one of them was one of his own sons. This unfaithful son was assisted in his disloyalty by six of his father's knights, to whom he had promised wealth from his father's strongbox or deeds of land if they would support him. The night came when they were to strike, but within moments of their appearance, the cry of 'Treason, treason!' rang through the keep." Miss Avery clutched Lady Felicia's hand at Trenholme's cry and gasped aloud. Manning and Lady Felicia were hardly less caught in the tale, their eyes trained upon Trenholme.

"Yes, and then?" demanded Manning.

"The conspirators knew they had been betrayed, but which one was the betrayer? They had no time to determine which among them it was, for flight was their only chance to survive. They fought their way out of the keep and past the gates, never thinking to ask themselves how they succeeded in winning their way past all their lord's mighty men. All they knew was that life lay across these fields and on to the sea and Ireland."

"Rather careless of this lord to let them slip through his fingers when he had been warned," Manning observed, his air of disinterest now flown.

"Careless? Or part of the plan?" Trenholme countered. "The traitorous son and his men fled for their lives over these very fields only to be met by his lord father and his personal guard. The lord cried out to his son to lay down his arms, but he answered his father with great curses and called his men to resist. They formed a circle, the better to protect each other's backs and railed against the lord and his guard, challenging them to 'come to' and fight. All, that is, except one. The betrayer, or rather the knight loyal to his lord, stepped from the circle and stood with his lord. Enraged with the man at whose hands his dreams had been slain, the son drew a knife from his boot and threw. It flew true, and the faithful knight fell dead at the feet of his lord."

"Oh!" exclaimed Lady Felicia and Miss Avery, their eyes as wide as the buttons on Manning's greatcoat. Darcy smiled. Yes, Trenholme was very good, indeed. It lacked now only the curse. There was always a curse. He looked away to Sayre and discovered a man who was no longer derisive of the tale being told. The hand grasping his walking stick was actually trembling! The other was occupied in loosening the knot at his throat while he attempted to take in gulps of air without attracting the notice of his companions. Good heavens, the man was clearly rattled! Darcy narrowed his gaze upon Trenholme.

"'Oh' indeed!" repeated the storyteller. "The lord knelt at the side of his fallen knight and pulled the knife from his body. Then he rose and faced his son. In the hearing of all he disowned him, called him traitor and worse. The rebels jeered and rattled their swords against their shields. 'These are the dogs that have sworn you fealty, bought-men you bribed with your own birth-right?' the lord asked. His son said nothing, but his eyes spoke everything that was in his black heart.

"Tonight, I curse you," declared the lord, "'and all who would sell their patrimony. To you it is given to hunt down such curs to join you here in this field forever.' With those words, he threw the bloody knife into the ground at the son's feet, and in an instant, they all were turned to stone."

Miss Avery cried out at Trenholme's end and moved to sit between her brother and Lady Felicia. Manning swallowed several times before he was able to summon up a laugh. "Sayre was right, Bev, a great deal of rubbish fit only for frightening children." The stones could now be seen across a small dale. The drivers turned the teams away from the main track into a smaller one prepared for the passage of Sayre's guests.

"A dreadful tale, Mr. Trenholme." Lady Felicia brushed at her coat. "It is no wonder that your grandsire desired to change it." She paused and then queried, "But why 'whispering'? Is there something you have not related, sir?"

"Why yes there is, my lady," Trenholme replied as if she'd reminded him of something he'd forgotten. "It is said that the rebel knights watch over the lands that make up the old lord's estate for any who would break up the holding or sell it off piecemeal. And, if they find such a one, he is given warning so he may mend his ways before they come for him."

"A warning?" Darcy asked, an appalling suspicion forming in his mind.

"Yes, Darcy, they whisper his name."

~~~~~~~&~~~~~~~
~~~~~~~

As the drivers pulled the teams to a halt at the base of the hill from which the Knights maintained their reputed vigil over the countryside, Darcy dismounted and handed the bay to a stable boy who had appeared rather suddenly from behind a less sinister outcropping. Evidently, the party had been preceded to the site by a number of Sayre's servants, for a sledge was now able to be seen to one side from which refreshments for the guests had been unloaded and a cheery fire prepared against their arrival. As he watched the occupants of the sleigh disembark, Darcy could not determine whether Miss Avery or Sayre was the most affected by Trenholme's recital. Once coaxed out of the conveyance, Miss Avery made obvious her wish to stay close to her brother by clinging to his arm. Manning, just as clearly, desired her elsewhere and finally sent her over to the fire with an order to "…drink something hot and try to stop behaving like a little fool." Sayre made straight for the fire as soon as he descended, demanding a flask of whiskey be produced immediately. No sooner was the flask in his hand then he availed himself of a prodigious gulp, all the while regarding the stones with a baleful eye.

Those who had not been privy to Trenholme's story strolled toward the path that lead up to the circle of weathered, lichen-covered stones on ground swept almost clean of snow by the wind. "Come, Sayre, are you not joining us?" Trenholme called out from among the other guests, displaying a glee in his brother's fearful loss of composure that Darcy found, under the circumstances, not only distasteful but disturbing. "P'rhaps we shall catch a whisper or two!"

"Go to the Devil," Sayre shouted back and turned away from the stones and his brother's laughing countenance.

As troubling as his hosts' behaviour appeared, Darcy was disinclined to indulge in further speculation upon it. The suspicion that had arisen in his mind concerning Trenholme's purpose during his tale was dismissed as unworthy and evidence of his own disordered thoughts rather than nefarious intent on the part of Trenholme. Sayre and his brother had always engaged in a certain rivalry as far back as Eton, he reasoned, and it most likely extended back to the cradle. That in the intervening years its animosity had increased was not to be marvelled at, although the turn it appeared to have taken was a curious one. He would not have credited it that either brother was of a superstitious nature beyond that of any man who was addicted to the gaming table. At least, when it came to stories of ghosts and their curses, he would have derided the notion, save that it was undeniable that Sayre had been profoundly affected. Even as Darcy looked on, his lordship downed another gulp from the flask, his nose turning a distinctive pink against an unnaturally pale visage.

Turning away to join those on the stroll, Darcy began up the short, steep incline to the top of the hill. At the head of the party, Trenholme acted as guide. Poole and Monmouth followed closely, as did Miss Farnsworth, who had tossed the train of her habit over one arm, thus exposing a shapely pair of ankles as she strode upward with the gentlemen. Behind them, Lady Sayre leant upon Lord Chelmsford's arm, Lady Chelmsford having decided to remain with the warmth offered by the fire, and the two appeared engaged in close, private conversation as they slowly made their way after the others. Having divested himself of his sister, Manning squired Lady Felicia toward the stones, taking every opportunity the terrain offered to put a hand to her waist in assistance. There was but one of the party unaccompanied in the climb to the Whispering Knights, Darcy noted, and she appeared to be waiting for him.

"You see, I am quite left behind, Mr. Darcy." Lady Beatrice smiled helplessly at him as he drew near her. She rose from her perch upon a fallen companion of the stone guards above them. "I fear the way is rather steep."

"Please, permit me to offer you my arm, my lady." Darcy extended his arm, suspect of what her true purpose in waylaying him might be. He invited her to continue up the path, in no doubt that she would enlighten him soon enough.

"Thank you, sir. I see your manners are those of a more polite century rather than the less formal ones of this." Lady Beatrice's lips pursed for a moment as she looked up to those who had so unceremoniously left her to fend for herself before turning a handsome smile upon him.

"You are very kind, ma'am," he replied smoothly. Lady Beatrice was not exactly a young widow, being perhaps just forty years old, but she could not be accused of looking her age. Rather, with her fine figure, delicate porcelain complexion, and gracious manner, she was the fulfilment of what was as yet only a promise in her daughter. Regardless, he was fairly confident it was of her daughter that she wished to speak. But whatever were her designs, Darcy was not to discover them as yet, for a call from behind them stopped their progress.

"M-my lady, Mr. D-darcy," gasped Miss Avery as she hurried toward them. "Your p-pardon, ma'am, but may I accompany you? I do not w-wish to stay with Lord…" she stopped and bit her lip. "That is, L-lord Sayre is not…oh, dear! I m-must see my b-brother!"

"Of course, my dear." Lady Beatrice withdrew her hand from his arm and laid it on the young woman's, drawing it through her own. "You may certainly accompany Mr. Darcy and myself; is that not so, sir?" Darcy nodded a curt assent as he looked back to the fire and Lord Sayre, who was still nursing his flask. Blast the man! Had he no better sense than to disgrace himself and then frighten his young kinswoman with his intemperate behaviour…all because of a legend? And Manning! He looked back up the hill to the baron, silently excoriating the fitness for society of one who showed more interest in another man's betrothed than in the safety and comfort of his own sister.

"Th-thank you, my lady," breathed Miss Avery in great relief. She disengaged her arm from Lady Beatrice and stepped lightly before them, whereupon her ladyship possessed herself once more of Darcy's arm.

"Poor child," Lady Beatrice commented, shaking her head. "Do you not have a sister near to Miss Avery's age, sir?"

"Yes, ma'am. Miss Darcy is a year or so the junior of Miss Avery." The thought struck him then how different Georgiana was from Miss Avery! Yes, his sister had been demur and still was somewhat shy, but never could he recall seeing the self-conscious timidity in her eyes that seemed Miss Avery's daily companion. On the contrary, her demeanour had ever been one that trusted in the goodness of the world that had been created around her…until Wickham had shattered it. Lately though, since her new-found contemplation of religious themes and the solace it seemed to have afforded her, Georgiana had exhibited a remarkable maturity in both mind and manner that far outmatched Miss Avery's thin veneer of social sophistication. He doubted they would ever be within Miss Avery's scope.

"She is not yet out then," Lady Beatrice asserted, continuing the conversation.

"No, my lady. Perhaps next year she will be introduced at court," he replied carefully.

"It was not so long ago that my daughter made her curtsy, Mr. Darcy. Such a trial, sir! When she was a child, Mr. Farnsworth *would* have Judith always with him, for he had—alas—no sons, and that meant in the stables and out in the fields, you may believe, not the drawing room." Her ladyship sighed. "That all ended, of course, with his accident. The poor man finally met a fence that he could not master and left me a widow." She glanced quickly at Darcy as he murmured the appropriate condolences. She then continued, "Judith did not immediately take to the circumscription of her former activities with her papa, but I am glad to say, by the time she made her curtsy she had been brought to recognize where her happiness lay."

Lady Beatrice slowed her pace, and with a sinking feeling in the pit of his stomach, Darcy did likewise. "I cannot deny that Judith is of a strong-minded temperament, Mr. Darcy. She is a little like her father in that regard, but she is yet young. She will, I am certain, respond to a firm hand and quickly settle down to the enjoyment of all those domestic accomplishments required by a gentleman of the highest position and influence."

Darcy's jaw tightened, as had his resolve during Lady Beatrice's excuse of her daughter's exhibition of a shockingly headstrong temper. So, she needed a firm hand, did she? And was it hoped that *he* would chuse to be responsible for the schooling of her? Evidently, it was what her mother wished. He could well imagine the scenes enacted within the Farnsworth household when Miss Farnworth's will was crossed. There might be some men who enjoyed bringing such a woman to heel, but he was certainly not of their company. Good Lord! He shuddered inwardly at the thought of a life spent battling Miss Farnsworth's temper. Any hopes the lady entertained in his direction were to be dampened at all costs!

"Undoubtedly, that will be the case, my lady, when the appropriate gentleman appears," he returned in as disinterested a fashion as he could summon.

"But you, Mr. Darcy, have had the raising of your sister and know your way in this regard, do you not?" her ladyship persisted. "I have heard wonderful things concerning Miss Darcy…"

"I thank you, ma'am," Darcy intervened in the midst of her praise, determined to put an end to any more notions of his ability or willingness to take on Miss Farnsworth. "But I believe that the rearing of a sister cannot at all be compared to that of such instruction as you say Miss Farnsworth should require at the hands of her husband. In that task, I believe, my experience would serve me but little."

"Well!" responded Lady Beatrice, withdrawing her hand from Darcy's arm. "Upon my word, sir, you are forthright!"

"Your pardon, ma'am, but you would not wish anything less than the truth in a matter regarding the happiness of your only child, I am sure," he returned coolly.

Her ladyship's eyebrows twitched upward in response to his statement before settling into a countenance graced with a speculative smile. "I see you have encountered your due share of matchmaking mamas, Mr. Darcy," she laughed throatily. "You handled me quite well, sir. Quite well, indeed."

As there was naught he could decently reply to such an observation, Darcy held his silence but with increasing unease at each step up the hill. Several times he detected measuring glances from the lady as they progressed, and when she stumbled over a rock upon the path and into his arms, he began to be alarmed at the possible meaning of her regard. When they reached the top, he quickly excused himself and strode toward the rest of the party.

Miss Avery had gained the crest before them and all but run to her brother, who listened to her briefly and with displeasure. "Bella, stop your damned stammering, girl, or I shan't listen to you. What about Sayre?" Miss Avery assayed to meet his demand, but he soon turned and called to his other sister, "Letty! Bella is in a state…something about Sayre. P'rhaps *you* can make it out, for I cannot abide her babble a moment longer!"

At his very public complaint of her, Miss Avery's face turned a pink that did not recommend itself to her other features and in haste left Manning's side. Striking out in the opposite way, she avoided the rest of the party and went off alone in the direction of a large, singular stone that brooded over the landscape some yards away.

Darcy watched her progress for a few moments before turning away to the rest of the party, his jaw clamped down in anger at Manning's callous display of contempt for his own flesh and blood. He really could stomach it no further.

"Shall we hear them whisper, Mr. Trenholme?" asked Lady Felicia, cautiously brushing the tips of her glove-clad fingers along the side of the largest stone.

"I cannot say that I have ever heard them," Trenholme confessed, "but I would hazard that we will not hear anything in broad daylight. Such things," he dropped his voice into a menacing register, "belong to the dead of n—"

An horrific scream of abject terror cut off Trenholme's words and froze the smiles on his listeners' faces as they seemed rooted to the ground by the awful sound. "Bella!" shouted Manning. Again, the scream was heard, jolting them out of their icy trance. Finding the use of their limbs returned to them, Darcy and Manning broke into a run across the ground that separated the stones. Heedless of Manning's claims, Darcy quickly outstripped him and, reaching the great monolith, rounded it to behold Miss Avery. She stood as one bewitched, her hands clasping and unclasping, her face drained of colour. If she recognized him, she did not show it, but continued her terrible screaming until Darcy was nearly upon her.

"Miss Avery!" Darcy stood between her and the stone, taking up the entire window of her vision. "Miss Avery!" he repeated and grasped her arms. Finally, she looked at him, her eyes wide with terror; and with a pitiful wail, she cast herself against his chest, burying her face in his coat and clutching at the lapels. Without a thought, he brought his arms around her just as he had done countless times to comfort Georgiana. "What is it?" he probed gently. She only shook her head and clung to him more tightly.

The others must be almost upon them, Darcy reasoned, as he looked back over his shoulder. What in the name of heaven had frightened this girl who trembled so in his arms? The King's Stone loomed behind him. Its ancient, weathered solidity challenged his sweeping gaze and silently compelled his attention, drawing it down…down to its piercing claim upon the earth. The blood in Darcy's veins turned to ice.

"Good God!" Manning's voice trembled with horror as he swayed back away from the base of the stone and looked up into Darcy's eyes.

"Yes," Darcy agreed tersely. Miss Avery still trembled and sobbed so into his coat that he doubted she could stand on her own strength. "Manning!" he called sharply to the baron, whose attention was once more transfixed by the grisly bundle at his feet. "Manning!" He had to shout again before the man's head came up, his visage almost as pale as his sister's. "Miss Avery is in need of you," he continued in a firm but subdued tone. "She must be taken from here immediately and the others warned away."

"Yes…of course," Manning agreed hoarsely, shaking himself as if to awaken from a nightmare before stepping toward Darcy and his sister. With more gentleness than Darcy had ever before seen him employ, Manning eased her grasp on Darcy and transferred her weight to himself. He held her tightly for a brief moment, whispering something in her ear and then bent down and took her up in his arms, pressing her face into his shoulder. With a nod to Darcy, he began to make his way down the hill to the fire below. As soon as Manning and his sister were seen, the rest of the party surrounded them. From his vantage point, Darcy observed Manning's vigorous refusal of any assistance. Sheltering her closely, he bore his sister free of their clinging curiosity and continued to the fire, the others trailing after him in agitated confusion.

Satisfied that they were well occupied, Darcy turned back to the monstrosity lying at the base of the stone. His stomach revolted at the sight, but he resolved to ignore it as well as the icy prickings down his spine that urged him to flee the task before him. What confronted him could only be called what it was: Evil, monstrous Evil. The bundle of blankets swaddling the tiny figure was stained with blood. Despite the cold, perspiration stood out on his forehead as he carefully drew off the first layer of swaddling, revealing the infant face turned away toward the stone. His gorge rising in his throat, Darcy gently tipped its head back then sucked in his breath, his eyes narrowing in surprise and thought. What was before him was certainly a mask. Made of a flesh coloured fabric and cunningly stitched, it was fashioned to imitate the face of a child. Its delicate, cherubic features stuffed with cotton wadding enhanced the illusion and completely covered whatever was beneath it.

"Darcy!" Trenholme's shout caused Darcy to look up just as its owner rounded the stone. "Darcy," he repeated when he saw him, "I say, what—Good God!" Trenholme's hand went to his mouth as he unwittingly repeated Manning's horrified exclamation, his shoulders jerking so convulsively that Darcy fully expected he would hurl his breakfast. To his credit, Trenholme regained control of himself and dropped down on his haunches beside him. "Is it…a child?" he asked in a halting whisper.

"I am not yet certain," Darcy answered, his voice constricted with the effort to contain his own trepidation. "Look here, Trenholme." Darcy pointed at the head. "It is wearing some sort of mask." Trenholme looked at him in stupefaction. "I was about to remove it when you arrived." At Trenholme's glazed nod, he took a deep breath and, reaching over, grasped the top and pulled it away. For a moment the two men could only stare in perplexity at the sight before them.

"Thank God!" Darcy closed his eyes and leaned back, embracing the flow of relief that was easing the tight hold he had maintained upon his nerve.

"It's a pig!" Trenholme croaked. Then, louder, his voice rising in anger, "It's a damn, bloody, baby pig! Oh, this is beyond everything! I'll not have it! Where is my horse?" He scrambled to his feet and would have run for his horse had Darcy not risen swiftly and caught his arm.

"Do you know who did this?" Darcy's piercing examination bore down upon the man. "Trenholme! Do you know?" Trenholme looked back at him in outraged anger, but he could not conceal from Darcy the shadow of fear in his eyes.

"What do you mean, sir? No! No, I certainly do not know who did this…this filthy…gaaugh!" He wrenched his arm from Darcy's grasp and fell back a few steps from him. "The Stones have always drawn those who hold with the old ways…as well as lunatics who dance around them in the middle of the night. Love potions, cures, curses—the whole lot—but not this!" He shook his head as he gestured toward the stone. "Never this!" Under Darcy's narrowed gaze, Trenholme turned away and stumbled down the hill to the others, leaving him to the solitary contemplation of their awful discovery.

He turned and cast one more look over the scene before the great stone. Although its horrors were materially lessened by the knowledge that an animal lay beneath the bloody wrappings, he could not suppress the shudder that passed through both his body and mind. *It had been meant to pass for a child!* Someone had prepared for and committed this hideous, unholy sacrifice pretending it was a child. The enormity of the evil of it was staggering in its implications, and they granted him no quarter in their assault on his own careful view of the world. It simply did not fit! Such execrable practices belonged to another age, millennia past, when men were slaves to superstition and cringed in fear before a capricious universe. This was the 19th century, for heaven's sake! Men have long been accustomed to rule by the dictates of logic, not some bloodthirsty deity lurking about ancient stones on an Oxfordshire hillside! The idea was totally irrational, absurd even, save for the terrible fact that stained the hillside at his feet.

Darcy looked away, down the hill, to the confused gathering at its foot. A roar from Sayre reached his ears. Although he could not understand his words, Sayre's meaning was obvious as all the servants scurried to pack the food and other amenities that had been provided for their master's guests. The outing, evidently, was over;

and it was expedient that he rejoin the others. There was nothing more he could do here.

Except for Trenholme, who brooded over a mug of hot cider at the fire, the rest of the party was divided into two groups near the sleighs. Manning had retired to one group, his sister still within his embrace. Around them, the ladies clucked or cooed over Miss Avery, trying to entice her face from the folds of her brother's greatcoat. The remaining gentlemen formed another group, but Monmouth and Poole, seeing his approach, broke from them and hurriedly strode over to meet him.

"Darcy, what happened?" Poole gasped out as he came to a halt. "Manning will only say it is something horrid, and Trenholme will speak to no one!"

"We apply to you, old man." Monmouth nodded his agreement with Poole's words. "The ladies are imagining all sorts of lurid scenes *a la* Mrs. Radcliffe. 'No such thing' I told them. 'This is England, not Italy or the deep reaches of Carpathia. Probably tripped over a dead rabbit or bird,' I said. But truly, Darcy, what happened?"

Darcy hesitated. *This is England.* He knew exactly what Monmouth meant by the phrase. Had not every man in the country used it at one time or another, or heard his father declare it? The French may brutally lop off the heads of their aristocrats and later follow a madman across Europe, but *This is England.* The Italians might form secret, murderous societies and regard poison as merely one more political tool, but *This is England.* Yet, above them on an *English* hillside lay a reality more maleficent in its authorship than any novel Mrs. Radcliffe had ever written.

Darcy looked into the faces of his old hallmates. A wave of disgust washed over him, as he detected neither concern nor compassion for Miss Avery in their importuning of him, but only a rampant desire for the satisfaction of their hungering curiosity. He would not feed it.

"If our hosts decline to discuss the incident," Darcy responded stiffly, "I must naturally respect their wishes and remain silent as well." He interrupted their vociferous protestations, "Excuse me, but the lad has my horse ready. Gentlemen." He bowed quickly and strode around them to his horse. The bay pricked up its ears at his approach and bent its neck to watch him as he gathered the reins and prepared to mount.

"Mr. Darcy." Miss Farnsworth brought her horse alongside him. "I fear, sir, that I must humbly beg your pardon. You were proved quite correct in your concern and, I confess, your advice as well." She smiled contritely. "My horse," she supplied at his vague return of her regard. Darcy inclined his head in weary consent—that she could speak of that now! —and vaulted into the saddle.

The sleigh drivers signalled to the stable lads, who stepped away smartly, and the party departed the cursed scene with a nervous chattering that drove Darcy to the rear of the procession until they should gain the track leading back to Norwycke. In his circle back, he brought his mount abreast of Manning's sleigh to inquire after Miss Avery. She was still pale as she shivered in her brother's arms, but some colour had returned. Her eyes remained tightly shut against the world, and wrenching sobs would overtake her as tears spilled down her cheeks.

She still mourns a child! The realization that Trenholme had not relieved her suffering with the truth of her discovery sent a hot surge of fury through his body. Cursing himself for not immediately seeking assurance that she was in possession of the truth, he leaned down.

"Manning," he ventured. His old antagonist raised eyes still shadowed with incomprehension at what they had beheld.

"Darcy," he sighed in acknowledgment. "How can I thank you? Poor Bella…thank God you kept your head."

Politely dismissing the baron's expression of indebtedness, Darcy continued, "Manning, it is of the gravest importance…you must know and represent the truth of it to Miss Avery—it was *not* what it appeared to be."

His hearer's brow creased in confusion. "But, I saw it…in all that bl—

"Quite." Darcy forestalled him describing the scene in the hearing of the sleigh's other occupants. "It appeared so and a-purpose, but it was not; I assure you. Miss Avery must find a great comfort in that."

Manning shook his head in bewilderment and then looked down into his sister's face. Gently, he caressed her cheek and the curls that had escaped her bonnet. "Why?" he breathed, and looked back up at Darcy.

Darcy drew upright, his jaw clenching as he looked back into the darkening distance behind them. Returning to the baron, he inclined his head. "I regret that I can be of no further use to you in that regard. Please convey my best wishes to Miss Avery." At Manning's nod, Darcy checked his horse, allowing the sleigh to sweep past them and cut through the clean, white snow.

By the time they had clattered across the castle's bridge and into the courtyard, he was stiff with cold and wished for nothing better than the solitude and comfort of a hot bath and, perhaps, a letter from sister or friend to stay his mind from further reflection on the events of the day. It had so preyed upon his mind that he could not have relayed anything about the journey back to Norwycke Castle save that a solemn twilight had crept over them, accompanied by a rise in the force and coldness of the wind.

He dismounted slowly and handed his horse over to a burly fellow already leading two others back to the stable. Although he and the bay had reached a mutual respect, both man and horse parted gladly in weary hope that their respective attendants were well prepared to minister to their needs. Apparently, Sayre and his other guests were of the same mind, for no sooner had bedchamber doors slammed shut than upraised voices and the sound of running feet on backstairs were heard throughout the guest wings.

Darcy laid a hand upon the doorknob of his chambers and turned it with fervent hope that Fletcher had not lost his talent for anticipating his needs. From the sounds echoing through the castle, hot water would be a very precious commodity in short order. His hope was fulfilled to more than his satisfaction.

"Fletcher." He sighed at the sight of his dressing gown laid out, "I believe you are truly priceless." He sniffed the air. "Food as well!"

"Yes, sir." Fletcher bowed. "Your bath lacks but one more bucket of hot water, which is on its way; and the food will keep warm until you desire it. May I help you, sir?" He reached for the edges of Darcy's coat and expertly pulled it over and off his shoulders. Brushing it lightly, he laid it down and turned to proceed to Darcy's waistcoat when he stopped short, his brow crinkled in question. As Darcy unbuttoned his waistcoat, Fletcher returned to the coat, picked up a sleeve, and turned the cuff around several times while examining it closely.

"Mr. Darcy!" he finally said. "There is *blood* on your cuff, sir!"

Darcy looked up from his task, "There was so much of it, I am not unduly surprised. Can it be gotten out?"

"Y-yes, sir," Fletcher sputtered, his agitation increasing, "but are you hurt, Mr. Darcy? Was there an accident? Why was I not informed?" Darcy regarded him with wonder, but it soon gave way to a guilty exultation.

"Can it be you do not *know*, Fletcher?" he demanded gravely, unable to resist the temptation to exploit this singular experience, the novelty of which expiated, to a degree, the grim circumstances upon which it was predicated. Fletcher's struggle to admit his ignorance of so great an event as the cause for blood upon his master's clothing would have been terrible to behold had Darcy not been almost giddy with weariness, hunger, and an unconscionable delight in having, at last, astounded his valet.

"No, sir, I do not, and I am sure it is none of my business if you are not hurt," Fletcher confessed stiffly. He dropped the sleeve and stepped 'round Darcy to remove the waistcoat. "I trust you are *not* hurt, sir?" he added quietly.

That Fletcher's concern was real, Darcy did not doubt; and he felt a twinge of shame for his teasing. "No, I am not hurt," he said over his shoulder. "It is not my blood; it is not human blood at all, but animal."

"Indeed, sir," Fletcher would not be drawn in again. Darcy sat down at the knock on the dressing chamber door. Fletcher answered it and motioned the boot boy to enter and proceed while he supervised the last bucket of water being added to the bath. His tasks complete, Fletcher sent him off, waiting until the ringing of his boots upon the stairs was no more before he closed the door.

"The bath is ready, sir, but have a care. It is quite hot." Fletcher moved to catch the shirt Darcy flung off as he walked toward the dressing room. A few moments more and Darcy was easing himself down into the bath. Steamy vapour rose from the surface and swathed his face as he leaned back and savoured the relief granted his body by the liquid heat. If only there were a similar remedy for the mind, he mused as he closed his eyes, but the scenes of the afternoon played out again beneath his eyelids: Sayre's fear, Miss Avery's hysteria, Trenholme's rage, and, most troubling, the bundle at the foot of the stone. What did it mean? Even Trenholme, who knew the stones as a magnet for the superstitious, was shocked and sickened, claiming that nothing like it had occurred before. If he was being truthful, the sacrifice must signal an attempt to manipulate fate in a vastly more serious way than the cure of warts! The illusion of child-sacrifice created by the mask indicated a grasping after power, a good deal of power. And, if power, would it not likely be directed against a rival "power" in the neighbourhood? Sayre, perhaps, who was already in a quake about the Stones? But why, and to what purpose? A groan of frustration escaped him.

"Mr. Darcy?" Fletcher appeared at the door. "Did you call, sir?"

"No," he sighed, "but you may pour the first bucket." Soon warm water was sluicing down his face and shoulders. He pushed his hair out of his eyes and blinked against the remaining drops.

"Your soap, sir." A bar of fine French-milled soap was thrust before his nose, accompanied by a washing cloth. Darcy fumbled for the soap, which popped from his grasp like a cork from a bottle and plunged, uncork-like, to the bottom of the bath. One of Fletcher's brows arched, but he turned away to the tray of grooming articles without comment. Darcy retrieved the bar and vigorously applied it, the silence between them deepening uncomfortably.

"The second, sir?" Fletcher's disinterested voice arose from close by. With a nod, Darcy steeled himself for the rinsing water. It came down gently, carrying the lather out of his hair in directed streams. When he had cleared all from his eyes, he looked up at Fletcher intently. He had grown rather used to his valet's uncanny prescience and bold repartee, as well as his conscientious service. This falter in an impressive record clearly discommoded the man and his own insensitivity had added the proverbial "insult to injury."

Excellent, Darcy! He silently congratulated himself. Estrange your most trusted ally just when he is most needed! Who else but Fletcher might be relied upon to untangle the webs being spun around them? Images of the villainy at the King's Stone flooded through him again. He needed Fletcher at his best, not sulking over a temporary failure and his own poor attempt at humour.

Darcy rose thoughtfully from the bath as Fletcher held out the dressing gown, guiding the sleeves up Darcy's arms and then left him for the dresser to bring out clean smalls and stockings. Donning the garments quickly, Darcy cast about in his mind how he might restore Fletcher's confidence and direct his talents without prejudicing his perception. Should he lay the whole before him? Doubtless, Fletcher would pry loose the story, or some version of it, from someone's maid or manservant. Would it not be more useful for Fletcher to be in possession of the facts and, therefore, free to observe the inhabitants of the castle unhampered by the shock of revelation?

As Darcy pulled on his black knit breeches and buttoned them over the silk stockings, his social obligations suddenly recalled themselves to his attention. They were to play at Charades tonight, he remembered joylessly, and he was supposed to be looking for a wife. In that, too, Fletcher could be invaluable. Darcy passed over the faces of the eligible young women he had met so far and discarded all save one. Lady Sylvanie. He could not say that she did not intrigue him with her otherworldly beauty and enigmatic eyes, but he also had to acknowledge that there had not yet arisen that irrepressible pull that had o'er taken him every time Eliza....

"Your neckcloth, sir. Are you ready?" Fletcher held out the perfectly starched article. Darcy nodded and sat down. Well, there had hardly been time, had there? The fact that his interest had been caught so quickly in their short acquaintance was certainly in Sylvanie's favour. Perhaps there was hope that his needs and requirements would soon be met acceptably, and he could go home. With that thought, Darcy felt a pang of longing for the comfort of home—of the woman he had imagined there, in every room. He knew his own desire; it was already engaged in the person of one impudent, exciting, lovely little piece of baggage by the name of Elizabeth Bennet, whose unsuitability reached to the stars. He was here at the command of duty. Duty necessitated that he remain at Norwycke with people whom he was fast coming to loathe.

"Your coat, Mr. Darcy." Fletcher's toneless voice broke into Darcy's thoughts once more. He slipped his arms into the frockcoat and shrugged it over his shoulders and then observed his reflection in the mirror as he pulled down his cuffs. It was newly made, and fit like a second skin, but he found no pleasure in it. He was almost ready and soon must depart his chambers for the drawing room battles below. How to span the breach and set Fletcher's nose a-twitching?

"Fletcher," he tossed over his shoulder while the valet applied the lint brush across his back. "You have read or attended a performance of *MacBeth*, have you not, Fletcher?"

"Yes, Mr. Darcy. It is strange that you should mention it, for I was thinking of it myself. Your coat reminded me, sir—'Out, damned spot!'" he laughed ruefully and then stiffened up again as the correct gentleman's gentleman he had been since Darcy's return. "Your pardon, sir."

"Not at all. But that was not the line of which I was thinking." Darcy waited until Fletcher came 'round him to flick the brush over the front of his coat. "Do you remember how the line goes, 'By the pricking of my thumbs…'?"

"'Something wicked this way comes,' sir?" Fletcher asked, more than a flicker of interest sparking his face.

Darcy fixed him with a darkling eye, "Precisely, Fletcher."

~8~

The Woman's Part

He was less than half the hall away from the drawing room when Darcy caught the first notes of music. The sound was unmistakably a harp. But as he drew closer to the doors something about its resonance struck him as unusual. His curiosity roused by the quality of the sound as well as the plaintive melody being performed, he was almost impatient for the ubiquitous satin-clad servants to open the doors. They opened finally upon a small group posed, to Darcy's surprise, not around the grand harp at the end of the room, but in a circle near the hearth. Most of the listeners were gentlemen; the ladies having not yet descended save for Lady Chelmsford and her sister, Lady Beatrice, who sat together on a settee whispering companionably. In contrast, Monmouth lounged against the mantle, while Chelmsford's chair was drawn in among the shadows at the other side and Poole sat on the edge of a divan drawn up nearer to the hearth, the attention of all of them fixed upon the harpist at their centre.

Lady Sylvanie acknowledged his approach with a cool, fleeting glance, but her fingers did not hesitate as she continued playing the music that had captured Darcy's attention. The small harp cradled against her shoulder gleamed in the firelight. The light reflected along its sweeping curves seemed to quiver in response to the graceful pluck of each chord. Darcy's gaze was drawn first to those shapely fingers as they called forth such sorrowing sweetness from the strings, but his attention was soon enticed along the performer's lithe arms to the curve of her pale shoulders and on then to her face. The lady's eyes were lightly closed, but not, he guessed, in concentration upon her performance. Rather, he had the sense that while they were closed to her surroundings, they opened instead to some secret place the music created. From the lift of one raven brow and the slight smile that graced her face, he suspected that she was barely aware of her audience. Her smile deepened as she played, and Darcy, conscious of the sensation of having once again caught a glimpse of a fierce faerie princess, caught his breath at the picture she presented.

He watched, fascinated, as her smile faded and her brow creased as if in pain. Her lips parted and there poured forth from them a song whose words he could not understand, but which he knew intuitively was a hymn of longing. The beauty of it swept over him before he'd time to prepare against it and forced him into a chair. *Gaelic.* His brain informed him of the language, but it enlightened him no further as to the song's meaning. Instead, the lilting words and haunting tune worked on him, recalling to his mind images and emotions of times long past: the exhilaration of galloping the fields of Pemberley atop his first pony, the wonder of boyhood rambles in the wood beyond the park, the companionable feeling of the fishing expedition to Scotland with his father the summer before his first term away at school.

Then the music changed, slowing to an altogether different key, and he was at his mother's bedside, his heart stunned with the aching fear of bidding her his last farewell, and, deeper still, the feeling of utter loss at his father's passing. Struggling to break from this turn in the tide of his emotion, Darcy closed his eyes in a determined frown against the music. As if in response to his wishes, the lady's voice began to drop, gentling, fading into silence as her fingers passed lightly over the strings. Had she noticed his discomfort? Darcy looked up at her from under hooded lids but saw that her head was bowed over her instrument.

"Breathtaking!" Poole exclaimed, breaking the silence as he applauded Lady Sylvanie's performance. "Absolutely marvellous!" In like opinion, the other gentlemen joined him in vigorous appreciation.

"What is it called, my lady?" Monmouth addressed her still bowed head. "Is it Irish? It sounded Irish." Darcy watched intently as Lady Sylvanie lifted her head, her face composed in soft complexion although her startling grey eyes were still withdrawn.

"Yes, milord," came her reply in quiet clarity, "it is an Irish tune." Her eyelashes swept suddenly up and captured Darcy's stare before he could look away. The smile in them was of such understanding he was tempted to believe that she was, indeed, a faerie, knowing his very thoughts.

"'Deirdre's Lament,'" she continued, her eyes piercing Darcy's, holding his even as he started at the name of the tune.

"I beg your pardon?" Monmouth responded.

Lady Sylvanie lowered her lashes, releasing him, before turning and giving her attention fully to Monmouth. "It is called 'Deirdre's Lament,' an old song, milord." The door to the room opened, and her audience looked with her as others of the castle's guests entered the drawing room. Lady Felicia and Miss Farnsworth entered arm in arm, followed by Sayre, his lady, and, at the last, Manning. With their appearance she made to put the harp from her and rise, but the protests of the three gentlemen near the fire stayed her. With an elegant nod of acquiescence, she brought the instrument to her breast and settled it against her shoulder once more as the newcomers found seats.

Darcy had not joined in their plea, too discomposed with what had passed between them to give order to the variety of sensations flooding him. Neither could he look away as her graceful fingers caressed the strings, nor even when her eyes closed as she gathered herself to begin, chary to guard against the effects of her last song. But the piece she offered them was entirely different from the previous ones. Its sprightly pace and bright notes suggested nothing more unsettling to Darcy than a country reel. The other listeners were impressed with the same notion as several pairs of feet tapped discreetly under gowns, and some of the gentlemen pounded out the lively beat on their knees. By her finish, Darcy could almost dismiss his former impressions as too fantastical, evidence that the events of the day had come near to exhausting his usual store of good sense.

Lady Sylvanie rose with becoming modesty and curtsied her acknowledgment of the enthusiastic applause of the room that, this time, Darcy joined. Beaming with approval, Sayre rose as well, took her hand, and presented her to the room. This second round, Darcy noted, the enthusiasm of the ladies was somewhat restrained, their applause tepid, while they darted looks at the continued show of appreciation by the gentlemen. He grinned to himself and applauded more loudly.

"Delightful, charming, my dear!" Lord Sayre inclined to his half-sister. "Now, upon whom shall I bestow your company for dinner? Who shall be the fortunate fellow?" Sayre took no notice of the lady, if she should express a preference, but looked about the room with the countenance of one who finally had found in his power the disposal of a coveted treat. His search passed briefly over his old hallmates and soon came to rest upon Darcy. "Darcy, it shall be you! Come, sir, and claim your lady, for supper is ready and you shall lead after me."

Rising immediately, Darcy advanced to Sayre. A quick look at Lady Sylvanie revealed that she did not regret her brother's choice, but neither could he have said she showed any sign of undue pleasure. "My lady." He bowed formally and offered his arm. Her manner, though quite correct, served him a twinge of disappointment, and her cool acceptance of his arm niggled at him. After such a look as she had given him earlier, he had thought to see more animation.

He led her to their accorded place behind Sayre and his lady and followed them to the dining room, using their promenade as an opportunity to assess her further. Her hand was light upon his arm and the blue-grey fabric of her gown fluttered slightly as they walked, drawing his attention to the pleasing curves of her form and the milky whiteness of her shoulders. Her richly plaited hair shone ebony in the hall candlelight and a refreshing scent of mingled sweet herbs and new rain tickled his nostrils. No, he decided, he was not at all averse to Sayre's choice. It was, in fact, exactly the opportunity he required to engage Lady Sylvanie further without that singling out of her that would only cause a wretched round of speculation. With these consoling thoughts, he relaxed a bit and his interest in the woman at his side rose.

It was not until all were seated at table that the absence of Miss Avery and Trenholme was noticed. Her brother's explanation that "Miss Avery did not feel well enough to come down to supper" was quickly accepted and with little comment. Sayre, on the other hand, could supply no information about his brother and sent one of the servants up to inquire if Mr. Trenholme would be joining them before signalling the others that they should begin serving the meal.

The first course served, Darcy set himself to the delicate task of entertaining his companion. He knew himself to be intrigued by her, but of the lady's willingness to be discovered, he was less certain. Her behaviour toward him had been all that was contradictory. One minute he was ignored and the next held in thrall by her Delphic eyes. Well, he must make a beginning…

"My lady…"

"My lady!" Manning's voice from the other side of Lady Sylvanie clashed with his in a bid for her attention. His eyes met Manning's briefly as she hesitated between them, but the rivalry Darcy expected to find in his expression was not there. Rather, he saw a man struggling with an unaccustomed emotion. Lady Sylvanie looked back to Darcy, a lift of her brow requesting his forbearance. He looked again at Manning and then nodded the withdrawal of his claim.

"My lady," Manning began again, his voice low and strained, "please allow me to thank you once more. Your kindness to my sister has greatly eased her distress. I left her sleeping peacefully, a thing I had not thought possible after this afternoon!" He glanced over at his other sister with a grimace before turning back to Lady Sylvanie. "You were of vastly more comfort than ever her ladyship was. *She* would not stay with Bella above five minutes and then would only plague her with questions…make her tell the whole horrid thing if she could, stupid woman!" He paused, then ended softly, "I am indebted to you ma'am."

"Lord Manning." Darcy could hear the lady's dulcet reply clearly although she was turned away from him. "How could I not offer whatever comfort was in my power to give to your poor sister? Such distress must engage my sympathy. That my efforts are deemed helpful is all the thanks I could wish."

"I shall not forget this," Manning insisted, "nor your part in it, Darcy. Lord, what a business!" He sighed and lapsed into silence. Then, picking up a fork, he turned to his meal.

Lady Sylvanie's brief, blush-tinged smile acknowledged the approval Darcy did not hide when she turned back to him, but the moment passed, and soon she was in full possession of herself. It was enough, though, to reveal to him that his companion had a woman's heart as well as an artist's soul, and he was pleased with his discoveries.

"We did not have the pleasure of your company this afternoon," Darcy began. "I trust you are well recovered, my lady? Or perhaps you conceal your discomfort?" he asked, remembering her glance of pain before beginning her song.

"You are remembering my song, Mr. Darcy." her eyes rested on him lightly, their fierceness banked. "Such perception! An uncommon quality in a man! Yes, I have recovered from my heedless indulgence of last night, I thank you. What you saw earlier was due entirely to the sad nature of the song."

"You are easily touched by suffering?" he asked.

"Easily touched by suffering?" she returned, surprised. "I do not take your meaning, Mr. Darcy."

Darcy motioned to Manning on her other side. "Your waiting upon Miss Avery in such a manner as to earn Manning's gratitude must make you very intuitive in regard to that condition of the human heart." She began to shake her head, refusing his compliment, but he would not allow it. He pursued his point. "And further, if a song can evoke in you another's pain…You cannot deny that, either, for I saw it."

"I see it would be pointless to deny, for you will have it no other way, sir." Lady Sylvanie looked discomfited as a blush coloured her fair cheeks again. "But it would appear that we have unknowingly joined hands in calls upon our sympathy, Mr. Darcy. Miss Avery credited you with her rescue and told me of your tender calming of her hysterics." She lifted her wineglass and looked speculatively at him over the rim. "Perhaps I am not the only one who is 'easily touched by suffering'."

"Perhaps." He smiled back at her and decided to take a different tack. "Your music—I confess it is not what I am used to hearing in drawing rooms the like of Norwycke Castle."

"I beg your pardon if you did not like it," she answered.

"You mistake me, ma'am," Darcy countered quickly, not certain whether she was teasing, or if he had offended. "Your music was all your brother declared and more. I liked it quite well. I meant that I have never seen a lady play a harp like that before, or sing in such a way. Usually, the grand harp is used to exhibit one's proficiency, and more formal arrangements are offered in company. Or am I mistaken in this as well?"

"You may declare it to be so with far more authority than I," she acceded, her eyes flashing momentarily in Sayre's direction. "I have not had the privilege of attending many drawing room recitals." Darcy followed her look, not sure of what to reply. Why *had* Sayre kept his half-sister virtually hidden from the world? Was it, as Lady Felicity had intimated, a means of spiting his father's widow? If that were the case, why was she being introduced to Society now, at an age that was perilously close to being labelled 'on the shelf'?

The doors to the dining room opened, saving him the necessity of a reply, for the attention of all the room was caught by the entrance of the missing Trenholme. Lady Sylvanie's nose wrinkled in disgust as she and Darcy, with the others at table, took in his dishevelled appearance. He had not changed out of his riding clothes, and his coat and waistcoat flapped unbuttoned about him. He had apparently worked at his neckcloth but with only that degree of success which had resulted in it loosening so that it sagged about his neck. Stumbling into the room, he almost went down once before falling into his seat between Lady Beatrice and Lady Felicity, who nervously edged their chairs away from the strong odour of Blue Ruin which emanated from the house's younger son.

"But that is neither here nor there." Lady Sylvanie recovered her poise and smiled at Darcy but not before he detected what he was tempted to think was a look akin to satisfaction. "You are curious about my harp, Mr. Darcy? It was my mother's, and it was she who taught me to play and sing the songs that you heard tonight. We spent many a long night sharing the music and stories of her people. She was Irish, you know, and a descendent of Irish kings. It was only right that I should learn her music."

"Yesshhh, she was." Trenholme's slurred voice boomed across the table. "Irish, that is. As Irish as the grass is green, Darcy! An' they're *all* outta kings, you know. Scratch 'em an' they bleed blue, evra one."

"Bev, you're drunk!" declared Sayre angrily.

"Completely f-foxed, my dear brother." Trenholme staggered to his feet and bowed, but the movement threw him off balance, and he tumbled back down into his seat. "An' you would be too, if you…no, mustn't say…where was I?" He rounded on Lady Felicity, who shrank from him in confusion.

"You were making as ass of yourself," snapped Manning, "and doing a damned fine job of it. Sayre, send for his man and bundle him off to bed before he says something he should not."

"I'll say wha' I like in my own h-home, Manning. It is still our home, ish it not, Sayre?" He stared hard down the table, trying to focus on his brother.

"Shut your mouth, Bev!" his lordship commanded, alarm spreading over his face, "or I swear, I'll have the servants pitch you out!"

"Right, then. Pitch *me* out, but keep tha' little, half-Irish b—"

"Trenholme!" Darcy rose menacingly from his chair. He would countenance the discourtesies that ran rampant about Norwycke no longer. "Keep a civil tongue in your head. I'll not have you abuse your sister further, no matter how…"

"Half-sister," Trenholme corrected him. "Never forget, half…. He rose unsteadily. "Well, Sayre, *that* should make you happy, eh? Defending her!" He turned to Darcy, motioning him closer. "She don't need it, you know. Little b—sorry, *her ladyship* can take care of herself."

"Which seems to be more than you can do." Manning rose and joined Darcy. "Lady Sylvanie looked after Bella with more compassion than…" He stopped and looked up at the ceiling, collecting himself. "Trenholme, you disgust me; and, if this is the manner in which we are to be entertained, I swear I will pack up Bella and return to London as soon as she is able."

"No need for that, Manning." Sayre broke the shocked silence at his lordship's declaration and then addressed his brother firmly. "Bev, your company is not required this evening. I *strongly* suggest you go to your rooms and let your man attend you."

Trenholme surveyed his brother and their guests with a defiant smirk until he came to his half-sister, whereupon his countenance suddenly flushed dark with anger. Seeing his reaction, Darcy moved closer to her. Looking down into the Lady Sylvanie's face for an indication of how he should assist her, he saw that her fierce, unflinching gaze had returned, the full power of which she was flinging back at Trenholme. Suddenly, Trenholme rose and threw down his napkin. "I shall leave you to it, then. I c-consider myself absolved. Here, you there!" He motioned to the serving men. "Require your assistance. Believe I am drunk." He flung an arm around the neck of the nearest one and leaning heavily upon him, stumbled out of the room.

The rest of that evening's supper passed in the sort of strained artificiality that Darcy detested. He could not quiet the turmoil in his mind at Trenholme's offensive behaviour toward his brother, his guests, and, most particularly, Lady Sylvanie, nor could he help but speculate on its connection to the vile business at the Stones. To Lady Sylvanie, his words had been of the cruellest nature. Darcy did not wonder that it must be the uppermost subject in the minds of everyone, but it made for poor conversation and the happy mood of the gathering was lost. After Trenholme's departure, Lady Sylvanie withdrew into her pose of indifference and Darcy could think of nothing to say to her that would not be considered an invasion of her privacy. Instead he was constrained to merely observe her as she conducted herself regally through the remainder of the meal, unbowed by the curious looks the other guests cast her and in a manner that he could not help but admire.

When it came time for the ladies to withdraw, Darcy rose courteously and helped her with her chair before assisting her to rise. She had not worn gloves that evening, so when she laid her delicate hand in his, its warmth and softness was not disguised. The sensation was, he found, very pleasant and the nature of her private, parting expression of thanks for his assistance was most gratifying. He resumed his seat with a smile that he could only just manage to mask before Sayre called them all to the sampling of his cellar's best.

"We may not dawdle long, I fear," Sayre continued after proposing a toast to the evening and downing a respectable portion of the brandy in his glass. "The ladies desire to play at Charades and if we are to have any peace later this evening," he winked, "we must present ourselves in the drawing room without undue delay." The gentleman groaned and laughed, but only the most desultory of small talk followed to flavour their time. A creeping impatience with his company drew Darcy away to one of the windows and the moonlight's stark illumination of the maze of hedges in the garden beyond it. The play of light and shadow against the snow reminded him of a chessboard stretched crazily askew, pinned to the earth here and there by the garden statuary. *And what piece am I upon the board?* As he sipped at his brandy, a curiosity took possession of him about how Lady Sylvanie was handling the gentle inquisition surely taking place among the females in the drawing room. He pulled at his fob and brought out his timepiece. *Another five minutes should certainly suffice for this obligatory masculine ritual.* He took another sip, this time taking care to enjoy the fire as it slid down his throat. *Not unlike the lady,* he thought to himself wryly, *cool and fiery.* He need not be concerned over how she fared with the other women, but he should like to watch her as she did so.

Sayre finally signalled the end of their exile, and with an heightened expectation, Darcy put down his glass and followed. As he had guessed, Lady Sylvanie sat in unruffled composure near the hearth, leaving him in no doubt that she had held her own against the more practiced drawing room strategists ranged against her. Lady Felicia's smile upon the gentlemen's entrance was rather forced in appearance, but Miss Farnsworth was seen to be deep in distressed consultation with her mother and aunt. Lady Sayre's relief and joy at the entrance of her husband was likely the greatest that his lordship had seen upon his lady's face in quite some time.

"Ah…well, my dear," Sayre began uncertainly. "It is to be Charades, is it not? Have the slips been readied?"

"N-no, Sayre," her ladyship stammered, "but it shall be done directly. Felicia, my dear, would you be so kind?" The gentlemen, in good form, scattered about the room among the ladies to await the assignment of teams. Darcy sauntered to the hearth and took up a position against the mantle behind and to the side of Lady Sylvanie, smiling down into her upturned face as she followed his progress.

"Do you enjoy playing at Charades, Mr. Darcy, that you smile so?"

"In general, I avoid activities that involve playacting, my lady. My smile is not for such games."

She arched a brow at him, "But you are playing at one now, are you not? The Drawing Room Game of feint, parry, and retreat. I believe that was a feint, sir, and I am expected to parry. Or is retreat the proper move? You must pardon my ignorance of the game. I am, as I told you, unskilled in drawing room etiquette."

"Your move should be determined by your strengths, not your opponent's expectations." Darcy's smile deepened as he warmed to her allusion to fencing. "Always move to your advantage."

"Strange advice for a man to give a woman, Mr. Darcy. I had rather understood that it was the object of the male of the race to allow as little advantage as possible to the female. Are you entirely sure you do not wish to take back your advice?"

Darcy chuckled at her acuity. "It is a dangerous gift; I admit! I suppose I might be considered a traitor to my sex, but I do not take it back." His grin faded slightly as he adopted a less frivolous tone. "I believe, ma'am, that it is advice you have already taken." He nodded toward the other ladies. "And with cause." He stopped, curious to see whether she would confide in him or dismiss his words as mere banter.

"Lady Sylvanie!" Monmouth's call interrupted the moment.

"Yes, my lord?" Lady Sylvanie looked over in question to the viscount.

"You are teamed with Darcy, Lady Beatrice and me." He waved the paper slips with their names written on them. "We shall make a splendid team, even if Darcy does remain as stiff as a statue, I have no doubt!"

Darcy rolled his eyes, as Lady Sylvanie laughed. "No doubt, indeed, Lord Monmouth."

Lady Felicia came over to them. "My lord viscount, you must be mistaken. Mr. Darcy's name cannot be among your slips, for it is here with mine." She held out her slips to Monmouth's view.

"His name is there, ma'am, but it is also among mine." He matched hers with those in his hand. "You must have put him down twice."

Lady Felicia looked dumbly at her slips and then at Monmouth's. "It is not possible," she declared in a voice small with confoundment.

"But true, nevertheless," Monmouth replied firmly, "and as I have only two other and Darcy would make a fifth in your team, I must insist on keeping him even if he is the veriest clodpole at Charades!"

"Thank you, Tris." Darcy bowed mockingly. "I, on the other hand, shall refrain from informing the room of your shortcomings; but should anyone ask about that unfortunate adventure commandeering the Northern Stage, I shall be forced to divulge all."

"Darcy!" Monmouth laughed. "That was eight years ago!"

"And your driving hasn't improved a wit, old man," Darcy returned dryly, his eye on Lady Felicia, who still puzzled over the two sets of slips in her hands. She continued to examine one and then the other, shaking her curls with a frown.

"I am certain that I wrote it but once," she said under her breath. "How came it to…" She stopped. Her chin came up sharply, her eyes narrowing, and focused on Lady Sylvanie. "Unless some other one added his name again." From his stance above and behind her, Darcy could not see Lady Sylvanie's face and therefore could only guess at what was displayed there in response to Lady Felicia's barely unspoken accusation. From the slight stiffening of the lady's shoulders and the sudden guardedness that flushed Lady Felicia's countenance, he would wager that the fierce princess had returned. A twinge of sympathy for Lady Felicia briefly surfaced but was quickly suppressed.

"My lady." Lady Sylvanie's voice was devoid of its music. "It is easily proved. Did you not write all the names? Then, examine the slips; see if there is one that is not in your hand."

"They appear all in the same hand to me." Monmouth peered over Lady Felicia's shoulder at the slips. "Give it over, my lady; it was a simple mistake—or a clever ruse. Regardless," he smirked, "you shall not have Darcy." A flash of hot indignation appeared in Lady Felicia's eyes and coloured her cheeks, but it was quelled immediately when she turned it upon Lady Sylvanie. Her complexion paled, and the look in her eyes reminded Darcy of a deer caught in the hunter's sights. Without a word, she curtsied hurriedly to all of them and retreated to the other end of the drawing room.

Monmouth traced Lady Felicia's quitting of the field for a few moments before looking up at Darcy, both brows lifted in surprise. "A rather easy victory, wouldn't you say, Darcy?"

Stepping around her chair, Darcy bent to catch Lady Sylvanie's attention. She tilted her face up to his, her grey eyes alight with amusement, but he sensed she also looked for an indication of his approval. His answering smile teased from her a laugh fraught with more delight than he'd heard her dare express before. "An easy victory, to be sure, Tris," he tossed over his shoulder, "but whose was it, I wonder?"

The evening of Charades passed quickly and, to Darcy's surprise, rather agreeably. Lady Felicia kept her distance from him and the other gentlemen in a manner more in keeping with his idea of what was proper in his cousin's fiancée. Monmouth and Lady Beatrice were engaging partners in the game, as inventive in their own mimes and poses as in the piecing together of their opponents'. He and Lady Sylvanie were less supple in their play parts than the other two but held up their end of the partnership with keen observations and swift identification of the themes and phrases of the opposition.

When the ladies finally rose to depart, Darcy felt a twinge of regret that this part of the evening was ended so soon. He had quite simply enjoyed himself, and he knew to whom it was due. Along with the other gentlemen, he took a place at the door to bid the ladies goodnight as they departed from the room. When it came Lady Sylvanie's turn to take her leave of him, he could not suppress the urge to take her hand and delay her just a moment. She looked up at him in smiling question. "Mr. Darcy?"

"A moment, please," he answered quietly. "The pleasure I had this evening is more than I had expected, my lady."

Her smile changed, shifting from one of polite inquiry to something else entirely, and as had happened often that night, he was captured by the mystery in her eyes. "As did I, sir," she replied softly, "much more." She sighed lightly before withdrawing her hand from his. "May I ask, do you play cards tonight with the other gentlemen?" At his affirmation that it was likely to be so she pursed her lips ever so slightly and then leant toward him. "Play facing a window," she whispered. At his incredulous look she explained, "It is an old superstition. It could do no harm, and it would please me to think you possessed some little advantage over the others in return for the pleasure of this evening."

"As you wish, my lady." He bowed to her again, and with a last smile at him, she passed out of the room.

"Shall we retire momentarily, gentleman," Sayre asked, "and meet in the library in an half-hour?" He looked round as they nodded and bowed their leave. "Good, good! I wonder shall we come to playing for that sword tonight, Darcy?"

"That is for you to decide, Sayre," Darcy replied absently, still somewhat entranced by his last view of the lady.

"Then, perhaps it may be tonight. We shall see, shall we not?" His lordship rubbed his hands together. Darcy bowed his leave and headed to his chambers for more comfortable attire in which to engage in the battles of chance that would end the evening.

His mind still occupied with review of the evening's pleasures, he arrived at his door, entered by his own hand and progressed to the dressing room before he even noticed Fletcher's absence. The candles were almost guttered out, although fresh ones were lined up neatly beside each candleholder. Clothes for the evening's gambling were laid out, as were a comfortable pair of shoes. All, indeed, was in readiness, but of Fletcher there was no sign. Even a call down the back stairs from the dressing room elicited no response. Perplexed, Darcy shut the door to the stairs and strode to the nearest branch of candles. He quickly replaced the near-spent ones with fresh and, grasping the base, turned to an examination of the dressing room. Everything was in Fletcher's meticulous order, down to the placement of his hairbrush and comb upon the dresser.

Uncomfortable with the mystery of his valet's whereabouts, Darcy put the branch of candles down upon a nearby table with a disturbed frown and began to pull at the knot of his neckcloth. Perhaps he had been unwise to send Fletcher on the scent of whoever had done the bloody deed at the King's Stone. The man was a wonder at gathering information, but the hand behind that abomination would hardly be free with the details. Given the violent evidence, he might well have foolishly put Fletcher in danger.

"Damn and blast!" he exploded, the curse directed at his careless use of an excellent man as well as the knot that man had tied about his neck. He went to the mirror and began again on the knot. "Patience, Darcy," he reminded himself and was rewarded with the knot coming loose. He unwound it and flung it off, his coat and waistcoat following, although not without some trouble and a few heated observations on the intelligence of the fellow who decreed that men's attire should fit so closely. Returning to the dresser, he pulled at his fobs, unpinned them and put them down on the table and toed off his pumps. He looked again at the door to the back stairs, but no sound issued from behind it of steps, either hurried or laboured. He shed his breeches and sent them to join his coat. Sitting down on the shaving chair, Darcy pulled on a pair of trousers and then rose to button them. He glanced again at the door, willing Fletcher to be on the other side, but it remained as it was. He sighed in consternation. There seemed to be nothing for it but to continue on to the library.

Lacking only his shoes and a waistcoat, Darcy walked over to where Fletcher had laid them and slipped his foot into a shoe as he reached for the waistcoat. A crinkling sound greeted his ears and something was definitely preventing him from seating his foot properly. He leaned down, scooped off the shoe, and brought it closer to the candlelight. There, wedged into the toe, rested a piece of paper. He pulled it out and, laying it under the light, quickly smoothed out the creases and read:

> Mr. Darcy,
>
> Sir, if you are reading this note I have not yet returned from pursuing the explanation for a Curious Occurrence that may have some bearing on your concerns. I set your coat sleeve to soaking in the washing room below stairs immediately upon your departure for supper and before I had set the dressing room to rights. When I returned above stairs, I found that your brush and comb were NOT where they had been left. What this may portend, I cannot yet say, but I intend to find out! I have made myself agreeable to his lordship's staff and am regarded with some awe by the ladies' maids and my fellow valets. (The fame of the "Roquet" has spread even to Oxfordshire!) That is, except for One, whom I shall watch tonight very closely. I hope to be back in attendance on you, sir, when your time with the gentlemen this evening is concluded and with Something of Value to disclose.
>
> Your very obedient servant,
> Fletcher

With some relief, Darcy took up the note and crumpled it before taking it into the bedroom and tossing it to the fire. The flames licked greedily at the titbit, reducing it to ash in seconds while he watched. So, someone had been in his rooms! Evidently nothing was missing; Fletcher would have known immediately if anything were gone. But why had he come if not to steal something, and then left after merely handling his hairbrush? And how had Fletcher come to suppose a connection between his hairbrush, of all things, and his discovery at the King's Stone? He walked back into the dressing room and finished readying himself for the night of gambling below. He would have to clear his mind of these matters if he were to return to these rooms unscathed by tonight's play; and, as loath as he was to appear to succumb to Sayre's enticement, he would very much like to win that exquisite sword. Darcy blew out most of the candles, leaving a few burning against Fletcher's return and, with a fervent wish that they should both have some luck tonight, left his chambers.

~~~~~~~&~~~~~~~

"Mr. Darcy! Mr. Darcy, sir!" Fletcher's urgent voice, and a tentative jab at his shoulder brought Darcy straight up in the chair with a start.

"Fletcher!" he began groggily, but a yawn interrupted him. "Where the devil have you been? What time is it?"

"It lacks a quarter until three, sir," Fletcher returned apologetically. "I beg your pardon, but it could not be helped. You found my note, sir?"

"Yes." Darcy rose from the hard chair he had chosen to ward off sleep and stretched until several joints protested with load cracks. "In my shoe! Singular place to leave it!" Staving off another yawn, he motioned to the dresser. "Now, what is this about? '...a round, unvarnish'd tale,' if you please!"

"As I wrote in the note, sir...when I had returned from the laundry I found that your brush and comb had been moved. It was clear to me that some person or persons had wantonly invaded your privacy." Fletcher's face was heavy with the import of his words. "Mr. Darcy, what would someone want with your hairbrush?"

"I cannot imagine, Fletcher," Darcy responded dryly before succumbing to the insistent yawn, "and I do not wish to play at *Questions* at a quarter until three in the morning." He leaned over and poured a glass of water from the bedside carafe.

"A charm, sir."

"What!" The water spilled over the rim of the glass as Darcy looked up in sharp surprise at his valet. "A charm! Are you serious?"

"Never more so, Mr. Darcy." Fletcher returned his incredulous look grimly. "Whoever invaded your rooms was looking for something with which to fashion a charm. Strands of hair from your brush
~~~~~~~

served the purpose quite nicely, but I fear that was not all that was taken." Fletcher paused, his jaw working in consternation before continuing. "I believe, although I am not certain, that the cloth with which I stanched the blood from your shaving cut two nights ago is also missing."

"Good Lord!" Darcy breathed, as he sank down on the edge of the bed. Yesterday he would have dismissed such a theory with contempt; but, after the events of the day, it made eminent sense. It was of the same nature as the abomination at the Stones. Against whom *that* horror had been directed he could not say with certainty, but of this there was no doubt that he was the target!

"Just so, sir," Fletcher responded, his eyes sympathetically meeting Darcy's as a man with his friend. "In truth, a 'thing of darkness.'"

Hot indignation swept through Darcy's chest. That anyone should think to control his fate, whether by natural or unnatural means, galled him to the very core of his being. So it had been with Wickham, the incessant manoeuvring and pressing, and so it was in this. That the origin of the "power" called upon in this attempt to compel him to bend to another's will was diabolical he counted as nothing more than evidence of the perversity of the mind from which it had sprung. It was the intent behind it that angered him to the quick.

He shot up from the bed, and with jaw hard-set and eyes dangerously narrowed; he walked the length of the room. "Of this detestable thing, *I*, then, am the object." He stopped at the door to the dressing room and peered intently at his brush and comb lying atop the dresser before swinging abruptly back to Fletcher. "But who is our Prospero and what does he hope to achieve with this? What does he want from me?"

Fletcher broke the momentary silence that had descended after his master's last question. "Sir, I would venture that there are two likely possibilities. The first is…"

"Money!" Darcy finished the sentence. "It takes no excess of intelligence to apprehend the dire need for coin at Norwycke Castle. But are you asking me to believe that Sayre is behind this?"

"I made no accusations, sir!" Fletcher shook his head. "I have no proof against his lordship or his brother."

"Trenholme! Now, there is a piece of work!" Darcy considered him with disgust. "But he was vilely drunk at supper and needed assistance to remove himself to his rooms."

"Or appeared so," Fletcher added thoughtfully. "But I say again, I have no charge to make against him or his valet, except for lack of attention to what is due his profession. *That* young man has nearly been my shadow ever since we arrived. Wants for sense, that one. To think I'd freely reveal my skills…." He sniffed with disdain.

"Neither Sayre nor Trenholme want for sense, and this business exhibits none!" Darcy interrupted his valet's fall into professional pique. "How should a trumpery charm 'charm' enough of my resources from me to stave off the losses and debts Sayre has incurred? He must know, the others, too, for that matter, that I never gamble to excess. Does our Prospero think to influence me to make him a *gift* of Pemberley with a bit of blood and hair?"

"More than 'a bit' of blood, sir, from your description!" At Fletcher's arched brow, Darcy stopped his pacing.

"The King's Stone!" Darcy's eyes widened. "Could this be what that was about as well?"

"It is possible, Mr. Darcy, certainly; or it may be something else entirely. But I do believe that the similarities between them indicate the same hand or hands." Darcy nodded his silent agreement with Fletcher's speculation, but its usefulness appeared to him to be limited.

"The other possibility…?" He let the question dangle.

A flush spread o'er Fletcher's face at Darcy's question, and after clearing his throat, he offered tentatively, "The other, a-hem, the other possibility is that it is a…ah, love charm, sir."

"A love…!" Darcy choked and drew breath for a swift and vehement rejection.

"Mr. Darcy, I beg you, do not discount it." Fletcher put up his hands to forestall his master's ire. "I have made some inquiries among the ladies' maids—discreet inquires, sir," he added quickly at the affronted look Darcy gave him, "and it seems that most of the unwed females at Norwycke Castle are…well…'on the hunt,' so to speak, sir."

"That information is *not* in the nature of a revelation, Fletcher," Darcy replied tersely. "The contrary would be more curious!"

"True, very true, sir, but it is the desperation of the hunt that catches one's attention." He paused, waiting for Darcy's permission to continue on this delicate subject.

"Go on," Darcy sighed.

"The unfortunate Miss Avery has had two unsuccessful Seasons," Fletcher began, ticking off a finger. "Lord Manning has given up hope in that venue, holding Miss Avery's shyness to blame, and is now trotting her around to the notice of his various moneyed acquaintances. If an offer is not forthcoming within a year, she will be packed off to a small estate in Yorkshire to live out her days in obscure spinsterhood.

The next," he continued, ticking off a second finger, "is Miss Farnsworth. Lady Beatrice is beside herself with anxiety that her daughter's headstrong temperament will land her in disgrace or make her repugnant to any man of position or reputation. The sooner Miss Farnsworth weds and is under a husband's control, the sooner Lady Beatrice may wash her hands of her and, by the way, concentrate on her own future."

"She hunts as well," Darcy stated baldly a fact to which he could well attest.

"Yes, sir!" Fletcher nodded in surprise, but did not question Darcy's knowledge. "The fourth is Lady Felicia."

"She is affianced to my cousin!" Darcy snapped at him in warning. Fletcher bit his lip and looked at him, commiseration apparent in every line.

"I know, sir," he quietly continued after a moment, "but the lady is not content with the adoration of your relative. She is accustomed to the attentions of a court of admirers of which you, sir, were at one time a member. That you are, of your own choice, one no longer, rankled her pride sorely. According to her maid, she has vowed to have you *and* your cousin."

With a black look of revulsion, Darcy turned away and leaned his forearm against the window, the honest darkness beyond it preferable to that which was being revealed within. The small chamber clock struck three. He waited until the echo of the last stroke had died away before asking, "And what of Lady Sylvanie?"

"Lady Sylvanie and her maid are a complete enigma, sir." Fletcher's voice tightened, evincing no little degree of agitation.

"An enigma, Fletcher!" Darcy faced him, folding his arms across his chest in bitter amusement. "This *is* a day filled with surprises! How so, an enigma?"

"The servants are unusually cautious concerning the lady and her maid." Fletcher clasped his hands behind him in an uncharacteristic show of perturbation and then, to Darcy's amazement, took up the pacing of the room that his master had ceased. "That is not to say I have not discovered some of their story, but more may well be…impossible!" he admitted with chagrin.

"Fletcher!" The valet abruptly halted his immoderate ramble and, colouring, presented himself in correct form before Darcy.

"As you know, sir, Lady Sylvanie is the offspring of the old lord and his second wife, a woman from an obscure but noble Irish family. Lord Sayre was delighted at the birth of his daughter, the young lady becoming quite his favourite, but he lived to enjoy her for only twelve years. His lordship's sons, though, did not look upon their step-mama with filial affection; and their half-sister they cordially despised, especially Mr. Trenholme who was closest to the girl in age. When his Lordship passed away, the new Lord Sayre packed mother and child off to Ireland with a pittance upon which to live and both he and his brother engaged to forget their very existence."

"Altogether infamous!" Darcy expostulated, bridling with anger as Fletcher spoke. "But I do not doubt you, for I had never heard of a second wife—or a sister—all the years I knew them at school."

"Such was the state of affairs, sir," Fletcher continued, "until a little less than a year ago when a letter arrived from Ireland announcing the death of the Dowager Lady Sayre. The message was accompanied by legal documents that Lord Sayre immediately placed in the hands of his solicitor, who forwarded notification of their contents to his lordship's most pressing creditors."

"Legal documents?" Darcy sat down upon the bed again, relieved to put his mind to the solving of a tangle not associated with acts drenched in bloody superstition. "An inheritance, or interest in some financial venture? It would have to be something substantial. "

"Land, sir," Fletcher supplied. "A legal suit over the ownership of some land initiated by Lady Sylvanie's Irish grandfather decades ago had been but lately settled in Chancery in the family's favour. The sale of this property might go some way in solving his lordship's financial problems."

"But, the land would devolve upon Lady Sylvanie, not Sayre," Darcy objected.

Fletcher shook his head, "The land was deeded to Lord Sayre in the dowager's will."

"To the man who dispossessed her!" Darcy snorted derisively.

"Indeed, sir, but on condition only. It seems that the property is not of such a value that the interest on its sale would afford Lady Sylvanie more than 'respectable' independence in the hinterlands of Eire. Therefore, the lady's mother made it over to his lordship to do with as he will on the condition that Lady Sylvanie be brought back to England and that he do all in his power to arrange her a marriage into a wealthy, prominent family, with the added proviso that the lady be freely agreeable to the match. When the deceased lady's solicitors in Dublin are informed of Lady Sylvanie's 'happy' marriage, the will's provisions will be enacted."

Darcy stared unseeing into space as his mind turned over Fletcher's discoveries. Of course he knew that the lady was in want of a husband just as he was in want of a wife. Fletcher's tale did no damage to his esteem of her. Rather, his sympathy was further engaged, and his admiration increased at the plight of the lady and her proud handling of the situation fate had dealt her.

"There is no mystery in this, Fletcher." His focus returned to his valet. "Her ladyship's mother furnished her daughter with a means to a future in the only way that her step-sons were likely to heed."

"The mystery, sir, is that the lady has refused to entertain any of the prospects his lordship has lured to Norwycke Castle, and no one can answer for it!" Fletcher answered, obviously vexed with the resistance he had encountered. "Neither his lordship nor his brother has yet been able to prevail upon her to choose a husband from among their acquaintances, or attend any public or private assembly in which to meet other eligible gentlemen. The two are said to be enraged with behaviour that can only make their own situation more desperate the longer the lady refuses."

The scene in which he had first encountered the lady flashed before him: Trenholme seething in a fit of anger while Lady Sylvanie calmly looked through him. The explanation for this curious exchange was now evident. Trenholme had been attempting to force her attendance among the gentlemen for the evening, and Lady Sylvanie had been in the midst of a cool refusal when he had entered the room. The lady's eyes had then met his, and the lady had stayed.

"From all I can observe, sir," Fletcher continued in the same vexed tone, "it is nonsensical that Lady Sylvanie would wish to prolong her stay at Norwycke Castle. Far more reasonable to expect that she would hasten to take advantage of the opportunity her mother has bought her. Yet she stays, and none can furnish a reason for her obduracy. On this there is absolute silence!" Fletcher fairly shook with irritation. "The lady confides in no one but her maid—an old and close servant brought with her from Ireland who, in turn, treats with none but her mistress. The household servants hold her in aversion and, when she is about, take care to be out of her way." Fletcher paused to heave a long sigh. "It is she of whom I wrote in the note, Mr. Darcy. The old woman bears watching, and that is what I was about for the better part of this night, but with little success. I very much doubt," he concluded abjectly, "that *I* shall be able to cozen anything from her, sir."

Darcy yawned again as the clock struck the quarter hour. The truth that lurked beyond Fletcher's information was too well masked to reason out while his brain and body insistently demanded the sweet relief of sleep. It required a clearer head than he was now possessed of. But the man's faithful service needed to be commended first; it was his duty to him every bit as much as taking a wife was his duty to his family's name.

"Well done, Fletcher," he dismissed him with unfeigned sincerity. "I could not have discovered a quarter as much had I a week! You have more than earned the sleep that is fast claiming us both."

The valet's anxious countenance relaxed at Darcy's words, but when he arose from his acknowledging bow, his face was once more deep with lines of concern. "Thank you, Mr. Darcy, but I cannot be easy about the matter. It is a veritable 'serpent's egg' that could well hatch at any time to your harm. With your permission, I will set up in the dressing room and lodge there until it is killed in its shell or we leave this place."

"You do not put any credence in these Othellian 'charms and conjurations,' I hope!" Darcy peered at him curiously.

"Certainly not, Mr. Darcy!" Fletcher protested. "Any unnatural 'power' called upon by such revolting fardels was rendered impotent long ago. It is the *natural* evil and the desperation behind such pitiable delusions that I respect, sir. I will not presume upon Providence when Heaven has furnished a warning."

"As you wish." Darcy was too tired to object to Fletcher's plan and not at all certain it was not a wise precaution. It had all become too deep to reject out of hand anything that would contribute to his advantage. He lay back on the pillows of the grandly ornate bedstead.

"Good-night then, Mr. Darcy." Fletcher bowed again. "And God be with you, sir," he added, closing the dressing room door softly behind him.

~9~

The Whirligig of Time

The very last person that Darcy expected to find upon entering the breakfast room late the next morning was the not-so-Honourable Beverly Trenholme. But when he entered, there he was—his elbows propped on the table and his head resting in both hands, a large mug of steaming black coffee set just inches away from his nose. His head came up momentarily upon hearing Darcy's footsteps on the polished wooden floor, but only long enough to identify their owner before dropping again into his hands.

"Oh…it is you, Darcy," Trenholme groaned as he gingerly rubbed his temples.

"Evidently," Darcy returned brusquely and went over to the buffet board to find something with which to break his fast. Trenholme's bizarre behaviour of the previous day coupled with Fletcher's discoveries made the man's company difficult to bear. If it were not for the rumbling of his stomach, he would happily have quit the room. In fact, Fletcher had asked whether he would prefer a tray this morning but he had refused in some little hope that something might cross his path that would lend rationality to the events of the day before. Instead, he was to be burdened with a sullen, reprehensible excuse for a gentleman as a dining companion.

Trenholme winced so terribly when Darcy set his plate and saucer upon the table that he was sorely tempted to let his silverware drop on the polished surface as well. But years of good breeding intervened against the impulse. Laying them down quietly, he took his seat with the intent of finishing quickly and ignoring Trenholme's presence as much as possible. His companion obliged him by remaining silent through most of the meal, entertaining Darcy only with intermittent groans and sighs as the bracing brew before his nose was slowly and carefully consumed. Left thus to the contemplation of his own situation in relative peace, Darcy chewed meditatively upon the country ham, boiled eggs and buttered toast that made up the selections upon his plate. His situation was one that a hasty removal from Norwycke Castle would appear to solve admirably, but such a course could be considered as nothing less than an insult to his host. This he was almost willing to brave save for what this desertion might portend for a certain lady. The protective nature embedded within his character that so sheltered his sister was awakened on behalf of the castle's beleaguered daughter. Although that impulse had not as yet brought him to the point of wishing to offer for her, he could not abandon her to the machinations of her relatives or, his lip curled in distaste, whomever was playing at sorcerer.

Offer for her. The thought returned to tease him. What would life be like with Lady Sylvanie at his side? In terms of breeding, manners and understanding she was well qualified to bear his name as mistress of his estate and mother of his heirs. He could not ask for a woman with a more austerely beautiful bearing who yet had something of poetry about her. As the daughter of a marquis, any gentleman of discrimination would consider her an asset to his consequence despite her lack of dowry. In addition to practical considerations, he was inclined toward her. Her company was preferable to any at Norwycke, certainly, and to most young women who had been pressed upon him as suitable mates. Then also, as his wife, she would have his protection from those who troubled her and the position and dignity she had been so cruelly denied.

His thoughts flitted then to more intimate aspects of the question. *She was fiercely beautiful, and her passion obviously ran deep; but would it turn to him? Would she ever love him, welcome him?* Absently, Darcy's fingers went to his waistcoat pocket. *What was this!?* Glancing quickly at Trenholme, who was still contemplating the interior of his eyelids, he dug a finger into his pocket and slowly withdrew the silk strands that had lain curled in its depth. *Elizabeth.* His vision of Lady Sylvanie as mistress of his heart and home melted away in the instant it took Darcy to acknowledge what lay in his palm.

"Reading your own palm, Darcy?" Trenholme interrupted his thoughts. Darcy closed his fingers about the strands and he tucked them back inside his pocket with a promise to himself of an interview with Fletcher on how they came to be there.

"Is that commonly done hereabouts?" he responded, gazing indifferently at Trenholme.

"Oh, no!" Trenholme snorted. "Tricking pigs up as infants and slashing their throats is more our line!" Darcy made him no rejoinder. The look of bitterness in Trenholme's face faded, only to be replaced with one bordering on desperation. "Darcy, what do you think it meant?"

"This is your country, man! You should know far better than I," he answered with an edge of irritation.

"My *brother's* country, which he is fast losing to the squeeze-crabs. You see how he is! I expect he will begin laying his bets with the family silver any time now!" Trenholme laughed, the bitterness returned. "If only…"

"Yes?" Darcy invited him to continue, curious whether Trenholme would confess to him the business of the dowager's will.

"Well, all is not lost…not completely. It is just a matter of the proper persuasion in certain quarters." Trenholme returned to a study of his mug of coffee, signalling that the subject was closed.

The polite response, Darcy knew, was an expression of good fortune, but he held his tongue. Such a wish might be construed wrongly and would, he was sure, redound upon Lady Sylvanie, the "quarter" to which Trenholme must refer. He tried a different tack.

"At the Stones, Trenholme, you said that what we saw was 'beyond everything.' Have there been other incidents of the like?"

"Like and not like." Trenholme eyed him over his mug. "There have always been superstitions and legends about the Stones. We have had visitors, even from the Continent, come and make a great deal of nonsense about them. Daffy, some of them, too, wanting permission to prance about them…well, indecently." He placed the mug carefully on the table. "And, of course, the locals in the villages hereabouts sometimes leave tokens—charms, that sort of thing—lying about, hoping for good luck of one sort or another." He sighed then laughed. "Perhaps *I* ought to give it a go, myself. Cannot possibly make things worse!"

"No ritual sacrifices, then?" Darcy persisted.

"I had heard that a rabbit was found a month ago." Trenholme shook his head slowly. "And then there was a kitten from the stable back in the fall, but they'd had their necks…" Trenholme's mouth suddenly snapped shut, and his focus reached past Darcy to the door of the breakfast room. Before Darcy could turn, Trenholme resumed in a queer, strangled voice. "Poachers! It was poachers; I've no doubt. Gamekeeper after them, you know, and they cast away the booty!"

"But, you said a kitten…"

"Poachers, Darcy, simple as that, no doubt of it at all!" He pushed back his chair and rose hurriedly. "Must forgive me…forgot something." In a moment he was gone, and Darcy was left staring in perplexity at his empty chair. What had Trenholme seen that had so unnerved him that he'd squealed like a trapped hare before taking himself out of his way? Turning 'round, he peered at the equally empty doorway. *Castle?* He was beginning to think it a madhouse!

Darcy found himself still quite alone after making a finish of his repast and downing several cups of coffee. He looked out the window and conceded that, as welcome a diversion as it would be, a morning ride was out of the question. The sky was overcast in a manner that warned of more snow, and the wind had kicked up so that the panes rattled in their frames and whistled 'round the corners of the castle in a most forlorn key. It appeared that he must amuse himself indoors this day, at least until some other guest or his hosts came downstairs. Where to go? His usual retreat of the library was denied him unless he retrieved a book from his own travel bag first. But he was too restive, and the activity he craved would not be satisfied with a book. He strolled out of the breakfast room into the hall and paused. The old armoury! He had wanted another look at the sword with which Sayre was baiting him during their nightly gaming. Mayhap he would make him another offer and be done with it. If what Fletcher reported was as true as the evidence seemed to indicate, a generous offer for it might not be refused.

Heartened by the thought, Darcy made his way to the armoury, encountering a servant here and there along the way but otherwise meeting no one. There was, of course, no fire in the room, rendering it chill; but the warmth of his enthusiasm for the weaponry displayed there was proof against its effects. The collection was, indeed, superb. The sword in which he was interested was one of several with impressive, documented histories. Still, the Spanish sabre was far and away the most exquisite of the lot, and Darcy grimaced to himself at the pains he might have to take and the coin he would undoubtedly have to expend in order to possess it. As he reached out his hand to run his fingers over the object of his desire, the door behind him clicked open. Dropping his hand to his side, he turned to receive the newcomer.

"Lady Sylvanie!" He bowed smoothly, but when he came up, it was to perceive that she was not alone. "Ma'am," he offered another bow to the stranger.

"Your reputation for politeness is well deserved, sir." Lady Sylvanie curtsied, a smile for him upon her face. "But this is merely my former nurse, now maid, Mrs. Doyle."

"Your servant, sir," Mrs. Doyle murmured as she curtsied.

"Ma'am," Darcy repeated with a nod to her. So this was the mysterious maid who had vexed Fletcher so! His valet's word that she was one to be watched echoed in his mind, and he determined to observe her closely. An initial, furtive examination disclosed nothing remarkable about her save that she was quite old and suffered from a hunched back that caused her head to hang down awkwardly, requiring her to look up from under her brows whenever she was addressed.

"We have interrupted your admiration of my brother's collection, I fear." Lady Sylvanie swept past him.

"It is a very impressive one, my lady." He turned, following after her, "It is probably one of the finest in the country save for the Regent's."

"You have seen the Regent's collection?" she queried him, her eyes alight with interest.

"No, my lady, not in person. I claim no intimacy with His Highness, but Brougham, a good friend of mine, had the privilege and presented me a copy of the catalogue, which," he added with a smile at her light laugh, "I read thoroughly. I am a collector myself, ma'am, although not in the same society as your brother."

"Which is your favourite, Mr. Darcy?" She waved her hand to indicate the entire room. "What piece would you chuse if you could convince Sayre to part with it?" Darcy's eyes were already upon it even as she spoke. "Ah, this one," the lady's voice dropped almost to a whisper as she reached out and ran her fingers over the top of the blade and caressed the intricacies of the hilt. "It is beautiful, Mr. Darcy. Have you held it, tried it?"

"Y-yes," he stammered, her closeness and her fingering of the sword strangely affecting his senses. "The first night, the night I arrived, he allowed me to test it in exercise. It is as well balanced as it is beautiful."

"A true work of art, then," the lady concluded softly. Darcy could only nod under the smoky intensity of her eyes turned upon him. "Perfect utility and perfect grace—a deadly beauty, crafted to kill exquisitely. Is it its beauty that makes such a thing admired by the world, I wonder, or simply that it is a man's weapon?"

Confounded by her words, he could find nothing to reply but only stared back into her eyes. Both were made mindful of this impropriety by Mrs. Doyle, who vigorously cleared her throat behind them, "A-hem, my lady, were you not intending to show the gentleman the gallery?"

"Yes, thank you, Doyle," Lady Sylvanie recollected herself. "You have not seen the portrait gallery at Norwycke, I trust, Mr. Darcy?"

"I have not had that pleasure, my lady. Will you guide me?" Darcy offered his arm, thankful for both the maid's interruption and a reason to put his body into purposeful motion.

"It will be *my* pleasure, sir." She curled her hand lightly around his forearm. Their passage through the halls of the castle was not rapid or direct. The warren that was the hallways of the old castle prevented such a modern transition from one locale to the other. On their way, Darcy was shown other rooms and halls that Sayre ancestors had built, modified or refurbished, the grandest of these being the ballroom over which, it was said, Queen Elizabeth had presided one evening in a surprise visit to her loyal retainer. Darcy could not help but wonder at Lady Sylvanie's enthusiasm for each nook and cranny through which she conducted him. The lady at his side took just such a pride in all she showed him that one would think she had been resident all her life and not lately recalled from a twelve-year exile in Ireland. Of that, she had not yet made mention, although she must know that he had known Sayre and Trenholme for years.

"At last, we are arrived." Lady Sylvanie's grasp on his arm tightened as they turned into a hall that in every way invited a promenade. Although the sky had darkened, a remarkable amount of light still illuminated the wide hall from the row of windows that extended down one side of the gallery and fell gently upon the paintings that lined the opposite wall. The Sayre family was an old one and portraits from almost every generation since the 1300's looked down upon them in stiff hauteur. Except for an occasional intrusion of work by a portraitist from the Dutch or Flemish school, it was not until they reached those of the last century that the portraits took on a more human aspect, and their subjects became real, identifiable people.

To Darcy's surprise, the lady knew them all, or was prompted gently by Mrs. Doyle, and happily pointed them out to him as they walked slowly down the gallery. But as they approached the far end, he could sense a disturbance in her manner. Her voice took on a higher tone and her bearing seemed to vibrate with restrained emotion. She brought them to a halt at a large portrait of a man, his wife and their two children. Darcy knew it must be of the former Lord Sayre and his first wife. The children were, undoubtedly, Sayre and his brother.

"My father, Mr. Darcy." Lady Sylvanie looked up at the face of a young man she had never known. "Or rather, Lord Sayre and his first family. You are aware, of course, that Sayre and I are half-brother and sister."

"Yes," he replied, gazing up at the portrait with her. "Although, I must confess that, as odd as it may seem, I never knew of your existence until this week, my lady. A sad affair, I understand."

"Oh, 'sad' does it no justice, Mr. Darcy." She smiled bitterly at him. "You must remember, I am half Irish, and so being, only a great tragedy will suffice to satisfy the Irish soul."

"Your pardon," Darcy offered sincerely, hoping to ameliorate the bitterness into which she seemed to have fallen. He was rewarded with an apologetic smile.

"No, you must pardon me, sir, and allow me to lead you on to happier times." She led him down the gallery to another large portrait, this one of a young woman with a child at her breast. The woman in the portrait looked to Darcy very like the one at his side.

"Your mother, my lady?"

"Yes," she sighed, "and here is another with the three of us." She brought him to a grandly-sized painting in which an older Lord Sayre, the beautiful woman of the other portrait, and a girl of nearly ten years of age gazed out at them with inviting warmth kindled by a love that the artist had captured with perfect feeling. "This was begun two years before my father's death." Her voice trembled. "He died suddenly, you know. We had no warning."

"My sincere condolences, Lady," Darcy addressed her with feeling.

"I thank you," she returned solemnly. "Some would scoff at a twelve-year held sorrow."

"Then they never knew the depth of felicity in true family feeling," Darcy quickly affirmed. "My mother passed away more than twelve years ago and my own dear father, five; so, I am intimately acquainted with such sorrow. In my case, both deaths were a result of lingering illnesses." His voice took on a slight tremor. "I was away at school during most of Mother's illness, but I shared my father's last years and bless Heaven that we had them together."

"You 'bless Heaven'?" Lady Sylvanie turned upon him a countenance suddenly full of anger. "Can you really mean what you say, or is the phrase merely a platitude you employ in polite society? Proper sentiment for proper persons!"

"My lady," Mrs. Doyle whispered forcefully as Darcy drew back, his brows raised at her vehemence. The maid sought to restrain her mistress with a hand upon her arm, but the lady heatedly shrugged off.

"I, sir, do *not* 'bless Heaven,'" she spat out contemptuously, "and I never shall, for Heaven is either cruel or powerless, as has been amply proved time upon time. You cannot tell me, Mr. Darcy, that as you watched your father slowly dying you did not have numerous occasions to think the same."

Darcy stared at her in consternation and shocked uncertainty at both the strength of her passion and the challenges laid against his own convictions. Such theorizing he had heard at University—the philosophy and theology rooms at Cambridge had been rife with such speculation. Then, yesterday, that 'thing of evil' at the Stones had shaken those basic assumptions he'd entertained about his world. Today, a beautiful woman with every reason to think ill of the world was questioning them. The lady had struck close to home, and the doubts he'd suppressed or left unanswered, his dissatisfaction with the economy of Heaven, were brought uncomfortably to the fore.

He cast about him for how to answer her demand, and strangely, the queer interview he'd had with his sister's companion, Mrs. Annesley, came to his mind.

The human heart is not so easily mastered. Trumpery will not turn it aside of its course…. Mr*. Darcy, do you give any credence to Providence?*

'…all things work together for good'… 'Sweet are the uses of adversity.' It was not in your power or mine to comfort Miss Darcy…you must look elsewhere.

"My lady," Darcy began stiffly, intending by way of an answer to repeat Mrs. Annesley's proverbs, but the anxiety with which Mrs. Doyle was regarding them gave him pause. He began again in a gentler tone, "Lady, I am ill-qualified to furnish you with a defence for the actions of Providence and confess that I have questioned them and continue to struggle with Its goodness and influence myself." A look of triumph appeared in the lady's eyes. "But a woman who knows more of this than I," he continued, "who has suffered far more than either of us, I daresay, recently expressed to me her confidence that *all* that happens is 'for good.'" Lady Sylvanie began to turn away, disappointment with him written clearly upon her face. "You turn away, but there is more, Lady." He reached for her instinctively and laid his hand lightly upon her arm. "I have seen the happy results of this conviction in her life and, more importantly, in the life of my sister."

Lady Sylvanie stood very still, her eyes roving over his face, searching for what, Darcy could not say. Then, with a lift of a brow she countered, "I am all delight that this woman and your sister are reconciled to their ill-treatment by Providence. But you, Mr. Darcy, will you grin at adversity and call tragedy 'good' because Heaven bids you do so?" She stepped closer to him, her eyes glittering, inviting and whispered seductively, "I know how it is. What you believe you must say before others, before the world. But you are not such a fool!"

In that moment, everything in Darcy urged him to answer her with what she wanted. "No," was such a simple word, and what man would not quickly aver that he was, most definitely, *not* a fool? He also knew, instinctively, that "No" would bring the lady willingly into his arms, that his question that morning of her welcome of him was fully answered. Her eyes sought him as her hand came to rest upon his arm; her breath trembled with passion as he, without thought, moved closer. Cascades of sensual delight broke over him as she laid her other hand upon his chest and, with parted lips, looked up into his eyes.

"Lady," he breathed low in both warning and pleasure.

"Mr. Darcy!!" Fletcher's voice boomed and echoed from the opposite end, down the gallery hall. "I say, Mr. Darcy!!" A small cry of rage escaped the lady as Darcy's head came up to see Fletcher walking briskly down the hall toward them, waving something in his hand. "Sir, it is a letter from Miss Darcy!"

Red-faced and breathing rapidly, Fletcher quickly traversed the hall to where Darcy stood, still waving the post he held clutched in his hand. The lady, meanwhile, had dropped her hands from him and retired a few paces away to engage in close, agitated conversation with her maid. After a flicker of a glance at the pair, Fletcher concentrated wholly upon his master and offered Darcy a bow with an extravagance quite out of his nature. The tilt of his brow when he arose made it all the more clear to Darcy that something was afoot. He accepted the missive with a curt nod, his mind clear enough from the heated impulses of the previous minutes to make him thankful for Fletcher's odd, yet timely, appearance and motioned his valet to stand while he glanced at the direction.

The flush of shame and alarm at what he had almost allowed cooled instantly and a frown creased his brow as he looked sharply back at Fletcher, whose shoulders returned him an almost imperceptible shrug. The direction was not in Georgiana's fine script; rather, it was in a much bolder hand that he recognised as Brougham's. Darcy's eyes returned to the letter. He *had* asked Dy to watch over Georgiana; so, it was not unreasonable to assume that a note from her might be franked by his friend and wrapped in a report of his care. *Good Lord, nothing was amiss, was it?* The haziness of his mental processes of moments before was banished as concern for what Brougham's news might be possessed him.

"My lady, ma'am, your pardon." He turned to address the women behind them but, on doing so, found it difficult to meet Lady Sylvanie's eyes. "As you have heard, an important post has arrived concerning my sister. I beg your leave to indulge in its contents without delay." By the end of his speech Darcy had regained his composure to the degree that he was able, once more, to look the lady in the face. She regarded him regally, her chin high with only a hint of the flush of passion that had so suffused her features earlier.

"Of course, a letter from a sister must be attended to at once," she replied lightly in dismissal. "We will have the pleasure of your company at supper, I trust, regardless of the news?"

"Very likely, my lady." Darcy bowed. "You will excuse me." The lady curtsied, as did her maid, but before he had completed his turn to leave, Darcy saw the old woman direct such a look of pure venom at his valet that he almost flinched. Feigning blindness to the malice he'd seen, he called Fletcher to attend him, and both men exited the gallery as rapidly as was seemly.

"How on earth did you find me, Fletcher?" Darcy demanded under his breath as they made their way back through the labyrinth to Darcy's chamber suite. "Do you know how to get back?"

"Yes, sir," he replied, then added ruefully, "these confoundedly confusing halls and passages were part of the reason for my lateness in waiting upon you last night. I followed the old woman there to that very hall, Mr. Darcy, and she with no candle! At least, none until she was in the gallery. Then, out comes a candlestick—from her pocket, I suppose—which she lit at the picture you were standing beneath."

"The one of old Lord Sayre, her ladyship and her mother?" Darcy drew a sharp breath.

"Yes, sir, the very one." Fletcher shuddered. "It was passing strange, sir. She held the candle high as she could and just stared and stared at the painting. I almost fell asleep waiting for her to move on, but I woke up smartly enough when the candle suddenly went out! I had no idea which way she had gone and was that afraid she'd discover me that I didn't even dare breathe."

"Hmmm," Darcy intoned and motioned Fletcher to walk beside him as they continued on. "And how did you know where *I* was?"

"The housemaids, sir."

"Housemaids now, Fletcher?" He looked at the valet disapprovingly.

"Housemaids are very good sources of information, sir," Fletcher sniffed, "as, like the Creator, they are everywhere present and never noticed by the gentry." Darcy's brow hitched up. "Your pardon, sir," he added quickly. Then, after a moment or two of walking in silence, "I promise you, Mr. Darcy, I have conducted myself as I ought."

"I trust that you did, Fletcher," Darcy sighed. "At the moment, I have more reason to take comfort in your conduct than—Fletcher!" Darcy halted and fumbled several fingers in his waistcoat pocket. Pulling out the embroidery threads, he waved them before his valet's nose. "You took these from my jewel case and put them in my pocket, did you not!"

"I-I noticed that you had left them in your case, sir," Fletcher stammered. "You have carried them with you since Hertfor—for a number of weeks." Darcy noted his avoidance of the shire's name, but said nothing. "In the midst of all this madness, I thought you should have them by you, sir."

"You told me that you did not believe in charms, Fletcher!" Darcy accused. They had reached his chamber door and he waited as Fletcher opened it. Once behind its heavy protection, Darcy went at once to the window and broke the seal on the post while Fletcher brought him a chair.

"There, sir." He set the chair advantageously in order to afford Darcy the best light. "And I do *not* believe in charms! Rather, there are those times that, to quote the Bard, 'the patient must minister to himself.'"

"Meaning?" Darcy looked up impatiently from the letters as he pressed out their folds on his knee.

"Meaning, sir," Fletcher took a deep breath and plunged forward into a speech that both of them knew might well cost him his situation, "that I put them in your pocket to remind you of the very different 'charms' of another young woman. One who casts others who style themselves 'ladies' very deeply in the shade."

"You take too much upon yourself, Fletcher!" Darcy glowered. "And you toe the border of insolence. You can have nothing to say concerning the woman I take as wife, whoever she may be."

"Yes, Mr. Darcy." Fletcher's countenance fell before his master's ire, yet he continued. "I know that I have strayed unpardonably beyond my sphere. But I hope to truly esteem whoever that fortunate lady may be and to see you content, sir."

His lips tightly compressed, Darcy eyed his valet with chagrin. "Perhaps I am not the only man in need of the contentment of a wife," Darcy growled at him, expecting a swift and voluminous denial. To his astonishment, the valet's face coloured up pink with a very silly grin.

"You know, sir? I had thought…but, of course…no, that cannot be. How, sir?" Fletcher's fidgets as he tried to speak were awful to see.

"Know what, man!?" Darcy bellowed, both mystified by his odd reaction and anxious to end the man's blathering so he could read his letters. There were two of them, as he has suspected, Georgiana's resting within the folds of Dy's.

"Annie," Fletcher finally gulped, "that is, Miss Annie Garlick, my intended, sir."

"Your intended! You are to be married!" Darcy crossed his arms over his chest and sat back in the chair as he surveyed his valet with amazement. "Fletcher, when did this happen and who is this woman?"

"Just before Christmas, sir. You remember I left Pemberley early to invest Lord Brougham's gift?" Darcy nodded. "Well, sir, the 'investment' was Annie. His lordship's gift was security enough to enable me to support my parents *and* a wife and family." He paused and cleared his throat, then straightened his shoulders with obvious satisfaction. "She said, 'Yes,' Mr. Darcy, but not until I have your consent and her new mistress is wed. So, I've said nothing, sir, as the lady has at present no eligible suitor."

"She is of good character, then? You would bring an asset to Pemberley?" Darcy knew his duty to his valet and to his own interests. Bringing in a servant from the outside was chancy enough, but bringing in such a one as a wife could be disastrous to Pemberley's domestic tranquillity.

"Of the best character, Mr. Darcy! A fine Christian woman." Fletcher fairly glowed. "As modest as she is lovely, and to that you can attest yourself!"

"I? Where could I have seen her?" Darcy sat up, his suspicions alerted.

"Last November, sir, in church in Meryton that Sunday. You must remember!"

Visions of that day arose in Darcy's mind with no effort at all: Elizabeth Bennet's melodious voice and dancing curls beside him as they recited from his shared book, the increased import that had curiously invested the familiar words they had read, the psalms they had sung. He sighed, "Yes, I remember the day, but—you do not mean the young woman you defended from that lout in the middle of the church, do you?" Darcy looked keenly at his valet, whose chin jutted pugnaciously.

"Yes, sir. My poor girl had no defender then, but she is safe now. Between your reputation, sir, as my employer and her new mistress's care, she is well and safe until she can come to me."

"My reputation..." Darcy repeated under his breath as he rose and stared out the window. Looking back up at his man, who was obviously in some anxiety for his word on his exceptional news, Darcy nodded. "You have my consent, of course, Fletcher, and my wish for joy," he pronounced firmly.

"Oh, thank you, Mr. Darcy! We both thank you, sir!"

Darcy held up a hand, "But you have met only half of your intended's condition for your marriage. It would seem the more difficult part is yet ahead. Perhaps you might put your not inconsiderable talents to assisting her in finding a husband for her mistress...*and allow me to read my letters*," he ended with emphasis.

"Yes, sir!" Fletcher bowed smartly, the silly grin returned to his face, and retreated to the dressing room door. "Thank you, sir!"

"Fletcher!"

"Yes, sir!" The door clicked shut and a blessed silence reigned in the room. Darcy turned to the window again, the letters unattended in his hand. It was snowing again. The flakes, large and wet, plashed against the pane as they flew from the darkening clouds. The walled garden below looked up in resignation as the new blanket was laid, further smothering the hopeful, dreaming seeds in the beds beneath.

What had he almost done! Fletcher's stunning confession and his happy exultation in the prospect of his future state of matrimony served to focus Darcy's mind amazingly. The temptation he had been offered, his unwarranted susceptibility to it, and the slimness of his escape provided him finally struck him like a blow to his stomach. Of what had he been thinking? Had he thought at all? Upon cool reflection, he very much doubted that "thought" had had anything to do with the encounter. He'd been drawn to her intensity and passion without consideration. The lady was beautiful, of that there was no doubt, and of acceptable, even honourable, lineage and station. Her intelligence, talent and grace were undeniable. Her infamous treatment at the hands of her family and his observation of her fierce defence of her new independence now she had returned had further attracted him, appealing strongly to his sense of what was just and right.

He had followed her, allowed them to be virtually alone together, and had almost succumbed to a strong, momentary desire to kiss her. Not only a kiss, he reminded himself, a chill creeping up the back of his neck, but a kiss conditional upon the denial of verities he'd assumed all his life.

The interview in the gallery and her open defiance of Heaven had finally roused him from the gossamer webs of his enchantment to the perilous storm that lay gathered behind Sylvanie's faerie-grey eyes. One embrace, one moment of weakness in surrender to the demands of passion and he would have put his family, his fortune, his very future into her hands.

Darcy laid his palm against the cold windowpane, welcoming the icy burn as he watched the snowfall with increasing speed. There would be no travel on the morrow, no matter how much he might desire to escape his situation. Not only had his purpose for coming to Norwycke Castle met with failure but the circumstances he'd encountered had served to harden his opinion on the unlikelihood of finding a woman who could drive the other from her residence in his mind. Fletcher had the right of it. Although she was present only in his mind, Elizabeth Bennet's shadow had eclipsed the Brilliants society had offered him, whether in the halls of the powerful in London or among old acquaintances in the country. Her winsome loveliness of character and person was the measure he'd held every woman against since their meeting—and every woman had been found wanting. It seemed as much a divine cruelty as Lady Sylvanie had declared, this unwilling attraction that bordered on an obsession over which his vaunted self-control could gain no lasting sway. What hope lay ahead for him, save to sacrifice all to gain what his heedless, traitorous heart was set upon? Could he do it? Or, having done so, would he regret the loss of all else he valued? Or should he stay his course, maintain that within which he had been born and bred, and eschew love and esteem to marry for his name. If not for himself, did he not owe his heritage to his children and theirs?

One of the letters fell from his hand. Darcy bent wearily and retrieved it, then sat once more on the chair Fletcher had thoughtfully positioned and brought Georgiana's letter up to the fading light. He hoped that all was well, at least, with her.

January 15, 1812
Erewile House
Grosvenor Square
London

Dear Fitzwilliam,

I received your letter of the 14th with great pleasure and assure you that I am as well and happy as may be without your company, my own dearest brother. Your friend, Lord Brougham visits often to assure himself that I am not languishing for company and to fulfil your charge, so he says, that he care for my welfare. Our Aunt and Uncle Matlock are quite charmed with his lordship and, as he is your particular friend, have given him permission to act as escort along with Cousin Richard whenever they are called away to their own affairs. I must, with shame, confess that you were quite correct about Lord Brougham, and that you have once again chosen well. His lordship is not so much a fribble as was my first impression. We have discoursed sensibly on any number of topics during his visits, and he has promised to squire me to lectures and private concerts that I had never dreamed to have the privilege to attend. His care for my happiness and schemes for the broadening of my mind are such that it is almost like having you with me, Brother.

I hope that you are enjoying your stay at Norwycke Castle and that Lord Sayre and his guests are the excellent, stimulating company you so enjoy. Our Aunt Matlock was rather surprised to hear from your letter that Lady Felicia and her parents are guests at Norwycke as well. Cousin Alex had expected her in Town but received a note that they were called away to deal with a family affair. Since the receipt of your news our cousin is not the best of company and can barely be in the same room with Cousin Richard, although why he is angry with him, I cannot say. Perhaps you know more of this, Brother, and could intervene? It distresses me so, to see them thus.

Dearest Fitzwilliam, I am selfish enough to wish that you are not having so enjoyable a visit that you will extend it too far behind the date you had set for your return. Although Lord Brougham is very kind, I miss you…dreadfully.

With prayers for your safe return,
Georgiana

Darcy carefully re-folded the letter and set it on the small lamp table nearby the bed. Dear Georgiana! It was wonderful how her sisterly words served to steady him, even as he read with resignation of his cousins' resumption of their quarrel over Lady Felicia. She "missed him dreadfully," even with Dy's overcareful attention to her well-being. And what did Dy mean by all this attention? Doing it rather brown, wasn't he?

The room was now in shadows; a lamp would be needed if he were to apprise himself of the contents of Brougham's letter. Darcy rose, lit the lamp by the bed, and took up his friend's missive as he settled once more into the chair.

January 15, 1812
Erewile House
Grosvenor Square
London

Darcy,

Pardon me for using your stationery, old man, but Miss Darcy just read me your letter and I knew I must write you straight away. You have landed yourself in a nest of vipers, my friend, for a greater collection of knaves, rascals, and simpletons could not be gathered from among our old schoolmates than are at Sayre's for this "do." I poked around Town after you left on Monday and found that Sayre is in the very devil of a fix—in a word, deep in Dun's territory—but his creditors are strangely silent on the matter. Only the merest whisper of a legacy through a sister's marriage could I turn up as reason for their odd restraint in bringing the matter of his debts to the authorities.

Had you any notion of a sister when we were at University, for I surely did not! Step carefully, my friend, for something havey-cavey is afoot at Norwycke! I would advise you to come back to London directly!

Miss Darcy is well and, I must add, delightful! What a credible job of raising her you have done, old man! I predict that she will have a very successful Season next year, but few, if any, of the young cubs in Town will interest her. They'll bore her into the ground or disgust her with their manners and "gentlemanly" pursuits.

Whatever your reasons for going to Norwycke, take my advice, Darcy, and come home.

Dy

P.S. Bye-the-bye, why did you ever allow your cousin to offer for Felicia? She is still determined to have you, you know!

With an oath, Darcy crumpled the sheet and shied it into the fire of the hearth. "Tell me something I do not know!" Everywhere he turned, the same message greeted him. Leave Norwycke! But he could not leave. The weather was against him in every way. The chamber clock struck out four, and at precisely the last note, a knock sounded at the dressing room door.

"Do you desire anything before going down to tea, Mr. Darcy?" Fletcher bowed after Darcy's call to enter.

"Why, yes, Fletcher," Darcy replied, his voice heavy with sarcasm. "See about getting the snow to stop, there's a good man!"

"The snow, sir?" Fletcher's puzzled countenance changed to one of concern. "Your letters, Mr. Darcy! Nothing amiss, I hope!"

"Not in London! All that is amiss is located precisely where we stand." Darcy laughed ironically. "It would appear that even Lord Brougham bids me hie myself away from here post haste, for in his words, I am 'landed in a nest of vipers!'"

"An apt description, sir!" Fletcher nodded sagely.

"Yes, well—I cannot hie myself away, can I? This blasted snow!" He walked over to the window where Fletcher joined him and both cast an eye upward.

"Well," Fletcher sighed as he drew back from the sill, "I can do no more than any mortal about the weather and that is to pray Providence for it to cease." Darcy snorted at his words. "Do you go down to tea, sir?"

"Yes, I suppose I must." Darcy saw and raised Fletcher's sigh. "I require nothing at present." He looked back at his valet from the bedchamber doorway but paused on the threshold, struck by something he had forgotten. "Except that you have a care when you go about below stairs. When you interrupted us in the gallery, the old woman cast you a murderous look. Considering my foolish behaviour, she may well blame you for her mistress' loss of my name and fortune."

"I will, sir," Fletcher replied solemnly, "and you, Mr. Darcy, should exercise like caution. For when the lady realizes that she has truly lost the game, I would assume the same prospects for your own comfort."

~10~
That Perilous Stuff

Tea was already begun, all of the gentlemen being well into their biscuits and cakes when Darcy strode through the drawing room doors. A brisk survey of the room revealed that all save one of Sayre's guests and relatives were present; even the timorous Miss Avery was in attendance. The only member of the party missing was Lady Sylvanie and her absence at this time Darcy could not but count as a blessing. The gentlemen greeted him with enthusiasm and the ladies hardly less so. Lady Sayre cast him a languid smile as he approached the tea table, but as he extended his hand for his cup a graceful feminine one intervened.

"Lady Felicia." Darcy acknowledged her with a grimace that he transformed into the slightest of polite smiles.

"Mr. Darcy, allow me," said Lady Felicia, taking his cup and amending it perfectly with sugar and cream. "No one has seen you for an age today, sir." She smiled archly as she offered him his tea. "Last night's gaming or Sayre's fine spirits?"

"Neither, my lady," Darcy replied tersely to her assumption of intemperance. Then, with a satirical lift of a brow, "I have been exploring the castle. Lady Sylvanie was so kind as to offer herself and her companion as guides."

The shadow of pique that he knew would appear did so in a brief flash, but the lady swiftly regained her composure. "Ah, Lady Sylvanie *and* her companion? Surely, Lord Sayre or Trenholme would be a more informative guide. Lord Sayre!" she called over Darcy's shoulder.

"My lady?" Sayre joined them.

"Mr. Darcy has been on tour this morning!"

"On tour? Of the castle?" Sayre regarded him warily. "I would not wander far, Darcy. This place is a veritable rabbit warren, and one can get turned about very easily. Bev or I would be glad to show you 'round." His face suddenly brightened. "In fact, that is a capital idea!" He turned to the rest of the room. "Shall we make a party after tea? Just a short go-round of the place and then cards with the ladies. What say you?" The agreement with his plan was general, if lacking in enthusiasm, but enough was expressed to set the event into motion.

"Where did you go, may I ask?" Sayre turned back to Darcy.

"Everywhere, it seemed: the ballroom, the gallery…Lady Sylvanie was an admirable guide for one so long separated from her home," Darcy replied lightly as he waited for Sayre's reaction.

"Yes, well…her mother, you see. Irish woman." Sayre stumbled through his explanation. "When my father passed on she wanted nothing more than to return to her own people. Couldn't abide England, she said, without my father."

"I see," Darcy replied meditatively. "It may well be my lamentable memory," he returned, availing himself of one of Dy's disarming expressions, "but I cannot recall the merest mention of a step-mama or sister while we were at school or university. How came that to be, do you suppose?"

"Been wondering about that myself," Monmouth broke in on his way back from the plates of cake. "The lady is a beauty, Sayre, nothing to be ashamed of, surely! Beauty always an asset to any man, sister or wife, is what I always say. Unless you've been hiding her on purpose, Sayre!" He looked at him curiously. "Big trout on the line, old man? Don't want any little 'uns snatching the bait, is that it?" Lady Felicia laughed nervously at Monmouth's witticism, her eyes examining Darcy with trepidation.

"Monmouth!" Sayre growled, his face growing red, "I'd forgotten how vulgar you can be! Really, my lord!"

Monmouth took no offence, but merely grinned at Darcy. "I am right, you see, Darcy. Wouldn't be at all surprised that the big trout is you! Although," he tossed back to Sayre, "I might do in a pinch. Title, you see. But the ready is better, and Darcy is a surer card than yours truly." Monmouth sketched them a bow. "My lady, Sayre." He then winked at Darcy. "Beware, Darcy, unless you have determined to have the lady. And if you have not, send her my way, there's a good fellow." Stuffing another piece of cake into his grinning mouth, the viscount moved on.

Darcy smiled thoughtfully at Sayre before excusing himself to the table of biscuits. After securing a nice selection of the confections, he ignored Lady Felicia's look of invitation and took instead a seat beside the lately recovered Miss Avery. Here, at least, was safety, for the shy girl offered him no more conversation than a grateful smile and a soft greeting when he sat down. Unfortunately, they were not to be left alone. He had barely consumed one biscuit and enjoyed one sip of tea when Miss Farnsworth and Mr. Poole approached them.

"Darcy, Miss Avery." Poole bowed. "So glad to see you recovered, Miss Avery. It must have been a terrible fright...." He let the sentence dangle, a hopeful gleam in his eye.

Miss Avery drew back and looked in confusion to Darcy, who, with a severe look, answered in her behalf. "Yes, it was, Poole; and very ungentlemanly of you to bring it up."

"But, Darcy," Poole protested, his voice rising, "no one will tell what happened! I call it a damn scurvy affair when a man's friends won't tell him what caused a lady in their company to fall into blind hysterics and three of them to look like they'd seen the Devil!"

Hearing Poole's outburst, Manning came swiftly to his sister's side and, taking her hand, turned to Poole. "It is not a fit subject for the ladies, Poole." He glared at him.

"How can that be, as it all began with a lady?" interposed Miss Farnsworth. Her chin came up with unbecoming stubbornness, her eyes glittering with an eager curiosity. "Miss Avery survived the sight; may not we survive the hearing?"

"Miss Farnsworth, I hardly think..."

"That may be so, Baron," she interrupted haughtily, "but I am not alone among the ladies in desiring an explanation of what happened at the Stones. Come, we are sensible women all," she cajoled, "and have heard any number of ghost stories since childhood. We are not so easily frightened." She looked about the room and focused on the house's younger son. "Mr. Trenholme!" Trenholme returned her regard cautiously. "You began the excursion with the story of the Whispering Knights. Will you end your tale with the truth of what occurred at the King's Stone?"

Trenholme cleared his throat. "I would prefer not, Miss Farnsworth. A tale is one thing; what was out there was quite another."

Lady Felicia, shivering delicately at his words, linked arms with her cousin. "My dear Judith, I find I am all the greater intrigued! Mr. Trenholme refuses to give satisfaction. That leaves only Manning and Darcy to relieve our curiosity." They turned together towards the two men. "How shall we persuade them?" Lady Chelmsford and

Lady Beatrice then added their requests to those of the younger women, but Darcy noticed that Lady Sayre did not join them. Instead, she, Trenholme, and Sayre exchanged furtive glances.

"No!" The word rang out in the drawing room and the insistence of the two men ceased. In amazement the room turned to the speaker and waited. "I-I will t-tell what hap-happened," Miss Avery was pale, but a tenacity akin to her brother's seemed to animate her before their eyes.

"Bella, it is not wise…" Manning declared.

"I l-left my brother's side in some distress," Miss Avery began, placing her hand on Manning's arm for support, "and ran to the b-big stone so that no one could observe my discomposure. I ran…p-past the stone, but stumbled a few feet away. As I recovered my b-balance, I turned and saw it." Miss Avery stopped and closed her eyes. A great, tremulous sigh escaped her. "On the g-ground…at the foot of the stone lay a b-bloody bundle of swaddling that looked, for all the world, like an in-infant…a babe!" She looked up at her listeners. "It had been offered up, like in the Bible, like those horrible Philistines! Oh, George!" She turned then, shaking violently, into her brother's embrace.

Horrified cries from the ladies rent the room as Miss Avery's allusion was finally understood. Darcy leaned forward, alert to the various reactions to the young woman's tale, as even the confident Miss Farnsworth turned pale and, abandoning her cousin, leaned on Poole, who himself was visibly shaken. "Good God," he swore in a strangled voice, "you don't mean a *human* sacrifice!" The room was quickly in an uproar at his voicing of what was in all their minds. Monmouth no longer grinned, but wore instead a very solemn, shocked expression. Poole set Miss Farnsworth in a chair and rounded on his object. "Trenholme," he demanded, his voice rising, "what is the meaning of this! You knew the danger and yet would not say!"

"Get a hold of yourself, Poole," Trenholme hissed. "You always were a henhearted little cawker! What good would telling you have done? D'you think someone's going to creep into the castle and gut you in your bed, man?" When Poole burbled his attempt to respond, Trenholme shook him off. "Besides, as Darcy will testify, it weren't a babe. It was a piglet from the farms. It only looked like an infant."

"A piglet?" Monmouth entered the fray. "A piglet in swaddling, Trenholme? A rather gruesome trick."

Trenholme's face darkened. "Trick! How dare you, sir!"

"Bev!" Lord Sayre addressed his brother with a firm and, Darcy suspected, restraining hold upon his shoulder.

"Damn me, Sayre, if I'll take the blame for this!" Trenholme twisted from his grasp and stalked to the fire.

"I've begun inquires in the villages surrounding Chipping Norton." Sayre looked first at Poole and Monmouth before turning to address the entire company. "But unfortunately, the weather has impeded those efforts and I expect that nothing will be known for several days. So distressing were the details of this horrific discovery that I determined that nothing should be said about it. Beverly was merely obeying my wishes in the matter. It is my doing entirely, that you were not apprised of the particulars."

Mollified by Sayre's apology, Monmouth inclined his head and lifted his tea to his lips, but Poole was not appeased. "My lord, your inquires aside, what does it mean? It was not done for nothing!"

"How should I know, Poole," Sayre answered, more than a hint of affront in his voice. "I know nothing of the Old Ways, so my opinion would be no more than a guess. In all probability, it is the work of some poor desperate creature and for a reason only to be found in a deranged mind. But I can assure you, sir, you are safe at Norwycke Castle." Sayre's assurances, though thin, were eagerly seized upon by the majority for the sake of the evening if not for their own merits and the company broke once more into conversational groups. Trenholme, though, remained at the fire and nursed his tea, a grim expression upon his face.

They know! Darcy was certain of it. Sayre, Trenholme, perhaps even Lady Sayre. They know who did it and probably why. The story about making inquiries was a tale, invented to fob off just such objections as were raised while protecting their interests. Which were what, exactly? As he worked on his tea and cake, Darcy shifted through the pieces of information he'd acquired and came up with only one answer, the perpetual one—money! But the answer did nothing to paste the pieces together into a recognizable image.

Miss Avery sat down once again beside him, shunning the false sympathy of the ladies for a quiet corner and another cup of tea. Manning stood by her like a guard dog, daring anyone to press his sister further on the matter. "I am indebted to you, again, Darcy," he offered quietly. Their eyes met in silent understanding over the top of Miss Avery's braided hair. "Since you've had the tour," Manning continued disinterestedly, "perhaps you would fancy another round of billiards. Allow me the opportunity to *even the score*, so to speak." Manning's choice of words and the lift of brow at the last clearly signalled his desire for private conversation.

"I am most obliged, Manning." Darcy accepted his curious offer.

"As soon as my sister is happily situated, then?"

Darcy nodded. "I shall meet you in the billiards room."

"Excellent!" Manning replied evenly. Speaking lowly to Miss Avery, he helped her to rise; and after making their apologies to Sayre, he escorted her from the room.

~~~~~~~&~~~~~~~

"Pardon me, sir, but you must remain quite still with your head held so." Fletcher nudged Darcy's chin a degree higher and, taking the ends of the neckcloth once more in hand, began the first intricate fold of his masterpiece. Darcy rolled his eyes in frustrated submission, but did not dare to reply for fear that doing so would necessitate that the torturous procedure begin again with another fresh cloth. He *had* promised Fletcher, he reminded himself grimly, and tonight, his valet had declared, was the night that *The Roquet* should make its appearance.

He glanced quickly at the man before training his eyes once more upon the ceiling. Although Fletcher's hands were going through the motions of tying his victorious white linen creation, Darcy could see that his mind was absorbed with the account he had just related to him of his interview with Manning around the billiard table.

Lord Sayre had not been best pleased when Darcy had quietly informed him that he would not be accompanying the party on the tour of the castle. His lordship's forehead creased in irritation as Darcy gave his reasons and offered his apologies, but it cleared considerably when he mentioned billiards with Manning.

"Well, if you are to entertain Manning, that is all right and tight," Sayre acquiesced with a forced smile. "We shall return from our little ramble just in time for the ladies to change for supper. Then we shall have a little round of cards with them, some music, and later it will be off to the library." Tapping a finger against his nose, he warned with a smirk, "I hope you will not bleed too freely around Manning at billiards, Darcy, for I believe you shall have an opportunity to raise quite a breeze later tonight."
~~~~~~~

~~~~~~~~&~~~~~~~~

"Does his lordship mean to put up the Spanish sword tonight then, sir?" Fletcher interrupted as he passed Darcy his stockings.

"Quite possibly," Darcy replied before looking him askance. "You know about—?" Fletcher's raised brow gave answer to his question. "Of course you do! Why am I surprised?" "I have no notion, sir," the valet replied.

Darcy had waited until such time as he could decently expect Manning to be in the billiards room and then made his own way to their assignation. When he arrived, it was to the solid thwack of ball hitting ball as Manning sent the spheres speeding across the green baize.

"Manning," he greeted him as he unbuttoned his coat and shrugged it off.

"Darcy." Manning straightened and put aside his cue stick. The baron advanced toward him and then, to Darcy's surprise, passed him, proceeding on to the door, and looked carefully up and down the hall before closing it. "I find myself doubly indebted to you, Darcy," Manning began when he turned back to him, "and I loathe being in anyone's debt. I wish to settle, here and now!" Manning waited briefly for him to reply, but then ploughed ahead before he'd uttered any of the appropriate phrases. "Something is not right, Darcy, and has not been right ever since those women arrived."

"Those women?" he repeated.

"Sylvanie and that antidote of a serving woman she brought with her! This whole business is too smoky by half." Manning scowled. "Yet Sayre will hear nothing to the contrary, *do* nothing to settle the matter, save continue his reckless gambling. Soon, he'll not have a feather to fly with. "

"Unfortunate, no doubt," he replied, "but what does Sayre's imprudence have to do—"

"With you, Darcy?" Manning shook his head. "Monmouth was right on the mark. *You* are the 'big trout' Sayre hopes will snatch the bait and solve his problems for him!" He leaned across the table and fixed him with a solemn regard. "Darcy, you should know that with the leaving of Sylvanie from his house for yours, a heretofore unknown piece of property in Ireland belonging to the late Dowager Sayre will be sold and seventy-five percent of the proceeds will fall into Sayre's profligate palm. *That* is what it has to do with you."
~~~~~~~~

"If I am satisfied with the lady, what is Sayre's windfall to me," he returned, taking another page from Dy's book and feigning boredom. "I have no need of any property in Ireland."

Manning's scowl deepened. "But Sayre does, or rather the money from it, and desperately. So desperately that he will not look into the circumstances surrounding the affair, which are more than strange." He walked back to his cue stick and, picking it up, began sliding it back and forth between his fingers. "Earlier, you asked Sayre about his step-mother and he told you that she had left England for grief of his father, did he not? That was a lie!"

"Continue," Darcy nodded and picked up the other cue stick.

"Sayre and Trenholme hated the woman and her child. As soon as Sayre succeeded to the title and control of his father's estate, he drove them out, sent them packing to Ireland with no more an allowance than would feed a mouse." Manning pounded the end of his cue into the floor. "Yet, eleven years later, that same woman has, on her death, left the man who dispossessed her a tidy property on the condition that his half-sister is brought back to England and married advantageously."

"Just as I had already related to you, sir," Fletcher pointed out, holding a new-pressed shirt wide and slipping it over his shoulders.

"An admirably canny lady." Darcy shrugged as he examined the disposition of the balls upon the table. "She played her cards well and secured for her daughter a chance for a future."

"Rather too well, I should say," Manning returned. "Think on it, Darcy! Ten years after ridding himself of his step-mama and sister, Sayre has succeeded in running his estate nearly into the ground and is in dire need of cash. Meanwhile, the cast-off sister has come of marriageable age. Then an unheard-of case in Chancery Court is decided, awarding the dowager a piece of land, and not long thereafter, the woman dies!" His eyes narrowed. "Everything is so very damned convenient."

"Not for the dowager," Darcy remarked, snapping the tip of his cue against the ball and sinking his call.

"Perhaps, even for her." Manning looked at him sharply. "Darcy, Sayre has no real proof that his step-mama is truly dead or that the property even exists!"

What!" Fletcher dropped Darcy's watch fob on the dresser at that bit. "You are joking, sir!"

"Fletcher, have a care!" he warned, "and no, that is what Manning said exactly."

"What! You are joking!" Darcy dropped the cue upon the table and faced Manning. "On what basis was Lady Sylvanie recalled from Ireland, then?"

"A copy of the dowager's will and the testimony of her solicitor—a cousin of some sort, I believe."

"And Sayre has sent no one to Ireland to secure the matter?"

"Oh, one was sent to deliver Sayre's invitation and send Lady Sylvanie home to Norwycke," Manning replied with a mirthless laugh, "but during his first two months in Ireland he wrote only of delays and difficulties with the cousin and the Irish courts. The dowager's family lands are particularly remote, it seems, making travel difficult and correspondence almost impossible. Then, all communication stopped. Sayre hasn't heard from the man in weeks nor will he send another to find what has become of the first."

"Hmmm," Fletcher intoned as he passed Darcy the fob and seals.

"Are you saying, Manning, that Lady Sylvanie has perpetrated an elaborate fraud upon Sayre, and he refuses either to see it or to do anything more to acquire the truth of the matter?" Darcy demanded incredulously. "It is beyond belief!"

"Is it, Darcy?" Manning met his scepticism with steely certainty. "It is what Trenholme suspects; although he, too, would rather believe that all will come right in the end and this phantasmal property will prevent his brother from ruining them both."

Darcy took a breath to reply, but held it instead while he searched the baron's countenance for any intimation of deceit. Manning had known exactly what he was about and had steadily returned his regard.

"I have not yet convinced you, I see," Manning sighed. He laid aside his cue and, clasping his hands behind his back had stepped away from Darcy to one of the few paintings that still remained upon the billiard room's walls. It was of the typical sort, a spaniel bitch serenely gazing out at the viewer as her litter gambolled about her. "What I tell you now, Darcy, I tell you only because of the exceeding debt your kindness to my younger sister has laid upon me. But in discharging it, I lay my other sister open to your derision and must have your word as a gentleman that no hint of what I will reveal to you will reach her ears."

Fletcher went quite tense at that point, so much so that Darcy could almost have sworn that his ears literally perked. "Yes, sir?" Fletcher prompted him, Darcy's waistcoat hanging loosely in his grasp.

"You have it," Darcy replied, extending his hand.

Manning took it in a crushing but brief grasp before looking away from him and establishing some distance between them once more. Then, he took a deep breath and began, "You know, of course, that Sayre and my sister have been married for six years now; and as is very obvious, she has given him no heirs." His jaw worked in grim designs. "Nor has she had even the cold comfort afforded by the tragedy of a miscarriage. In short, nothing has come of the union, and although it is not apparent, my sister grows despondent—despondent enough to turn to other means."

"Mr. Darcy! Good heavens, sir! He must mean..."

"What can you mean, Manning?" he demanded. "Speak plainly, man!"

"In plain speech, then!" Manning made no attempt to hide the anger that the necessity for this confession suffused in him. "My sister believes that Sylvanie or that hag of hers can work some sort of miracle that will allow her to conceive. I do not know in what manner she convinced her or what promises were exchanged, but Letticia has put herself entirely in Sylvanie's hands in this. I think Sayre half believes her as well. For Letty's sake, for the coin he hopes to realize from the sale of the Irish property, and the outside possibility of producing an heir, Sayre will do nothing to gainsay his sister or appear to delve too closely into her affairs until he can safely dispose of her in marriage." Manning's gaze swung back then to meet Darcy's, piercing the guard he'd thrown up at such an incredible tale. "Believe what I have told you, Darcy, or dismiss it; I consider my debt to you repaid, sir, 'in toto!'" And with a curt bow, Manning had left the room.

"Almost finished, sir." Darcy could feel the whole construction draw his collar tightly around his throat as Fletcher made the anchoring knot. He swallowed largely a few times to prevent the knot's creator from drawing it so that he could not breathe or converse and devoutly wished that he could see the man's face.

"Done, Mr. Darcy. You may look down—slowly, slowly, there! Perfect!" This time when he rolled his eyes, Darcy made sure Fletcher saw him. Fletcher allowed himself a fleeting smile before turning to retrieve his master's frockcoat.

"Well, Fletcher?" Darcy asked as he pulled down the corners of the coat and began buttoning it up. Fletcher had dressed him all in black again, as he'd done for the Melbourne triumph, and as Darcy examined himself in the mirror, he found the entire effect as imposing as he could wish for such an evening as he anticipated.

"Commanding, sir, and elegant. Just what is needed this evening, if I may be so bold, sir."

Darcy snorted and shook his head. "You are most likely right, but I was more interested in the opinion you have reached concerning Manning's story. I believe he was telling the truth, at least as far as he knows it."

"I agree, sir. Such intimate details of one's family are not tossed about lightly, and Lord Manning is particularly closed about his affairs. His man is quite free about his lordship's female conquests, but, on any other matter, he is strictly silent."

Darcy strolled over to the dresser in search of his jewel case. The emerald stickpin that matched his waistcoat would do nicely. "You know what that means, then?"

"A great deal, sir. At the least it establishes that Lady Sylvanie, or more likely her maid, was the one who came into your rooms to discover something with which to fashion a charm. And it was, as I suspected, a love charm, sir. Given her ladyship's advances earlier today and," Fletcher cleared his throat as his master winced, "a-hem, your response, sir, I've no doubt she puts great store in its power."

"Yes, that…at the least," Darcy agreed as he retrieved the case from the drawer and laid it atop the dresser. "But more to the point, it goes a far distance in explaining Sayre and Trenholme's very peculiar behaviour and their present treatment of Lady Sylvanie. Sayre will do anything to see her married according to the terms of the will. Meanwhile, Trenholme chafes at Sayre's restraint of his animosity at being beholden to a woman he has always despised.

"And fears, sir," Fletcher interjected. "Mr. Trenholme fears the lady, the maid, or both as he fears that his lordship will gamble their patrimony out from under him. It is a wicked fearfulness, Mr. Darcy, that seems everywhere in the castle."

Darcy opened the case. The emerald stickpin lay glinting in the candlelight atop carefully wound silk threads. He retrieved the pin and, looking into the small mirror to one side, thoughtfully positioned it in *The Roquet's* folds. "You have not mentioned the most ghastly aspect of this shocking state of affairs," he looked over his shoulder.

"The Stones, sir?" It was more a statement than a question.

"Yes," Darcy affirmed quietly as he turned to his valet, "the Stones."

Biting down on his lower lip, Fletcher slowly shook his head. "Such a bloody, evil deed, sir! Could a woman…pretending that it was a babe…?" Fletcher looked up at him, his face stricken by the implications his thoughts were forming. "I can hardly credit it, Mr. Darcy."

"Nor can I," Darcy sighed. "Yet all our information points in that direction. Lady Sylvanie or her companion."

"Or both," Fletcher added. "Could it not be, perhaps, that someone else…an agent of one of them…did the deed at the Stones?"

Darcy frowned. "Unlikely. The sacrifice was either a demonstration of power or a bid to gain it. The one who hoped to acquire something from it was the one who performed the deed." He turned back to the jewel case, his gaze fixed on its contents. "Remember that first night we were here, Fletcher, and we saw a figure in the garden? Could it have been Lady Sylvanie?"

Fletcher drew out his response, "Y-yes, Mr. Darcy, it could have been a woman."

"I believe you are right, and I also believe that things cannot continue long as they are." Darcy reached out his hand and lightly brushed the coil of silk; then, coming to a decision, he plucked them from their resting place. Fletcher's eyebrows lifted in surprise.

"A good-luck charm, Mr. Darcy?" he asked in disbelief.

"Neither do I believe in charms, Fletcher," he returned, "but in this maelstrom we have stumbled upon, I find myself in need of an anchor, some still place of goodness and good sense. He held out the strands in his palm, "These slender threads remind me that there is such a place in the world."

"And so there is, sir." Fletcher nodded gravely.

"Stay within call tonight, Fletcher. No rambles." He headed for the door. "And I shall require your attendance in the library tonight."

"In the library, Mr. Darcy? Like Lord—'s valet?" Fletcher's face was a study of pleasure and surprise. "Very *good*, sir!"

~~~~~~~&~~~~~~~~

Supper was a light-hearted affair, an incongruous bark of frivolity that rode lightly on the wake left by the uneasy tide of revulsion that had arisen from the disclosure earlier that afternoon. As he looked down Sayre's massive table, Darcy was struck once more by the shallow nature of his companions. Once they had recovered from the shock of what had been found at the Stones, they dismissed it from their minds so easily, as one more *on dit* to add to their store. Sayre and Trenholme he could understand. Neither wished anyone to think on the incident further, both setting themselves to the distraction of their guests with a rare commonality of purpose. Manning remained somewhat taciturn, but for all his dark warnings, he was not averse to exchanging razor-edged quips with the others at table. Evidently, he had also decided to renew his flirtation with Lady Felicity, for he was often to be seen whispering at her ear and receiving pretty encouragements to continue doing so. Even timid Miss Avery smiled, almost flirting with Poole, who also enjoyed the attention of Miss Farnsworth on his other hand. Only Lady Sylvanie showed herself subdued.

He watched her covertly throughout the course of the meal. At every story or sharp jest, with every lift of his wineglass, his glance would flicker in her direction, only to see the same look of regal serenity, touched now and then with a faint, cool smile. Despite his knowledge, he began to waver. Later, he watched her openly as she delighted them once more with her harp. The sweet lull of her music caused him to question his own memory. Was this the woman who had challenged him so intently in the gallery and then offered herself to him in the next breath? Could he really believe that those slim, supple fingers that charmed such music from drawn strings were also capable of performing dark, violent acts on a night swept hill? The images were irreconcilable, but in what other direction could his information lead?

"I say, could we not have some dancing, my lord?" Monmouth queried when Lady Sylvanie had laid aside her harp. "Surely there is
~~~~~~~

someone among our company who could play a reel tolerable enough for dancing." Darcy need not have stifled his groan, for it would never have been noted above the ladies' exclamations approving Monmouth's plan. Lady Chelmsford was immediately petitioned to furnish the needed music. Assured of her compliance with the scheme, Lord Sayre rang for more servants to come clear the middle of the room and roll up the carpets.

Darcy rose from his seat and moved apart from the excited fluttering of the ladies as they went giddily about smoothing their skirts and adjusting each other's plumes. Finding Monmouth and Trenholme lounging near the hearth he made no effort to disguise his dismay at his former roommate's suggestion.

"I'd forgotten your dislike of dancing," Monmouth laughed, "but my friend, look at how it has stirred up the ladies." He paused and they all looked over to the other end of the room. "Such animation! Such flash and dash! Like a flock of exotic birds all a-quiver with anticipation, eager to try their wings with us."

"Ladybirds, ready to tease and pout," Trenholme smirked. "Glad to oblige them."

"Oblige them we must and still remain gentlemen," Monmouth agreed, his eyes glittering with expectancy as he surveyed the field. "Which means, Darcy, that you are required to uphold the honour of the breed and dance and flirt outrageously, or we shall all be put down as very dull dogs indeed!"

"I am certain worse things could happen," he snapped back at him, but Monmouth only laughed.

"Then what are you about, sporting that knot of yours if you don't intend to fascinate the ladies!" he retorted and left him for the other side of the room. Trenholme followed lazily.

Dancing! Darcy sighed to himself, dismissing for the moment Monmouth's comment on Fletcher's knot. Well, perhaps it was a fortunate turn after all. The level of intelligent conversation available was sadly lacking, the company being in no way distinguished by their interests or expertise. Such a glaring lack was not faulted on the dance floor, but a failure to engage in flirtation most certainly was. The ladies, he knew, would expect gallantry and a hint of naughtiness in his address as they met and parted throughout the sets. Just the thought of putting himself forward so with the collection of ladies present made him tired. Another sigh escaped him as he warily surveyed the room. Truth be told, the only partner who appealed to him was the very one he suspected of masterminding a vast and cruel fraud. A thought struck him. *Would not her wall more likely be breached by his attentions than his suspicious distance? If he appeared to fall into Sayre's hopes for him, might not something slip out, something that would help him unravel this iniquitous tangle of pain, avarice, and fear?*

He looked again to the ladies, now beginning to pair off with the gentlemen. It was not hard to discover Lady Sylvanie on the edge of the lively circle, standing aloof to its excited currents. Her companion had appeared during his inattention and was now engaged in setting her mistress to advantage. The hunched old woman reached up awkwardly and unpinned a single, lush curl of her mistress's ebony tresses. It fell down seductively over one white shoulder, twining past her bosom and brushing her waist. It was wantonly beautiful, and if it had not been for the coolness of the grey eyes she turned upon the room, Darcy knew that Poole, Monmouth, and even Manning would have been immediately paying her court. They could not have helped themselves, he judged, had she turned upon them the look she now directed at him. She held him intimately with those eyes, and he nodded his silent acceptance of her invitation. Only briefly was the contact broken when her maid distracted her with a tug at her sleeve, passing her something from her pocket, which Sylvanie smoothly tucked into the recesses of her bodice's neckline.

Steady on, he warned himself, as Doyle made her final, neat adjustments to her mistress's *toilette*. His right hand went inside his coat to the pocket, his fingers making immediate contact with what he had deposited there in advance of just such a need. He took a deep breath and in his mind's eye he saw her. Oddly, it was not the Elizabeth of the Netherfield ball whose stillness enveloped him. Rather, it was the one whose shoulder grazed his arm as they shared his book and whose curls he'd set into joyful dance by the breath of his singing that long-ago Sunday morning. *Goodness and good sense.* He moved forward, no longer mesmerized or, he vowed, deceived by ebony glory, soft white shoulders, or faerie-grey eyes.

"May I have the honour?" He bowed and was rewarded with a rare, true smile as Lady Sylvanie extended her hand. He grasped it lightly and turned her out into the middle of the room, joining the others who had already formed lines, and awaited the opening measures of a country-dance. The reel was a lively one, affording Darcy no more opportunity for communication with his partner than could be had by a knowing glance and a lingering brush of fingertips, but he concluded that the lady appeared more confident of him at its end than she had been at its beginning. It was enough, in all events, to dispose her to accept the offer of his hand in the next, which was of the more stately, intricate sort and, therefore, more suited to his purposes. Seating her decorously, he went in search of refreshment for them both and encountered a beaming, expansive Sayre near the table.

"Darcy, my good friend, what a picture you and Sylvanie present!" Sayre nudged him with his elbow. "And I have never seen her in such looks, so it must be your doing." Darcy murmured something polite, but Sayre would not have it. "No, sir! You complement each other perfectly in every way; *that* is easy enough to see."

"Smooth as cream with you." Trenholme came up from behind them and nodded in Lady Sylvanie's direction.

Darcy feigned a study of the selection of refreshments. "Cream, Trenholme? Not precisely your description of the other evening."

Trenholme's countenance froze for a moment and then relaxed into a self-deprecating grin. "Foxed, Darcy! You saw me. Drunk as a lord. Don't know what fool thing I'm saying when in my cups. Ask Sayre." He looked meaningfully at his brother.

Sayre laughed uneasily. "You know Bev, Darcy! It's not called Blue Ruin for nothing!" He went back to his former subject. "But Sylvanie is a beautiful woman, is she not? Accomplished, intelligent… carries herself like a queen."

"She *is* beautiful," Darcy granted him, knowing what would come next. Sayre's smile grew wider.

"Private, as well," he continued. "Doesn't plague a man with demands for gewgaws or entertainments, I promise you. Quite content on her own at home. And in her own home," he suggested slyly, "she'd keep everything in good order and her husband satisfied…in every way."

Darcy's grip convulsed upon the sharp edges of the cut crystal stems of the glasses he held, barely containing an impulse to throw their contents into Sayre's leering face. It never varied in content, this jostling for position and connexions through the ironbound conventions of matrimony, only in its vulgarity. Had Elizabeth's mother in Hertfordshire exhibited any more brass, after all, than had Sayre? He bent his will to the assumption of a casual interest in the game. "Her dowry? What could her husband expect from the marriage?"

"Five thousand clear, after the sale of some property." Sayre had the grace to look apologetic. "I am a bit at sea at the moment, you must understand, and cannot promise more until my ship makes port. Incompetent business manager. Fired him! You know how it is, Darcy."

He nodded. Yes, he knew exactly how it was! "Interesting." He gave Sayre to interpret that however he wished. "But the lady awaits." They all looked to Lady Sylvanie, who was in the midst of an exchange with her companion. "You will excuse me, Sayre…Trenholme?"

"Certainly, certainly, old man." Sayre waved him away jovially, as if permitting him a rare treat in allowing his attentions to his sister. Trenholme's feelings about their exchange were less discernible.

As Darcy approached them, Lady Sylvanie's companion drew a respectful distance away, retreating to a dark corner of the drawing room. Darcy offered her a polite nod and received a curtsy from her in response before extending a glass to her mistress. "My lady," he addressed her softly.

Her smile was slow; he could have traced its progress from her lips and through her cheeks until it came to rest in her brightened eyes. "You honour my companion, sir," she commented approvingly as she took the offered refreshment. "In all the time since I have returned home and of all the guests Sayre has entertained, only you have treated her in a civil, gracious manner."

"Why should I not?" he inquired of her as he took the seat beside her.

Lady Sylvanie's smile hesitated, "Indeed! But that is not the custom of Sayre or anyone else I have encountered. To them, servants are so many hands and feet and nothing more." She peered at him intently. "With you, I gather, it is not so."

"How so, my lady?" Darcy wondered, caution racing coldly through his limbs. Of course! What a fool, to forget that she would have set about gathering information about him, just as he had done concerning her! The hair and bloodstained cloth in his dressing room were not the sum of what could be found out about him in a surreptitious visit. What had she discovered?

"Your valet, sir," she returned. "In a word, a 'singular' man."

"'Singular' is an apt description for Fletcher, I grant you." He tilted his face down to her as he brushed the edges of *The Roquet*. "He is somewhat of an artist in his profession, but sadly, I am a very unwilling canvas. I do not know why he stays with me." What did she want with Fletcher? Had she or her companion discovered his other abilities or had his interruption in the gallery merely raised their ire?

"You do not?" Lady Sylvanie's smile returned. "The mystery is easily solved. Either you pay him a very handsome wage or he stays for love of you. I suspect that if you treat Doyle, who is nothing to you, with such care, you likely treat your own servants with even better courtesy." She sipped lightly at her punch. "You have their loyalty and their love. A rare thing in this world, Mr. Darcy."

"I suppose it is," he answered, uncomfortable with the perspicacity of her words.

"You suppose! Ah, your reply reveals much, my dear sir." Her intensity of manner increased. "You are so accustomed to it, that you give it no thought. You do not question why your valet has taken up residence in your dressing room, for example."

"Fletcher has his reasons." Darcy's mind raced for a likely excuse. "He is very particular, an artist—as I said—and found the distance between his accommodations and mine to be injurious to his standard of attendance upon me."

"I see." Lady Sylvanie tilted her face up to his, her lower lip caught delicately. "Do you suppose his loyalty and love will make way for your wife, should that happy lady come into being, or will he always be that close by you?"

"My wife, my lady, will have no cause to complain of Fletcher's attention to his duty," he replied stiffly, "nor will my valet's wife suffer neglect for cause of his duty to me."

"I am glad to hear it for your future wife's sake. The jealousy of servants against their master's new wife is a formidable obstacle to a woman's happiness. In the end, one or the other must lose."

Sayre's call to the floor prevented Darcy from responding to the lady's words, and he did not regret the intrusion. Her words were not lost on him, and he fervently hoped that his disavowal of Fletcher's propensity for interference in his personal life had convinced the lady.

Darcy rose and offered Lady Sylvanie his hand to the floor, escorting her to their place in the set. Her countenance and carriage were austere as she faced him across the correct distance in the dance, but the emotions her bearing hid had unwittingly communicated themselves to him through the fingers she had laid upon his arm. She seemed inordinately excited and pleased with his partnership, more like a debutante than a practiced woman of three and twenty, and he wondered how she contained the energy that he felt pulsing through her fingertips.

Lady Chelmsford struck the first chord and the company bowed to each other. Darcy stretched out his hand for the petite-promenade and once again was impressed by the strength of the lady's hold upon his hand and the tremors of nervous excitement that betrayed her outward poise at each instance of contact between them.

"I daresay you find country dances more to your taste," he opened as they met and then circled each other back to back.

"True," she answered. "The stiffness of the patterns is so restrictive, so confining. Do you not agree?"

"Confining?" he returned as he rose from a bow and took her hand. They both turned to the head of the room. "I had never regarded them so. Rather, I would call them orderly and precise, even mathematical."

The lady smiled, a beguiling light suffusing her face. "Mathematical dancing! How droll you are, sir!" It was now her turn to pass behind and around him. Darcy could feel the air between them stir with her amusement as she performed the passé and faced him once more. "Dancing is not for the mind, Mr. Darcy; it is for the body and the expression of emotion. Do you never wish to kick over the traces, live outside of order and precision? Or is mathematics sufficient for you?"

"Do you accuse me of having no feelings, my lady?" He returned her question in a bantering tone.

"Oh, no, sir!" she hastened to correct him. "I am convinced that you are possessed of feelings—all those of the orderly and precise variety!"

"A very dull dog, then," he concluded for her.

The lady laughed. "No, I did not say it!" She looked at him speculatively and then murmured when next they faced each other, "I think that you would very much enjoy life beyond the conventions, Mr. Darcy. The exhilaration, the power of life lived on the crest of passion, is life worth the living."

The fierceness of her words, in combination with his suspicions of her, set the fine hairs at the back of his neck on end as cold caution seized him again. With effort he continued to draw her out. "Power, my lady?"

A low chuckle escaped her. "Yes, power." Her demeanour changed suddenly, as if she had come to a decision. She looked up at him intently, "Is there something you wish, Mr. Darcy, that as yet you have not been able to obtain?"

Darcy's alarm increased "My lady, I do not have the pleasure of taking your meaning."

"Something you desire but is denied you. Something that—the sword!" Lady Sylvanie exclaimed triumphantly. "The Spanish sword in Sayre's gun room!" The smile that caressed her lips was one of poetic satisfaction. "He baits you with it, does he not? Yes, that is perfect." The steps of the pattern separated them briefly, giving Darcy little time to formulate a response. Should he encourage her or take steps now to end her mischief in Sayre's household? The first did not appear to present any danger. Her choice of a test was innocuous enough and would hurt no one, for how could she possibly determine the turn of a card? His second option was more problematical. What did he have to present to Sayre but her wild assertions from the gallery and now these from this evening?

The pattern brought them together for a final promenade, and as Darcy took her proffered hand in his, her slender fingers gripped his tightly. "You shall have the sword," she pronounced with icy firmness, "I so will it."

Darcy bowed to Lady Sylvanie in the final step at the dance's end, but the curl of his brow he affected upon his rising expressed his sceptical reception of her pronouncement. "My lady, if you think to prevail upon Sayre to relinquish the prize of his collection merely upon your desire of it, I beg you will abandon such a course," he drawled in words designed to provoke her. "Whatever your 'will' in the matter, he *will* not, I assure you!"

Raising her chin to his challenge, Lady Sylvanie laid her hand upon his arm and regarded him with a brilliant eye. "I will ask nothing of Sayre," she whispered, her ebony curl brushing his sleeve. "You shall see; he is easily bound." She turned to him as they neared her chair and signalled that she did not wish to rest. Instead, her hand caressed his arm. "His fortune at play tonight will force him to put it on the table." She looked up at him from beneath elegant dark brows. "And when it is yours, we shall hold a *private* celebration and speak, perhaps, of future possibilities."

Both Darcy's brows rose briefly at her suggestion, but he delivered a smooth, "As you wish," in reply before bowing and making a strategic remove. Availing himself of another glass of punch, he slowly navigated his way past a very smug-looking Sayre and through the rest of the company, retreating to a quiet place in the shadow of a window. Raising the glass to his lips, he turned to the moonless dark and swallowed half of the concoction of sweet liqueurs as his mind reeled at the recent exchange.

Good Lord, not only was the lady very likely guilty of perpetrating a far-reaching fraud upon her stepfamily, but she truly believed she had the power to bend events to her will! The bundle at the foot of the King's Stone sprang unbidden to his mind, its ghastly purpose now clear. It had been a calling forth, a bid for the bestowal of power from a cast-down prince, and the supplicant was acting, sure of her answer. That such a thing were possible Darcy could not accept, but neither could he completely banish it from consideration. For, if Sylvanie believed herself so empowered, the influence of that belief alone was capable of wreaking untold havoc. What should be his course? A short, bitter laugh escaped from him as he considered the coils of intrigue his simple matrimonial search had woven.

Sweet are the uses of adversity. Again, it appeared, he was confronted with the mysterious workings of Providence. *Well, my dear Mrs. Annesley, explain this to me once more, if you please!* Darcy almost wished he had her in front of him to make an answer, but he must, it seemed, muddle through on reason and common decency alone.

~11~
Gentleman's Wager

Darcy emptied the contents of his glass and turned just as Poole approached to demand his making of a fourth couple with Lady Beatrice. Placing the glass on an available tray, he traversed the room to the ladies' side, offering his hand and as pretty and meaningless a speech as he was able. The lady gracefully received his meagre compliments with perfect understanding, and they took their places in the square. As he anticipated the start of another country-dance, he looked for Sylvanie, but she was not among the dancers.

"Called away, Mr. Darcy." Lady Beatrice turned to him in the beginning courtesy with a knowing smile. "Lady Sylvanie and her serving woman left shortly after you parted, should you desire to know." Darcy felt a flush rise to the level of Fletcher's blasted knot.

"Indeed," he replied indifferently and proceeded to ignore her speculative glances throughout the dance. It was not until some time later, after the last dance of the evening's gathering was announced, that Lady Sylvanie returned, although without her companion. Darcy espied her from the corner of his eye as he set Miss Farnsworth into a turn under his hand. When the last chord sounded he hurriedly performed his bow to the lady, but Lady Sylvanie's eyes had already passed over him and come to rest upon Sayre. Her chin high, she accosted him in conversation with Lord Chelmsford and drew him apart with a show of humble insistence. Too distant from their exchange to overhear her words, he could not misinterpret their effect, for it was plain that what the lady said had not found a home with her listener. Sayre's face turned first wary, then displeased. He looked about the room in agitation as his half-sister continued to speak. Then something she said arrested his attention. He blanched. His eyes flicked to Darcy and then back to her as he bent to whisper something. Lady Sylvanie nodded and the colour returned to Sayre's face. He nodded back curtly, and the two parted.

Darcy was certain the exchange had to do with the sword. The lady had demanded her brother put it down in play and, it appeared, had won the day. But to his surprise, the prized weapon had nothing to do with the announcement Sayre called the room to attend. "Gentlemen, gentlemen!" he boomed above the sea of conversation, "*AND* ladies!" The room quieted. "It has been brought to my attention that the dancing has so pleased the ladies that they are persuaded that the evening should not yet end. It is proposed that tonight, if they so choose, the hardy females among us be welcomed to observe the gentlemen in our night's battle of chance."

Along with the other men, Darcy stood in astonished silence at the proposal. Ladies present during a night of gambling? He'd heard whispers of such at parties hosted by His Highness's closest friends, but what was this? In contrast, the young ladies seemed very taken with the idea, and it was their enthusiasm that recalled the gentlemen from their dumb surprise into a tentative, then zealous display of approval of the scheme.

"Sayre!" shouted Monmouth above the hum, "I propose your metaphor be turned to fact and that the 'battle' be engaged in the honour of each gentleman's own lady!" He turned a wicked grin upon the twittery bevy of silk and added, "Of course, each lady must favour her champion with a token to display on the field, something intimate of her person, to spur him on, a charm—as it were—to provide him luck at the table." The outcry from the ladies that greeted his demand was one of deliciously scandalized delight, and immediately the women set about in frantic searches of their costumes for ribbons, lace, or handkerchiefs which might answer Lord Monmouth's requirement.

It was then that Lady Sylvanie came to him, her lips curled in a derisive smile that invited him to join her in amusement at the scrambling and posturing of the others. Without a word, she brought from the warmth of her bodice a scrap of white linen bound into a small bundle with a strip of leather, and taking a pin embedded in her dress for the purpose, pinned the token to his lapel, directly atop his heart.

"What is this, lady?" Darcy asked in a whisper. For all his suspicions of her, her closeness and their intimate contact were still not easily dismissed.

"My favour, Sir Knight, were you not listening?" she teased him.

"But you could not know that Monmouth would suggest such a thing. This 'favour' was not lately made."

"No, not 'lately' made, you are correct," she smiled as she tested the charm's security on his breast, "but of far greater worth than the trumpery now being exchanged. You see, everyone believes in luck. It is merely a matter of degree…or daring."

"'Dare' I ask what it contains?" he returned, hiding his distaste behind a show of wit. Given what he suspected of her, the possibilities were revolting.

"This and that," she answered lightly. Then looking up at him through thick, black lashes she added, "It will not fail us. Later, when all is well and we are private, I will show you."

Sayre's voice called them all to order with a command to the gentlemen that they escort their fair ladies to the library. The excited pairs took their places, and it was soon seen which of the females had dared to accept the invitation. Lady Felicia's presence on Manning's arm did not surprise Darcy in the least, nor the disclosure that Miss Avery would be retiring at her brother's command. Lady Chelmsford also declined to pierce the mysteries of the gaming table, declaring herself too fatigued to begin a new amusement. Miss Farnsworth had bestowed her favour upon Poole, Lady Beatrice's hand rested on Monmouth's arm, and Lady Sayre clung to her lord. To Darcy's mind, she appeared somewhat agitated, and he could well imagine that Sylvanie's interference in her designs for the evening had not been received with equanimity.

Sayre and his lady took the head of the line and the company proceeded to the library under their lead. Darcy cocked his head in wordless invitation to Lady Sylvanie and offered his arm. With equal hauteur, the lady obliged him and they took their station. Their procession to the library was stately and conducted with only a solitary lamp held high by a manservant to light their way through the shadowy corridors. Aside from the two servants who opened the library's doors, Darcy saw not a single soul but those of the company.

The library itself was transformed. The bare library shelves had been arranged with candles, a hearty fire crackled in the hearth, and around the room were set chairs and tables for the ladies. To one side the board, which usually supported only the stronger beverages, now boasted the lighter fair favoured by ladies as well as the sterner stuff required by the gentlemen. In addition, serving dishes of sliced bread and cold meats, along with chicken salad and fruit, competed with the tall amber and green bottles for the company's attention. But most compelling was the repositioning of the gaming table. It now occupied the middle of the room, and all else was arranged around it in receding circles. The gentlemen's chairs were already drawn up and at each place rested a card. A quick survey confirmed Darcy's expectation. His card placed him facing the nearby window. He looked back at the woman on his arm who returned him a percipient smile. But even as he nodded his understanding, the smile suddenly fled her face; and her hold on his arm convulsed, her attention wholly caught by something behind him.

"Good evening, sir…my lady." Fletcher's welcome voice came from behind Darcy's shoulder. *Thank God!* Darcy exhaled deeply while the tension of the evening abated. He turned to acknowledge his trusted ally.

"Fletcher?"

"Mr. Darcy." Fletcher bowed deeply. "All is in readiness, sir." He rose and met Darcy's eyes only briefly before adding in a meaningful accent, "I have seen to all myself." If he understood Fletcher aright, then he had examined the tables and chairs for hidden compartments and assured himself of the inviolate purity of the packs of cards that lay unbroken in their seal-bound boxes. "Good man." Darcy nodded his approval. "May I prepare a plate for you, sir? Or her ladyship?" Fletcher's gaze passed blandly from Darcy to Lady Sylvanie. "A glass of wine, perhaps?"

"My lady?" Darcy inquired, looking down into Sylvanie's face. Her eyes, he observed, were stormy and narrowed upon Fletcher in an alarming manner, and her hold upon his arm had not diminished since her first sight of him. To his supreme credit, neither Fletcher's face nor his posture indicated notice of the lady's animosity. Nor did he flinch from his purpose, for he stood his ground with his inquiry and waited in seeming polite, disinterested silence for a response.

The tension of her clasp lessened, and with a brief glance at him, she answered, "A glass of wine is all I shall require for the evening."

"Very good, my lady." Fletcher turned to his master. "Sir, his lordship has ordered broken open a bottle that has aroused some interest among the gentlemen. Would you care to examine it before I procure you a glass?" The polite disinterest Fletcher had turned upon Lady Sylvanie still ordered his features, but new as they both were to this sort of game, Darcy did not need a sign painted for him.

"My lady," he addressed her carefully, "may I escort you to a chair before seeing to this bottle?"

"You may," she answered smoothly and indicated a chair immediately behind and to the right of the one assigned to him at the table. "I shall be most comfortable. We both shall, as you come to understand." She lightly caressed the token at his breast and then, with a secret smile, allowed him to conduct her to her place. Repressing a shudder at the dark, conspiratorial temper of her words and the satisfaction of her countenance, he seated her and strode directly to Fletcher at the board.

"Yes?" he hissed to him as he took the bottle Fletcher handed him and feigned a serious contemplation of the label.

"Something is happening, sir. The old woman had everyone in a state over the preparations for this game tonight. Is it not unusual for ladies to be present, sir?"

"Yes, in my experience; although I've heard—but that is not to the point. The servants are disturbed, you say?"

"Indeed, Mr. Darcy, but not only due to the sudden change. The snow ceased some hours ago, and servants caught in Chipping Norton by the storm have finally gotten through to the castle. It is the rumour they've brought, sir, that has the under-household in such a ferment." He paused and his eyes fell upon Lady Sylvanie's token. "What is that, sir?" he whispered in a horrified voice.

"Lady Sylvanie's 'token' for luck tonight at the table. Forget it, man! What is this rumour?" The effort to keep his voice and body from expressing his agitation was near choking him.

His gaze still focused on the token, Fletcher's voice quavered. "The rumour, sir, is that a child is missing, a boy-child of one of Sayre's poorest tenants. A babe, really, not yet old enough to walk."

"What!" he hissed and looked involuntarily to Lady Sylvanie. The lady cocked her head in question at him in such a way as to communicate that her patience for his conversation with his valet was wearing thin. *A child missing! Good God!* Darcy's stomach turned as he warred against the fear rising in him that the scene he'd come upon at the Stones was about to be played out in truth. If this was so, the danger of the situation was now multiplied, but he could not multiply himself, nor could he send Fletcher out to turn over the entire castle single-handedly. Neither could he call upon Sayre. What did he have but his suspicions and servants' gossip? He saw his only course and set it into motion. "I must take my seat, and you must attend me; but I will send you on various 'errands' during the game. See what you can learn, but for God's sake, Fletcher, take care!"

"Yes, sir." Fletcher breathed deeply and nodded, then indicated the bottle. "Do you wish anything, sir?"

"Not this!" Darcy dismissed the ancient bottle of Scotch whiskey. "A thimble of port for now will suffice. Your news..." He left the sentence unfinished and dismissed Fletcher to procure the wine and port and turned back to the room.

The other gentlemen, glasses in hand, were taking their seats at the table while the women floated toward theirs, giddy with excitement at their daring in attending an activity from which they had heretofore been excluded. Lady Sylvanie waited for him, her pose one of patient calm; but when he took his seat, she reached out her hand, her fingertips brushing his, and he knew that the fire he had detected during their dance was returned. He forced himself to respond in kind to her smile, but in truth, he could now barely stand to be near her. Uncomfortable at the realization that she would be always at his back throughout the night's play, he was again thankful that he had thought to require Fletcher's attendance.

In a few moments, Fletcher approached them at the table, two glasses in hand, and Darcy marvelled again at the impassivity in his face and demeanour. "Mr. Darcy, my lady," he murmured as he handed them their glasses. Then, at Darcy's nod, he took up a position on his master's left.

"Does your valet stay with you?" Lady Sylvanie asked in a tight voice, belying the smile on her lips. "I was not aware that such a thing was done."

"No more so than the presence of gentlewomen," he replied evenly just as Sayre, sitting opposite him, rapped the table for everyone's attention. Chairs were pulled up to the large, round gaming table that Sayre had specially commissioned in more prosperous times. Manning took the chair to Sayre's left and Poole appropriated the next at Darcy's right. On Darcy's left sat Monmouth, followed by Chelmsford. As had been his custom, Trenholme did not join them at the table but hovered about the rim of play, anxiously watching his brother while soothing his fears with liberal amounts of whatever libation lay at hand.

"There now, shall we begin?" Sayre reached for one of the packages of cards and offered it to Manning. Manning obliged him, taking it and breaking open the seal before handing it on to Poole, who shook the cards from their wrapping and passed the deck back to Sayre. "Is Primero agreeable?" He looked 'round the table and, encountering no opposition, began to remove the unneeded 8s, 9s and 10s. The amendment completed, he then shuffled the deck and dealt out two cards each.

Darcy picked up his cards. The 4 and 7 of spades—a Numerus of 35—possibly the beginning of a Fluxus but not enough to tempt him to place a bid. He flicked his hand to pass as Manning and Poole had before him. Monmouth and Chelmsford did the same. Evidently, no one was feeling lucky as yet. Sayre dealt out the remaining two cards each and placed the deck to one side. A wave of expectation flowed around the table as the ladies bent forward to see what their champions had drawn. Darcy's gaze flickered through the assemblage about the table, assessing the expressions of each lady's face as the gentlemen brought up their new cards and arranged them in their hands. The other players did the same, and Darcy experienced his first satisfaction with the evening when their glances rested briefly on the lady behind him and turned quickly away. No, they would gain nothing by observing Sylvanie, of that he was more than confident. He palmed his two new cards and assessed his hand: an ace of spades and a 2 of diamonds joined the other cards in his possession, now a Numerus of 51. He still had the outside possibility of gaining a Fluxus from the draw, but if the cards came his way, he held in his hand the majority of the lesser Maximus as well. He decided to pass and see what the draw brought him.

Manning passed, discarding two cards and drawing two, but Poole placed half a crown on the table and bid a Primero 30, an obvious underbid. Darcy passed as he intended and discarded the 2 of diamonds, and against all odds, he drew the 6 of spades in one draw, satisfying the requirements for both a Maximus and the more powerful Fluxus! He counted his hand, hardly daring to breathe, and came to an incredible total of 69, only one point short of a perfect 70. A light sigh of satisfaction accompanied by the rustling sound of skirts being rearranged drifted to his ears from behind him. Darcy's shoulders stiffened. Did Sylvanie mean him to credit *her* for the cards in his hand? He steeled himself against any such temptation to nonsense as he regarded his incredibly fortunate hand. No, neither the lady nor her devilish token had anything whatsoever to do with it! He set his cards face down on the table.

Monmouth staked Poole's half-crown and threw in a crown with a bid of Primero 36, to the delight of Lady Beatrice, leaving Chelmsford to pass and exchange two cards. The play was now to Sayre, who staked Monmouth and advanced two guineas with a bid of Primero 40. Manning looked from under hooded eyelids at the coins on the table and, with a careless smile, tossed out two guineas and another two along with a bid of Primero 42. Poole met it, and the play came back to Darcy. Two guineas pinged against the pile of coins on the table, followed by two more as he announced a Maximus 55. Poole flinched, but Monmouth gamely staked Darcy's bid. Chelmsford passed again, replacing only one card, and the play was back to Sayre. His lordship staked the two golden boys as did Manning, who peered sharply at Darcy and then advanced three more. Loosing his nerve, Poole passed, discarding a card and drawing a replacement.

It was now back to him. Manning obviously held much more than a Primero 40, but unless he held a Chorus, he had him. Without referring to his cards, which still lay on the table in front of him, Darcy leaned forward and placed three more guineas in the centre and advanced another five.

"Too deep for this hand," Monmouth drawled and passed. Chelmsford followed. Sayre bit his lip and hesitated for a few moments, but finally his fist closed around his coins and he met Darcy's five. Manning's gaze flicked between him and Sayre. Five coins joined the pile, but no more. With no one bidding, the hand was ended. Darcy carefully turned his Fluxus face-up on the table. He felt rather than saw Fletcher's startled response, but it was nothing to the reaction of the others.

"Good Lord, Darcy, a damned perfect hand!" Manning looked at him speculatively while the others exclaimed over the cards and then glanced over his shoulder at the lady.

"But one, Manning." Darcy corrected him, solidly meeting his gaze.

"But one." Manning accepted the revision and set about gathering up the cards for the next round. Sayre fell back into his chair, his eyes trained on Sylvanie, while Trenholme whispered heatedly in his ear. Darcy leaned back and motioned to Fletcher, who removed a purse from his coat pocket and proceeded to take possession of his portion of the winnings. Monmouth leaned around him and snorted, "Anticipating so good a night that you've brought your valet along to hold your purse, have you?" The question was tinged with disfavour.

Darcy suppressed a grimace at the jibe. Deciding, instead, to take the offensive, he returned dryly, "Been long away from London, Tris? It is all the crack to bring one's man to the table. Lord—'s valet even arranges his cards for him." Monmouth's visage darkened at the pricking, telling Darcy that his shaft had hit a mark he had only suspected might exist after reading Dy's letter. "A pit of vipers," he'd said, "knaves, rascals and simpletons." Well, Dy had certainly had it right. He usually did, confound the man!

"Darcy, we're waiting!" Sayre had dismissed his brother and now winked at Darcy broadly. "Your lady, sir!" At Darcy's questioning frown, Sayre motioned behind him. "Honour your lady, Darcy, so we can get on with it!" Darcy shot a glance at Fletcher, who returned it with widened eyes but no suggestions. With all the room's eyes upon him, he rose and turned to Sylvanie. Her hand rose languidly from her lap and slipped softly into his.

"You win me honour, sir," she said in a voice that invited him to more than possession of her hand.

"Your servant, my lady." Darcy clasped her fingers briefly and bowed over her hand but offered her no more personal a salute. A disappointed groan was voiced among the gentlemen as he took his seat, but the complacency with which he met their dissatisfaction discouraged further comment. Manning began dealing the cards for the next hand.

As the evening progressed and play became more intense, Darcy's winnings increased respectably. He did not win every hand, but overall he was more than ahead in the number of coins Fletcher was required to scoop up from the table. He also managed to send his valet on various "errands" in the course of play, but each time Fletcher returned with nothing more to report on the rumoured missing child or the activities of Lady Sylvanie's serving woman, who seemed to have vanished. If they were to discover anything, it would appear it must be from Sylvanie, and that fell to him alone.

One by one, the other men at the table dropped from play in favour of flirtation with their ladies or observation of the contest that was now reduced to Sayre, Manning, and Darcy. Trenholme would sit with them occasionally, but his anxiety over his brother's losses and his animosity toward his half-sister soon sent him back to the board for another glass, followed by an increasingly uneven pace about the room. Finally, Manning called for a break, to which Darcy gladly agreed. He rose and stretched in an attempt to work the stiffness from his muscles. Lady Sylvanie, who had risen during the last hand and refreshed herself with a turn about the room, now came for him and drew him to the window out which he had gazed earlier. The moon was now up, and it shone full and stark, every bit the stern mistress the ancients had imagined her.

"The moon is full," the lady observed softly. "Even she is with us tonight."

"Lady," he began, adopting a laconic tone, "what could the moon's interest be in tonight's all-too-mortal diversion? We are merely men playing at cards."

"Men do nothing 'merely.' You will come to understand that… in time," she responded.

"But you desired that I see the moon full. Why? Is there some significance in it?" he pressed her. If she regarded it as an omen, a signal for action, he must know.

"Have you never heard that the full moon blesses lovers caught in its beams, Mr. Darcy?" she laughed throatily. "But I had forgotten, such unmathematical a notion you probably dismissed years ago!"

This romantic turn was not getting him anywhere! "I have heard no mention of Sayre's sword tonight, my lady. Perhaps it is *your* notions that will be disproved tonight!" He flicked a finger at the linen scrap on his lapel. Lady Sylvanie's lips pursed in momentary displeasure, but she set her countenance to rights with a tight smile.

"He has not yet lost deeply enough, but it will not be long." She spoke with conviction as she looked into his eyes. "You see how Trenholme paces and worries him. He will put down the sword within the hour."

Darcy searched her face for some sign, some indication that she hid a darker secret behind her eyes than credence in the contents of a linen-bound charm and the force of her own will. The woman before him did not shrink from his examination. "Come," she whispered finally, "Sayre is about to begin."

After escorting the lady back to her seat, he took his own and reached for the cards, nodding to Sayre and Manning, who sat in readiness to receive them. The luck went very badly for Manning in the first two hands. As he played his cards, he continually shot narrowed glances at Lady Sylvanie and then back at his hand, his jaw set stiffly. Finally, after betting heavily on a Fluxus only to lose it to Darcy's Chorus, he threw down his cards, invited Darcy and Sayre to "cut each other's throats, if that was their purpose" and withdrew to the more agreeable pastime of allowing his wounds to be dressed by the amiable Lady Felicia.

"It is just the two of us now," said Sayre. He reached for a new package of cards and shoved them toward Darcy, who took them but made no move to free them from their wrapping.

"Should you wish to cry 'Draw!' I would not object," Darcy offered. Hearing him, Trenholme sat down heavily in Manning's seat and in a whiskey-soaked slur implored his brother to agree, but Sayre would have none of it.

"Draw, Bev? When has a Sayre ever cried 'Draw'?" his lordship replied in disdain and turned his back upon him. A murderous look crossed Trenholme's face at his brother's rebuff, and he lurched unsteadily out of the chair and departed to smoulder in anger in a dark corner of the room. "Now then, Darcy," Sayre's smile was as false as his good cheer, "no more talk of leaving the table with the winner undecided." He indicated the much-diminished pile of coins, which lay about him on the table. "I believe I have the wherewithal to mount a successful campaign. But as the hour is advancing and the ladies are tiring, I will bow to the necessity of bringing the issue to the point. I propose a different game and higher stakes. What do you say, sir?"

Darcy hesitated. His winnings for the evening were substantial. With no more than the ready cash of his quarterly portion added to it, he had no doubt he could bring Sayre to his knees but to what purpose? Sayre's ruin might be Sylvanie's objective, but all he really desired of him was the sword. The sword! That was the solution! Darcy glanced at Lady Sylvanie. Her eyes, urging him to accept Sayre's proposal, decided him. He would act and, with that action, end this charade on his own terms.

"Your proposal is accepted on the condition that I name the stakes." He might have shouted his counter-offer for the hush that came over the room.

Sayre's cheer faded, to be replaced by wariness that extended to his lady wife and his brother, who now abandoned his corner and drew near Sayre's elbow. "What do you propose, Darcy?"

"You may name whatever game you like, and I will put up the entirety of tonight's purse..." He paused for the gasp that circled through the room, "...against your Spanish sword."

"No!" Lady Sylvanie cried, but Darcy ignored her, his eyes trained upon Sayre.

"What do *you* say?" He pressed Sayre to respond.

With the eyes of the room upon him, his lordship's jaw quivered and then set. "Done!" A wave of excitement rippled through those gathered as Sayre shouted for one of the servants to go immediately to the gunroom and, on pain of the loss of his skin, bring the sword carefully to the library. He then turned back to Darcy and slapped his hand down on the table. "Picket," he announced.

"Agreed." Darcy broke open the new package of cards and gave them to Monmouth, who had retaken his place on his left. The 2s through 5s were quickly dispatched and the deck was passed to Poole to shuffle. While the noise of speculation rose about the room, Darcy noticed Fletcher at the door, returning from his latest "errand" about the castle. Excusing himself, he stepped quickly to the empty bookshelves, motioning to Fletcher as he did that he should join him. "News?" he demanded as soon as Fletcher rose.

"Sir, I believe a delegation of some sort is on its way to the castle. Torches have been sighted in the distance from the direction of the village."

"A delegation! Why do they come? What do Sayre's people think?"

Fletcher's mouth pulled into a grim line. "The servants who brought back the rumour about the child left their prejudices along with their coins at the taverns in the village. Her ladyship's companion, whether rightly or no, is credited with the child's disappearance."

"Then it is a mob, more like—disorganized, dangerous, and unpredictable," Darcy responded, "or we would have had the local magistrate here hours ago warning of it. Did you observe these torches yourself?" Fletcher nodded. Darcy thought for a moment. If this mob were convinced that someone at Norwycke had taken the child, it would not easily be deterred. "Any sign of her ladyship's woman?"

"None, sir," Fletcher replied ruefully. The situation was deteriorating rapidly. If the old woman had hidden herself and the child, the only person likely to know where they were in this cranny-ridden edifice was Lady Sylvanie. If, the thought chilling him, the babe was not already past finding. Had the price of the sword been the life of the child? He prayed it was not so.

"Stay by me and I shall inform Sayre," he ordered. "If he organises his servants to meet this 'delegation,' you follow along and discover their grievances. If he ignores it, apprise me of its progress toward the castle. I will endeavour that Lady Sylvanie does not leave the room, but if she does, you are to follow her. She is our only hope of finding them both."

"Very good, sir." Fletcher bowed his obedience, but concern was written plain on his face as he rose.

Darcy discreetly caught the attention of his host as he sat down beside him. "Sayre, I have it on good authority that you are about to have visitors."

"Visitors!" Sayre responded loudly. Trenholme's head came up straight at the sound. "At this time of night?"

At that moment the library door opened again, this time to admit Sayre's ancient butler, who advanced upon his master as rapidly as his age allowed, bowed, and began to speak before Sayre could object to the interruption.

"My lord, a number of torches have been seen on the road from the village. Is it my lord's desire to send a man out to discover what may be the cause?"

Sayre blanched under his red displeasure at his butler's interruption. For a few confused heartbeats he was dumb, his eyes wide. Then he rallied and pounded a fist into his other palm. "Cause! The cause is no mystery! Damn Luddites! They've come here as well," Sayre fumed. Alerted by his lordship's tone, several of the others interrupted their conversations to attend, but he waved them away. Darcy stared at him, a deep frown upon his face. Luddites? No one had heard of any of those ragged revolutionaries this far to the South, and although he could not be certain, Darcy could not recall any of the sort of industry the Luddites targeted being part of Sayre's holdings. "Gather some of the menservants and see to the drawbridge," his lordship ordered.

"But my lord," the man remonstrated, "the bridge hasn't been drawn since my father's day and *that* when he was a boy! I doubt it will work, my lord."

"Try!" Sayre bellowed. "And if it will not draw, then barricade the entrance. And send someone for the magistrate! Let him handle it! I am engaged in important business and do not wish to be disturbed further!"

The old retainer bowed and retreated to the door, only to be met by a younger version of himself entering with the prized sword cradled in silk wrappings. The two exchanged looks, and to Darcy, it appeared that the older acquiesced to the younger. An agreement had been forged, and it did not look well for Sayre or any other member of the household.

~12~
This Thing of Darkness

Alarmed by Sayre's angry rumblings, the other gentlemen, who gathered now about him, demanded to know their cause. "Barricades!" Lord Chelmsford roughly caught his younger cousin by the arm. "What is this, Sayre?" Manning quickly joined him and in the strongest of terms required that he also be informed.

"It is nothing!" Sayre glared at them both, then hissed, "The ladies, gentlemen! You are frightening the ladies!" That, at least, observed Darcy, was true. "Drawbridge, barricade, and magistrate" had been words clearly discernible across the room, causing the ladies to gather in a knot around Monmouth and Poole, their fear-widened eyes set in faces now paled beneath their artful paint.

"What is it, Sayre?" Her ladyship spoke barely above a whisper, advancing uncertainly upon her husband.

"It is nothing!" Sayre repeated, shaking off Chelmsford and Manning to gather his lady's hands in his own. "Some ruffians," he admitted when confronted with her searching gaze, "but the servants will deal with them, and the magistrate has been sent for. There is nothing to fear." Lady Sayre's anguished eyes travelled from her husband to rest upon Lady Sylvanie.

"Why?" she asked plaintively, her voice catching in a sob. "Why tonight? You promised it would be tonight."

"Hush, Letty." Sayre began drawing her toward the library's door. "All will be well. You should retire…I shall instruct your maid to bring you something soothing, but you really should retire for the evening." They were almost to the door when her ladyship seized hold of her lord's arm.

"You will come to me tonight, Sayre? Later—even if I should fall asleep. You *will* come! Promise me!" Sayre's reply was lost in the sound of the door opening. The murmur of instructions being given to a footman was all Darcy could hear, but it did not signify, for his attention was engaged elsewhere. After Lady Sayre's outburst, the eyes of the room had briefly turned to Lady Sylvanie, but interest in the drama being enacted between the Sayres had drawn them away again. With everyone's attention focused on the couple, she had retreated into the shadows of the library, carefully making her way along its perimeter to the door.

She is going to bolt! His conviction was certain, and putting action to thought, Darcy strode purposefully across the room. "My lady," he addressed her with feigned solicitude, "you cannot be so concerned with Sayre's 'ruffians' that you would desert us?"

"N-no, of course not," she replied, clearly angered by his interruption of her design. "Lady Sayre will desire my presence as she prepares to retire. I should go to her."

"It did not appear to me that it was *your* presence which she desired tonight." He cocked a brow at her.

"I assure you, she does, sir!" The lady's ire rose. "I…I promised her as much."

"Ah, yes. She did mention a promise; a promise *you* had made her." Lady Sylvanie's lips curved into a small, triumphant smile. "But, my lady, there is also a promise that you gave to me, that you should be 'my lady' this evening. My object is now at hand; therefore, I cannot allow you to leave."

"But, you do not p-perfectly understand." Lady Sylvanie struggled to control the tremor in her voice, whether from anger or fear, he could not discern.

"Does any man?" he countered wryly, then softened his voice to coax, "Come, Lady Sayre is well taken care of by her maid and serving women. Sit with me, and when I win the sword, you may go where you will. Or do you no longer maintain faith in your talisman…or the strength of your will?" His challenge stirred up the fire in her countenance, but that flame warred with an uneasiness she could not disguise.

"Darcy!" Sayre's call prevented him from pressing his advantage with the lady. He turned back to the room and Sayre who was already seated at the table. "We are ready to begin, if you would be so kind." Unable to resist the lure of the game or the nature of the stakes, the other gentlemen had successfully quieted their consciences on the fears of their ladies and were once more ranged around the table for first-hand observations of the contest.

"My lady?" Darcy offered his arm in a manner that communicated he would not brook denial. "It appears that our presence is *unquestionably* required." He rigidly schooled his countenance against any revelation of the cold uncertainty that gripped his chest at her hesitation. Fletcher had not yet returned, and if she refused him, she would certainly disappear into whatever hidden corner of the castle contained her missing companion. A small, fleeting smile was all that betrayed his profound relief when the lady placed her hand on his arm.

"Mr. Darcy," she acquiesced, pronouncing his name with terse, reluctant grace, her delicate jaw set hard. He led her back to the gaming table and her seat behind his right shoulder. Bowing over her hand, he then turned to the assemblage, nodded to Sayre and took his own chair. Glittering in the light of the candles, the Spanish sabre lay on the table between them, entwined in the silk scarf that had protected it in its passage through the halls of the castle. Beside it lay Darcy's purse, full to nearly overflowing with his night's winnings.

"Shall we begin?" Darcy looked straight into Sayre's eyes and was not ungratified to see him flinch from his stare. The man was unnerved, and why should he not be? An angry mob advanced on his estate; the strained loyalty of his staff was uncertain; his estate was in financial ruin; his relations held him in animus; vile, unchristian acts had been performed on his lands; his lady lay undone in her chambers above them; and now his prized possession was on the table. Pity for the man threatened to soften Darcy until Sayre reached for the cards. The hard, avaricious gleam that suffused his face once the instruments of his destruction were in his hand drove the impulse from Darcy's heart. If Sayre would sacrifice all to his passion, then so be it. He would not pity him but would reserve it for those of his household toward whom it was due. He wondered briefly how many of the servants and housemaids he might be called upon to absorb into Pemberley.

A click at the door brought Darcy's chin up, and out the corner of his eye he observed the welcome form of Fletcher returning from his "errand." "Your pardon, sir," he offered Darcy as he took up his accustomed place at his left, then, "Excuse me, sir, this seems to have been mislaid." He bent down and appeared to retrieve something from the floor. "A 'golden boy,' Mr. Darcy. Gone missing," Fletcher straightened and laid a bright, golden guinea on the table, "and Shylock without the door. I should be more careful, sir." Darcy nodded and tossed the coin into the purse. Fletcher's message was clear. The mob had gathered because of the missing child and was desirous of no less than blood for blood. He looked down at Lady Sylvanie's "favour," still pinned to his breast. He would have none of it. Whatever the outcome of the game, the lady must have no claim upon him. With deliberation, he pulled at the decorative pin, and as the talisman fell into his hand, a frustrated, angry gasp came from beside him.

"Madam." He turned and, with a cool smile, deflected the fire in her enraged eyes before dropping the linen scrap into her insistent hand. Turning back to the table, he nodded to Monmouth who stood ready with the coin for the toss. "Heads," he called as his hand, of its own volition, drifted to the embroidery threads inside his waistcoat pocket. *Goodness and good sense.*

Darcy won the toss of the coin and removed the 2s through 5s. He then shuffled the deck and offered Sayre the cut. That formality performed, he began dealing out the cards in tierce until both of them had received their dozen. Laying the last aside, he retrieved his hand, and quickly touting up his Ruff, Sequences and Kinds, he chose his discards, closed his fan and regarded Sayre with a raised brow. Across the table, with the purse and sword dividing them, Sayre arranged his hand in a heavy silence that was dutifully observed by all the gentlemen dispersed about them. He licked his lips; bit the lower and then the upper before breaking the quiet that had descended upon them.

"Blank," he coughed and then repeated himself. "B-blank." Trenholme groaned softly in the background, eliciting a sharp command from his brother to "shut his jabbernob." Darcy nodded his understanding and marked down Sayre's ten points in compensation for his unusual lack of court cards. His opponent studied his cards with an assiduous eye and, with jaw set as stone, discarded six cards and reached for replacements in the Stock. One, two…Darcy betrayed no surprise in Sayre's decision to replace half of his hand, but with a steady, disinterested regard, he waited for him to arrange his new cards. When they were finally ranked to his satisfaction, Sayre then reached for the next two cards in the Stock, and as was his privilege, noted them and set them back down. Relaxing somewhat, he leaned back into his chair.

"Darcy," he invited with a fine show of noblesse oblige, indicating the depleted Stock. Darcy pushed his discards over to join Sayre's and snapped up three from the Stock. Briefly noting their value, he set them atop the others in his hand, and lifting the last card, he committed it to memory and placed it back on the table.

"Your bid?" Darcy's modulated voice still carried across the room and seemed to echo off the library's bare shelves.

"Forty-eight." Sayre looked keenly up at him after laying out his Ruff of spades. The attention of the room shifted from the cards on the table back to Darcy.

"Fifty-one," he returned, displaying the diamond-pipped cards.

"Fifty-one it is," breathed Monmouth. "Gentlemen, you are both down for five points." Darcy gathered up his cards and waited for Sayre's next play.

"Six cards, ace high," Sayre announced and splayed them out in front of him.

"One Quart," Monmouth announced. "Four points to Sayre for a total nine."

"The same." Darcy pulled out his Sequence for Sayre's perusal. His lordship's gaze flashed expertly over the cards. A brow twitched.

"No winner," Monmouth reported, "but a Quint for Darcy for fifteen points, making a total of twenty. Gentlemen?"

"A Quatorze of Queens." Sayre threw down each royal lady as if they were at fault for his previous deficiency.

"Of Jacks." Darcy displayed his cards.

"To Sayre." Monmouth looked at Darcy with concern and put Sayre down for fourteen more points. "Twenty-and-three." His lordship's smile was more of relief than triumph and he hurriedly pulled out an additional Ternary for three more points. "Twenty-and-six, then." Monmouth touted up Sayre's points. "To Darcy's tw—"

A disturbance at the library door drowned out Monmouth's announcement, and the sight of Norwycke's ancient butler entering into the room brought Sayre to his feet. "What is it now?" growled Sayre before he'd had a clear view of the man, then, "Good God, man! What the devil has happened!"

At Sayre's first protest, Darcy had risen and swung around his chair, alert for any eventuality. He now stood by Fletcher, and the two of them exchanged warning glances as the old retainer stumbled further into the room. The man was a fright. His neckcloth, half undone, dangled down over his thin chest, and his powdered wig was aslant. His rheumy eyes were stricken with fear and, oddly enough, thought Darcy, sadness.

"My lord…my lord," the man gasped.

"Yes! Speak, man!" Sayre thundered.

"I could not, my lord! Served you, your father, grandfather…all my life. Could not betray—"

"Betray! Who betrays me?" Sayre's voice raged and echoed against the library's walls, wavering between anger and fear, and caused the ladies to demand what was the matter.

The old man swayed in the face of his master's fury. "The servants, my lord. They will not take up your defence at the castle gate. Some," he gulped, "some have said that they'll not defend the evil within from the righteous anger without. Give up the child, my lord, I beg you!"

"Oh, my God!" cried Trenholme.

"Child? What child?" roared Sayre. The question was taken up by the rest of the room as they rushed to Sayre, but Darcy swivelled around, intent on a quite different object.

"Fletcher! Where is Lady Sylvanie?"

While the whole of the room formed a clamorous circle about Sayre, Darcy and Fletcher scanned the shadowy recesses of the room in search of the lady. Several of the candles, he noted, seemed to have been extinguished, casting the edges of the great old room into darkness.

"There, sir, at the door!" Fletcher's clear voice galvanized him into action, and soon both men were circling around the other distraught, fearful guests in a bid for the door. That achieved, they stepped together into an empty hallway, lit only in one direction by a few feeble candles. Which way had she taken? "Mr. Darcy, I fear—" his valet began.

"Yes, into the darkness. Come!" Darcy plunged forward, Fletcher beside him, racing into the deepening shadows. They quickly reached a juncture with another corridor sunken almost completely in night. Another decision! "Listen!" Darcy commanded and endeavoured to quiet his breathing and the beat of blood through his veins. Faintly, the tapping sound of a woman's slippers disturbed the unearthly somnolence that seemed to hang heavily in the air. "There!"

"She is making for the older portion of the castle." Fletcher's whisper echoed eerily as they turned in pursuit of the sound. "She'll be the very devil to find if—"

"Then we must enlist the aid of Providence," Darcy said over his shoulder as he took the hall at a rapid stalk, his ear cocked against the tapping of his quarry.

"I have, sir, and regularly since we arrived at this...place."

As most men born to privilege, Darcy had long become accustomed to the presence of servants about their duties in even his most private apartments; therefore, the utter lack of any of that class in their traversal of the castle impressed him as singularly ominous. The old butler had spoken the truth. Little—if any—aid in defence of Norwycke could be expected from Sayre's people, and once emboldened by the numbers outside, it was more than possible that they might also take up the hunt for Lady Sylvanie and her companion. He and Fletcher must reach them first or who knew what outrage might be committed to haunt the halls of Norwycke and the consciences of its inhabitants and guests?

Ahead of them and around another corner, a door was heard to shut with a soft click. Rounding it first, Darcy was confounded by a Stygian darkness that, try as he would, he could not pierce. Evidently they had passed below ground. "A candle! Fletcher, did you see any candles?"

"A moment, sir!" Darcy heard his valet fumble about his clothing, and in short order, a candle was shoved into his hand. "Hold it before you, sir." Darcy stretched out his arm. Never before had the sound of a flint being struck been so welcome.

"You *brought* a candle?" Darcy caught Fletcher's eye in wonderment as the flickering candle created a hesitant pool of light. His valet merely returned him a crooked grin before both of them turned to survey the passage into which they had followed Lady Sylvanie. From the look of it, they were in a long-unused portion of the castle's storehouse, for a series of doors set in stone walls marched along the corridor as far as the meagre light of their candle could illumine. Holding the candle high, Darcy took a few exploratory steps down the corridor, his ear cocked to the side to catch any sound, but all was silent.

"Mr. Darcy," Fletcher called in a low voice, "the candle! Please, sir!" Darcy returned swiftly and handed him the candle.

"Have you discovered something?"

"When you walked before me, sir, I noticed—there! Do you see, sir?" Darcy peered down in the direction of Fletcher's finger. Footprints! Vaguely outlined in the dust of the abandoned hall were his own footprints where he had preceded Fletcher down the passage. If his could be detected, then could not Sylvanie's be also? Darcy straightened and, taking the candle, lifted it high again, searching for a disturbance in the dusty passage that was not of his own making.

Precious minutes ticked by while he ranged to and fro across the corridor but his careful search was finally rewarded.

"Here! Fletcher!" he shouted in triumph. Then, hoping that the door would not be locked from within, he pulled on the handle. The massive door, swinging back obediently on noiseless hinges, opened upon a room that seemed unusually bright after their dark passage through the castle. Both Darcy and Fletcher blinked and squinted as they stepped inside, their one small candle ridiculously faint against the light that now surrounded them.

"Darcy!" Lady Sylvanie appeared suddenly out of the penumbra cast by the many flaming candles. She advanced upon him, an imperious look upon her face. "You should not have followed me!"

Stung by her continuing hauteur in the face of her impossible situation, Darcy drew up and matched her will with his own. "My lady, 'should' or no is immaterial," he declared icily. "I am here and here to warn you that you can proceed no further. You endanger your brother's life, the well being of his guests, and the future of the servants of this house with this detestable course! Give over! A mob is at the very doors of the castle. Release the child to me, and I will see to it that you and your companion leave Norwycke unharmed and bound for wherever you will."

"*You* will see…!" she sputtered at him.

"You have my word on it, but you must understand this." He leaned over her, his eyes piercing, commanding, "I do not negotiate. Your game is played out, and you have lost!"

"You are mistaken, sir, if you think to frighten me or engage my sympathy for my 'brother.'" Lady Sylvanie's lips curved in derision. "What sympathy did he have for me when he packed my mother and me off to a cold pile of stone and moss in Ireland? Did he care that we almost starved?" Sylvanie's voice rose higher. "Does he quake before his god at the remembrance of what he has done to his own father's wife, his own sister, who shared his blood?"

"Sayre has, indeed, much to answer for—"

"And answer he shall! Tonight he was to have been called to account, if you—"

"If I had ruined him, as you hoped?" Darcy bridled. "What else? Was I to offer you marriage after I had brought him low?"

"If I wished it," she replied. Her eyes flashed insolently, then narrowed upon him. "And I may still." She turned from him then, hugging herself as she stepped away. "I *will* have vengeance, Darcy! I *will* see Sayre brought down!" She turned back to him, the faerie fierceness he had admired when they first had met glowing now with unnatural fervour. "It is promised me, and no one will deny me now!" Darcy looked at her in wonder. So deep, so unforgiving was the lady's resentment of her past and her family that she had set herself at war with all the world. If she had ever been whole, her looks and words warned him that now she was not. She had become instead a flawed, broken creature for whom the world was not atonement enough for her pain.

"You would destroy Sayre and all around him then, lady? Those innocent of your mistreatment as well as the guilty?"

"Have you never desired revenge, Darcy?" Lady Sylvanie's voice dropped almost to a whisper. Against his will, he stepped closer to catch her words. "Has no one ever hurt you, almost destroyed you?" Darcy froze, a chill frisson travelling as lightning up his back. "Taken what was most dear to you..." One name, excluding all other thought, burned in his mind. "...twisted it, defamed it beyond recognition or redemption?" Bitter anger rose from his heart so suddenly it almost choked him.

"Yes," she drawled softly, "you have. You desire it still. What is its name?" Wickham's smirking face arose before him as it had been when he had discovered them at Ramsgate—the triumphant mien, the satirical eye—then again, in Hertfordshire. "Remember it, Darcy! Think on what was done to you, to those you love. The betrayal, the pain." Georgiana! He saw once more the sorrow-laden shadow that had been his sweet, innocent sister before...Wickham. He had come so close, so very, very close to destroying them all.

He has been so unlucky as to lose your friendship. The accusation in Elizabeth Bennet's voice and in the eyes she had laid upon him arose in his mind's eye and flayed him anew. He saw himself that night, mute before her charge, his last opportunity to recover himself in her esteem—ruined! Wickham! A deep groan formed in his chest.

"You have suffered its bitterness long enough, borne the pain of it beyond endurance!" Lady Sylvanie's words drew him. "Reason will not soothe, logic does not answer; they have no power. Embrace passion, Darcy. Embrace 'th'unconquerable will, and study of revenge.' I can guide you, help you—comfort you—in the way!"

Revenge! The temptation she offered grew in his mind, and for a moment, Darcy allowed himself a glimpse into the desire that had lurked deep within his heart from the first time Wickham had deceitfully shamed him in front of his father to Georgiana's months of pain.

"But, the child, your ladyship," Fletcher's soft plea broke through Darcy's heightened senses and arrested Lady Sylvanie's flow of words. "Have mercy, dear lady!"

Lady Sylvanie hesitated, and then turned from him to face Fletcher. "The child will come to no real harm, save for a few plucked hairs and several nights away from its mother. Its usefulness is nearly at an end. Lady Sayre will be convinced she has conceived before the week is out, and then the child will be returned." She laughed, "Can you imagine! That cow! She believed my tale that if she suckled a peasant's child and swallowed some herbs, she could cure the barrenness of her womb. As if I would help her against my own interests!"

"Lady, you have no week." Darcy recovered himself from the mesmerism of her words. "You have only minutes before the mob that confronts your brother at this very moment descends into this hall in search of that child." He advanced upon her, determined to force the issue. "I say again, my lady, give over. It is all ended. Bring him to me now, or your safety can in no wise be certain."

"Give over! When all is within our grasp?" The voice rang out strongly and echoed against the chamber's stone walls. A door set low in the wall and down a few steps behind Lady Sylvanie opened, and the bowed shape of her companion ascended the stairs, a child limp in her arms. "The time is at hand, and we stand in no need of *your* feeble help!"

"Doyle!" Lady Sylvanie gasped sharply as the old woman pushed her aside and faced Darcy.

"Mr. Darcy has worked it all out, have you not, Mr. Darcy? Or is it your manservant who has pieced it all together? Clever man," she sneered, "but not clever enough. Men never are." Darcy's astonishment at her boldness was nothing to his doubt of his senses when the crippled serving woman seemed to grow before his eyes. Her preternatural increase in stature was matched by a decrease in age as, with a mocking smile that was now level with his face, she untied her widow's cap and threw it from her. Hair black as night touched lightly with streaks of grey, tumbled down about her shoulders.

"Lady Sayre!" exclaimed Fletcher, in awe at the now straightened figure that stood defiantly before them.

"Yes, Lady Sayre," she answered him, but did not take her eyes from Darcy. "Not that plaything upon which my step-son has lavished the title. Twelve long years it has been, and all would have been set to right already tonight, Mr. Darcy, if you had acted as you were bid." Her eyes slid to her daughter. "He is right in one thing, Sylvanie. We must leave now, but we do not leave empty-handed, defeated. We will have our full measure of—"

With her attention diverted from him, Darcy made to seize the child; but as he made his move, the woman brought a small, intricately carved silver dagger to the child's throat. "Mamá!" Lady Sylvanie cried as Darcy froze, his eyes flying to meet hers in alarm. "What are you doing?"

"'*Une femme a toujours une vengeance prête,' ma petite*!" Lady Sayre replied with a laugh. "Stand away from the door, sirs!"

From the corner of his eye, Darcy could see Fletcher slowly moving around them. "What will you do with the child once you are free of Norwycke, ma'am?" Darcy demanded, centring the lady's attention upon himself.

"I think you know, Mr. Darcy."

"Another visit to the King's Stone? It has been you; has it not? Rabbits, kittens, *pigs*..." Lady Sayre's lips twitched as he catalogued her activities. "It was you I saw that first night, returning from the Stone and your latest—" his face darkened with disgust. "In point of fact, the entire plan has been yours from the beginning. Tell me, is Sayre's agent still alive, or is he buried in some forgotten place in Ireland?"

"Tell him it is not so, Mamá," Lady Sylvanie looked desperately at her mother, but she did not reply. "The child is in no danger," she declared again hotly as she turned to Darcy, "and the man was paid off. I saw the purse! He is somewhere in America!"

"Truly, my lady?" Darcy addressed Lady Sayre in a voice heavy with sarcasm. "Sayre's man is living happily in America, and the child will remain unharmed?"

"Tell him, Mamá!" Sylvanie's eyes glistened with anger. At that moment a shout echoed faintly from somewhere in the castle.

"The rabble from the village has breached Sayre's defences," Darcy observed calmly to Lady Sayre. "Most likely they are ranging through the castle as we speak. Madam, I believe you have run out of time."

"Sylvanie, leave us!" Lady Sayre ordered, her eyes flaming.

"Mamá, I cannot *leave* you—"

"Go, now! You know where!" cried Lady Sayre. With a low wail, Sylvanie shook her head, tears streaming down her face. "Sylvanie, obey me!"

"Mamá," she sobbed, and turning away, she stumbled out the door into the black corridor. They listened to her running footsteps until they faded into the darkness.

"You have destroyed her; you must know that," Darcy whispered.

"You know nothing," Lady Sayre spat at him. She shifted the child in her arms. Throughout the whole of their interview he had not stirred. Darcy decided he must be drugged and that it was a mercy. If the child had struggled, he would probably be dead. "You do not know what it is to love someone to distraction, to bear him a child," she continued. "To raise his ungrateful sons, gladly suffering the snubs of his relatives and friends, only to lose him to a stupid accident and an incompetent surgeon." Fletcher had by this time made his way to a table covered with candles and made a motion of tipping it to his master. Darcy nodded.

"And then Sayre sent you and your daughter to Ireland where, for twelve years, you plotted this elaborate scheme of revenge."

"Yes, just as I thought: a clever man and almost my son-in-law. Think of that! But I can stay in your delightful company no longer, sir." She moved to the door.

"Now!" Darcy shouted. With a great clatter, Fletcher sent the table over as Darcy leapt the distance to Lady Sayre and laid hold of the hand holding the silver dagger. Fletcher was soon at his side and, with several strong, quick tugs, wrested the child from Lady Sayre's startled grasp. A wild scream of rage erupted from the lady, and for a brief time, it was all Darcy could do to maintain his hold on her without doing her an injury. Finally, he was forced to exert such pressure on her arm and wrist that, with a cry of pain, she dropped the dagger to the floor.

"Your pardon, my lady." Darcy released the pressure but retained the lady's arms in an unforgiving hold. More shouts and the sound of boots hitting the stone floor outside the chamber caused the three of them to look toward the door. Trenholme's face was the first to appear in the doorway, followed by Sayre's and Poole's.

"Oh, my God!" Trenholme almost fell as he tried to back away out of the chamber. "Lady Sayre!"

"Here!" demanded Sayre, pushing his brother aside. "Darcy! What are you—ah!" Sayre's eyes nearly started out of his head as his step-mamá's visage came into view. "But, you're dead! The letter…it said you were dead!" he squeaked.

"And I am, Sayre. Dead and returned to haunt you," Lady Sayre laughed cruelly, and then under her breath launched into a string of arcanum that caused Sayre and his brother to go white with fear. More footsteps were heard, and Monmouth poked in his head.

"Lady Sylvanie?" he looked at Lady Sayre in confusion.

"Her mother," Poole supplied.

"Mother? That cannot be, Poole; her mother's dead! Does look dashed like her, though! Cousin, maybe."

"Tris," Darcy interrupted Monmouth's speculations. "Lady Sylvanie has escaped down the corridor. Perhaps you could find her and escort her back?" Monmouth grinned and saluted him before ducking back out and taking up the new chase. He peered over Lady Sayre's shoulder to Sayre. "The mob, what happened?"

Sayre looked at Darcy vaguely, as if in a dream, but Poole stood ready. "We stopped them at the drawbridge, Darcy. Showed 'em our pistols and some of Sayre's musketry. That held them until the magistrate came with his bully-boys." He motioned to Fletcher, who still held the insensible child in his arms. "That the brat they wanted?"

"That is the child, yes. Fletcher, it might be wise to see to returning the child to his parents," Darcy instructed. "But take care still. Perhaps a note to the magistrate first?"

"Yes sir, Mr. Darcy." Fletcher inclined his head and, with a tired sigh, wound his way out of the crowded room.

"Sayre!" Darcy next addressed his lordship sharply. "Sayre, what do you want done with her ladyship? Sayre! Do you hear?"

"Done?" Sayre continued to cringe from the figure of his stepmother, who had not ceased her mutterings as she stared at him with a fixed hatred. "Done?" he repeated weakly.

~~~~~~~&~~~~~~

"And then what did that pompous lobcock say? I always said he had more squeak than wool!" Colonel Fitzwilliam downed the last of his brandy and set the glass on the mantle in his cousin's study. Darcy had been home from Oxfordshire for a week, but military duties had kept Richard from Erewile House until today. It had been just as well. He'd not been ready to tell the tale. He had even succeeded in resisting Dy's subtle questioning, causing his friend to
~~~~~~~

shake his head at him and roundly declare that he was "the most unamiable person of my acquaintance" to deny him what must be "the most delicious scandal of the season." Even now, he had been judicious in his recounting of the affair to Fitzwilliam. Nor had Georgiana teased him with pleas for a recital of his visit. One look at his face and she had ordered a great quantity of tea and cakes to be brought to his study. She had then proceeded to make him comfortable in every way, plying him with the sweets and stroking his arm as they sat together on the divan, softly telling him of her activities while he was away. He'd very nearly fallen asleep on her shoulder.

"Sayre? Neither Sayre nor Trenholme were of any help, so shocked—or guilty, I know not which—that they were useless. So, we bundled her up to the living quarters where Chelmsford and Manning met us, pistols still in hand. A decision had to be made, but you never saw such a collection of craven idiots! Finally, Manning could take no more and declared that he didn't care whether she was Lady Sayre or not but that he was sending down to the village for the magistrate to take her into custody; and he wished her in hell or Newgate for what she'd done, whichever came first."

Richard let out a low whistle. "Manning was ever a nasty piece of work even if he did hint you on." Darcy tipped his own brandy glass in agreement and took another swallow. It furnished him an excellent excuse to pause in his story. What came next would be difficult. His cousin allowed him his silence, busying himself at the hearth with the poker. Had Georgiana warned him before he came up? Probably. He opened his mouth to begin, but the words were not there. Richard noticed his frown and, sighing at the sight, asked quietly, "What happened, Fitz?"

"When Lady Sayre saw that Manning had swayed the others into a decision, she erupted into an horrific rage. It was the most hellish thing I have ever seen, Richard. She twisted and turned so, then finally, she brought her heel down onto my foot with such force that I lost my grip on her."

"That was all she needed," Richard supplied. Darcy lips formed a thin, straight line as he nodded.

"All and enough. She lunged for Manning. I thought she intended to knock him over, so wild was her leap; but instead, she went for the pistol he had tucked into his breeches. In an instant, she had it cocked and swept the room. Manning yelled out that it had a hair-trigger, and I will confess, I dove for cover just like the rest."

"The only sensible thing to do," Richard approved.

"Yes...well." Darcy swallowed and looked pensively into the amber liquid that remained in his glass. Then, with a snap, he downed it. "She laughed at us then, laughed and cursed us all. As soon as we heard her footsteps running down one of the corridors, we recovered ourselves and went after her. We hadn't gotten far, Richard, when a shot rang out. It echoed over and over—it seemed to last forever."

"Oh, Fitz!" Richard's face creased with concern.

"We found her in the Gallery, in front of the great portrait of her, Sayre and Sylvanie."

"Oh, my God, Fitz! It must have been horrible!" Richard laid a hand briefly on his cousin's shoulder. "What of Lady Sylvanie?" he asked, obviously attempting to turn his thoughts away from the image his words had recalled.

"None of us saw Monmouth return from his chase after her. But he must have, for the next day it was discovered that he had left, kit and carriage, sometime during the night."

"Foul play?" Richard asked.

"In a manner of speaking." Darcy motioned toward the Post lying on his desk. Fitzwilliam sauntered over and picked it up.

"What am I looking for?"

"The notices. Third column, the seventh one down."

Fitzwilliam read: "Lord Tristram Pellington, Viscount of Monmouth, gladly accepts the congratulations of his friends on his marriage to the Lady Sylvanie Trenholme, sister to Sir Carroll Trenholme, Marquis of Sayre and late of Norwycke Castle, Oxfordshire." He looked at Darcy in astonishment. "He *married* her?"

"She can be very persuasive," he explained. "*Very* persuasive."

"Hmmm." Fitzwilliam's response was sceptical. The clock on the mantle struck ten, and with its last strike, he looked out the window into the night and then back to his cousin. "Snowing again. I must be off if I am to appear at services tomorrow morning. Her ladyship," he offered sheepishly at Darcy's incredulous look, "ordered me to accompany her and pater to St.—'s tomorrow or she'd have my guts for garters. See you there, I suppose?"

Darcy shook his head slowly. "No, there are things..." His voice trailed off. Then, "No, I shall not. Will you escort Georgiana for me?" Fitzwilliam looked at him in surprise, but forbore to comment.

"Certainly! My pleasure, Fitz." He made for the door, picking up his coat and hat on the way. Then, turning back to his cousin he offered, "It will fade in time, you know. I daresay that by the time we go down to Aunt Catherine's, it will be little more than a bad dream. Try not to dwell on it, old man," he ended sincerely and let himself out the door.

Darcy grimaced to himself as he turned away from the door and walked back to the hearth where he poured himself another brandy. Richard's advice would generally be considered reasonable if, in fact, he were suffering guilt or shock over Lady Sayre's suicide. But although it had been horrible, he was feeling neither. He had done all that was humanly possible to discover and prevent what had happened at Norwycke. No, what preyed upon his mind was not the consuming desire for revenge that had been played out in the halls of Norwycke Castle, but that desire that he had seen in himself for those brief moments under Lady Sylvanie's tutelage. He hoped to God that it wasn't so, that he did not truly desire what he'd glimpsed in his soul, but comfort continued to elude him.

He sat down on the divan, and stretching out his legs before him, stared into the fire. A tapping sound brought his head up. That sound was followed by a shuffling at the doorknob that warned him of his visitor. Soon Trafalgar was staking proprietary rights to the rest of the divan. Darcy reached out to fondle the dog's ears. "To what do I owe this visit, Monster? In trouble again?" Trafalgar merely yawned widely and winked before settling down, his head claiming a place in Darcy's lap. "A clear conscience, have you?" He stroked the dog's head then checked. Shifting a bit, he reached inside his waistcoat pocket and brought out the coil of embroidery threads. Holding them by the knot, he shook them out until the strands separated; and then, slowly, he held them up, watching them in silence as they danced brightly in the firelight.

Quoted Works

~~~~~~~~~~~&~~~~~~~~~~~

Jane Austen. *Pride and Prejudice*

Bible. *Romans 8: 28-30*

John Milton. *Paradise Lost*

Jean-Baptiste Molière. *Tartuffe*
"A woman always has her revenge!"

William Wilberforce. *A Practical View of Christianity*

William Shakespeare:
As You Like It
Hamlet
King John
Julius Caesar
Macbeth
Merchant of Venice
Much Ado About Nothing
Othello
The Tempest
~~~~~~~~~~~

Darcy's Story Begins
In
An Assembly Such As This

Ten thousand a year and a large estate in Derbyshire! That was all Mrs. Bennet desired to know of Mr. Fitzwilliam Darcy before she began to entertain hopes that one of her daughters would attract his attention. Who is Fitzwilliam Darcy, the hero who is absent from two thirds of *Pride and Prejudice*? Pamela Aidan answers that intriguing question as she takes the reader into Darcy's world, a world very different from Austen's country neighbourhoods and rural gentry. Set vividly against the colourful history and political background of the time of the Regency, Aidan chronicles Darcy's supervision of his naïve friend Charles Bingley and his growing fascination with Elizabeth Bennet, culminating in the disastrous ball at Netherfield and his subsequent return to London with the express intention of forgetting Elizabeth.

And Concludes
In
These Three Remain

The third and final book begins at Rosings Park, picking up the events from *Pride and Prejudice* as Darcy and Elizabeth Bennet meet once more and Darcy's proposal is soundly rejected. Darcy's astonishing revaluation of himself and those habits of mind and convention in which he has always put his trust are merely hinted at in Austen's story but form the very heart and soul of Pamela Aidan's novel. With the support of his old university friend, Lord Dyfed Braugham, an enigmatic figure in his own right, and his sister Georgiana, Darcy embarks on the difficult task of reordering his life into that of the gentleman he wishes to become. A chance meeting with Elizabeth on his Pemberley estate and the reappearance of his enemy, George Wickham, make trial of Darcy's solemn resolve. The outcome, Darcy knows, will reveal what kind of man he truly is.